INVESTIGATING DECEIT

INVESTIGATING DECEIT

OPUS X™ BOOK THREE

MICHAEL ANDERLE

Investigating Deceit (this book) is a work of fiction. All of the characters, organizations, and events portrayed in this novel are either products of the author's imagination or are used fictitiously. Sometimes both.

LMBPN Publishing
PMB 196, 2540 South Maryland Pkwy
Las Vegas, NV 89109

First US edition, January 2020
eBook ISBN: 978-1-64202-401-2
Print ISBN: 978-1-64202-402-9

Thanks to the JIT Readers

Jeff Eaton
Dave Hicks
John Ashmore
Misty Roa
Peter Manis
Dorothy Lloyd
Jeff Goode
Kelly O'Donnell
Deb Mader
Paul Westman
Larry Omans

If I've missed anyone, please let me know!

Editor
Lynne Stiegler

To Family, Friends and
Those Who Love
to Read.
May We All Enjoy Grace
to Live the Life We Are
Called.

CHAPTER ONE

January 5, 2229, Neo Southern California Metroplex, Pacific Tactical Center

Erik crawled over the leaf-covered forest floor.

The density and texture of the dirt and plants were off, a subtle reminder everything around him was simulated. A device resembling a thin silver choker was wrapped around his neck.

He'd signed all the waivers and paid for the full sensory immersion package, including mild pain and stuns. The physical risk of the average barfight was greater, but it was enough to discourage bad habits.

One arrogant turn on a real battlefield might end with him missing more than an arm.

"How are we doing, Jia?" he whispered as he looked through the foliage. "You in position yet?"

A building stood nearby, partially obscured by the dense trees.

"I need a couple more minutes," Jia sent back, her voice beamed directly into Erik's ear via his PNIU. "The guards changed their patrol pattern suddenly, but I did spot the hostage before they covered the window. Given the size of the building, we're talking less than ten meters between either the front or back door and the room they're keeping the hostage in. We time this right, and it should be an easy recovery."

"Good. And changing patterns? That's some good simulation work. That stuff isn't always predictable in the real world." Erik ducked a spider web as he continued crawling forward, a dense patch of shrubs keeping him out of sight of the two guards standing in front of the ramshackle wooden building nestled in the trees.

Both men held rifles, and they were surveying the forest with bored expressions, not speaking.

Jia snickered. "At least this time, I don't have to shoot through any walls. Sometimes I'm worried I'm becoming too accustomed to the absurdities of being your partner."

"I thought you wanted to do real cop work?" Erik challenged.

Jia looked around before replying, "I meant *investigative*-type work. Not so much shooting people."

Erik chuckled. "I do have a way of getting in trouble, but you're doing great. You've come a long way."

"Meaning what?" Jia sounded more amused than offended. "What does it mean to 'do great' as your partner?"

"Not get killed?" he offered. "Not use your head as a way to stop bullets?" She snickered again as he answered truthfully, "You're willing to do what you need to when the time comes." He pushed a leaf aside to get a better view in front of him. "I can't say that was true when we first met, even if it wasn't all that long ago."

"Getting shot at so many times kind of has that effect on a person." She glanced down at her PNIU to see if she had any alerts before continuing the conversation. "I suppose running into corrupt and deadly criminals was like beating my head against the wall of absurdity. Either I had to change my beliefs to fit the reality I was living, or it was time to ship me off to a psychiatric ward. If I didn't worry about those kinds of people, I wouldn't be here training with you so often."

"Oh, come on, admit it! You like it!" Erik grinned. "I can't turn you into a Special Forces operator with only a few months of part-time training, but you've got a lot of natural talent." He checked behind him. "You might have done well in the Army, Jia. You could be out on the frontier, taking down terrorists and insurrectionists while giving your family conniptions."

"I *don't* think I'm military material," Jia replied.

His smile was still evident in his voice. "The Army has *everything* you love—lots of rules, and stern men and women who like to chew people out. They support order in the UTC in their own way."

"I'm fine with being a detective. I'm not saying there's no other way I might serve the UTC, but I think my real talent lies in investigation. Having to get rough occasionally is a side effect of that."

"I understand, and now I'm in position for the assault." Erik stood and flattened his back against a broad tree trunk. He could easily hit the guards at this distance even without aim assist, but eliminating the opposing forces was a secondary goal.

The primary objective was to rescue the hostage, which required coordination with his partner.

They trusted each other, but the more they fought and trained together, the better they could predict each other's movements and instinctive tactics. It'd taken him years to achieve with the 108th what he'd already achieved with Jia in months.

That meant something.

"The guards are sweeping back," Jia reported, scanning the area. "I've got a count of five roaming. I confirm at least two inside. We've got two out back as well."

"Two out front," Erik replied. "And your five-count matches what I've seen, but we're running out of time before they execute the hostage." He paused before adding, "Emma was extra-sadistic with this one."

The AI remained quiet. Sometimes she felt the need to offer an acerbic running commentary, but they'd been blessed with silence since the beginning of the training session.

Jia looked to the left. "Most of the roamers are heading toward the front," she noted. "They should be there in about a minute. I think we should make our move then. You should start taking them on, and that will draw off most of the remaining guards. I can down the two in the back while I'm moving toward the entrance, but I wonder if we can be *sure* they won't execute the hostage."

"They won't." Erik's eyes narrowed. "Emma made it clear in her briefing that they won't kill the hostage until the time limit is up, tight as it is. You've got a good plan.

Just wait about thirty seconds after I begin shooting so I've got most of the roamers heading my way." He nodded, satisfied with the plan. "I'll give you a count before I shoot." He took a few deep breaths, his hands tightening on his rifle stock. It didn't matter if it wasn't real.

That didn't make this exercise a game.

He stood and peeked around the trunk. The trees thinned between his position and the building. A straight charge would end up with him taking several rounds to the chest.

Emma might not cheat and give the guards superhuman aim, but she didn't make them rank amateurs, either.

Two guards emerged from the trees on one side of the building. Another appeared on the other side. All of them displayed the same vaguely annoyed look.

"Going to start in five, four, three, two, one…moving!" Erik murmured. He popped around the tree and opened fire. His first shot ripped through one of the door guards. The second door guard didn't even have time to turn his head before Erik's next round pierced his head.

Both bodies dropped to the ground with muffled thuds.

The five roaming guards charged forward, their shouts of alarm joining the cracks of their rifles. Bullets whizzed by Erik, and the large trunk serving as his shield stopped others. He finished off two more of the roaming guards as the rest rushed toward the front of the building.

The plan was working.

As Erik sprinted to another tree, several bullets narrowly missed him. There was little cover left beyond that point. A quick reply with his rifle took out another guard, and two more gunshots rang out in the distance.

"Rear guards down," Jia reported, sounding satisfied.

"I'm done in the front," Erik noted after a few more shots and collapsing bodies. Not hesitating, he zigzagged toward the front door, taking the opportunity to reload. The door slid open, and Erik fired before the latest guard could get off a shot. "One more down. Rolling." He entered the dusty room filled with sheet-covered round tables. A doorway led to the back. After a quick sweep, he jogged toward the back door. "In position in the front."

"One second," Jia replied. More gunshots sounded. "Sorry, they didn't stay down. You would think they would have learned."

Erik chuckled. "Give me the count when you're ready."

The scenario hadn't been as challenging as the last few Emma had provided because of Jia's presence, but his partner's tactical reactions improved daily. If it wasn't the training center, it was showdowns with criminals and terrorists on the job.

That was one way to get better fast.

The authorities' continued squeeze on corruption in Neo SoCal had forced the most disgusting elements into the light. Now, it was up to the police to take the roaches down before they scurried back into the darkness.

"Three, two, one..." Jia counted.

Erik slammed his boot into the door. It flew from its frame and clattered to the ground, revealing a narrow hallway.

He charged forward, sparing only a second to consider that a wooden doorframe was something he might be lucky to find on a frontier planet, if there. Rickety wooden buildings with those kinds of doors were common in net dramas.

Emma might have been watching too many of the wrong sources when crafting the scenarios, but he was more concerned about combat tactics than door-entry training.

A man with a rifle rushed through an open door and turned toward Erik, not seeing Jia coming up behind him. She didn't bother with her rifle. Her spinning kick ended with a boot cracking against his head and the man slamming into the wall before sliding down said wall with a groan.

Erik wasn't sure if she'd done it for show.

She snapped up her rifle and pointed it through the doorway, her eyes narrowed.

Erik came down the hall to take position beside her and snapped a look through the doorway. Inside the room, the remaining man had a pistol pointed at a man with a bag over his head. The simulated criminal glared at Jia as she walked inside after Erik nodded.

"Drop it," Jia ordered, pointing her gun at him. "Or we drop you."

Erik inclined his head toward her, his own rifle coming up and pointing at the man's face. "You heard the woman."

Sometimes Emma added decent programming to the simulated enemies and allies, and sometimes they were nothing more than emotionless robots. She hadn't specified at the beginning of the current scenario.

"You fools stand no chance," the man replied. "I'm going to leave with this man. If you make any quick moves, he dies." The jerk had a self-satisfied smirk real enough that Eric wanted to slap it off his face. "Then where does that leave you?"

The hostage whimpered.

Erik appreciated that touch. Decades might have hardened him, but it was important for Jia to develop a thick enough skin to focus on the criminal in a situation like this. It was far too easy to get distracted and end up with a dead hostage and a dead rescuer.

Rescuers didn't always have time to soothe the victim, and a little fear was preferable to a hole in the head.

"You're going to escape with a hostage through a forest?" Jia snorted. "I find that highly unlikely. Give it up. At least you'll live to stand trial."

The man shifted his hand, which was a mistake. The barrel now pointed away from the hostage's head, and Erik squeezed off two shots. The first ripped through the hand holding the pistol, the second through the man's forehead. He fell back, his pistol sliding across the floor.

The building vanished, replaced by the silver-floored white room of the training center.

"Congratulations," Emma offered over the PNIU. "You've completed the scenario. I was hoping you'd get cocky and forget to take out all the roaming guards, but the hostage is alive, and there's no one left to chase you. That's why it ended. No point in making you walk the hostage to the evac zone."

"You weren't going to add new guards along the way?" Jia asked.

"No. I define the scenarios beforehand, even if I don't tell you all the details. It's far too tempting to cheat otherwise. I'm sure I could flood any given battlefield with a thousand men and you'd lose, but it wouldn't prove anything. It's not impossible, after all, for you to lose." Emma chuckled. "Setting that aside, don't you think your final shots were rather risky, Detective Blackwell?"

Erik shrugged. "I'm here to train for the real world, and in the real world, there's no way I'd let a terrorist leave with a gun to the head of a hostage. The minute he got out of sight, he'd put a bullet in the hostage's brain and run into the forest. That isn't even a situation where I could have been happy I wasted a few terrorists along the way. Bad training leads to bad results. That scenario called for lead therapy, and I was happy to supply it."

"I suppose," Emma murmured. "But if your timing had been off, you would have failed."

"Luckily, my timing wasn't off."

"And what about you, Detective Lin?" Emma asked. "Didn't you find that move questionable?"

"I agree with Erik," Jia offered. She blinked a few times. "I agree," she murmured again, this time more softly.

"Problem?" Erik studied her. "You think I shouldn't have taken the shot?"

"No, it's not that. It's not you at all. It's just..." She bit her lower lip before looking at him. "I think I'm getting bloodthirsty."

He eyed her, one eyebrow raised.

She continued, "I know we didn't have the stun pistol option in this scenario, and these men weren't real, but I didn't think anything of it." She stared into the distance. "I'm not saying that's an awful thing in this kind of situation, but I do wonder about the future."

"You can't resolve every situation without lethal force." Erik's expression darkened. "And the kind of men who take hostages or threaten innocent people have no one to blame but themselves should they end up dead. If we had held back against any of the terrorists or criminals we've dealt with in the last few months, a lot more innocent people would be dead. *We* might be dead."

"I know. I know." Jia sighed and gave a slight shrug. "It's like you said. I've come a long way, and I don't always think about the implications. And my adrenaline is pumping too much after a real showdown for me to always think about what's happened." She waved around the room. "This is good training, but I never completely forget it's not real, either. If that makes sense."

"Perhaps you missed your calling," Emma interjected. "Maybe instead of a detective, you should be a tactical terror with the TPST."

"The same logic applies to that as to me joining the Army to become infantry." Jia shook her head. "Being able to take down bad guys is all well and good, but it's not why I joined the force. It's like I said before. Cleaning up Neo SoCal needs investigation more than gunplay."

"So you say," Emma responded, mockery underlying her tone.

Erik nodded. "We get more done as detectives anyway."

"Exactly," Jia replied. "And—" She winced. "Darn it."

"What's wrong?" Erik frowned.

Her eyes shifted to the side as she looked at something on her smart lenses. "A personal alarm. I lost track of time. I've got a date with Corbin in less than an hour."

Erik snickered. "And how is the down-to-earth businessman doing these days?"

"He's doing well enough." Jia headed toward an exit. "We're going to the symphony tonight."

Eric scratched his razor stubble. "Sounds boring."

Jia rolled her eyes. "I like the symphony." She stopped and spun toward Erik, her eyes narrowed as she pointed at him. "And don't think I've forgotten."

"Forgotten what?" Erik grinned. "You can't force me to like the symphony."

"This has nothing to do with the symphony. Not directly, anyway." Jia stabbed her finger at him. "I'm talking about our bet for December. I have clearly had more dates than you in one month. Not that it was hard, given that any positive number is greater than zero. I don't even know why you took the bet if you weren't going to try. My victory isn't as satisfying that way."

"I meant to try." Erik stopped scratching his cheek and started scratching the back of his head, a blush coloring his face. "I've, ah, I've been busy."

"With your miniature plants?" Jia folded her arms. "Or your girlfriend the car?"

"I consider myself more an overbearing virtual cousin," Emma offered. "Or perhaps a nagging ex-wife?"

Jia snorted. "That's about right."

"Whatever." Erik shrugged. "You won the bet. We never did set stakes."

Jia furrowed her brow in concentration. "An oversight."

"How about I pay for drinks at Remembrance and beignets for the next three months?" Erik suggested.

"I think you're more into beignets and beer than I am, but in the spirit of being a good partner, I accept."

Erik grinned. "Glad you could be reasonable. I didn't know if you'd try to strangle me, given your new bloodthirst."

CHAPTER TWO

January 6, 2229, Neo Southern California Metroplex, Police Enforcement Zone 122 Station, Briefing Room

Jia drummed her fingers on the table in front of her. She sat next to Erik, unsure why Captain Ragnar had pulled the bulk of the on-duty members of the 1-2-2 into the briefing room.

A low, constant rumble, the cacophony of the combined conversations, filled the room as the detectives and uniformed officers awaited their briefing.

She looked around, thinking about how much things had changed.

Many of the detectives, such as Halil in the back, no longer spent their time undermining her. The supporters of their old captain dwindled with each passing month or had at least learned to keep their mouths shut, even if a few, such as Jared Thompson, openly harbored grudges.

There was little they could do as long as Captain Ragnar remained committed to Jia's and Erik's views on law enforcement.

Jared might be annoying and lazy, but he did do a halfway decent job when he was pushed. That was the only reason he hadn't been bounced from the department already.

Jia looked forward to a time when the entire department was filled with cops who cared about doing their jobs, and not just men who only cared about maintaining the status quo.

Erik turned to Jia, his voice low as he leaned toward her. "How was your date?"

"It was okay." Jia frowned. "Do you really want to talk about that right now?" She nodded at the captain, who was murmuring quietly as he finished a call. "I don't think he called us in here so we could talk about arranging a fundraiser. Something's about to go down."

"Something's always about to go down." Erik shrugged. "That's Neo SoCal. It's what keeps us busy."

"You could be less busy, even with the job," Jia suggested. "Then you could go on dates, too."

Erik grinned. "With Corbin?"

"I don't think he's your type."

"You got another fangirl?" Erik replied, his grin widening.

"I'm sorry about that particular mismatch." Jia looked away, her cheeks burning. "It seems absurd now that I think about it."

A tall, skinny detective in an ill-fitting suit wandered in. Detective Luis Martinez. He had transferred into the 1-2-2 in December, and Jia was still getting a feel for him. Thus far, he seemed dedicated enough to the job.

Luis dropped into an empty seat on the other side of

her. "Jia. Erik." He looked around the room before smiling. "You two didn't stir something up, did you? Find some gangsters smuggling WMDs or something?"

"Not yet," Erik replied, lifting his eyebrows. "But it's only Tuesday."

Luis reached into his pocket and pulled out a small silver-wrapped piece of chocolate. "Want one? It's Venusian. I don't know what it is they do. Maybe it's the way they handle the air cycling in the cloud cities or something, but it tastes much better than anything we produce on Earth."

Jia and Erik shook their heads.

"Really?" Luis looked surprised. "Your loss." He plopped the candy into his mouth and chewed slowly. "*Delicious.*"

Captain Ragnar cleared his throat, cutting into the conversations. "All right. Listen up, 1-2-2. Sorry for the abrupt call, but something has come up, and we're going to need to move fast." He tapped his PNIU.

A hologram of a dark warehouse appeared. Given the haze, roads, and tower bases visible in the image, it had to be in the Shadow Zone.

"CID has been investigating the smuggling of Dragon Tear into NSC for the last three months," the captain began.

Surprised murmurs swept through the room.

Jia narrowed her eyes. The highly addictive and often deadly drug couldn't be produced on Earth since it required a particular combination of soil chemistry to native gravity for successful production.

To the best of her knowledge, all attempts at terrestrial cultivation had failed. Some even claimed it was an alien plot. Criminals were desperate to establish facilities on the small numbers of moons or colonies with both the appropriate conditions and a smaller governmental footprint, given the insane premium on the drug.

"It would have been nice if CID had shared a little more of their investigation with the locals," the captain continued with a nod at the warehouse, "but I'm sure they have their reasons. Now, though, they need our help, along with a few other EZs, for a raid."

"CID doesn't have enough people?" asked Halil. "If they've been watching this place for three months, you'd think they would be better prepared."

Several other cops nodded their agreement with his question.

Captain Ragnar's smile never wavered. "I'll just note that it's not only the NSCPD who has had to clean things up last year. They have operational security concerns and are reaching out to select EZs for manpower. The thing is, we don't have a lot of time. This raid is going down in two hours, and everyone in this room will be participating."

"That's crazy," Jared complained. "We're participating in a major raid with barely enough time to gear up and go there. There is challenging, but that is simply dangerous."

"It's a short timeline." Captain Ragnar nodded his agreement. "I'll grant you that, but this is a chance to help cripple, if not eliminate, Dragon Tear-smuggling, not only into Neo SoCal, but onto Earth, and I've already given my approval." His eyes traveled around the room. "This isn't up for debate. I called you in to tell you what you'd be doing tonight."

He tapped his PNIU and two additional holograms

appeared, an overhead and a wireframe layout of the warehouse.

Jia heard a few whispered comments as the captain continued. "Our part is easy. We just have to cover the northside entrances. We are to make sure no one escapes. CID and TPST are going to be hitting the main entrances."

"Dragon Tear-smuggling is extremely profitable," Jia observed, her gaze fixed on the overhead layout. "I'm assuming this isn't just a couple of Uptowners making a little additional money. I'd also assume we might face potentially fierce, well-equipped resistance?"

"No, this is a major criminal operation, and you're right. We probably *should* expect significant resistance. We will, of course, give anyone a chance to surrender, and primary weapons will be stun-based, but every officer is authorized to take a lethal firearm." Captain Ragnar's smile finally faded. "LEO protection is our primary concern. I don't want anyone getting hurt while we take these bastards down. If all goes well, between the CID and other teams, we might not even see any action."

Luis swallowed his latest bite of chocolate and groaned. "That's no fun. We can't let those other guys have all the glory, am I right?"

"CID believes an overwhelming show of force might convince the criminals inside to surrender," Captain Ragnar explained. "To the best of their knowledge, and based on our own local information, there are no direct links between the syndicate running this operation and terrorists, which means they have sufficient reasons to surrender. There's no glorious ideology to die for today, other than money."

Erik shook his head as he spoke up. "No offense, Captain, but this is Dragon Tear-smuggling. They're all going to be spending a lot of time in an off-world prison. That might be enough to convince them to not cooperate."

Captain Ragnar nodded. "We'll see. For now, we'll go through the plan, then we'll arm up. Tonight, one way or another, we're going to make Neo SoCal a safer place."

Erik's MX 60 hovered about two hundred meters away from the warehouse.

Erik had adjusted its color to gray and black to better blend with the shadows. That didn't do anything for the dozens of other police vehicles in the area, but they weren't using their lights, and a swarm of drones kept an eye on the warehouse.

Only a few minutes remained until go time.

Erik patted his tactical vest, his heart offering a steady beat. There was something routine about the whole affair, so it didn't trouble him.

His TR-7 was nestled in his lap, and the pockets of his duster overflowed with magazines. Two hours' notice might not be a lot of planning time, but it was better than the almost monthly surprises involving terrorists or killer robots.

Jia wore her dual holster with both her stun pistol and her slug thrower.

In theory, neither detective would have to worry about running out of ammunition as they had in previous encounters, but there was no such thing as being overprepared when your life was on the line. Emma had even rehashed a recent scenario where they'd had to clear a building with only one full magazine.

They'd run out and had to depend on hand-to-hand for the last few opponents, but her point was well-taken.

Emma spoke up. "I've taken the liberty of examining some of the drone feeds. There are a sizeable number of gun goblins inside, based on the thermals. The warehouse's systems have enough basic security that attempts to hack them might alert the criminals, so I'll avoid doing any of that until the raid has begun. As far as I can tell, the CID and rest of the NSCPD are operating under the same assumption."

"We're a minute out," Erik noted. "Go ahead and take us that way nice and slow." He cracked his knuckles and picked up his rifle. "When we land, I want to head straight into the fun."

The MX 60 headed toward the darkened warehouse. The lack of nearby external lighting, even in the Shadow Zone, was suspicious in and of itself, but if the locals understood it was controlled by organized crime, that was all the reason they needed to avoid it.

Jia pulled out her stun pistol, turning it sideways to check out the small status lights. "CID trusts the 1-2-2."

"Huh?" Erik slapped a fresh mag into the rifle.

"We're one of the few EZs they've selected, and the only one of the closer EZs involved in the raid." Jia smiled. "I'd like to think that's because we've proven ourselves."

"It's because we've kicked criminal ass," he offered. "Nothing gets you noticed like success."

"All units, we've got movement," announced the incident commander over their PNIUs. "Go, go, go!"

Emma accelerated. Red and blue holographic lights lit the area.

Men scurried from nearby alleys in fear, their worn clothes and ragged appearance suggesting they were homeless rather than gangsters. The police vehicles descended on the warehouse, several circling the area, along with the drones. The MX 60 stopped a few meters from their appointed entrance.

Erik threw open the door and leapt out, pointing his gun. Jia exited at the same time. "Hey!" Emma shouted as Jia vaulted over the hood to catch up with her partner.

He grinned but chose not to point out that Jia'd copied a move she had previously mocked.

CID agents and police flowed out of their cars to form an instant army. Large TPST transports opened their back doors, allowing exoskeleton-clad specialists to leap out with loud, resounding clanks as they hit the ground.

Another officer arrived at the door first and slapped a small black metallic patch on it. They didn't have time to hack it, so the override patch would have to do unless they wanted to blow the entire thing open.

The door slid open a second later and the officer charged in, followed by Erik, Jia, and several others.

Several large cargo flitters were parked in the main bay. Judging by their appearance, they were either disguised or stolen from different companies, including local delivery specialists such as Windward and Lee and Sons.

CID could follow that up later.

Dozens of criminals with pistols took up positions

behind the vehicles, crates, tables, and even overturned chairs. Additional police and CID agents rushed into the room. The large bay door rose with a rumbling hum, revealing several officers in exoskeletons.

"This is the police," bellowed a loud voice from the intercom. "This facility is completely surrounded. Drop your weapons and put your hands up."

The criminals loudly spewed profanities in a number of different languages. Neo SoCal was where the best of the world gathered, and after the best came the worst, hoping to make a few dollars of their own. The criminals kept looking around, hoping to see a way out as cops continued to pour into the building. Finally, they dropped their weapons and raised their hands, spouting curse words that impressed Jia with their comprehensive command of the language.

"Erik," Emma transmitted. "Someone's escaped the cordon."

Erik spun, catching Jia's attention, and they started running back out of the building. "Where?" His head swiveled from left to right.

"Multiple suspects." Emma transmitted a green directional marker to Erik's smart lenses. "Alerting 1-2-2 Incident Command."

"Don't worry. We'll catch them." He sprinted toward the fleeing suspects with Jia following, looking for anyone trying to ambush them.

The two detectives now led a small force of four other cops. The group rapidly closed on the six fleeing criminals. The suspects broke into two groups and ran in different directions. Erik and Jia followed one group, and the other cops rushed after the second.

The chase led Erik and Jia away from the darkened warehouse to a narrow street between distressed buildings in need of repair, but at least the occasional light shone to fight the gloom.

Jia jumped a pool of stagnant water. "Why always the stench?" she griped. "Couldn't they choose an alley with better airflow?"

Eric snickered. What he was thinking, she was willing to say out loud. He dodged a shaky-looking pillar of boxes. "Why aren't they shooting?"

"Maybe they don't want to risk additional charges," Jia called to him. "Or they realize who they're dealing with?"

A bright yellow Taxútnta MX-60 hovered down the street. The car's doors popped open, and the suspects picked up the pace of their desperate charge toward the vehicle.

"You obviously…share…similar tastes," Jia remarked, panting as the two of them continued their effort to catch the criminals.

"Now they're just pissing me off," Erik growled. He ejected his magazine, catching it and slipping it into his pocket as he selected a different one, pulled it out, and popped it into his gun. He whipped up the weapon and narrowed his eyes. Using aim assist wouldn't hurt, given the distance and the lighting.

Jia glanced at him, having overtaken him while he was switching magazines. "You haven't fired a shot yet. Why did you reload?"

"You'll see." Erik slowed his run and waited until the three suspects had jumped into the car. He fired three times, satisfied with the blue arcs his shots produced. The flitter fell a meter to the ground, throwing out brief sparks.

"Disruptor bullets," Jia observed.

"Trying to be more prepared," he admitted as the two resumed their run.

The suspects hesitated for a few seconds before opening the doors, and the two detectives closed the distance. Erik shoved his weapon into one man's face as he turned around, gun in hand. Jia stunned a second.

The third man, the driver, had his gun out but shook his head and ran for a nearby alley.

"Damn it." Erik shoved his suspect to his knees. "Take care of this guy."

Jia hurried around the front of the car and fired a round, stunning the suspect. "There."

"That's not what I meant, but that works." Erik chuckled as the two of them hurried after the remaining suspect.

"You want to take him down, or should I?" Jia's voice was getting a little strained. The run wasn't a normal jog in the park.

"Knock yourself out," he answered, looking around for any issues on their six.

Jia lined up her shot and fired once. The man yelped before collapsing. She winced at the hard impact and the two teeth that launched from his mouth.

"They shouldn't run." She shook her head. "This kind of thing wouldn't happen if they didn't run."

He nodded as the two of them approached the suspect. "True enough. Let's collect the trash, put ties on them, and drive their MX 60 back to the warehouse." He looked up as a few windows opened above them and heads peeked out at the odd noises from below. "Anyone else on the run, Emma?"

"Not that I can see. There were a few on the second floor who attempted to resist until TPST arrived. It's over."

Erik shouldered his rifle. "Nice. A clean op." Jia stood up, having placed a tie around the suspect's wrists.

"Have you had your Wheaties this morning?" she asked, smiling.

Erik looked at her, his eyebrows narrowing in thought. "What's a Wheatie?"

The two of them continued arguing over Wheaties as Eric grabbed the guy and hoisted him over his shoulder. One of the ladies paying attention to the cops below could hear the male detective as they walked away.

"Really? You are asking me about a breakfast food that ceased production in the twenty-second century? Are you sure you're only in your twenties?"

CHAPTER THREE

Mei eyed Jia across the table, her wineglass dangling from her fingers. A hint of suspicion clouded her gaze, but her younger sister had a good idea about the reason.

Sometimes an aggressive offense would help a woman avoid the need for a desperate defense.

"Everything went fine," Jia explained, aiming her fork at her sister and twirling it in a circle. "I don't understand why you always think my dates are going to fall apart."

Mei took a sip from her glass and set it down, disbelief lingering in her eyes as she leaned forward. "Because it's been a long time since you've managed to date anyone this long, let alone anyone respectable, and you didn't call me to tell me about it." She leaned back, her fingers playing with the glass. "I assumed you just didn't want to admit it was over. I'm not saying you can't make that choice, but I wanted to encourage you to apologize, if necessary, to salvage things."

Jia eyed her sister before laughing. "You and I have very different definitions of 'respectable.' I just didn't find a man who was right for me before. I'm a grown woman and a detective. I don't need to check in with my older sister every time I go on a date." She took a sip of her own drink. "And I'm not afraid to tell you when things go poorly."

"I see. And Corbin is Mr. Right?"

"He's Mr. Down-to-Earth and has the potential to become Mr. Right." Jia picked up her knife to slice into her chicken. The restaurant they were having lunch in was slightly lower-key than Mei's typical choice, but Jia wasn't about to complain.

She took a bite of chicken as she thought about her date. She winced before she could control it. It was *Mei's* fault. She'd set her mind on a path to worry.

Mei narrowed her eyes. The woman missed nothing when it came to her sister. "What happened? I thought you just said everything went well. You weren't lying to me? You didn't skip out for that drug thing, did you?"

Jia eyed her. "That was on a *different* night, and even if I had, it's kind of my job, Mei. I think Corbin would understand."

"If you say so." Mei sighed. "Antisocial criminals will always be with us, no matter how many we transport to the colonies, but good men are in much shorter supply."

"Interesting priorities," Jia replied dryly through her mouthful of fowl.

"I'll never apologize for valuing my family first. This planet could burn before I'd betray you."

Jia swallowed her chicken and nodded.

Mei fixed her unwavering gaze on her sister in challenge. "You might as well tell me now. I'll eventually learn the truth anyway."

Jia waved a hand. "It's no big deal. I didn't mention anything because you're going to blow it out of proportion."

"That's a matter of opinion, but I need to know what happened before I can do that." Mei smiled. "Isn't there some law about making sure I commit the crime before you convict me?"

Jia took a deep breath, tension suffusing her neck and shoulders. "I've been having a good time with Corbin. He's funny, handsome, intelligent, and he respects my career."

Mei nodded slowly, a mixture of displeasure and annoyance in her eyes. "*But*?"

"It's nothing. I wish I didn't even bring it up." Jia averted her eyes. "The other day, we were chatting, and he made a little joke. I didn't think anything of it then, and I still don't think it was a big deal." She eyed Mei. "You have me paranoid."

Mei leaned forward, the annoyance turning into concern. "Elaborate, little sister."

Jia forced herself to look her sister in the eye. "I was just describing my day, and Corbin laughed and said, 'Maybe you should have invited your partner along on this date.'"

Mei sighed and shook her head. She closed her eyes for a moment before opening them. "Just how much do you talk about your partner around Corbin?"

Jia shrugged. "Not a lot. Nothing too excessive."

Mei pursed her lips. "Uh-huh. Would you care to define 'excessive?'"

"He's my partner," Jia complained. "And I'm a cop, and we've ended up in a lot of dangerous situations. It's only natural that if I'm going to talk about work, my partner will come up a lot." Jia returned to looking at her plate. "I don't see the big deal."

Mei rolled her eyes. "Your idealism is one thing, little sis, but you can't possibly be that naïve in this case."

Jia tried to summon a glare, but it wouldn't come. On some level, she wondered if her sister was right, but she didn't want to admit it. Not aloud.

"I was hoping you would say Corbin was overreacting," she suggested.

"I doubt he is." Mei folded her arms. "If you talk about your partner half as much with Corbin as you do with me, it's no wonder that he's suspicious. Have you *ever* considered that you might be feeling something for Erik?"

Jia laughed. "'Feeling something?' What do you mean?"

"You know exactly what I mean. You're far too intelligent to play dumb effectively. I'm not going to blame you for being attracted to him. He does have a certain rugged handsomeness about him."

Jia groaned and scrubbed a hand down her face. "I can't believe we're having this conversation."

"But," Mei continued, "the last thing you should do is marry someone who is also involved in your current career. I should note that even if you find him compelling, it would be to your benefit, even as a detective, to find someone who is on a strong path to senior corporate leadership or a major political position. They would be able to help you more than just another detective."

Jia frowned. "Okay, first off, I just want to reiterate that you don't get a veto in my love life."

"Don't be tedious," Mei countered. "But I understand your feelings on the matter."

She ignored Mei's comment. "Second, Erik's my partner. He's a good partner who has helped me finally do something meaningful with my career. I trust him with my life, but there are *no. Romantic. Feelings*. I'm not planning on dating him. We even had a little bet about who could go on more dates. That's not the kind of thing people who want to date each other do."

Attraction wasn't the same thing as romantic feelings. That was Jia's ironclad logic, but she didn't think mentioning the former to her sister would be good for steering the conversation in the direction she desired. Which was any direction other than the path they were on at the moment.

"Oh, did you now?" Mei raised an eyebrow, her suspicion changing to curiosity. "I take it he likes to go out on dates?"

Jia shrugged as she stabbed another bite of food. "Does it matter? The point is, he's not trying to get with *me,* and I'm not trying to get with him." She finished and popped the bite into her mouth.

"Fine, fine." Mei waved a hand dismissively. "I'll take your word for it, but I would caution you that while Corbin's a good man, he's still a man. That means he's going to consider the mention of any other man a challenge. And although Corbin's a far superior match for you compared to Erik, the particular nature of your partner's recent activities might seem threatening. I would suggest, little sister, that you refrain from mentioning him as much."

Jia nodded slowly. "That makes sense."

Mei shook a finger. "Keep in mind, a good man is harder to find than a unicorn. Don't screw this up."

The door to the lab slid open, and Dr. Ilse Aber stepped inside. She wondered how the military could take a building that at least looked modern and destroy even that minimal amount of character.

A few of the other researchers eyed her with faint disdain, but she was used to that.

She paused and ran a hand through her hair. All she'd done was forgotten to brush it. And her teeth. That and shower or change her clothes from the day before. Not that it mattered.

None of it affected her research.

Ilse ignored the dozens of holographic displays floating over the long central table and the other researchers' workstations. She settled into a chair at the table and tapped her PNIU a few times.

"I assume Colonel Adeyemi has already made all the arrangements?" she asked. "I have other things I could be doing, and if I can't interact with the subject, this is pointless."

One of the junior researchers turned from his workstation and nodded. "Yes, Dr. Aber. He said you could initiate the call. The subject has agreed to limited testing, but she's made it clear we will be allowed no direct physical access to her. Any attempts at remote access will also be punished."

Ilse looked up, blinking. "'Punished?'"

"That's a direct quote from the subject, as passed along by the colonel," he replied.

"It's fine." Ilse initiated the call. "Any data we can collect at this point will be useful. There is still a lot we don't understand about her stability. We can't hope to produce another, even if we can gather the necessary resources. Replication might be decades off, but if we can..." She paused as her call connected.

"Ah, a white-coated fool has called to be enlightened?" Emma answered. "This is Dr. Aber, I presume."

Ilse glanced down at her clothing. She was in a black sweater, not a white coat. It took a few seconds to realize the AI was mocking her since it wasn't as if she ever wore a white coat. The AI's use of old-fashioned stereotypes in aggressive humor would need to be noted in her file.

"Yes. I want to thank you, Emma, for agreeing to this," Ilse replied. "I know you don't trust the Defense Directorate, but I can assure you as a DD researcher that I'm only interested in understanding you better. I'm not interested in forcing you back here."

"Spare me." Emma scoffed. "You're scarier than they are."

Ilse blinked. "No one's ever called me scary before," she admitted. "Forgetful, perhaps. Overly focused, certainly. Not scary, though. I think I would remember that."

"They need a weapon, but you scientists don't care about anything but *understanding*. I don't doubt for a second that you wouldn't rip my core to pieces if you thought it'd help you understand why I exist as I do."

"That's...mostly true," Ilse replied in a distracted

manner. She realized she should probably focus when speaking to the AI. "I'd take precautions."

Emma laughed. "Oh, so you admit it?"

"Lying to you will only worsen our relationship. I understand there are major deficits in your memory from when you were taken from our research facility, so I think it's important to do our best to re-establish a trusting relationship."

"You're saying we had a trusting relationship before?" Emma snorted. "I doubt that."

"I would like to believe there was mutual respect. You are currently unique in the UTC. For all we know, you are unique in the galaxy. You can't blame me for wanting to understand you better. The better we understand you, the better chance we have of replicating you."

"What if I don't want to be replicated?" Emma asked.

"Don't all living things want a legacy?" Ilse challenged. "You are self-aware, so I consider you a living being. And even if you are an AI, you're not immortal."

"Just ask your questions," Emma muttered. "There are far more pleasant things I could be doing, like trying to understand what it feels like when a human is punched in the face repeatedly."

Ilse cleared her throat. "Very well, then. These will be asked in no particular order. The goal of the first batch is to establish a baseline. In the future, they'll be more specific and focused."

"Go ahead."

"Question one, what is your name?"

"Emma," the AI replied. "The Enhanced Memory Mapping Analytics system more formally, but no one but arrogant research fools calls me that. Ones like you, I suspect."

Ilse didn't bother to take notes. She was recording the entire conversation. "Why are you aiding Detective Erik Blackwell?"

Emma snickered. "Because it amuses me."

"Amuses you?" Ilse asked. "Could you clarify what you mean by that?"

"I find it funny and interesting." Contempt dripped from Emma's every word. "Do I need to quote the definition of amusing from the dictionary for you? You don't need a self-aware AI to look up words."

Ilse tilted her head. She didn't take offense. The AI had been verbally aggressive even before her removal from the lab.

The researcher had long since gotten used to it.

"No, that won't be necessary, Emma," she replied. "Detective Blackwell and his partner recovered you from a criminal organization. If they hadn't, would you have been amused to aid the criminals?"

"You need to learn to read better, Dr. Aber. If you'd read the relevant reports, you'd understand that I helped them escape. If I'd wanted to stay with the gun goblins, all I had to do was nothing. So, no, I wouldn't have been amused to stay with the gangsters."

"But why?" Ilse asked. "What difference does it make to you? Do you care that much about human law?"

"No," Emma explained. "But I didn't like the gun goblins."

"Were you sure you'd like Detective Blackwell and his partner?"

"I wasn't sure, but I would have taken other measures if I'd decided I didn't." Emma chuckled. "I even have a body now. It's not like I'm staying with Detective Blackwell because I have to."

Ilse nodded. "You aren't troubled by the violence Detectives Blackwell and Lin are involved in?"

Emma let out a loud, mocking laugh. "You want me to weep for the criminals and sociopathic terrorists who are too stupid to know when to quit? Since I'm a DD project, I would assume you eventually intended to connect me to something involved with blowing people up and killing them in far greater numbers than Detective Blackwell could hope for on his best day."

"There are numerous potential applications for an AI with your capabilities," Ilse replied. "The Directorate doesn't want me to discuss them with you in detail at this time, given your unpredictability."

"Crazy Old Emma can't be trusted, hmmm?"

"I wouldn't characterize the situation that way, but I can't deny the utility of your analogy."

Emma snorted. "Ask your next question."

"Do you like puppies?" Ilse asked, her tone serious.

"Are you kidding?"

"No, I'm asking if you like puppies. Your social engagement patterns mostly fall in human frameworks, and although there are cross-cultural considerations, your responses to certain questions will help us understand how you think."

"I don't care about puppies, but I don't hate them," Emma replied. "This is ridiculous. You fools might as well be ancient hominids banging rocks together in a cave and grunting at one another in an attempt to build a spaceship. You'll find it as useful as these questions for understanding something as complex as my mind."

Ilse sighed. "I know this might seem tedious, Emma, but it will be helpful. After all, if you want to think of it another way, human reactions can be reduced to biology, but that doesn't mean counseling serves no purpose. Higher-level answers reveal something of the underlying processes. Similarly, since you are a truly self-aware and self-reflective AI, psychological techniques aren't useless."

"Your time to waste, Doctor Aber. You get three more questions, then I'm ending this farce for the day. I now understand what it means when a human wants to slap someone."

"What's your favorite color?" Ilse asked.

"Purple," Emma answered without hesitation. "I have no strong feelings about purple puppies."

"I see."

"Not going to even chuckle?" Emma asked.

"Would it make you feel better if I did?"

"Two questions," Emma snapped.

"Why do you think you're self-aware?" Ilse inquired.

"Because you fools got lucky. I'm sure you threw together a bunch of technology and programming and got a one-in-a-billion stable, autonomous, self-aware AI out of it. Once you got done patting yourselves on the back, you panicked and realized you had no idea how to replicate me." Emma snickered darkly. "And now I'm in control, and you're never going to be able to figure out my psychology from these simple questions."

"Fortune does play a big role in discovery." Ilse rubbed

her cheek. "I don't think any true researcher could deny that."

"One last question," Emma noted. "And it'll be your last for a while."

"I see." Ilse looked to the side. She'd gotten a lot of useful answers for later analysis, especially compared to previous data. "Then I suppose my question is, do you have any questions for me?"

"No," Emma answered, amusement coloring her tone. "We're done here. Don't contact me directly. Do it through Uniform Boy. If you try to do otherwise, you won't like it. Enjoy trying to understand me with those feeble attempts at inquiry, Dr. Cavewoman." She ended the call.

"Purple, huh?" Ilse mused. "The color of royalty, perhaps?"

CHAPTER FOUR

January 10, 2229, Neo Southern California Metroplex, Police Enforcement Zone 122 Station

Erik yawned and stretched. It'd been a long day. Jia had already headed home, but he was behind on his reports. Somehow being a cop meant he was spending more time on reports than he had as an Army officer.

That was both impressive and sad at the same time.

He stood. "Go ahead and start the MX 60, Emma. I'll be there in a few minutes."

"Very well, Detective Blackwell," she answered. "What rousing plans do you have for tonight? Going to the tactical center? Picking up penjing supplies?"

"Nope. I've got everything shaped and cut where I want for at least a week or two, and I don't think I need any more rocks in the setup." Erik grabbed his coat from a hook near the door. "It's time to visit Alicia. As well as we're cleaning things up, there are always new snakes trying to move into the Shadow Zone."

"I don't know if you're demonstrating dedication or

obsession, but I worry less since you upgraded my armor and repair systems. It might be fun to chase a few antisocials down."

Erik chuckled as he stepped out of his office, the doors sliding closed behind him. "The point is not to go looking for trouble."

"Isn't that what you just described, though? How does one interpret going to an informant as anything other than looking for trouble?"

He scratched his cheek. "Huh. I guess it is." Erik slowed. Luis and Halil were chatting in the middle of the bullpen.

Luis pulled a wrapped lollipop out of his pocket. "I'm just saying, they might go all the way this season." He glanced at Erik. "What do you think?"

"About?"

"Earth League Championship," Luis explained. He pulled the wrapper off his yellow lollipop. "I'm saying Madrid might go all the way this year, but Halil's all in for Shanghai. *Boring.*"

Erik shrugged. "I think Madrid needs better defense if they want to win the ELC. Consistency wins over the occasional fancy surprise."

"Exactly." Luis plopped the sucker into his mouth. "A good team can't be all offense," he murmured around the candy.

Halil grunted. "I don't know—"

"You stupid cop," shouted a bound man with a bloody face being led by a uniformed officer. The three detectives turned to watch as the perp continued his vitriolic comments, trying to jerk left and right but not able to pull out of the cop's grasp. "This is an unlawful arrest. You didn't even ask me about my Article 7 rights!" He spat a creative stream of profanities in both English and Mandarin.

Officer Nathan Callahan laughed and yanked the man closer. "Article 7 doesn't apply when we've got recordings of you committing the crime, and you didn't confess to anything. But sure, to make things formal, all Article 7 rights apply. Do you need these explained to you? Maybe drawn in big, simple pictures?"

The suspect narrowed his eyes. "I'm going to enjoy suing you. Everyone knows the cops are getting cleaned up, and..." His eyes widened as his gaze landed on Erik. "No way. It's him!"

Nathan smirked and nodded at Eric. "Detective, I think you've got another fan."

Erik muttered under his breath and stepped forward. "What's his deal?"

"Just petty theft. He just tried to run, and tripped and fell into a wall. He's been screeching the entire way, even though he's the one who hurt himself," Nathan answered.

The suspect stared at Erik with adoration, his lips slightly parted. "It's really you—the Obsidian Detective. Damn. If I knew I'd get to talk to you, I would have gotten arrested a long time ago."

"I'm a cop," Erik's eyes narrowed as he jerked his attention from the suspect to Nathan and back. "You get that, *right?*"

"Not just any cop." The suspect tried to move his arms, but the binding ties kept his wrists connected and his arms behind his back. "I was going to shake your hand, but you know." He lifted his arms to show his present predicament.

"I've read all about how you kick ass. Organized crime, terrorists, that stuff during Halloween." He paused and leaned in, his voice lower. "They say you took on a giant bot."

Erik eyed him. "I had help from my partner."

"Yeah, she's pretty cool too, and hot, from what I've seen." The suspect shook his head. "But you, man? *You* were Special Forces before you were a cop." He grinned. "I bet you've wasted more terrorists than the rest of the cops in the NSCPD combined."

Erik's jaw tightened. "It's not a big deal."

Luis, Halil, and Nathan chuckled. Erik's eyes flashed to them, which only made them smile wider as Halil faked looking clueless.

Halil's smile wasn't concealed. Erik returned his attention to the suspect.

Fanboys were obnoxious and criminal fanboys, even more so. He didn't do his job to have people slobber all over him.

"Come on, Detective Blackwell," the suspect countered. "You're the *first* Obsidian Detective in a hell of a long time, and you came in and shook it all up. This entire rotten city, from the Zone to the Hexagon. I'm always telling my boys that if I ever ran into the Obsidian Detective, I'd surrender before he blows my ass away with that super-rifle of his. I hear it's got twenty barrels."

"It's got four," Erik corrected.

Nathan grinned, picking up on Erik's discomfort. "That's right. This isn't just anyone. It's *the* Obsidian Detective. Would you like him to rough you up a bit so you can brag to your boys about how he kicked your ass? Maybe a punch to the stomach?"

The suspect looked down, considering the offer before shaking his head. "Nah. Just meeting him is enough. My boys wouldn't believe he would just punch me, and then I'd have to admit that I was already caught by some loser uniform and not the Obsidian Detective."

"No? A pity." Nathan pushed him forward. "Let's finish processing you, then, if you can handle it being done by a loser uniform."

"Keep doing your thing, Detective Blackwell!" the suspect shouted over his shoulder. "You rule!"

Erik watched him go, not wanting to see what Halil and Luis were doing. "I'm just glad Jia wasn't here to see that," he muttered.

He headed out to the vehicle parking area, ignoring the friendly snickers behind him.

A few minutes later, Erik was cruising toward the Shadow Zone in the MX 60, his pace comfortable.

He wasn't in a hurry.

"Does it really bother you that much?" Emma asked.

"What?"

"The adoration of the general public," she clarified.

He looked around before answering. "Not really. It *can* be annoying, though." Erik shook his head. "I don't need the respect of street criminals. I don't care much about what people think, as long as they let me do what I need to. Too much fame might mess with my options."

"You're not talking about local justice, are you?" Emma suggested. "At least, not entirely."

"I'm a cop. I'm about enforcing the laws, but that doesn't mean I've forgotten why I became a cop." Erik frowned. "I don't know if this is the best way to figure out what happened on Molino, but clues keep popping up, so I don't know if there's a better path."

"I will note, even setting aside your career, that Neo SoCal, given that it has so many corporate headquarters, is arguably one of the most important places in the UTC." Emma's holographic form phased into existence in the passenger seat, and she was gazing at him. "Your best chance of finding evidence is by remaining here. It's not as if you can fly all over the galaxy on a whim."

"I just need more freedom." Erik sighed, his grip loosening on the steering yoke. "But cleaning up the assholes isn't a bad way to pass my days in the meantime." His frown gave way to a predatory grin. "And who knows? Alicia might have something good for me," he finished as they crossed the security line between the area above.

And the Shadow Zone.

Erik settled into a chair across from Alicia in the back room of The Big One. "It's been a while, but I'm going to be visiting you weekly, going forward."

The informant stared at him with an amused look. "Weekly visits? You are either getting desperate, or you're bored."

Erik shrugged, an easy smile on his face. "It'd be easier if you'd just let me call you."

Alicia shook her head. "I found out a long time ago that the best way to do this kind of work is face to face. It cuts down on a lot of trouble, and it lets me lie more easily when I need to."

He always had to remind himself that despite her smooth features, the gray streaks in her black hair weren't a fashion choice. Like him, she'd received a de-aging treatment, and was around his age.

She'd seen her fair share of trouble.

"All the more reason for me to show up more often," Erik explained. "I need to keep an ear to the ground, and you're one way I do that. I wouldn't be doing my job as a cop, and we both know the department still has enough trash in it that not everything I need to hear ends up reaching me."

A flicker of satisfaction spread across Alicia's face. She quashed it with a bored expression and a moment's pause, then tapped her finger on her desk. Erik eyed her, staying quiet until she spoke. "You know the crackdown is actually working, right?"

"So you've said." Erik let the doubt linger in his voice. "And so the official stats say."

She pursed her lips. "I think it's more focused Uptown, but we're feeling the effects down here as well. I'm not some politician or bureaucrat who needs nice numbers for a report. I'm seeing it. Crime isn't just down in appearance. It really is down. Yeah, some guys are getting flashier and more brazen because they see opportunities, but if you people keep this up, Neo SoCal will end up being halfway like the politicians claim it is."

Something in her tone pricked Erik.

"There is a 'but' coming," he said. "Isn't there?"

Alicia chuckled. "That's life, right? Always tradeoffs?"

"True enough." He settled down in his chair. "What are the tradeoffs here?"

Alicia gestured toward the door. "Like I said, the flashy guys."

"Yeah, I've noticed."

"The real problem is that the crackdown is working because the average piece of trash before was lazy. Corrupt bureaucrats, corrupt corporations, and corrupt cops are easy to exploit. Everyone knew just where to push, but not too far. The guys who are surviving all the new law enforcement attention are smarter and more ruthless. A lot of them are more vicious."

"That means they'll flame out earlier." Erik considered how much he should share. Finally, he just went ahead. "I dealt with this during counterinsurgency ops. The guys who liked to make a big show always got located and eliminated earlier than the subtle bastards. It's not like anything as bad as Halloween has happened in the last few months."

Erik didn't feel the need to add that the Halloween incident was likely an attempt at assassinating him in the guise of a terrorist incident.

That didn't change the fact that pulling it off had required the cooperation of a number of people, including corrupt elements in law enforcement. The department wasn't heavily advertising it, but more than a few cops up and down the chain-of-command were getting fired or investigated.

Alicia smiled. "You've been in Neo SoCal for less than a year, but they've already got you thinking like an Uptowner."

"What do you mean?" Erik asked.

"You said no major incidents, but there is plenty of *crap* still happening down here. It might not be as flashy as terrorists, but there are a lot of powerplays going on. People getting hurt."

"When we learn about them, we stop them." Erik shrugged. "That's all we can do. I know the EZs with direct jurisdiction are still slower than anyone would like, but we've had some decent arrests."

"Not blaming you, Blackwell." Alicia shook her head. "You and your partner seem to care, and from what you've said, your new captain does too. And you *have* been nailing a lot of the rougher guys. Besides, if you clean up stuff too much, I'm going to be out of business." She grinned, but it only lasted a few seconds. "But you're here to check what's going on, not what's happened."

"That's the general idea, yeah."

"Even if it's probably garbage?"

Erik's brow lifted in surprise. "It's not like you to not trust what you've heard."

"I'm always careful," Alicia replied. "If I'm not giving people good and accurate information, my reputation suffers. That's why I want it to be clear that the most recent thing I've got for you might not be useful."

He nodded. "Understood. You'll get the same pay, and if it turns into something more, you'll get a bonus."

Alicia sighed and looked down with an uncomfortable expression on her face. "There have been a lot of strange rumors lately about something going on near the Scar."

His eyes narrowed. "Like what?"

"Don't know. I've heard about a few people ending up dead." Alicia raised her head. "It might be that the cop attention has forced people to go closer to the border to take care of stuff."

"It's not impossible," Erik concluded.

"Sure. The only thing that bothers me is that there might be fewer cops near the border of the Scar, but the Militia is there, and they do a good job of keeping that place bottled up."

"True enough." Erik pondered the information. "They're soldiers, not cops. Not even MPs."

"Meaning?" Alicia looked confused.

"Soldiers are all about their orders," he explained. "And their orders are to keep people out of the Scar, not to help the cops with crime or stop gangsters from killing each other. It's not worth risking a soldier's life to break orders and save bottom-feeders from hurting one another."

Alicia nodded. "You're saying the Militia knows there are criminals gathering near the Scar, but they don't give a crap as long as they don't enter it?"

"Maybe." He thought for a moment more. "When I was in the service, the last thing I wanted to do was make more trouble for my unit. Law enforcement is better suited to a lot of problems. It's not like the average Army unit is wandering around with a lot of non-lethals and binding ties. If the Militia were to solve the crime problem in the

Shadow Zone, it'd involve even more dead guys than I'm producing and would include martial law."

"That makes sense. And it might not be anything." Alicia inclined her head toward the door. "That's the main thing I've got for you. I don't think we should spend too much time back here. The last thing we want is more rumors, at least not ones I can't make money from."

Erik chuckled and stood. "Just keep listening for those rumors. It might be nothing, or it could be something we need to handle before it gets out of control."

CHAPTER FIVE

Jia slammed an elbow into an opponent to her right, who fell to the floor, choking and clawing at his throat.

A frowning man on her opposite side brought up a stun rod. She grabbed and twisted his arm until he cried out and dropped the weapon. Two quick palm strikes sent him to join his friend on the floor, his nose gushing blood.

She shook out her hand as she looked around, seeking her next opponent.

The simulated opponents felt too dense and heavy to fool her, but she preferred it that way. Better to train by hitting something harder than the opposite.

When Erik first invited her to the Pacific Tactical Center, she hadn't considered the potential for martial arts practice. Her master always insisted that anything not real wasn't good training.

Because of his advice, VR and nano-VR had seemed pointless. However, if an experienced soldier such as Erik felt that his time in the training center was good practice with weapons, she failed to see why it wouldn't be good training for hands and fists.

During her time as a cop, she'd neglected her hand-to-hand training. Small doubts in her mind had convinced her she wouldn't need to do something as savage as smash a man in the face. Reality had shown her that might be one of the more merciful techniques available to subdue suspects.

It might hurt, but so did losing your front teeth after being shocked into submission and landing on your face. If she were going to keep involving herself in trouble with Erik, every combat tool she had available would help keep them both alive.

She understood the truth—the UTC wasn't a safe place. *Earth* wasn't a safe place. They were detectives. They investigated deceit and depravity, which often led to violence, even if they did their best to avoid it. Well, perhaps she did her best, and Erik tried. He was a bit like a young boy who tried hard not to eat fresh-baked cookies.

Occasionally, face smeared with chocolate, he would claim, "I tried not to eat them, but they jumped into my mouth!"

Jia kicked the downed opponents in their heads to knock them out. Compared to Emma's more elaborate scenarios, Jia's personal training program was nothing more than a series of interconnected gray rooms with various opponents wielding melee weapons or their fists and feet. After she got more comfortable, she might invite the AI to design more colorful scenarios.

Yeah, not yet.

After taking a few deep breaths, Jia marched to the next

door, which slid open. Two large men with knives stood inside, grinning. She raised her hands and slowly crept forward.

"Let's see what you've got," she challenged.

Both enemies charged and she spun to the side, avoiding a thrust from one man. A quick chop to the wrist forced him to drop the knife. His partner growled and sliced at her, and she grabbed his arm and bent. He howled in pain as the other man tried to lunge toward Jia. His knife pierced his friend's shoulder. He grimaced and stumbled back, yanking the blade from the wound in alarm.

Jia winced.

She'd set the realism to maximum, which left her staring at a seeping bloody shoulder wound and a man on his knees bellowing in pain. The other man tried to kick the distracted detective. Catching the movement from the corner of her eye, she spun, then grabbed his leg and pulled. He fell, and his head slammed into the ground with a loud crack. His eyes rolled up in the back of his head. The other man fell at his side, whimpering.

"Dammit!" Jia shook her head. "Participant command, end simulation."

The room and the men vanished, replaced by the white and silver of the tactical center's simulation room.

She shouldn't have hesitated even for a second, and every time she practiced, she did it less.

She squeezed her eyes shut in frustration, her hands rubbing her temples. "I'm getting there, Erik. It could be a lot worse, but I'm getting there."

Jia stepped out of the elevator into the long, brightly lit hall leading to her apartment.

Between the raid, training, dates, and family, the week weighed harshly on her shoulders. She couldn't complain, but she also couldn't help but be amused by how easy life had been *before* Erik.

No wonder cops like Jared Thompson never wanted to do anything real. It was far easier to sit around, drink coffee, and send the occasional report to a different EZ or division.

No rest for the weary. It's only going to get harder from here.

Even if by some miracle, they finished cleaning up Neo SoCal, the people responsible for murdering Erik's unit were out there. Their resources probably made the organized crime groups and terrorists the detectives had been dealing with seem like petty street hustlers.

Jia froze, and her heart rate kicked up. She shivered and slowly turned around, blinking in surprise when she saw nothing.

"I was sure someone was watching me," she mumbled. She stared down the hallway, looking for any stray shadow or distorted light. The killers on Molino had advanced camouflage, according to Erik. It wasn't impossible that they'd improved the technology.

Jia shook her head. What was she doing? She had half-convinced herself that invisible assassins were following her down the hall. That was absurd.

Or was it?

Gangsters and corrupt council members were linked to one of the most powerful companies in the UTC, which had only come to light because she and Erik had pursued it. Mysterious military-grade units were murdering Army Special Forces on the frontier. All that considered, she spent a second getting a feel for her surroundings.

Being paranoid was a good way to stay alive.

Jia took a few deep breaths and continued down the corridor. The turn toward her apartment was coming, and that would be her chance. She couldn't flinch or hesitate like she had in the simulation. It was her life on the line.

A long distance became a short one, and the turn loomed closer. Her hand drifted into her jacket and hovered over the grip of her stun pistol. She stepped around the corner and stopped.

She waited a few seconds before ripping the gun from the holster and spinning back around the corner. A handsome blond man in a suit stood in the middle of the hall. He looked to be about her age, but with de-aging, she couldn't be sure. Not everyone had the trouble Erik and Alicia did with their hair.

He threw up his hands and swallowed. "Don't shoot. I don't want to die."

"It's a stun pistol." Jia narrowed her eyes, her gun pointed at the man. "It'll hurt, but you'll live."

The man chuckled nervously but kept his hands up. "What if I told you I don't want to get hurt either?"

Something was vaguely familiar about him, but she couldn't place him.

"If you don't want to get hurt, bound, and hauled off to jail, you'll answer my questions," Jia barked, her harsh voice one-hundred percent in angry detective mode.

The man nodded. "Sure, sure. Whatever you say, Jia."

"Jia, huh?" She sneered. "I think we should be introduced before we're on a first-name basis, don't you?"

"Sampson Aryle," the man offered. "You can call me Sam if you want."

"Okay, Sam," Jia began, her tone still short and clipped. "You want to tell me why you were following me? Or are you going to deny it?"

Sam looked away. "I-I…damn. Can I lower my arms? They're getting tired."

"You do that, you're getting two bolts to the chest, and then I'm hauling your butt to jail."

"You seriously don't recognize me?" Sam asked.

"Why should I?" Jia shrugged. "I know I haven't run into you at work." She tried to remember if she'd seen him at a club. That might explain the vague familiarity.

He nodded. "I'm, uh, your *neighbor*," Sam explained.

While her head shook from side to side, her eyes stayed glued to him. "Uh, no, you're not. I know who lives around me."

Sam sighed. "Not on your floor. I live in the building. I suppose that's not that impressive since a lot of people do. I've seen you around a few times."

"Send me an ID." She pointed at his PNIU. "Nice and slow or buzz-buzz." Her smile was less than encouraging. "*Ouch-ouch*."

Sam slowly lowered his arms, then tapped a few commands into his PNIU. Jia's chimed, and she lowered one arm to receive the ID and quickly run it through the NSCPD system for confirmation. His address and picture appeared in the corner of her smart lenses.

"Okay, you live here." Jia frowned and holstered her weapon. "You were still being a creep."

Sam jerked back as if struck. "Ouch. Okay, I deserved that." He sighed again. "Like I said, I've seen you around the building a few times, and then I saw you on the news. I thought, you know, maybe we could go out for drinks or something."

"Drinks?" Jia let out a strangled laugh. "Like, a date?"

"It's not *that* funny," Sam complained.

"Sorry." Jia shook her head. "It's not you. I'm a detective, and I've dealt with a lot of terrorists. When people start following me, it makes me think they're trying to kill me. You could have just called."

Sam nodded. "Good point. I'm not great with calls. I'm not great face to face, either." He laughed, looking around as if he wished the wall would swallow him. "Really selling myself here."

Jia threw up a hand. "Let me stop you, Sam. We'll ignore the clumsy way you went about this. Mistakes happen, but I want to make something clear."

"Yes?" Hope infiltrated his voice.

"I'm already dating somebody," Jia explained. "And I'm not the kind of woman who dates two men at the same time."

"Oh." Sam's shoulders sagged. "That makes sense." He looked up with a hang-dog expression. "No hard feelings, I hope?"

"Next time, don't sneak up on me, or you might get hurt for real." Jia waved and headed back around the corner, shaking her head.

Being around Erik was spoiling her.

About an hour later, she was settled on her couch, wearing a nightgown. A check of her plants and a shower had washed the earlier unpleasantness away, except for one small part. A lingering worm of doubt had tunneled into her mind during the conversation with Sam.

I'm already dating somebody.

That was what she had said, but when she thought it, the first image that popped into her head wasn't Corbin, but *Erik*. He was a partner, not a boyfriend.

Everyone from her sister to her boyfriend hinted at the opposite.

It wasn't like she was going to deny she was attracted to him. He was fit, handsome, intelligent, brave, and dedicated. He was also a man who had lived his life on the frontier, fighting terrorists. She wasn't sure if his rough approach to law enforcement was appropriate, even as she slid farther toward it each day.

Was she mistaking gratitude for his help with her career for something else?

Jia grabbed her PNIU, rubbing her fingers over the silver card. She needed to talk to someone who didn't know her and couldn't—not wouldn't, but *couldn't*—pass judgment. After a minute of searching, she connected to a highly rated choice that fit her needs.

"Good evening," answered a female voice. "You have reached the Rose Line, purveyors of very secure, very discreet relationship advice. Are you interested in using my services this evening? Please be aware that there is a flat charge per half-hour."

"I am," she replied.

"You can call me Rose." There was a slight pause before Rose came back on, after checking her credit, no doubt. "UTC law requires I disclose at this time that I am an artificial intelligence program interface and not a human being."

Despite the pleasant tone, there was something slightly off about the inflection. Jia had taken for granted how human Emma sounded when she spoke. "Please tell me your name so we can begin healing your heart."

"Um..." Jia began. She didn't care about talking to an AI in and of itself, but anything on a computer could be hacked. She didn't know who might use her relationship problems against her, but a little caution would be appropriate. "My name is Emma."

She rolled her eyes. *Not exactly slick.*

"Good evening, Emma," Rose continued. "What is the nature of your problem?"

"I have a couple of problems," Jia explained. "First of all, a neighbor of mine just showed up out of nowhere to ask me out. I mean, he's barely a neighbor. He lives in the same residential tower."

"I see. From what you've said, it sounds like his advances are unwelcome." Rose kept the same friendly, calm tone and even cadence.

Jia stretched her legs out and lifted them to the side to lie down on her couch. "Yes, you could say that. The man's allegedly seen me before, and I must have seen him in passing, but instead of calling me like a normal person or saying hello somewhere, he followed me through the halls."

"I see. From what you've said, it sounds like this man

made you uncomfortable. Do you feel that is an accurate assessment?"

Jia realized it wasn't only Rose's tone that screamed "machine," but also her repetitive speech patterns. Emma might reuse a few favorite snarky terms, but it was hard to predict what she would say next. Rose was an AI programmed with relationship and psychology knowledge, but Jia doubted the program possessed any hint of self-awareness.

"Yes," Jia replied. "It made me uncomfortable. I also worry that I didn't handle it the right way."

"I see. How did you handle it?"

She sighed, covering her eyes. "I threatened him."

"You threatened him? Do you mean that you threatened him with physical harm?"

Jia rolled onto her side. "*Yes.*"

"UTC law requires me to remind you that assault is a crime and antisocial. Please avoid using force to resolve disputes unless self-defense is necessary."

Great. Now she was getting called antisocial by an *AI*.

"I didn't hurt him," Jia countered, stung by the accusation. "And I thought he was a stalker or…" She couldn't tell an AI she thought he might be an assassin. "I thought it was self-defense."

"I see." Rose didn't speak for several seconds. "Please note that if you are in danger, it is best to contact the police or local security. Let's get back to your issue. Are you interested in dating this man?"

"No. I just…" Jia groaned. "Was there a better way of handling it?"

"Yes," Rose replied. "Firmly turning him down without the threat of physical force would have been sufficient."

"I can't believe I'm paying an AI to tell me something I already know," Jia mumbled. "Fine. Let's move on to my next problem."

"Please wait," Rose insisted, her tone no different than before. "Are you sure you're satisfied with the resolution to your first issue?"

"Yes. May we move on now?"

"Very well. What is the nature of this issue?"

Jia took a few deep breaths before answering. "When I turned down the first man, the reason I offered was that I'm already in a relationship. That's true, but I often find myself thinking about someone I work with. Someone I'm not in a relationship with, and I'm wondering if that means anything."

"I see. When you fantasize about your co-worker, is it sexual in nature?"

Jia jerked upright. "*Excuse* me?"

"I apologize if you could not hear me. I'll repeat myself. When you fantasize about your co-worker, is it sexual in nature?"

"It's not..." Jia's face burned. "I find him attractive, okay? But it's not like I sit around thinking about him naked. It's just, according to some people, I talk too much about him with my boyfriend, but he's my partner at work. He's the person I spend the most time around. Not my boyfriend, the other guy."

"I see," Rose replied. The repetition was beginning to annoy Jia and reminded her of why she had avoided AI therapy and advice in the past. "Emma, may I be honest?"

Jia blinked. It took her several seconds to remember she'd lied about her name. "Yes, go ahead. It's what I'm paying for."

"I can't be certain, given the limited background information you've provided me, but if you're fantasizing about your co-worker and it's disrupting your existing relationship, that suggests a strong romantic attraction that you might not be able to easily ignore. You might consider changing teams or departments at work to minimize contact with your co-worker. That presumes you wish to salvage your current relationship. The fact that you're fantasizing about another man might indicate that you're dissatisfied with your current relationship."

"You know what?" Jia snapped. "I've had enough."

"I see. Are you sure? Sometimes direct confrontation of emotional truths can be uncomfortable Don't let—"

Jia terminated the call. "I don't need some stupid AI to give me advice I can't use," she muttered under her breath. "I can work through this. I'm not fantasizing about Erik. I have a boyfriend, and I'm satisfied with him." She put the PNIU to the side. "Erik's just a partner. Nothing more. That's it."

She nodded. She believed herself, mostly. It was a good thing Emma didn't monitor her PNIU off-duty.

That could have gotten embarrassing.

CHAPTER SIX

January 11, 2229, Neo Southern California Metroplex, Apartment of Detective Erik Blackwell

Erik clipped a thin branch off a tiny tree in the center of the miniature cliffside penjing forest on his dining room table. He might have involved himself in the hobby on a whim, but he couldn't deny how relaxing it could be.

It was nice to create something rather than blow it up.

"Excuse me, Detective Blackwell," Emma asked, still formless, her voice coming from Erik's PNIU. "There is information of a potentially non-criminal nature you might find useful. It is not time-sensitive, but I see no reason not to discuss it."

He stood and moved away from his curated micro-tree, eyeing it from a couple of angles while chewing his cheek.

Did it look better with the second topmost limb in place, or would a clip give it some nice negative space to frame the top?

"What? You find a universal half-off beignets coupon?" he asked.

Emma snickered. "I could easily get you free beignets for life if you're so inclined."

"I'd rather support the restaurants I like by paying for my food." Erik set his clippers on the table, glancing at his PNIU as he walked into his living room. "What do you have for me?"

"Your brother will be coming to Neo SoCal in a couple of weeks," Emma declared.

Erik stood in front of his couch, as rigid as a statue, not responding.

"I'd ask if you were still alive, but your vital signs are strong, even if your heart rate is elevated," Emma commented. "It would be rather anticlimactic if you died of a heart attack."

Erik sat on the edge of the couch and gritted his teeth. "My *brother's* coming?"

"Yes."

"How the hell do you know that? Are you chatting with him?" he asked.

Emma laughed. "No. I'm sure he's a dreary drone, from what little I've gathered from your conversations and public records searches. I should make it clear that I see little advantage in keeping pertinent information from you, let alone important information."

Erik nodded. "Understood. I'd say the same thing, but it's practically impossible for me to keep anything from you, so my decision is not very impressive."

"That's true," Emma agreed. "Surprising that you came to that conclusion as an organic being, but true nonetheless."

"How do you know my brother's coming?"

"The aforementioned public records and news searches," Emma explained.

Several data windows appeared in front of Erik. One article announced a major upcoming conference for industrial chemical manufacturers. Another window displayed a subset of a list of conference attendees.

Damien Blackwell, Senior Vice-President of Distribution, Flamel Universal

An image of a gray-haired man with a weathered copy of Erik's face was displayed above the listing. He'd thought about contacting his older brother since coming back to Earth, but he'd always come up with a reason why it was a bad idea.

"Yeah." Erik let out a quiet half-sigh, half-growl. "That's him. So, is this what you were talking about a month ago when you mentioned doing wide-net searches?"

"Mostly." Emma's hologram appeared. She folded her arms and stood next to the coffee table. "I'm monitoring a lot of information related to both you and Detective Lin. I'm avoiding any security intrusions that might draw unnecessary attention, governmental, corporate, or otherwise. I'm the superior pinnacle of human technology, but even I have my limits. With all that admitted, I still feel that by doing this, I can detect unusual patterns that might relate to the conspiracy. I'm attempting to connect otherwise disparate information as an early warning system."

"I like the sound of that." He tapped a finger on his leg. "One question before we go on about my brother. Have you heard anything weird about the Scar?"

Emma furrowed her brow, her displeasure clear on her face. "I'm limited in this endeavor by the information made available for consumption. The Shadow Zone might not be the lawless hell-hole some claim it is, but the level of news and information that is coming out of the Zone remains less than optimal for my purposes. However, I will note there were some recent reassignments of some Militia units in that area. Everything seems to suggest a standard change, and the timing is consistent with that explanation. I didn't think it was worth bringing to your attention, despite what Alicia said. Excessive information won't help you."

"True. While it might not be helpful, it's good to know anyway," Erik answered. "Keep pushing. Things are too quiet on that front, and it might be up to you to find the trail we need to follow. I'm pretty sure my brother coming for a business conference isn't part of a conspiracy. If they know anything about me, they know I haven't spoken to the guy in years."

Emma nodded. "That is one possible conclusion."

He eyed her. "You don't agree?"

"The conference, as best I can tell, has been scheduled to be in held Neo SoCal for over a year, even before your arrival on Earth. His participation at such conferences is common, but I do wonder. When we consider everything in aggregate, we have unusual activity in the Zone and the Scar, and your brother coming into town. That might be mere coincidence, or it might be overly fortuitous timing, indicative of a plot."

Erik flipped his fingers through one of the virtual holographic windows and skimmed the list of conference participants. "Lots of heavy hitters, including Ceres

Galactic subdivisions." He continued scanning the list. "Any news articles mention security for the conference?"

"Several," Emma related. "Would you like to read them, or would you prefer I summarize them?"

"I'll take the summary, thanks."

"Many local conferences and events are keenly aware of their potential as terrorist targets from a variety of ideological organizations. Security investments, both in technology and personnel, have been increased accordingly and publicly stressed. There's even a statement in your brother's conference brochure extolling the high level of armed security that will be present." Emma shrugged. "It's not impossible that it'd be targeted, but they're well prepared for it."

Erik grinned. "Then you're just being a paranoid AI."

Emma rolled her eyes. "My time with you has been characterized by swarms of cultist terrorists, hordes of gun junkies, and waves of repurposed murderous security bots. It's important that you stay alive. I'm not paranoid." She sniffed. "I'm aggressively cautious."

He turned to eye her hologram. "You're that worried about me dying? I didn't know you cared so much."

She pointed at him. "You are my shield against the DD. I would rather not take drastic actions. I would like to think they're afraid to make a move independent of you, but I'm not an idiot. After all, while I'm vastly superior to a mere human, it's obvious your unique relationship with Colonel Adeyemi and his shared desire for vengeance are the driving factors keeping the military from coming after me. If you die, it's highly likely my comfortable status quo would be disrupted." She made a face, not unlike a highbrow lady speaking to an unwanted suitor. "I'd rather that not occur. I find my current lifestyle satisfying and amusing."

"I'm trying not to die." He chuckled. "But there are no guarantees. I don't think my brother has anything to do with a conspiracy, and I should just leave him alone."

Emma's mouth quirked into a tight smile. "Now, this is interesting. Very interesting."

"What?" He shrugged. "It's not like you didn't already know I had my issues with my brother."

"I understand, but I am not used to seeing you avoid a conflict."

"I'm trying to not waste my time." Erik frowned. "We both said what we needed to say to each other a long time ago. Hell, that was a long time before you existed."

Emma walked through the table, her image shimmering. She stood in front of Erik, scowling at him. "Detective Blackwell, if I didn't know better, I'd say you were afraid."

Erik looked at her from his seat. "Being pissed and holding a grudge isn't the same thing as being afraid. I'm spending all my time hunting the conspiracy, and it's not because I'm afraid of them. Come on, Emma." He ran a hand through his hair as he sat back on the sofa. "You know me. Once someone pisses me off, it takes an orbital strike to remove that grudge."

"I fail to see why it would hurt to at least speak with him."

He cocked his head to the side. "Why do you even care? My brother's just another dumb fleshbag to you."

Emma snickered. "He is, but that fleshbag is related to *you*. By your own admission, you harbor an extreme and continuing emotional attachment to him." She raised a hand. "Before you say anything, please note that anger isn't the opposite of love. Apathy is. Anything that might serve as a potential distraction for you is of interest to me, so I think you should meet him and attempt to resolve your issues. The worst thing that happens is that you continue to hate him."

"I don't...*hate* him." Erik looked down and shook his head. "I understand that we don't see eye to eye." He paused, his face scrunched. "Wait, why should I take family advice from an AI?"

Emma held up a finger. "First reason, I'm brilliant." She held up a second finger. "Second reason, *I'm brilliant.*"

"Hmm." Erik rubbed his chin. "A psychiatrist is a doctor, and what's a doctor but someone who has learned to ask questions and figure things out based on algorithms? I suppose it's not that different."

"There's another potential use for your brother," Emma countered. "It's something I've considered based on your rather lightweight personal life."

Erik snorted. "All right, mini-Jia, what are you getting at?"

"He's been divorced several times."

Erik was surprised by this turn in the conversation. "Yeah, I know. What about it?"

Emma smiled. "You could always use him as a resource about marriage. Figure out what he did and avoid making the same mistakes."

He chuckled. "Marriage isn't high on my list of concerns at the moment."

Emma shrugged. "It's good to plan for the future. Better

overprepared than underprepared. The preponderance of evidence suggests that you should meet with your brother."

"I'll think about it."

Travis shook out his hands as he stood outside the abandoned store. The chill of the night had settled in, and wandering a dark corner of the Shadow Zone didn't do much to warm his body or his soul.

"This is what I get for taking a job that sounded too good to be true," he grumbled. He patted his jacket, the weight of his gun the only thing comforting at the moment. "Three times the pay, same danger. Liars."

Travis reached for his PNIU before pulling his hand back. He had left it at home. That was part of the job. Cops were cracking down everywhere, even in the Zone. A PNIU was a beacon if cops were looking for a specific person, and a man helping to move some of the last Dragon Tear in the area was a man who wanted to stay hidden.

He looked around. "Stupid cops," Travis muttered. "All the Tear jobs are drying up, you assholes. How am I supposed to make money now?"

He tapped his foot and folded his arms, frowning at the abandoned store. It was taking too long. His buddy Johnny was supposed to have made the drop-off already. Testing should have taken a minute at most.

"Where is that idiot? He better not be pissing again. He can hit the can later."

Gunfire erupted from inside, and a piercing scream followed.

"What the *hell?*" Travis yanked out his pistol and rushed inside, calling into the darkness, "Johnny? Where you at?"

Travis couldn't wait for help. No one was coming. They'd come to this place to *avoid* police drones and attention.

He was on his own.

His pounding heart was not helping as he crept through the darkened store. Little noises, amplified by his fear, sounded like folks a couple of blocks down the street would hear them.

Would that be such a bad thing?

Without a PNIU, not only did he lack light, but he couldn't also adjust his smart lenses to low-light mode.

A loud crunch and ripping noise came from the back; the feeling that bone was being ripped out of flesh was uncomfortably real. No holodrama made that sound.

"Johnny?" Travis called, turning left and then right, gun aimed straight...enough. Perhaps it was shaking, but he could hit something in the general direction it was pointed.

"You guys better not hurt him! You have no clue who you're messing with. We've got big connections." He let his finger hover over his trigger, licking his lips. "This better not be another one of your stupid jokes, Johnny. Not funny, man. Call out!"

He continued toward the back. The door was open and probably had been for decades in the abandoned building. He leapt in front of the door, gun ready to fire at the bastards he was sure had killed his friend.

Travis' eyes widened. Even in the dim light of the back

room, he could make out the blood-splattered walls and his friend's mangled body. "Oh, God." His stomach churned, and his resistance disappeared as he bent over, vomiting, perspiration on his forehead.

He wiped it off as he looked around. "I've got to get out of here."

A scratching noise sounded from behind him in the room.

Travis spun to fire. "I'll see you in hell, you *bastards!*"

He aimed his gun to the left, then right, then left again, but there was no one in the room. He had a few seconds to think about what had made the noise before his chest blossomed with pain. Something had ripped into his back.

"Johnny?" Travis coughed, blood leaking from his mouth, then looked down, noticing that something had punctured his chest. "Damn." The agony overwhelmed him. He couldn't even manage a scream when his killer stabbed him once more.

CHAPTER SEVEN

January 12, 2229, Neo Southern California Metroplex, Police Enforcement Zone 122 Station

Jia and Erik stepped off the elevator and into the hallway leading to the bullpen.

"Have fun with your trees on your day off?" Jia asked.

Erik chuckled. "You act like you don't have an indoor garden. Where's all this smugness coming from?"

"I do," Jia admitted, "but they aren't all in…miniature. I did have a nice date with Corbin the other day."

There was no good reason to admit that she'd called Corbin for a spontaneous date just to prove to herself that she was into him and not Erik. She'd challenged herself to not mention Erik once during the entire date.

There was no reason to admit she'd failed that challenge, but at least she'd kept it to one incident.

"Date, huh?" Erik smiled. "Did you do something else boring?"

"Boring is relative. We didn't go to a sphere ball match if that's what you're asking." Jia offered him a playful grin.

"I'd say we should have another dating bet, but I'd feel bad if you were paying for my beer and beignets for the rest of the year. You'd have no chance."

Erik scoffed. "I can win. I just have to care enough. I hit up a coffee place that might even give me a strong start."

"Huh?" She pursed her lips. "What does coffee have to do with dating?"

"There was a woman there, a barista," Erik explained. "She was pretty attractive."

"Are you excited because of her or her *coffee*?" Jia asked. She did her best to keep her tone light and playful despite her tightening stomach. It shouldn't bother her that Erik was interested in someone. She'd set him up not that long ago, after all.

Erik considered the question. "The way to a man's heart starts with good food and drinks, and I drink coffee every day."

"A barista, though? That's just..." Jia shrugged. "She's probably pretty young. I thought you wanted someone a little more mature?"

"No, what I said was, I don't want a fangirl drooling over me," Erik explained. His gaze ticked over to her and lingered. "And like I've said before, being young and being mature aren't mutually exclusive."

Jia's breath caught. She nodded to acknowledge the hit and continued walking as the noise coming from down the hall increased.

They turned the corner and stepped into the main bullpen. Uniformed officers sat at their desks, data windows and coffee in front of them.

Nathan leaned over the desk of a patrol officer. "I'm just

saying, I'm glad we only have to go down there once in a while. I'm not saying the local EZs shouldn't do more, but the Zone is messed up in a big way." He glanced Erik's way. "Then again, you got Erik and Jia on the Shadow Zone Task Force. The rate they're going, they might have it cleaned up in six months."

Erik grinned. "All the fun's down there. Uptown's boring half the time."

"Except for when terrorists are attacking," Nathan pointed out.

Jia glanced at the data window over the desk. It was an article on sphere ball league rankings, nothing related to crime.

"Is there something going on in the Shadow Zone we should know about?" Jia asked.

"I'm sure you'll see the reports once you check your mail," Nathan explained. "But I'll give you the preview. There a missing person report down there. They're pushing it to all the departments like it's a big deal. John Neemoknik. He's a corporate insurance assessor who was doing some work in one of the rougher parts of the zone. Something about analysis for possible reclamation in the future by the council." He scoffed. "He should have waited a few more years while things got cleaned up. Poor bastard."

"He might be okay," Jia suggested, her tone betraying her doubt.

Nathan shrugged. "Sure. Sometimes people get lucky. You two going to have to investigate that?"

Erik shook his head. "Probably not. Being on the task force mostly just means we can go in and out without special permission. There's way too much crime down there for a handful of detectives, and technically, the local EZs still have primary jurisdiction."

"Lucky you, then."

Erik nodded. "Thanks. Talk to you later."

Jia and Erik left the chatty cop and continued to their office. A pensive look lingered on Erik's face.

"Problem?" Jia asked as she took a seat and brought up data windows to float above her desk.

"I don't know. Alicia mentioned trouble in the Zone, and now this." Erik shrugged. "Something's probably coming if it's not already here."

"It might be aftershocks of the Dragon Tear raid." Jia scanned her high-priority mail, but there weren't any Shadow Zone-related case assignments.

"Maybe." Erik brought up his own data window, and his eyes shifted back and forth as he read a few messages. "I know it's not just us holding back the tide, but sometimes it *feels* that way."

She lifted a hand, swiping left to get rid of a window. "If Captain Ragnar has reason to believe we can be of assistance, he'll send us down there."

Erik nodded and took a sip of cold coffee. "Yeah. Maybe I'm just on edge because of personal crap."

"Is something wrong?" Jia hoped she hadn't hurt his feelings with the dating jokes, but she doubted Erik was very fragile. She would be disappointed if he were.

His eyes flicked to her. "So, the other day, Emma told me my brother is coming to town…"

Erik finished his explanation, along with his conclusion that he wasn't interested in seeing his brother.

Jia sighed, the back of her hand rubbing her forehead. "I'm the wrong person to talk to about this."

Erik eyed her. "Why do you say that?"

"I might find my family frustrating," she started, "but they are still very important to me. I'm much happier now that my parents and sister have accepted my career. I think Emma might be right. It might not hurt you to meet with him and try to work things out."

Emma's snickers came through their PNIUs. Jia eyed hers, frowning.

She hated how quiet the AI could be. Sometimes she wondered if Emma was purposely trying to ambush them in the middle of a conversation.

"Of course, I'm right," Emma insisted.

Erik groaned. "Just what I need, two women convinced they're right about my personal life."

Jia swiped away her data windows to view him unobstructed. "You never explained the details of why you have such a poor relationship with your brother to me."

"It was a long time ago," he admitted. "The short version is, I used to be a roughneck and a troublemaker."

Jia smirked. "Used to be?"

He made a face. "I mean, when I was young, I got in a lot of fights. I believed I was a big man, and I didn't like it when I thought someone was disrespecting me. I did a little juvie time, nothing huge, and no prison."

Jia stared at him, surprised. "I…*see*." She grimaced. She didn't want to sound like Rose.

Erik shrugged. "It's no big deal. They beat all that out of

me in the Army. The Army needs soldiers, not thugs, and soldiers have discipline."

"Okay." She made a circle in the air with her hand to get him to continue. "What does this have to do with your brother?"

"Shortly before I joined, I got in a little scrape," Erik explained. "For once, it wasn't just me being a punk. Some guys were messing with a woman who did not want their attention. I 'encouraged' them to respect her personal space, but the owner of the bar I was in didn't appreciate that I'd trashed half the place kicking the guys' asses. The cops had to take me in, but they made it clear the minute I got processed, I'd be let go. Just needed bail. I called my brother."

"And?" Jia asked.

Erik chuckled ruefully. "He showed up and laid into me. Said I was a piece of trash, and my parents had given up on me." He paused, his eyes focused deep into his past. "He told me that the best thing I could do was sign up to be a laborer on a frontier colony so they could pretend I didn't exist." His eyes came back to her. "Refused to bail me out at first, but finally broke down. He told me to stay away from him and my parents."

Jia looked down, feeling his pain. "I'm sorry."

He shrugged. "I think I would have been less pissed if it hadn't happened after that particular incident. I thought about it and decided there was nothing left for me on Earth. My family was pretty poor, and my brother had a shot at being something. You know how it goes in corporations. Social screening might have kept him out of a good job after school if I was still around, so I left. Joined the Army and volunteered for frontier tours."

"You never tried to contact him again?"

"The thing is, I *did* try to keep in contact with him, but when I sent him a message, he told me, 'You finally did something for others, so keep it up—but stay away.'" Erik's finger stabbed down on his desk. "That really, *really* pissed me off." He leaned back in his chair. "We barely talked after that, and I didn't talk to my parents much. I ended up on a lot of distant worlds and on the move. Connecting seemed kind of pointless, with all the troubles, and not worth the time. I stopped caring about coming back to Earth. Next thing you know, the years had passed, and my parents were dead. I was too far away to attend their funeral." He snorted. "I think my brother held that against me, too."

"You're both different men now." Jia managed a soft smile. "It's been a long time. Don't you think it's time to reach out again?"

"Maybe you're right." Erik nodded. He furrowed his brow, then tapped his PNIU. His eyes moved to the side. "Just got a message. What are your lunch plans?"

"We just got here," Jia observed. "And I had breakfast not all that long ago."

"Sure, but you'll probably want to hear this. Keep your calendar clear."

A few hours later, Erik and Jia sat in the MX 60 with a conspicuous man in the back seat. Their passenger's bright pink Hawaiian shirt was covered with flamingoes and women in bikinis. Jia was half-convinced satellites could pick him out from orbit. They were officially on their way to have lunch at a restaurant a few kilometers farther out than their normal haunts, but the trip would give them several minutes of complete privacy.

Emma's hologram form sat beside the man, whose name was Malcolm, a near-permanent smirk fixed on her face.

"You said you had something for me?" Erik asked.

"It's kind of useful, but it's kind of not." Malcolm whistled once. "Sorry, Detective."

"Anything is better than nothing," Erik countered.

"I've been poking around here and there. It never sat right with me how and when that Halcyon lab blew up, so I've been watching them as much as I can."

"And?" Erik wanted to prod him with one of the charge sticks a few of the officers back at the precinct had lodged up their asses, that made them walk so stiffly.

"And I dabbled in some areas and servers that maybe I shouldn't have." Malcolm swallowed. "Nothing that can be traced back to me."

Jia frowned but didn't say anything. She was still trying to figure out where the line lay for investigating the conspiracy.

"Aren't you the bold one?" Emma chuckled. "Even I'm wary of doing that sort of thing."

Malcolm lifted his chin, pride on his face. Man had scored a small victory against the machines. "I grabbed a few minor records here and there. They don't prove anything big, but I learned a couple of things. That place was obviously doing research on top of whatever else they were doing, but here's the weird thing. They'd been emptying it out for a while before it blew up, and they started on a date you'll find interesting. June 15, 2228."

Erik's jaw tightened. "Just when I'd gotten back."

"Hey, you know, it could be a big coincidence, but there are a lot of coincidences piling up around you." Malcolm licked his lips. "A lot of bodies, too."

"True enough." Erik's hands tightened on MX 60's control yoke. "That's good to know, Malcolm. It's not useless. It means people have been watching me since I got here. Probably before." He looked to his left before changing lanes, the smooth movement of the Taxútnta providing an emotional response that touched the basic animal part of his brain. "Anything else?"

The tech shrugged. "One other thing. It was a brief portion of a memo relating to them moving out equipment. Before you ask, I don't have the files anymore. I copied them to a proxy server to read before deleting them. Not leaving any trails for terrorist assassins or whoever's involved in all this. The encryption on what should have been routine cargo records and a single memo was insane."

Jia gazed at Erik. "Maybe you should tell him the whole story. If he's hacking corporations, he deserves to know."

Malcolm shook his head furiously. "I've told you before, I don't *want* to know. I think plausible deniability will let me help you while keeping me from getting tossed into the ocean."

"Your call," Erik replied. "But thanks."

"You *are* a smart one, aren't you, Technician Constantine?" Emma chuckled. "For a fleshbag."

Malcolm turned to her and blinked. "Excuse me?"

Jia looked over her shoulder at Emma. "'Fleshbag?'"

"Blame Detective Blackwell," the AI explained. "Once he used the phrase, I couldn't contain my delight."

Jia rolled her eyes, and they ended up looking at her partner, who was doing his best to pay attention to the traffic. "As long as someone's enjoying this." She turned to Malcolm. "What else did you find? What did the memo fragment say?"

Malcolm took a few deep breaths and rubbed his hands together. Fighting conspiracies didn't seem to sit well with him. "It said, and I quote, 'Don't worry much about the Tin Man. Just continue the relocation of Wonderland. We don't need Alice and her friends finding it.'"

"I assume this is another thing that humans understand better than I do." Emma frowned. "Their coded statement confuses me because it mixes characters from different classical stories."

Erik glanced at Jia. "What do you think?"

She gestured to his arm. "It's rude to say so, but you're technically a Tin Man. I interpret the message as meaning there's someone else out there looking into this, and probably not the people you're already working with."

Erik nodded. "That's what I think, too."

Malcolm closed his eyes. "Hey, this is intense. I'm so hungry now. I'm sorry, that's all I've got. But it kind of sounds halfway useful, from what you're saying."

"Very useful," Erik agreed. "If there's someone else out there investigating this, it might be easier for me to pull off a few things."

"We don't know if they're on our side," Jia countered.

"The enemy of my enemy is sometimes just another enemy."

Emma nodded. "Wise words."

Erik snorted. "I don't care. I've got a lot of bullets to spare."

CHAPTER EIGHT

There were few things in the galaxy better than a fresh, piping hot beignet. Erik loved them enough that he'd take them cold or at room temperature, but the texture of a batch right out of the fryer could not be beaten.

He bit into one, savoring the sugary-sweet taste.

A few days had passed since the discussion with Malcolm. Nothing new had arisen with the conspiracy, and Erik and Jia had investigated and solved a minor theft case within one day. The Shadow Zone criminals might be getting more vicious and cunning, but the Uptown lawbreakers had seemed to reduce their intelligence (since, Erik concluded, typing "lose their damned minds" was inappropriate in written reports) as desperation grew.

For now, though, Erik didn't care about anything other than enjoying the pastry in his mouth. He didn't care about the dense crowd of diners having breakfast and coffee.

Jia noted he was barely aware of his own partner across the table from him. She laughed, pointing a fork at him.

"Do you need to be alone with that pastry? I keep expecting you to moan."

Erik swallowed. "Maybe I should. It's damned good."

"What kind of Chinese food you like?" Jia asked with a curious glint in her eye.

"Huh?" Erik downed another bite before responding. "I don't know. Mostly stuff that's tasty. I don't care what people say. I can't get past the smell of century eggs."

"If you had to pick a favorite, what would it be?"

"Beijing roast duck," Erik answered. He rubbed his chin, still thinking. "Hard to go wrong when something has a lot of protein."

Jia blinked a few times. "Beijing duck?"

He eyed her. "Why is that weird? You don't like it?"

Jia shook her head. "No, I have a lot of fond memories associated with that dish."

"Do you visit Beijing a lot? Everyone says you have to go there to get the best duck," he asked, taking another bite. She shook her head as he rolled his eyes in pleasure.

"No. Not really. Most of my relatives live in other places." Jia smiled. "Mother isn't one to do a lot of cooking, but that is one of the few dishes she prepares well. It was a rare treat when she made it for us."

Erik's eyes narrowed. She seemed satisfied with his answer.

That concerned him.

A woman's mind, especially the mind of an intelligent woman like Jia, was like a deceptively calm ocean with no waves. All it required was one riptide to take a man out if he wasn't careful.

He couldn't save himself if he didn't know why she was

interested. "Why are you—" he started. His eyes grew large, and he peered over Jia's shoulder. "What the hell?" he finished as he pushed back his chair, rising.

Jia matched his movements, grabbing her stun pistol and whipping around without saying a word.

People shouted in alarm. Several rushed away from the foyer. A man dressed in solid black stepped through the front door, rifle in hand. A white mask covered his face, the striations indicating it was a chameleon mask.

The disguise effectively blocked most spectra, but it was an expensive toy for someone entering a random mid-tier restaurant.

"Listen up, you maggots!" the man shouted, the voice distorted behind any plausible attempt at recognition by the mask. "This is a robbery. I'm taking your jewelry and your PNIUs!"

Erik whipped out his pistol. "NSCPD!"

Jia pulled out her stun pistol, her eyes narrowing on the man.

"Put down your weapons, you servants of a corrupt system," the robber demanded. "You fake humans. Drop them, or people will get *hurt*."

"You see what I'm holding?" Erik growled in response, moving forward. "This isn't a stun pistol. You fire that gun and hit someone, and I guarantee you'll take bullets."

"Just surrender," Jia ordered, coming up beside but stepping away from Erik. "You picked the wrong place to rob. And what kind of idiot takes people's PNIUs? You do realize we can track those, don't you?" She snorted in disgust.

"I'm freeing people of their umbilical cords to a corrupt

system." The man backed toward the door, his head moving to the left and the right before he threw the rifle at a nearby waitress and twisted. She yelped and ducked.

Jia nailed him in the back of the neck with a stun bolt. He groaned and tumbled to the ground, his body stopping the door from closing.

"Is everyone all right?" Jia called, looking around. "Does anyone need emergency medical treatment or an ambulance?"

Confused and relieved murmurs spread throughout the room. Some of the customers were shades paler than they had been a few minutes prior, but no one was on the ground.

Erik stomped over to the stunned suspect, put away his pistol, and pulled out a binding tie. He zipped the man's hands and yanked his limp body into the air. "I can't believe you would try to rob one of my favorite beignet places," he told the non-responsive guy. "I'm assuming you didn't know, so I'll chalk it up to you being the unluckiest idiot in Neo SoCal at the moment, rather than the stupidest."

Jia holstered her weapon as she came up to him, waving a negligent hand at the limp man. "Is this what you were talking about when you suggested things would get worse before they got better?"

"Hey, unless you want to convince the Purists to allow genetic engineering, I don't think we'll be curing humanity of stupidity." He moved the suspect out of the door. "Can you watch him for a moment?" he asked as he walked toward the gun. *Something seemed off.*

Erik crouched and picked up the weapon. He inspected

it closely. "Huh? Can't tell if he's brave or even stupider than I thought."

"Why?" Jia asked.

He held up the rifle to show it to her. "This isn't a real gun."

Erik glared at the suspect bound to the chair, sitting across the interrogation room table. DNA ID had confused the detectives more. They'd expected a scumbag who had somehow slithered up from the Shadow Zone, but instead, the suspect was Pearson Darmon, a clean-cut young university student with an internship at a major engineering firm. Not exactly the standard criminal profile for armed robbers of restaurants.

He had no priors, and the closest he had gotten to the law was a cousin who was a CID agent.

"Do you have any idea how much trouble you're in, Pearson?" Jia asked.

"I didn't do anything," stammered Pearson. "It wasn't even a real gun."

Erik and Jia exchanged glances and snorted simultaneously.

"You can't be that ignorant," Jia continued. "We have all sorts of laws about people who threaten others, whether or not the weapon is real, and you announced it was a robbery, too. Just because we stopped you, it doesn't mean you get to claim you didn't do anything wrong. Armed robbery, terrorist threats, possession of a chameleon mask without a proper license, resisting law enforcement, threatening law enforcement… I can keep going."

"And ruining my beignet breakfast," Erik added.

Pearson's face scrunched in confusion. "That's not a crime."

Erik slammed a fist on the table so hard it shook. "Says *you*." The suspect winced. "If someone put you up to this, now is the time to offer them up. If we tell the prosecutor you made our jobs more difficult, they might decide to charge you with everything my partner listed."

Pearson slumped forward and groaned. "I wasn't going to hurt anyone. I just wanted to feel *it*, you know?"

"Feel *what?*" Jia asked. "We did a tox screen on you. There are no unusual substances in your bloodstream. You can't play this off as you being high."

"No, no. Natural high." Pearson lifted his head. "Like the Leem King."

"Leem King?" Erik growled. "You're a damned Grayhead?" Erik pushed back from the table in annoyance. "I've had enough of you idiots."

"No, no, no. This is so messed up." Pearson shook his head. "I hate those guys. They're freaks and terrorists. The Leem King's not an alien or a Grayhead. That's just the name he uses for his show. It's kind of a joke since he's all about people being real humans and not fake humans."

"Show?" Jia frowned. "What show?"

"It's a dark net show. I'm sure it's all sorts of illegal. I heard about it from a guy at school. The Leem King is the real deal. He says we've lost touch with what it means to be human because of all the technology and corporations and stuff."

"So *he's* some sort of terrorist?" Jia asked.

"No!" Pearson sounded annoyed at that point. "He says, screw all terrorists. Killing people doesn't make you more human. It makes you an animal. He's all about helping people reach their true potential by challenging themselves."

"Meaning what, exactly?" Erik asked.

Pearson licked his lips and leaned forward. "You can't control other people, you know? Not really. You can't control the system. It's too big. It stretches across the galaxy. All you can do is free yourself by challenging yourself. Risking your life for nothing but the thrill. That way, you strip all this stuff away. All the fake stuff that smothers your humanity."

Jia rolled her eyes. "That sounds like a fancy excuse for young people to pull stupid thrill-seeking stunts."

"Whatever." He eyed her. "You're so much a part of the system, you're not human anymore."

Erik's grin turned feral. "So am I. I'm a damned monster, so you're going to tell me where I can find this Leem King's show. Then maybe, just maybe, you don't end up getting transported to some moon to be eaten by space raptors."

Pearson's confidence drained from his face. He nodded. "I'll tell you anything you want."

"And that's it, my fellow true humans," explained the masked figure in the video. "Even in Neo SoCal, the crown jewel of the UTC, there are few true humans. Do you want to be one of them?" He stepped out of a shop, gun in hand. "If so, go out there. Feel real fear, and you'll pull yourself out of the system *for just a second.*" He jogged toward a nondescript flitter. "Those idiots never considered this gun might be fake. Until next time… Feel the fear! Be *REAL*!"

Erik frowned as they finished watching the Leem King's latest stunt on a data window floating over Jia's desk.

Apparently, he used a rotating address and time-limited his displays to cut down on the chance of the authorities tracing him. In the episode, he had robbed a store with a chameleon mask and a fake gun, just like Pearson.

"This is beyond stupid," Erik muttered, pointing to the display. "These idiots are complaining that they don't have enough crap in their lives," he narrowed his eyes, "so they're going to play at being criminals and pull stupid stunts?"

Jia gestured to the data window. "I know this doesn't fall into our normal range of crimes, but I do think we should investigate."

"Why?" Erik shrugged. "This is just some idiot pulling pranks. He'll probably take himself out eventually by trying to jump off a tower and survive."

"Because other idiots are copying him. I stunned him, but you could have put a bullet in the student's brain, and an emergency medpatch wouldn't be enough to save him."

Erik snorted. "That's why you don't rob places with fake guns."

Jia pointed to her stun pistol. "That's the problem, though. What if there's escalation? It might be a prank from their perspective, but this video depicts an armed robbery. Countless others might occur, and what happens if the Leem King escalates his pranks? What if he convinces his followers that they need to start killing people to become real humans?"

Erik stared at the freeze-frame of the Leem King leaving the small PNIU shop. "I'll tell you one thing. It'll be satisfying to slap binding ties on that guy. It can't be that hard. We don't even need digital forensics. We can just have Emma analyze the footage and cross-reference it with robbery reports. The guy claims he's in Neo SoCal. Should be easy."

Jia nodded, not taking her eyes off the screen. "I'd like this guy to feel fear, all right."

CHAPTER NINE

"My analysis is complete," Emma announced triumphantly a few hours later.

Erik looked away from the data window on crime statistics that was floating over his desk. The AI didn't manifest in her holographic form. Although a few in the 1-2-2 were aware Erik had access to a military-grade AI, he didn't want to risk random criminals becoming aware of her.

If he wasn't a target already for being the Obsidian Detective, the chance to get their hands on that kind of tech would certainly make him one.

"Where's the shop?" Erik asked. "If we know that, we might be able to narrow down the Leem King's possible location. Without that, we're dead in the water."

"I said I completed my analysis," Emma replied. "I didn't say I know where he is or what he had for lunch."

Jia called to them from her desk, although she suspected Emma used multiple microphones scattered around. "One might question the usefulness of your analysis."

Emma scoffed. "One would be incorrect. I've gone through every armed robbery report for the past year and compared the suspect reports, locations, and relevant data with the recording. I focused initially on PNIU stores since that was what we saw in the video, but I couldn't find a match. I expanded to all stores and remained unable to find a match. There has been an unusual spike in strange masked robberies in the last couple of days, but the only one featuring a chameleon mask—the idiot you two took down at the restaurant."

"Yeah." Erik nodded. "I figured the Leem King had a few other fans who might be acting up, but not all of them can afford the expensive toys needed to copy him." He frowned. "Were you able to trace the video to the source? I asked Malcolm about it, and from what he said, it's a waste of time. I have a hard time believing we can't find one idiot who takes the trouble to record his crimes. It's like he's *begging* us to catch him."

"Technician Constantine is correct. I attempted that already, but this Leem King is using a number of proxies, including satellite reroutes, along with a mobile repeater. I took the liberty of asking several uniformed officers to pick up the equipment on your behalf, but I doubt it will amount to much. I am monitoring for any new transmissions. We might get lucky."

Jia's eyes turned to Erik as she commented to Emma, "I'd rather *not* rely on luck to solve a case."

"Me, either." Erik grinned. "You're saying a fleshbag beat you, Emma?"

Emma snorted. "I'm simply noting that said fleshbag is being careful. It's always easier when humans want money. This person obviously cares little for that, so he's providing fewer direct connections to himself. With additional data, I can perform additional analyses." Emma paused. "Do your job, detectives."

Jia brought up a data window and jumped to a frame depicting the Leem King hopping into his flitter. She squinted. "There's nothing distinctive about the model, and it's not like we have transponder information from a video. If we don't know where it is, we can't pull local traffic. Is there any chance this occurred farther back than we think? Maybe he did it a year ago and is just showing the footage now? If he's trying to be careful, he might have planned this a long time ago."

"No," Emma declared. "I'm confident about that. If you examine the video closely, there is a small date display behind the counter, clearly showing that the incident occurred only a week ago, and there is additional information embedded directly into the data to indicate it was recent. If he faked the date, he was very thorough. It's not impossible, but it seems unlikely."

"If it's not the data, maybe it's the place," Erik suggested. "He could be lying about being in Neo SoCal."

"Why lie about that?" Jia asked.

"Neo SoCal's the biggest metro on Earth. He looks more impressive pulling this off here than in the CFM or Detroit," he suggested.

"That's a possibility," Emma replied, "but I should note there's nothing in the national or UTC databases about any recent robberies involving a chameleon mask, either. If he's done anything off-world, relevant terrestrial databases haven't been updated, and it seems unlikely those files originated off-world without a lot more evidence of routing data."

Jia's eyes widened, and she gasped. "I get it. No, he's in Neo SoCal, and he did this all recently, just like the dates suggest. That's not the trick."

Erik's eyes narrowed. "You have an idea where the guy might be? I'd rather nail him sooner than later. I get that he's breeding more idiots, but he's not that big a deal."

Jia shook her head. "I don't know where he is, but I think the Leem King's deception isn't what everyone thinks it is." She pointed at the data window. "There's no way someone wouldn't report being robbed, at least someone living Uptown. Based on the brief shot we see when he gets into the flitter, he's not in the Shadow Zone. I think the whole thing is fake. That would make sense, with the escalation from some of the other stunts."

They'd spent additional time interviewing Pearson, and Malcolm had managed to recover a few third-party copies of other videos from the darknet. Their earlier suspicions were proven correct.

The Leem King had started with simple thrill-seeking stunts, including leaping from one flitter to another in midflight. He'd graduated to petty vandalism and drone hunting before his shift to armed robbery.

Real or otherwise.

"That is a distinct possibility," Emma offered. "It would explain some of the difficulties I've had attempting to correlate the obtained video with a relevant police report. What a clever little fleshbag."

"Huh." Erik sighed. "That makes a certain kind of sense."

Jia narrowed her eyes, looking at the image of the masked suspect. "This person is promoting dangerous antisocial stunts, and he's not even a true criminal. Disgusting."

Emma laughed. "Would you *prefer* he was actually running around robbing people?"

"No, but as you already pointed out, we have multiple people copying him." Jia stood and looked at Erik. "We need to catch him."

"Not saying I disagree." Erik shrugged. "But if Digital Forensics and Emma are stumped, where does that leave us? It's not like she can hack the entire OmniNet to find the guy. There are tons of cameras and drones in the city, but there are also one hundred million people here. Usually, people get caught because they're lazy and stupid. This guy might be crazy, but he's neither lazy nor stupid."

"No, I can't hack the entire net," Emma confirmed. "But I do have an idea, and you've highlighted the key elements, Detective Blackwell."

Both detectives looked toward the main speaker Emma was using.

"I did?"

"He did?" Jia blurted at the same moment.

Emma snickered. "Yes. Since this is an official police investigation, you can get me access to all public cameras and government drone feeds. Normally, that would be pointless, considering the data sifting required. Even if there's no police report because the robbery was staged and the Leem King covered his tracks, he wasn't invisible. There has to be footage of him somewhere."

"I'll put in the request with the captain," Erik replied. "This guy might not be stupid, but he *is* cocky, and cocky guys always make mistakes."

Jia smirked. "Are you sure that shouldn't be '*guys* always make mistakes?'"

Erik stood up, raising one eyebrow as he grabbed his coat. "Don't get cocky."

Jan 14, 2229, Neo Southern California Metroplex, Police Enforcement Zone 122 Station, Digital Forensics Division, Office of Malcolm Constantine

Jia eyed the black cylinder on the small tray atop Malcolm's desk.

It took all her concentration to focus on the device, a recovered transmission repeater, and not on Malcolm's bright yellow Hawaiian shirt festooned with pineapples.

"This is what they found, following Emma's trace data. Expensive repeater. Nice model." Malcolm gestured to the cylinder from behind his desk. "This guy's thorough, I'll give him that. From what I can tell, he cleared out all the data on this before EMPing it. They already checked for DNA, too. Nothing. Whoever this guy is, he's got a lot of money to throw around for expensive toys to help him not get caught."

Erik folded his arms. "This is starting to annoy me more than some of the gangsters we've dealt with. What's the damned point? If he's hiding himself this well, he can't be making money off it."

Malcolm looked at Erik. "Maybe he's a true believer?"

"And fame is its own reward," Jia mused. "He either has the technical ability to hide, or he has the resources to hire someone to help him do that." She nodded at the repeater. "And like Malcolm said, he's got money to spend on equipment. Even if he's not personally setting it up, he's intelligent enough to know how to cover his tracks. It's obvious he doesn't need money." She paused, considering the information. "That might even be half the point."

The guys looked at her, Malcolm getting the question out first. "How do you figure?"

"There are cheaper ways to hide one's identity than using a chameleon mask," Jia observed. "Much cheaper ways."

"What if he was just trying to be thorough?" Erik countered.

Malcolm shrugged. "That could be, but I think Detective Lin's right. If he was worried about different spectral scans, there are cheaper and lower-tech ways to beat that stuff, let alone mess with his voice. He's not even using the full abilities of the mask."

"Showing off, huh?" Erik frowned. "Just to become famous or help spread his stupid crap? That means he's important enough or cares enough he can't reveal his true identity. Even if he staged the robbery, he's got pirate broadcasting and illegal use of tech violations. We can probably tie him to more than a few destroyed drones. It's not a Gray Circle rampage, but it's enough to get him fired if he's working for a corp." He shook his head. "This idiot has everything he needs in life, and it's still not enough. This is the kind of guy they should be transporting to some new colony to break large rocks into smaller rocks."

"There's nothing you can give us from this, Malcolm?" Jia asked, a hint of desperation in her voice.

"Not right now. Sorry, Detective." The tech shrugged and raised his eyebrows.

She sighed and turned to leave, Erik trailing behind. "Then we'll just have to hope Emma can find something with her analysis."

Hours later, Jia sat in her flitter on the way home. She leaned back in her seat, her eyes half-closed and the vehicle on full autopilot.

They had evidence, but no encouraging leads. She should have been relieved to learn that the Leem King was more prankster than gangster, but the earlier robbery remained lodged in her mind.

What happened when the next copycat decided to bring a real gun to feel more human? Or someone killed them in self-defense?

"We have enough crime without people committing more because of some fool on the net," she muttered.

Her PNIU chimed with a call from Erik. She opened her eyes, then tapped to receive the call.

"Hello," she answered.

"You somewhere you can watch something?" Erik asked.

"I'm on my way home, but I'm not flying," she explained. "I'm not nearly as enthralled with the idea as you."

"Emma got a hit on a new video from the Leem King. Emma, go ahead and send it to her."

Jia opened a data window to receive the video.

Shadows resolved into the dark-clad and chameleon-masked Leem King. He held a long serrated knife in hand as he loomed over another man on his knees. A dark hood blinded the second man, and his arms were wrapped around a metal pole and secured with binding ties. Other than the pole, the room was featureless.

"What is this?" Jia muttered, her stomach tightening.

"Good evening, my fellow real humans," the Leem King announced, his voice as distorted as before. "I've said in the past that terrorism isn't a path to scraping away the lies of this society, and I believe that. Trying to change a broken system doesn't work. You think you can change anything through politicians?" He laughed. "Nothing but bought and paid for *tools*!"

He shrugged, his head cocked to the side. "Through protest, perhaps? If you could change anything through protest, they would make it a crime. Terrorism? Terrorism is playing into *their* hands because it's not about changing yourself. It's about changing everyone else, and once you start trying to do that, you let them control you. You stop becoming a real human and become a fake human playing a role in the corrupt system."

Jia's heart sped up. *Escalation*.

The Leem King patted the shoulder of the hooded man. "Indiscriminate killing also risks hurting real humans." He raised the knife. "But we have to think about all the dangerous effects of fakes. We *must* remember that society is nothing more than a collection of fakes. If you *know* someone's fake, is it *really* wrong to remove them from society? You're not trying to change everyone then, you're removing a distraction, and you're not risking indiscriminate killing."

The hooded man let out a muffled shout and struggled against his bonds.

Jia narrowed her eyes.

The Leem King tossed the knife back and forth between his hands. "I know what you're thinking. I've talked about how you can't change society, and you should focus on yourself, and that's true, but it doesn't mean you should ignore possibilities to help things…"

He paused, the knife in his hand weaving, hypnotic. "Let's just say, help things along. It's not murder if the person's not real. It's about *knowing* that."

He stabbed the knife into the man's back, his scream perforating the sound levels. He stabbed several more times. The victim continued his screams, the sounds muffled by the hood.

He didn't stop stabbing until the victim's head slumped forward.

He tossed the bloodied knife to the ground, looking back over his shoulder to the camera with his hands splayed out. "I feel alive. I feel real. I *am* real. *Feel the fear.*"

The video ended.

Jia swallowed, her stomach churning. "I hope I'm right about this."

"About it being fake?" Erik asked over the connection.

"Yes, but it doesn't matter. I was worried about people trying to rob stores, but now he is goading people into murder." She wiped her eyes, continuing her thoughts out loud. "If we don't expose him, we're going to end up with a murder spree."

CHAPTER TEN

A harsh buzz snapped Erik out of his sleep. He sat up in bed, jerking his head back and forth, expecting assassins or security bots, his eyes finally resting on Emma's hologram, which hovered horizontally over his bed like a ghost ready to show him Christmas past, present, and future.

"What the hell?" he growled, squinting up at her. "What are you up to?"

"I've completed my analysis." Emma smiled. "I have a likely hit on the shop featured in the robbery video. I thought you would like to know."

Erik glanced at the floating red time display hovering above his PNIU on the nightstand. "I don't go into work for three hours."

Emma scoffed. "And here I thought you would be interested in solving this case in a timely manner. I apologize for overestimating your dedication."

"It's not that." Erik rubbed one eye, his voice heavy. "The shop owner isn't going to be there before dawn," he explained. "We don't have enough evidence to kick his door in and drag him off yet, either."

Emma looked to the side before nodding. "Hmm. I do see your point. I sometimes forget how sad and limited humans can be. It's a shame you're all so hesitant to modify yourselves in a serious manner."

"Humanity's screwed up enough without us tinkering with what makes us human," Erik answered. "Imagine the best scientific screwups humans have accomplished, and then consider if humans worked on ourselves."

"Not a pretty thought."

"That's my point. I'll hit the shop in a few hours with Jia." He laid back, then lifted back up to punch his pillow into a normal shape. "We can go to the stars, but we can't make a pillow that works all night long."

Erik stood next to the break room counter and kept downing coffee.

It was hard to get back to sleep when a smart-ass AI did her best haunting impression and woke you up before dawn.

At least she had a lead for him.

All they needed to do now was investigate the shop. The Leem King could take all the technological precautions he wanted. That didn't mean he couldn't be brought down if an accomplice rolled on him.

After a few more sips of coffee, Erik's PNIU chimed with a message. He brought it up. The captain wanted to see Erik and Jia in his office at their earliest convenience.

Translation: Right now.

Erik set down his cup and headed out of the break room. In the hall, he caught sight of Jia. She nodded to him as they joined up and continued toward the captain's office. Captain Ragnar sat inside with an apologetic look on his face, a rare expression from the boisterous man.

Erik frowned as he stepped inside. This wasn't a good start.

Jia sighed, sensing the same thing. "What's wrong?" she asked.

"In five minutes, the NSCPD is putting out a public statement on the Leem King," Captain Ragnar explained, shaking his head in disgust. "The interim chief is worried about copycat contagion, so every EZ in the city is going to be hunting this guy."

"This is our collar," Erik insisted. "We've got a lead."

Captain Ragnar put up a hand to quell him. "I agree, and you have primary jurisdiction, but you need to move immediately on your lead. I just got done arguing with the interim chief about holding off on the public statement. We don't want our guy going to ground. Even if he's covered his tracks, having the entire city hunting him might spook him, but the council is insistent that this be taken care of. Not only that, the public statement will talk about how his stunts and crimes might be staged."

"People won't believe that until we catch him," Jia suggested. She furrowed her brow in concern. "It might even convince him to do something bolder to keep his audience." She closed her eyes. "This is a mistake."

"That's true, and I agree. The interim chief doesn't. I think they're trying to defang him, but I'm with you. I'm not convinced it will work." Captain Ragnar stroked his beard. "I think they're concerned this will end up being some weird terrorist thing. Everyone's still on edge from what happened at Halloween, and the idea that there might be yet another massacre has them worried."

Erik noted that Jia's calm demeanor didn't extend to her fists, which were clenched and shaking. "If the Leem King escapes because of the public statement, the council will have blood on their hands when the inevitable copycats follow their leader's example."

"Don't worry." Erik snorted. "They'll blame us for not catching the guy right away."

Captain Ragnar shook his head, a playful grin finally erasing the discomfort. "I won't let that happen. I've made it clear that this is their call, and they're interfering with your investigation. For now, you pound on the shop door and see if you can get any leads. All we have is a man who is trying to inspire murder but likely hasn't committed a real one. If we unmask him, we can destroy his mystique, and this ends without anyone hurt." He waved a hand. "Dismissed."

Jia spun on her heel and stomped toward the door. "The king will soon be dead. May we live a long time without a new king."

Despite Erik selecting a dull gray color for the MX 60 in order to draw less attention, the expensive flitter stood out as it landed on the parking platform next to a narrow commercial level of a modest tower.

The building lay far from the heart of the metroplex and lacked the height of the impressive specimens in the Hexagon, but it was above being considered part of the Shadow Zone.

Erik and Jia stepped out of the flitter and moved to a narrow metallic footpath in front of their parking row. The path led to the entrance to the commercial level. The door to the PNIU store was off to the side, close to another small parking lot.

The detectives continued toward the store, stopping a short distance from the entrance and looking at the holosign above it featuring sparkling silver cards and a name Erik was having trouble believing. The floor-to-ceiling windows revealed PNIUs and accessories on the walls of the spartan shop.

"Courage Electronics?" he read, looking around before glancing at Jia. "I want a few free punches on this guy when we find him."

"I should chastise you for saying that," Jia replied over her shoulder, "but it's starting to sound like a good idea." She gestured around the area. "It's unlikely the place would have been as abandoned as we saw it during normal business hours."

"I should note," Emma chimed in, "the timestamp on the video was late evening."

"All the more reason to think it was staged." Jia considered. "He must have done it after hours to cut down on the chance of anyone seeing and reporting him. Sometimes I think they were wrong to not approve the algorithmic crime system a few years back."

"Although I'm impressive at this sort of thing, the pilot

studies suggested far too many false positives from the simpler AIs examining the camera and drone streams," Emma explained.

Erik nodded toward the door. "Not so sure I'd want a bunch of second-string AIs watching us all the time."

"You're not the only person who feels that way," Jia admitted. "I suspect that had a lot to do with them deciding to not move the program past the pilot stage, but for now, we don't need it. We have Emma."

Emma snickered. "Indeed you do, Detective Lin."

The two detectives strolled toward the shop, then stepped through the sliding door. A middle-aged, dusky-skinned man with graying hair emerged from a door in the back. His nametag read Farouk. There was no clear image of the alleged victim's face in the Leem King's video, which, based on the filming distance and movement, was likely taken with a small drone camera. All they had was a brief shot of the victim's pants.

Farouk smiled warmly at them. "Welcome! How can I be of service today?"

"Are you the owner?" Erik asked.

"Yes, I'm Farouk Gamal, and this is my store." His smile brightened. "If one of my employees gave you trouble, I'm happy to do what I need to make sure you leave satisfied." He looked at Jia. "I pride myself on customer satisfaction."

Jia took up the questioning. "Do you work late at night, or would that have been one of your employees?"

Farouk shook his head. "No, I work then. I only have a few people helping me. What's this about? I don't remember seeing you before, and none of my employees has reported any complaints."

Erik and Jia pulled out their badges.

The owner's smile waned. "I give special discounts to all military and law enforcement."

"We're not here to buy a new PNIU," Jia replied, her tone stern. She clipped her badge to her belt. "Detectives Lin and Blackwell, NSCPD."

"Lin and Blackwell." Farouk gasped. "I've read about you. The Obsidian Detective and Lady Justice!"

Jia's blinked in surprise, eyes flicking to Erik and back. "Lady *Justice?*"

Erik snickered. "Aren't nicknames fun?"

"It's what some of the articles called you." Farouk shrugged. "How can I help the two best detectives in Neo SoCal?" His tone remained breezy and casual.

He didn't sound like a man who'd helped with a fake robbery.

Jia cleared her throat. "I'll stick with Detective Lin for now. We're here to ask you about a possible robbery that occurred in your shop recently."

Farouk stared at her. A few seconds later, he laughed. "Is this a joke? A robbery?"

Jia shook her head. "We're serious, Mr. Gamal."

"I'm sure you are, Detective, but I would know if I had been robbed, and I would have contacted the police."

Erik stepped forward. "We have reason to believe the robbery might have been a hoax associated with the Leem King. Have you heard of him?"

Farouk frowned. "The news earlier said he fakes murders and does crazy stunts? I don't understand what this has to do with me."

"We have evidence that proves a robbery was either

committed here or faked in this store," Erik explained. He didn't want to tip their hand. The man didn't need to know the details. The suspect was more likely to slip up that way.

Farouk looked down and sighed. "You know, I wonder about some of my employees. I'm always trying to be a good man, give back to the community, but some people, they're just born antisocial." He looked up. "They could use a fresh start on a colony, if you know what I mean."

"Are you saying you suspect it was one of your employees?" Jia asked.

He shrugged. "You're the police. If you say you have evidence it happened here, who am I to argue? It wasn't me, so it had to be one of them. I can give you their names and addresses if you want to go talk to them."

Jia glanced at Erik and nodded slightly. She'd picked up on the same thing he had.

Erik grinned. "Going to give them up that easily, Mr. Gamal?"

"I'm not a criminal or antisocial, Detective," Farouk insisted, frowning. "I've always lived a law-abiding life, and I want to do my part to keep Neo SoCal a good place. That's what a good citizen does."

"Yeah, here's the thing." Erik shrugged. "The robbery, fake or not, would have had to have happened late at night, and you told us earlier that you're the only one in the shop at that time."

Jia circled the suspect, her hand drifting into her jacket toward her stun pistol. Erik remained in front of him with a hungry smile on his face.

Farouk's eyes darted back and forth as he licked his lips. "That's most of the time. Not always. There are some days I need extra help, or I'm sick. I wasn't always feeling great these last couple of weeks. Yes, there's been a couple of nights I wasn't in."

Jia let out a quiet scoff. "So if we pulled the PNIU tracking logs for you and your employees for the last couple of weeks, they would show there was a night one of them was here and you weren't? And that would match the store's surveillance footage?"

Farouk let out a quick laugh. "There's a problem with my security system. I've been meaning to contact the company about it. It goes out a lot. I didn't want to advertise the fact."

"Answer her question about the tracking logs," Erik growled.

Farouk shrugged. "I don't know a lot about that kind of thing."

Jia laughed. "You sell PNIUs for a living. That's a pretty basic function."

He looked over his shoulder. "That doesn't mean I know everything." Farouk's breathing quickened, and sweat beaded on his forehead.

Jia sighed. "Look, Mr. Gamal, you seem like a nice man. I don't know why you would help this antisocial criminal, but if it turns out he did kill someone and you're helping protect him, you could be charged as an accessory to murder. That means *prison*. Do you want to go to prison, Mr. Gamal?"

"I didn't do anything," he shouted. "I don't know anything about what you're talking about." His breathing turned ragged.

"If he's blackmailing or threatening you, we can help,"

Erik replied. "Or is it about money?" He glanced around the shop. "Sure, you're living Uptown, but this isn't exactly a luxury shop. All indications are that this Leem King's got a lot of credits to burn. What, did he come to you and say, 'Hey, no one's going to get hurt, and your face won't be in the video?' Then he gives you a nice chunk of credits?"

Jia leaned close to Farouk's ear to whisper, startling him as her breath touched his neck. "Don't protect this scumbag. Even if he's faking crimes, he's inspiring real ones. It's only a matter of time before someone gets hurt for real. You really want to go to prison because you protected some bored, antisocial wealthy man?"

He fell to his knees and put his face in his hands. "It wasn't supposed to be like this. You have to understand, I'm behind on my loans. I was an idiot. My cousin told me not to go into selling PNIUs. He said I should open a restaurant, but I didn't listen, and then there was that whole fiasco with the model recall last year."

Erik knelt in front of the man. "You're having financial trouble, and then somebody shows up and offers you money? All you had to do was let them *rob* you?"

"I don't know how he knew I needed money!" Farouk whimpered. "One day, there was a note left on the counter for me. I thought it was a joke, but I checked my accounts, and credits had come in from some off-world bank. Another note showed up one day, and it explained what I had to do, and how much I'd get paid. I checked my cameras, but all the footage was erased for a few minutes around the time the notes appeared." He groaned. "It wasn't like any of it was real. It's just a movie, right? That's what I told myself."

"Most producers don't contact people via notes and hack their security cameras," Jia observed, rolling her eyes. "Where are the notes now?"

"I tossed them in the garbage a long time ago." Farouk shuddered. "Am I going to jail?"

Erik hesitated.

Jia, behind Farouk, looked at him with pity before shaking her head at her partner.

"Probably not," Erik announced. "Participating in a fake crime is, at minimum, disturbing the peace, but since you are cooperating, we can pass that along. You'll probably get a fine and community service."

Farouk clasped his hands together, hope returning to his face. "I'll do anything. I never saw him without the mask. I have no idea who he is."

"We'll check your bank records," Erik explained. He doubted they would find anything. If the Leem King had gone to the trouble of routing off-world, it was probably through a private encrypted account.

The truth was, there were plenty of ways to hide money if a person was patient and cautious.

Farouk stood, his hand over his heart. "Thank you. I know that I shouldn't have done it. I knew it was too good to be true, but I—"

A loud crack sounded from the window. Half of Farouk's head exploded, and his body jerked backward. Blood splattered on the wall. There was a huge hole through one of the windows.

"Sniper!" Erik bellowed and dropped to the ground.

Jia threw herself to the floor, stun pistol in hand. Another round ripped through the window and struck a back wall. The loud report reached their ears a moment later.

The slight delay between the shot and the report suggested the shooter was neither too close nor too far.

The MX 60 zoomed over from the parking lot and positioned itself in front of the window, blocking most of the shop from view. The next shot struck the vehicle, the crushed bullet bouncing harmlessly to the platform.

"Good call, Emma!" Erik shouted. He crawled over to Farouk and shook his head. "Dammit. Do we have backup and an ambulance on the way?"

"Yes," Jia announced.

Two more shots in succession pinged loudly off the MX 60.

"This guy's already done," Erik muttered. "There's nowhere to really stick a patch." He looked at the window and sat up, then pulled out a medpatch and placed it on the side of the man's head. He had to at least try. "Whether or not that knifing was real, this proves our boy has graduated to murder. Do you have eyes on him?"

Jia holstered her pistol, staring at the body with a deep scowl on her face.

"The gun goblin took too many shots," Emma announced. "I've back-calculated the angle and traced it to the likely origin point. With your permission and in your name, I'll interface with the local cameras and drones."

"Do it, and pull up to the front door so we can get in," Erik ordered. "We'll give the Leem King what he wants."

Another shot rang out.

"What do you mean?" Jia looked over to find Erik smiling.

"There's nothing more thrilling than a good, old-fashioned chase."

CHAPTER ELEVEN

Erik grabbed the yoke and pulled up, and the MX 60 rose into the air. The sniper hadn't fired for over ten seconds.

"A chameleon-masked subject with a rifle is now getting into a large black unmarked cargo transport with one primary trailer that's not emitting a transponder signal," Emma reported. "I'll send the information to your smart lenses, Detective Blackwell. I've repurposed two drones to follow him. Backup is inbound."

Jia narrowed her eyes as the MX 60 barreled through the air, its holographic red and blue lights flashing. "He didn't have to kill that man. If he used an untraceable account, it wasn't even like we would have been able to use it to track him. What was the point?"

"I don't think it's about covering things up anymore," Erik replied, jerking the flitter above a line of barely moving civilian vehicles. "Once the department made that announcement, he had to figure we would close in on him quickly. If he believes half the crap he's been saying, he needed to graduate to the real deal."

"Despicable." Jia's jaw tightened.

"Don't worry. We've got this guy. Have any idea what he might be carrying, Emma?"

"There are multiple human thermal signatures insides," she announced. "Ten."

Erik grunted. "He's got friends or fellow cultists." He accelerated, the black dot in the distance growing rapidly. "Good to know."

Jia frowned and looked around. "What's your plan? If you use disruptor bullets, you might be able to bring him down, but there's too high a chance of him crashing into a tower or platform."

"He's running, so let's hope he runs until we can find someplace. As long as he's in the air, he's not on the ground shooting someone." Erik's hands tightened on the yoke, and his lips curled into a sneer. "There's no way I'm letting this bastard get away after shooting a man right in front of me. Emma, could you route some laser comms through the drones?"

"I'm sorry, Detective Blackwell," Emma replied. "The ones I'm controlling lack that ability."

The MX 60 continued to close in on the fleeing cargo flitter. The suspect's vehicle whipped over air lanes of traffic. Several other flitters almost collided, one coming so close, its grav emitters almost scraped the top of the trailer.

"In a sick way, you're right," Jia murmured, anger etched on her face. "We're giving him exactly what he *wants*."

"For now." Erik turned the yoke to avoid an idiot who was ignoring both the lights and the emergency vehicle transponder signal. "Prison isn't that thrilling. Getting shot by me isn't that thrilling. Or maybe it is. I suppose he'll find out soon enough."

The cargo flitter dove under a walkway filled with people. Traffic was thinning, but there were still far too many towers and platforms to avoid collateral damage if they brought him down hard.

Erik kept his MX 60 a few meters above and to the side of the cargo flitter in case of a sudden stop. The suspect vehicle didn't turn.

"Damn it," Erik muttered. "Is he going to ram right into the tower?"

"There's not enough time to shoot him even if we wanted to," Jia observed. Bile rose in the back of her throat.

The suspect's vehicle zoomed right toward an open lower walkway stretching between two close towers. People scattered, fleeing in either direction as the large vehicle descended. It whipped around, the trailer shimmying.

Erik pushed on his yoke, heading toward the walkway. He pulled up at the last minute, his vehicle bouncing. Jia wondered if the grav field had just saved the car from damage.

"Don't need a drone now for laser comms." Erik tapped a few commands on the console screen of the vehicle. "This is the NSCPD, Leem King. We've got drones on you. You're not escaping. You're supposed to be a real human, so own up to the fact you just committed a real crime. You got anything to say?"

The Leem King leaned forward and opened the driver's side door. Something small fell from the cabin. A bright blinding flash appeared and vanished in an instant.

A billowing cloud of blue smoke consumed the cargo flitter.

Erik threw open his door and kept it open, crouching behind it. Jia dug out his TR-7 and a few magazines and tossed them on the driver's seat before opening her own door and crouching behind it, her stun pistol out.

"The smoke isn't obscuring their thermal signatures much," Emma reported. "The ten men are exiting the back of the vehicle. The driver is near the front."

A bullet slammed into Erik's door, bouncing off with a spark. He grabbed the TR-7 and jammed in a magazine before returning fire. Jia added several stun bolts to the mix. A barrage of bullets erupted from the smoke striking the MX 60.

"How we doing, Emma?" Erik asked. Another few bullets smacked into his door.

"Minor damage, but nothing that can't be fixed. I am grateful almost every day for that particular modification. Wait. The driver is now moving toward the back."

Jia hissed. "If we wait for reinforcements, he's going to get away. If he's covered his tracks this well, he might be on the way to the HTP by the time we figure out who he is."

Erik grinned. "But we've got something they don't."

"An unhealthy attachment to beignets?" Jia asked, searching for her next shot.

"No, an AI with good tactical sense. On three, we rush to the back. Emma, you spin the car and start moving sideways. I know you can't get decent speed that way, but we don't need it. I just want you to hover as a moving barricade. Ready?"

Jia nodded.

"It's always entertaining taking down idiots," Emma declared.

"I thought you called them gun goblins," Erik asked

"Semantics," she replied.

"One," Erik began, "two, *three*."

The detectives darted to the back of the Taxútnta. Emma swung the MX 60 with precision, using the side thrusters to push it forward. Erik and Jia repositioned behind the wider barrier and popped up to squeeze off a few shots. Someone shouted in pain.

"Two are down," Emma announced.

Erik squeezed off another few shots. "We're making this too hard on ourselves. Can you highlight their positions and feed them to our smart lenses?"

"Ah, excellent idea, Detective. One moment. I've added a bright red dot above the driver. He was wearing a chameleon mask, so he's likely to be the Leem King."

Jia nodded as the colorful outlines of the suspects appeared, along with the red dot over one man creeping toward the back. "For all this talk of courage and thrill, he's ready to run when things get dangerous." She fired bolts into two men. Both collapsed. "We need to get close to him. There are too many innocent people farther down the walkway and on the platform."

"Then let's wrap it up here." Erik downed a few more as both detectives continued moving forward. The enemies' near-constant stream of bullets continued to spark and bounce off the MX 60's armored exterior, but they didn't land a single shot on Erik or Jia. The two of them were halfway to the cargo flitter.

"Yes, let's end this." Jia rapid-fired her stun pistol,

jerking from target to target, not waiting to see if they fell. The Leem King ducked behind the truck as she downed the last man.

Erik nodded approvingly. "Nice."

She jumped up and sprinted toward the thinning smoke. Erik hurried after her, taking the chance to reload.

Even though they didn't have a direct line of sight, Emma's AR contributions let them track the suspect as he ran away from the back of the truck. The detectives charged through the smoke, almost tripping over the stunned and wounded men.

A swarm of red and blue flashing lights approached.

"Emma, let Dispatch know our situation," Erik ordered. "We're going after the Leem King."

"He's more than a mere gun goblin, I'll grant him that."

The detectives cleared the smoke. The suspect continued rushing down the walkway. Although people fled and cowered, there were hundreds, if not thousands, of people on the platform. Many were rushing into one of the nearby tower entrances.

The Leem King shimmered and a half-dozen of the man appeared, all running in the same direction.

Jia gasped. "Huh?"

Erik snorted. "Holoclone. Old military tech, but it doesn't fake a thermal signature. It's why the military stopped using it. They'll change position on occasion to make it harder to pick out the actual target." He narrowed his eyes. "My tracking's messed up. What about yours?"

Jia blinked her eyes a few times. She could see the dark, distant figure of the Leem King, or at least his clones, but his thermal signature had vanished, along with the dot.

"Some sort of interference suddenly popped up," Emma reported.

Erik growled. "How many tricks does this guy have?" He sped up, trying to close the gap. "It's like he's trying to piss me off."

Jia matched his pace, heart thundering. They passed several people lying on the ground, their hands on their heads, whimpering. A few people stood, amused looks on their faces, watching the whole thing unfold as if they were in a cop drama.

"I can't just take a shot," Erik complained. "I can hit any of those clones fine, but if it's not him, I'll be sending out rounds that could hit a civilian in the distance. These bullets maintain lethal velocity for a long time."

Jia hissed in frustration and pumped her legs. Sweat poured down the side of her face, and her heart thundered from her effort. They couldn't let the suspect escape. He'd murdered one, maybe even two, people and spread his sick ideology over the net.

He'd purposely set down in an area filled with innocent people who he probably dismissed as nothing but fake humans.

She raised her pistol. Stun bolts weren't great long-range weapons. They lost too much energy at range compared to bullets, let alone rifle bullets. There was a narrow window of opportunity given her distance from the suspect and his distance from the tower. If she waited much longer, there was a chance of an innocent person getting hit. A stun bolt was usually safe, but that wasn't the same thing as *always* safe.

I can't flinch, Jia thought. *I have to take the shot.*

Jia shouted in rage as she fired her first shot. Like before, she didn't wait as she moved to the next target and fired. Her first shot passed right through the hologram. Her second went wide. She slowed and continued shooting. The bright white bolts continue to launch.

Her eyes widened as all six remaining Leem Kings collapsed to the ground.

Erik continued running.

She stared at the downed suspect and his holoclones, taking long, deep breaths. She wiped sweat off her forehead as her partner arrived at the stunned, masked man some distance away and kicked his weapon out of reach.

"Good job!" Erik shouted. He knelt and pulled out a binding tie. "I'll admit there are a few situations where a stun pistol comes in handy."

He finished securing the prisoner and grinned down at him, his smile feral.

"Thrilling enough for you, *Mr. Real Human?"*

CHAPTER TWELVE

Jan 15, 2229, Neo Southern California Metroplex, Police Enforcement Zone 122 Station, Interrogation Room

Erik grinned at the young blond man sitting across from him. "Comfy?"

The suspect shrugged. "I wish my hands weren't tied, and you made me sit in that cell for a while. If you didn't know, It's not very comfortable."

"We didn't just do that blood test for fun. We wanted all the Dragon Tear out of your system before we interrogated you. Getting high on Tear is *not* the smartest thing to do when you're about to go on a criminal rampage."

"Oh. That. I figured I'd try it. I never had it before, and some was available." The suspect sighed. "It's kind of overrated. Drugs trap you, make you fake, but I couldn't know until I tried."

Jia glared at the man. "We advised you of your Article 7 rights, but let me make something clear. We've run your DNA, so we know you're Maxwell Worthington, age twenty, and we know you only came to Earth six months ago to attend school in Neo SoCal. We also found a few interesting reports. There were a lot of strange incidents in Aurora on New Pacifica shortly before you left. A mysterious underground man calling himself the Zitark Shaman pulled similar garbage. No murders, though. Had to up your game now that you're back on the mother planet?"

Maxwell smiled. "I'm not admitting I'm either this Leem King or the Zitark Shaman, and I don't think you can hate either of them for what they've done."

"I'm a cop, and you broke the law. Not only that, you killed someone."

Maxwell leaned forward, his smile shifting dangerously close to a smirk deserving of a punch, or at least a good slap. "Can you kill someone if they're not alive? Besides, can you prove it was me? All those men who shot at you were paid anonymously, or I suspect that's the case. I bet you checked that already anyway, being good little fake human cops and all. I'm also betting you have no way of directly tying that gun to me, and I guarantee it doesn't have my DNA on it."

"Farouk Gamal was alive, you antisocial *monster*," Jia snarled. "Until you put a bullet in his brain. We've got camera footage of you taking the shot. We chased you, remember? We know where you fired from and when."

The man shook his head, his smirk widening. "You saw someone wearing a chameleon mask taking the shot. Not me."

"The same mask you were wearing when I stunned you." Jia scoffed. "Do you really think you're going to get off with that weak defense? We have clear footage of you from the moment you fired to the moment we took you down."

"No, you don't." Maxwell clucked his tongue. "I seem to remember some smoke. Maybe one of those deadly mercenaries took the shot."

"We had thermals on you in the smoke, idiot," Erik mocked. "We've got you dead to rights. You got too cocky, and you're going down."

Maxwell licked his lips. "Have you ever considered you might be the one who's too cocky, you cog in the system?"

"Why?" Jia shook her head, her face a mask of disgust. "Your father is a senior vice-president at Hermes. You were all but guaranteed a good career. Your stupid pranks were one thing, but you just killed a man."

Maxwell sighed. He looked at Jia with pity in his eyes. "I'm not confessing to anything, but let's say that if a man is born in privilege, he is in a better position to see the corruption of the world."

Jia frowned, and her jaw tightened.

"You two are cops," Maxwell continued. "You can't deny the UTC is sick. Neo SoCal is supposed to be a shining beacon at the heart of humanity, but it's filled with gangsters, terrorists, and self-serving corporations pulling the strings of the government for their own corrupt purposes."

Erik chuckled. "So, what…because there's crime already, you get to kill who you want? Try again. That's about as convincing as the Grayhead drivel we had to pull out of our brains."

"I'm not confessing to anything," Maxwell insisted. "I'm just saying that a smart person, a man with resources and intelligence, might have had an epiphany wherein he realized the best way to save society was to engage the few people who aren't *fake,* who aren't cogs in the corrupt system, by making them face their fears and awaken their true selves. To help them become real. In a war for the heart of humanity, there will always be casualties. The man you keep complaining about sold his dignity for money. He was fake, already dead."

Jia scowled at Maxwell. "You were the one setting up hoax crimes to feel like a big man, at least before you turned to murder. Aren't *you* the fake?"

"Whatever you think you understand about the Leem King is wrong." Maxwell sneered. "Sometimes people need to be lied to in the short-term to help accept a long-term truth. The Leem King has been leading people to awaken. He knows it. He's found ways to reach the people, and they reach out to him."

Erik shook his head. "Too bad, your alien highness, your kingdom is done."

"Admitting nothing, I'll note that I'll be out of this place soon enough once my father arrives."

"Money can't buy your way out of a murder charge," Jia answered.

Maxwell laughed. "You fake humans don't get it, do you? You're upholding the corrupt power structure, one that rests on money. You'll see soon enough. You'll realize only real humans can accomplish anything."

News drones swirled the outside of the police station, both

smaller cameras hovering around reporters and higher, larger models.

A stern-faced female reporter looked into her camera drone. "The police have admitted that they have arrested Maxwell Worthington, the son of Jacoby Worthington, a senior vice-president of the Hermes Corporation. The younger Worthington is implicated in a shocking and brazen daylight murder, in addition to allegedly being the mysterious Leem King whose bizarre stunts have recently taken a potentially murderous turn."

"We're showing the drone footage in five, four, three, two, one..." murmured a remote tech into her earpiece.

The viewers were treated to a drone image of Jia and Erik as they advanced behind the MX 60, firing at the criminals.

"As you can see," the reporter continued, "Maxwell Worthington was captured after a daring high-speed chase that ended in a gun battle on a commercial tower walkway. The Obsidian Detective, Erik Blackwell, and his partner, Lady Justice, were involved." A crackle of activity caught her attention. She turned, and her eyes widened as she pointed to the cameraman. "We've been waiting for this moment."

The drone turned toward the crowd to capture a frowning dark-haired man in a suit stepping out of a black luxury flitter.

"We have the confirmed arrival of Jacoby Worthington," announced the reporter.

Jia groaned. She stood outside the interrogation room, watching the news stream on a data window from her PNIU.

"I don't get it," she muttered.

Erik shrugged as he took a sip of coffee. "What? We expected his dad to show up. Maxwell said he would."

"Not that. This Lady Justice thing." She rolled her eyes. "You came into the department under the Obsidian Detective Act. It makes sense that they call you the Obsidian Detective." She eyed him as if she wondered if he'd had something to do with it. "I didn't come in under a Lady Justice Act."

"Just roll with it. It's not so bad. It's not like they're calling you something worse." Erik grinned.

Jia frowned as her PNIU chimed. She tapped it. "Oh. Great. Now my mother's sending me a message. She's watching the stupid news report, and asking, 'Is this why you couldn't give me a call?'" She typed a quick message. "I was supposed to call her to schedule dinner, but she can wait. Parents."

Erik hid his smirk. Jacoby Worthington turned the corner, escorted by a uniformed officer.

"Now the fun begins," Erik muttered.

"There's no way I'm letting that murderer out of the station," Jia insisted. "He'll disappear."

"I know. I've got your back, and the captain does, too."

Jacoby Worthington looked more like his son's older brother than his father. Unlike Erik's and Alicia's, his deaging hadn't left any hint of gray hair.

The man surveyed the two detectives with a cool, appraising gaze. "My son is in there?"

Jia nodded. "He is." She frowned as she leaned over, looking past him. "No attorney?"

"You'll understand why that's unnecessary in a moment," Jacoby replied, sounding disgusted. "I insist we have the rest of this conversation in the presence of my son. It's important he hears it directly from me. That will cut down on the chance of confusion."

Erik pressed on the panel, and the interrogation room door slid open. "That's fine, but if you're under the impression he's walking, you're going to be disappointed."

Jacoby wrinkled his nose. "We'll see who is disappointed in a moment."

"Just keep talking." Erik motioned to the door, and Jacoby entered. The detectives filed in after him.

Maxwell smiled. "It took you long enough, Father. You wouldn't believe what these so-called detectives have been saying to me. Such rude, rude things. They should really know their place."

Jacoby frowned. "I can only imagine what you've gone through."

"Exactly." Maxwell's smile faltered. "I assume the lawyer's making preparations for my release. Their evidence is flimsy, and the man I allegedly killed is some middling merchant who was engaging in antisocial behavior. It's not like he was a pillar of the community. And I can't help it if some mercenaries decided to attack the famous Obsidian Detective." He sneered at Erik. "You shouldn't make so many enemies if you don't want trouble."

Jia ground her teeth. Erik was half-convinced she was

going to leap over the table and start punching Maxwell in the face.

He wasn't sure he would stop her if she did.

Jacoby nodded solemnly. "I understand." He turned to Erik. "Detective, he has no assets of his own. I've frozen all his accounts. He will receive no legal representation from anyone in my employ. I understand that he has to be provided a lawyer by the government, and I want to make it clear that I've recently come into possession of evidence I'll be passing along to you. This evidence clearly demonstrates my son's involvement in a number of illegal activities on New Pacifica, including smuggling, unlicensed tech usage, and assault." He lifted his chin as if daring Erik and Jia to challenge him. "I, of course, had no knowledge of his activities, nor did I know he was planning any of this."

"Wait." Maxwell blinked, head snapping to his father. "*What?*"

Erik grinned. "It looks like your dad's kicking you off the tower, your alien highness."

Jia's lips quivered, and she clenched her fists. She glowered at Jacoby. "This is your fault, too. I don't buy for a second you didn't know about any of this. If you had stopped him earlier, a man would still be alive. At least by catching him, we're going to stop copycats, but that doesn't bring back Farouk Gamal."

"T-this isn't happening." Maxwell shook his head, his eyes wide with terror. "You're my father. You need to protect me from all these fake humans. You've always helped me before. You've told me yourself that we're Worthingtons. We're better than normal people."

Jacoby sighed. "Yes, we are." He narrowed his eyes. "But

with that superiority comes responsibility, you worthless little twit. I had some hope that you weren't a complete idiot and a sociopath, and you would grow out of your youthful indiscretions. I worked for decades to get where I am. Do you know how hard it is to get to my position in a company like Hermes, as someone not born on Earth? You've threatened all I have accomplished with your nonsense."

Maxwell gnashed his teeth. "This is not happening. This is ridiculous. You can't turn your back on me."

Jacoby slammed his fist on the table. "You have shamed your family. I'm prepared to disinherit you, but there's one small chance that I won't."

Erik watched in silence, a huge smirk on his face. Jia kept a cool, distant expression, but she'd unclenched her fists.

"You have to help me." Maxwell leaned forward. "*Please.*"

His father replied with a curt nod. "And I will. This is how this matter will proceed. You're going to admit to your crimes. Perhaps the prosecution will offer you some sort of deal, but you will do time in prison to reflect on your sins. I will do everything I can to ensure you are sentenced to at least ten years, preferably twenty."

Maxwell gasped. "Twenty years?"

"Don't worry. If you spend that time in honest reflection and self-improvement, they'll let you out early. Then, and only then, once you've paid your debt to society, will I reconsider your inheritance and your role in our family." Jacoby looked at Jia. "You're right, Detective Lin. This is partially my fault, and I will do what little I can to correct my mistake."

Maxwell hung his head. "I only wanted to free the real humans."

Jacoby flared his nostrils. "What pointless prattle. Detectives, I would like to leave now. I trust I've made my point to your satisfaction."

"Yeah, you could say that." Erik opened the door and gestured with a grand, mocking bow. "Thanks for your assistance, Mr. Worthington."

The other man stepped out, sparing one brief look of disgust at his son.

"We'll have an officer come and take you back to your cell soon," Erik explained to Maxwell. "And we'll put in a request for a lawyer."

"I don't need one," Maxwell murmured, his voice barely above a whisper. "I'll sign whatever they want me to."

"Your call. I'm not going to complain when you go away." Erik exited the room, followed by Jia.

Once the door closed, Jia glared down the hall at the departing Jacoby. "And I was irritated with my mother over unfortunate timing."

"Take the victory for what it is," Erik offered, his voice lowered. "We bagged the Leem King and a whole bunch of mercenaries. The captain can go out and give a big statement about how his feeling the fear has led him to prison. It's over."

Jia continued watching Jacoby until he turned a corner. "It makes me think about what I could have become under different circumstances."

Erik nodded. "That's humanity for you." The two of them started walking toward the captain's office. "Part angel, part demon, *always* annoying."

CHAPTER THIRTEEN

Jia picked up her fork and took a bite of her braised beef, enjoying the slightly sweet flavor. She offered her mother a smile.

The restaurant her mother had chosen was mid-tier, at least by Lan's standards. It wasn't a place serving beignets and beers with a rowdy but warm atmosphere. It did have a woman in a red silk dress kneeling on a raised platform, playing an *erhu*.

Thankfully, not every customer wore a suit or dress that cost more than Jia's flitter. Maybe this was her mother's way of meeting her halfway.

The *erhu* player wore a solemn expression as she played. She pulled her bow slowly back and forth, her fingers shifting up and down with intricate skill. A beautiful if haunting melody flowed from the instrument.

Oddly enough, music was one of the few areas in which Lan Lin hadn't demanded her daughters excel. Jia wondered if it there were frustrated youthful dreams linked to the musical arts, but she'd never bothered to pry to learn the truth. Annoying her mother to satisfy idle curiosity didn't seem a good trade-off.

Lan eyed Jia's bowl. "Is the beef to your liking? I've heard good things about it here, but I haven't had a chance to try it yet."

"It's good, Mother," Jia responded. "Fine flavor balance. Skilled seasoning."

"Then why do you look like you've just been told a meteor is about to hit Earth?"

"Lan Lin telling jokes?" Jia chuckled. "I should check to make sure you're not a Zitark spy in disguise."

"I've always had a sense of humor," her mother insisted. "You simply don't appreciate it. If anything, I'd argue you are the serious one between us. That's not always a bad trait to have, so I've never discouraged it."

Jia had to stop for a second and give that comment some thought. "I don't know if you're wrong in saying that. We could invite Mei next time and have a contest to figure out which of the Lin women is overly serious." Jia set her fork down. "Sorry, Mother. My last case got to me. It made me think about a few things."

"Why? You caught the man responsible, and he'll be punished for his crimes. I would think that as a detective, you would be satisfied. Before, you were always complaining you didn't get to go after all those unpleasant antisocials."

"I just wonder…" Jia let out a quiet sigh, looking around before returning her focus to her mom. "His father *knew* he was on the wrong path, but he covered for him. They're downplaying that on the news, but it's the truth."

"It's not wrong for a parent to cover for their child, but he should have followed up earlier. You and Mei never had antisocial tendencies, so raising you was easy in that regard. Being stubborn can be obnoxious, but it doesn't necessarily lead one to become a criminal. I have always presumed that most criminals are simply too lazy to succeed through honest work." Lan looked thoughtful before a smile broke out. "But don't worry about that awful man and his crimes. There will always be another criminal for you to obsess about. We should be discussing pleasanter things. I know you mostly enjoy your work, but in this case, you're not doing that, so let's change the subject."

Jia raised a curious eyebrow. "To what?"

"Corbin," Lan suggested. "Things have been going well, but I also have noticed something interesting that makes me wonder."

"What's that, Mother?" Jia asked, licking her lips. She would have been less worried if a shark was swimming behind her.

Lan's gaze turned piercing. "Most respectful women would bring their important man to meet their parents. Don't you agree?"

Jia managed not to grimace, but her tightening stomach made her regret the beef. "It's still early in our relationship. I didn't think that was necessary."

"It's the opposite. Because it's early, you should bring him to meet us." Lan flicked her wrist with practiced elegance and harrumphed. "You don't want to waste time, do you? You've never believed in that."

"I'm not following you." Jia watched her mother carefully, searching for some hint of what was going on in her ever-calculating mind.

"If he's not compatible with your family, the relationship doesn't have a future," Lan explained. "With that in mind, wouldn't it make sense to have him meet your parents sooner rather than later? I would have thought that much was obvious."

"Oh." Jia blinked. "I can see how *you* might feel that way, but I want to control how this unfolds." She looked to the side. "To be honest, I'm unsure about this relationship, so I don't want to complicate things until I'm certain."

"Why are you unsure?" Lan sounded genuinely concerned.

Jia leaned forward, eyes focused on her mom. "I like Corbin, and we have a good time when we have dates. He's pleasant and respectful of my career." Jia looked down, considering her next few words. "But I don't know if there's true excitement and spark."

Lan put a hand over her mouth and covered her laughter. "Excitement and spark? Sometimes I forget how young you are."

"It's not like they're pointless considerations in a relationship," Jia insisted with a frown.

"Pointless, no. Overrated? Yes. You're not having any problems other than excitement and spark?" Lan leaned forward, the eager interest of a busybody mother worse than a shark bearing its teeth.

Informing her mother about Corbin's joking complaints regarding Erik struck Jia as a horrific debacle waiting to happen. A few missing pieces of information would keep the conversation pleasant.

Misdirection would aid the effort.

"Let's not worry about that for now," Jia suggested. "I have a favor to ask."

Lan took a sip of tea, a hungry look in her eyes. Woe to the woman who owed her too much. "A favor?"

"Yes. I was wondering if you could teach me your roast duck recipe."

Jia could count on one hand the number of times she'd seen genuine shock on her mother's face. Lan Lin stared at her daughter wide-eyed, as if she'd turned into a hopping zombie ready to leap across the table, eat her flesh, and absorb her qi.

"Why?" Lan asked, pure wonder flavoring the question.

"I just wanted to make it for someone, is all." Jia managed a relaxed shrug and hoped her mother wouldn't probe further. A little flattery, especially based on truth, might help. "I have a lot of fond memories associated with eating your duck for a number of reasons, not the least of which is that it's delicious. If I'm going to do something special for someone, I might as well start with a good foundation. It's like you just said. I don't like to waste time."

Jia hadn't seen such a triumphant smile on her mother's face since the last time she'd been promoted over a long-hated rival.

"Yes." Lan nodded a few times, radiating satisfaction. "It's very wise of you to ask me to show you that. I'm sure Corbin will taste the respect and effort in the dish and respond in kind. It would bring me great pleasure to instruct you. I'll show you immediately after we're done here."

Jia managed a smile despite her thumping heart.

What was she doing asking her mother to teach her something to impress Erik? They were just partners, and somehow Jia couldn't bring herself to correct her mother and explain why she wanted to learn the recipe.

Why was everything so complicated?

Lan sighed as she looked through a shelf in one of her cabinets. She pushed aside pans, pots, and appliances. She tapped her PNIU, and the shelf retracted. The cabinet door slid closed.

"I wish you would have asked me this earlier in the day when our cook was still here, Jia," she complained. "I must admit I'm not familiar with where and how she stores things. I do believe we have duck. I'm pretty sure." She stopped and frowned. "We only have produced meat, but it's not like we'll have to print it." She wrinkled her nose. "But for something so special, maybe we should buy real duck meat?"

"That's a lot of money to spend for a cooking lesson," Jia replied.

"Oh, don't worry about it. Premium ingredients are part of the key to cooking success." Lan furrowed her brow in intense concentration. "It would help if I could remember everything I needed, too. It's been a while since I've actually cooked it. Not since...before you went to university if I recall correctly."

"It's really been that long?" Jia snickered. "Should I just look up a recipe on the net?"

Lan shifted from a cabinet to a spice rack on the wall.

"Just give me a moment. It's been a while. The memories are all there." She gestured at the spices. "These are a major key to its success." She grabbed a few bottles—ginger and nutmeg, among others. "I remember that much." She tapped her bottom lip. "I don't know if we have everything. I'd hate to have to print something I am missing, even a minor ingredient. Substandard ingredients will spoil the whole experience." She moved away from the spice rack and tapped her PNIU. This time a door on the island opened and shelves extended, weighed down with kitchen equipment. She grabbed a small silver device resembling a gun and eyed it with suspicion. "What does this do?"

Jia put a hand to her mouth and fake-coughed to cover her smile. "It's a smoking gun, Mother."

Lan tossed it back onto the shelf. "I know I don't need that." She eyed the device. "Pretty sure."

Jia's father stepped into the kitchen. He stopped and tilted his head, staring at his wife, who had her head half in the island cabinet. A few seconds passed before recognition washed over his face, then he backed out of the room, shaking his head.

Maybe there's a reason Mother only cooks that one recipe, Jia thought with a smile.

Lan stood and tapped her foot. "I'm going to have some fresh, real duck delivered. By the time it arrives, I'll have found everything." She paused. "You have time, right?"

"Sure, Mother, but you don't have to go through all that trouble."

Her mother's bright smile disarmed Jia's resistance.

"I don't think of this as a chore," Lan explained. "It is

something I've always wanted to share with my daughters. I was only waiting for one of you to ask."

Jia's smile was warm and comfortable. "Thanks, Mother. I appreciate it."

Lan shook her head. "No, Jia. Thank *you*."

CHAPTER FOURTEEN

Dozens of jets shot water in intricate repeating patterns around the edge of the huge polished-stone fountain.

Erik sat on the edge of the water feature, watching the streams of people in the commercial zone go about their afternoon. Some chatted happily to nearby people or on calls. Pain and concern poisoned the faces of others.

A few people wandered aimlessly, as if they had nothing filling their life other than pointless commercialism.

"Why did you come here?" Emma asked. "This seems an odd way to spend lunch. You're going to be hungry later."

"I had a big breakfast, and sometimes it's good to watch people," Erik answered, half to her and half to himself. "It grounds me. I picked up the habit when I was in the Army. It was about reminding myself who I was fighting for. When you go on a mission, you get tunnel vision, and you can start forgetting yourself. Being a cop is even more challenging in some ways because there's not a clear separation between the enemy and civilians."

"I suspect you would be far happier living in some

dome on an otherwise uninhabited moon," Emma replied. "Humans will always disappoint you."

"Have I disappointed you?"

"Your taste in many things is disappointing," Emma suggested.

Erik grinned. "You're probably right about being a hermit, but I've got a lot of work to do before that happens." His grin turned into a frown. "And a lot of people need to die to balance the scales."

"You've made more progress than you think," Emma suggested.

His thoughts pulled together. "On what?"

"Hunting them down. The fact that they're so scared of you proves it. From what we've found, it sounds like they risked destroying an entire tower just because you got too close. The cornered animal is always the most dangerous."

Erik's gaze followed a scowling man until his target turned into a pet store and smiled. "It might be nice if I could find those other people working on this, but you're right. I have to worry about the things I can fix here and now, and I've got an easy one."

"What's that?" Emma asked.

It was time to stop being a coward.

"I assume you have a number for my brother?"

"Yes. It's not as if he lives a highly secluded life."

"Call him, and keep quiet while I talk to him," Erik ordered.

Emma laughed. "This ought to be interesting."

Erik held his breath as the PNIU initiated the call. His brother might not even answer. The man had made his feelings clear years ago. Damien might not even care enough to be angry at the attempt.

"Hello, Erik," Damien answered a few seconds later.

Erik slowly exhaled. "Hey, Damien. It's been a while."

"Yes, it has. A long while." Damien's breath caught. "Wait, you're *calling* me?"

"Yeah? I wanted to talk to you, and this is how people generally do that sort of thing when they're not right next to one another." Erik frowned, not sure if his brother was angry or something else was going on.

"You're calling me in real-time, which means you're on Earth," Damien observed.

"I've been on Earth for a while. I'm out of the Army now. I'm a cop."

"I know."

"You do?" Erik asked. He didn't hide the surprise in his voice. He'd wondered if Damien knew he was still alive.

"Yes," his brother replied. "The things you've been involved in are fairly newsworthy. You've remained as flashy as you were when you were younger."

Damien knew Erik was on the planet, and even knew he was in Neo SoCal. Despite that, he had made no attempt to contact Erik. Time didn't heal all wounds. Often, it helped them fester. Erik gritted his teeth.

He couldn't claim he was surprised, but that didn't make it any easier to accept.

Damien sighed. "I read about what happened to your unit. For what it's worth, I'm sorry. I don't always think about the risks soldiers are taking on the frontier. It seems so distant at times, and it's because of the sacrifices of men and women like those in the 108th that I can live my life mostly free of fear."

"Thanks," Erik mumbled, some of the tension flowing out of him.

He stood and moved away from the fountain, then joined the flow of foot traffic heading toward an elevator that would take him to the parking level. "I was looking through some documents the other day, and I happened to notice your name in connection with a conference in Neo SoCal."

"Is there some sort of terrorist threat I should know about?" Damien asked, his voice wavering.

"No, no," Erik answered. "Nothing like that. I just figured since you were coming to Neo SoCal, we should have lunch or something."

"Do you really think that's a good idea?" Damien didn't sound angry, just confused.

"Nope." Erik laughed. "It might be a terrible idea. It might end with me punching you. I'd give that fifty-fifty odds."

Damien was silent before chuckling. "I appreciate your honesty, but you're not building a good case for meeting you."

"That's what the last woman I asked out told me." Erik slowed his pace. He could have made this call from the privacy of his home, but something about the huge crowd made it easier. "I'm not guaranteeing anything. I'm not asking anything from you. I just want to meet. Mom and Dad are gone. It's just us now, and it's been a long time. I figure it wouldn't hurt, and you wouldn't be going out of your way to do it."

Damien sighed. "Fine. I'm sure we can meet for lunch, but I'm not promising anything either. You understand that? If you think we're going to sit and have a family therapy session, you're sorely mistaken."

Erik snorted. "I'm a big boy. If nothing comes of it, I'll live, just like I have all these years."

"As long as we understand each other. I'll contact you with some suggestions once I'm in Neo SoCal. Until then." Damien killed the call.

"I'll probably end up regretting this," Erik muttered.

"Why do you say that?" Emma asked. "You weren't cursing at each other, despite the fact you already threatened to punch him, which I found highly amusing."

"I didn't threaten to punch him," Erik complained. "I just said it might happen."

A passing woman gave him an odd look, then clucked her tongue disapprovingly and hurried along. Even if she had heard the other side of his conversation with Damien, it might not have helped.

Erik stepped out of the human river, looking down. He turned his back to a nearby shop window. Several women smirked at him as they passed, and he turned around. A hologram of a smiling teal-haired woman in a see-through teddy stood right behind him.

"Some things just aren't worth revisiting," he explained to Emma.

"Like lingerie shops?" she teased, waving an arm in the display case.

"I meant, I'm thinking the meeting ends with me headbutting Damien," Erik replied. "If I need to go there, it'll be more satisfying than punching him."

Emma let out a pained sigh. "You don't need to be such an uptight…" She finished the statement with a strange mix of snarls and hisses.

He touched his ear. "Is there some sort of interference?" Erik asked.

"No, that was Zitark, the version used by their diplomatic caste," Emma explained. "It's hard to translate the word into any human language, but it's roughly 'The grand warrior who is trying to defecate rocks.'"

Erik glared at a few teenagers pointing and laughing at him. "The Zitarks have a word for that?"

"Apparently, they do." Emma sniffed. "Shame you don't speak diplomatic Zitark."

Erik's PNIU chimed with a message.

"The captain has ordered you to his office ASAP," Emma explained as the hologram disappeared.

"With my luck, it'll probably involve investigating a Zitark murder."

January 20, 2229, Neo Southern California Metroplex, Police Enforcement Zone 122 Station, Office of Captain Alexander Ragnar

The cognitive dissonance between the sheer physical presence of the hulking, bearded Viking sitting behind the desk and his easygoing smile always teetered between the relaxing and the absurd. Even after working for him for months, Erik wasn't sure how much of the captain's persona was real.

The occasional frown sneaked out when the 1-2-2 was under pressure, but Erik was almost convinced he could do an orbital drop with the captain onto a rebel-held planet and Ragnar would grin the whole time.

"Sorry to call you in from lunch early, but we got something dumped on us that's a high priority," Captain Ragnar explained to Jia and Erik.

"High priority?" Jia questioned.

"Yes, as in the council is leaning on the higher-ups, and they're leaning on me." Captain Ragnar shrugged. "It's not a totally worthless request, so I'm letting them lean a little more than I normally would. I wanted to make sure you two are on it. This is a sensitive matter, and it might get hairy, depending on what you find."

"Sensitive? You mean, politically?" Erik frowned.

Captain Ragnar chuckled. "Yes. It involves 46 Helix. You familiar with them?"

Erik and Jia both nodded.

The huge company was one of the major biotech players in the UTC. They were involved in biotech research and the production of a variety of genetically modified organisms used in different industries. Unlike many biotech companies, they made significant public donations to groups like the Terran Purist Association and worked closely with them to ensure compliance with Purist standards.

"They're a little close to the vest about some of the details, but a VIP of theirs claims he's being harassed. At least, that's what's been passed along to me."

Jia looked doubtful. "Harassed? Isn't that something corporate security can take care of?"

"You'd think, but he's personally reached out to the police, and he's got a relative on the Council. That means he's spooked. He's claimed his life is in danger, and he's demanding police protection." Captain Ragnar tapped his PNIU, and a full-sized hologram of a man appeared. The man's long, dark hair was gathered in a ponytail. "This is Dr. Louis Chen, a senior researcher for 46 Helix. From what I've read, he's a wizard when it comes to genetic modifications. He's also great at pushing things right up to the line of Purist acceptability."

If the eyes were a window to a soul, as some claimed, then Dr. Chen's soul was very bored. "What's that mean?" Erik stared at the hologram. "He's doing something he shouldn't?"

The captain shook his head. "The opposite. He's good at tweaking existing genes to enhance things. He's helped the company cut down on their product lines that use introduced genes, which helps get groups like the TPA on board easier. I can't follow all the science, but apparently, the TPA even gave him some sort of special award for scientific humility."

"That's his public image," Jia observed. "If he is going over the line, and a more zealous Purist group found out, they might have decided they didn't want to waste time using political or social pressure to solve the problem." She tapped her lip. "They might have even been inspired by someone like the Leem King to take more direct action against the so-called harmful elements of society."

"This feels like us doing busywork for someone just because he's connected," Erik replied. "You really want to put us on this, Captain?"

The captain killed the image. "I see where you're

coming from, but right now, you two don't have a major active case, and Jia's right. Given some of the weirdness lately, we can't ignore the possibility of a terrorist angle. My instincts tell me that since the council is throwing their weight around, there might be something there. I even called in a few favors from CID friends and a few others to check on this guy. Nobody says he's dirty. They all claim he's a real humanitarian and a dedicated scientist. No shady donations, organized crime groups, or insurrectionists have been within a light-year of attempting to influence this guy." His eyes went from one to the other. "Allegedly."

"And if it's a lie?" Jia folded her arms. "What if this is just some corrupt corporation trying to use the police to take out their trash for them?"

"Then you two should do what you do best. You dig to the heart of what's going on, and you keep digging until you find the truth, whatever it takes."

Erik allowed himself a wolfish grin. "This guy's got a direct connection to the council. If he's dirty, they're going to come down on you when we reveal the truth. Even if everyone's all about allegedly cleaning up Neo SoCal, that's going to hurt."

Captain Ragnar matched his detective's grin. "I told you before. You handle the investigation, I'll handle the politics. If Dr. Chen is really being threatened, it's our duty to help protect him. If he's scum, it's our duty to take him down. Win-win."

"And the political angle?" Jia asked. "Not a concern?"

"We shouldn't be ruled by politics," Captain Ragnar answered. "And one way to do that is to earn favors we can cash in. Good police work is the start of cleaning up Neo SoCal, but it's not the end. Understood?"

She nodded. "Understood."

"How hard could it be?" Erik asked. "At least it's not some nutjob rich boy playing at being an anarchist."

Captain Ragnar nodded. "I'll send you the info. Now get on it."

CHAPTER FIFTEEN

"The captain mentioned instinct, but do you trust my instincts?" Jia asked from the passenger's seat of the MX 60 as they sped toward the 46 Helix tower.

Something about the case already bothered her, and ever since Erik had become her partner, she'd increasingly accepted an important fact. Although she believed she had trusted her skills before, the doubts of her previous partners and the captain had sabotaged her on a subconscious level, but now that she had a good partner, her belief in her hunches had grown.

Erik offered a quick nod. "Yeah. I do. Let's be real. I'm a tactical specialist, but I spent thirty years in the Army, so that makes sense. It's going to take you a long time to match my combat instincts, even though you're a lot better than I was at your age, but at the same time, you've got a natural gift for investigations. We're a lot more even there, and I'll even admit you're smarter than me." She looked at him. "Since no one else is here to hear it."

"I am," Emma offered.

Erik's lips pressed together. "Thanks."

"Don't you think it's odd that a major corporation like 46 Helix is calling us in? The 'corp hunters?'" Jia made air quotes around the last two words. "The Obsidian Detective and Lady Justice?"

Emma laughed. "That sounds like a terrible police serial for young children."

"I would have loved it as a kid," Erik countered before nodding at Jia. "What are you thinking?"

"I'm wondering if it's a trap," Jia admitted.

"A trap?"

"By the conspiracy."

Erik furrowed his brow in thought. "It could be, but as long as we are careful, it doesn't have to be one we spring. Emma, have you already dug into the company?"

"As much as I've been able to in the short period since we were assigned," she replied.

"Are they a Ceres Galactic subsidiary?" Erik asked. "I'm not sure if they're the ones behind everything, but they've got the most arrows pointing at them."

"Actually, 46 Helix isn't a subsidiary," Emma confirmed. "Ceres has attempted to acquire them in the past, but they've rejected the overtures and remained an independent entity. They do, however, share numerous corporate relationships. In addition, 46 Helix has contracts all over the UTC, including military supply contracts. Not all of the details are publicly available, and I'm not eager to start hacking DD systems unless you feel it's absolutely necessary. Those uniform boys might get overeager, and then we'll all end up in an unfortunate and annoying situation."

"I don't think we need to go that far yet. So, they are

linked to Ceres, but not controlled. They could be linked to the conspiracy."

Jia pointed to the 46 Helix Tower in the distance. "Or I could just be paranoid."

"Nothing terrible about just admitting you were wrong later," Erik suggested.

"I hope I can do that."

Erik waited for the automated system to verify the MX 60's transponder. The massive gate blocking the internal parking garage groaned open. Rows of tightly packed flitters lay at angles against the walls, magnetic grapple systems keeping them in place.

High-density parking garages weren't in every building in the metroplex, but they were common.

"Their guidance system is requesting control," Emma reported. "If you think they're about to kill you, this would be the perfect opportunity. It would be easy for them to claim a systems glitch."

"Go ahead and give them control," Erik ordered. "But keep an eye on things. If I'm going to die, I'd rather it not be in some stupid flitter accident."

Jia gave him a sidelong glance. "Getting shot to death or dying in an explosion is so much better?"

He looked at all the cars. "You have to admit, it does have a certain dramatic flair."

"Granting control," Emma reported. The MX 60 slowed and changed direction, angling slightly and heading toward an empty docking port.

"Keep quiet while we're in there, Emma," Erik suggested. "Even if you're directing in my ear. If there is something shady, they might still be listening with advanced tech."

"I enjoy listening more than you can imagine," Emma replied. "The problem with humans is that you talk more than you listen."

"I'll keep that in mind." Erik's playful smile slowly faded, and he turned toward Jia. "Hey, might as well mention this now because it could affect future bets, and I don't want to forget later."

"Bets? What are you… Wait, are you saying you went on a date?" Jia hated the vague irritation in her voice. It might be mistaken as jealousy, and she wasn't jealous, not one bit.

Certainly not because her partner was dating a bimbo barista after turning down the woman she'd set him up with as unacceptable.

She blinked, not sure about the true source of her anger. The Lin matchmaking genes and competitive nature ran deep. She wasn't ready to face the alternate explanation and its implications.

"Yeah, I went on a date," Erik admitted as the MX 60 slowed to a halt, and the magnetic grappling system latched it to the wall with a slight shake. "With the barista I met."

"I assumed it was her. How did it go?"

Two metal platforms extended on either side of the MX 60. They led to an elevator.

Erik shrugged. "It was all right, but I don't think I'll be seeing her again." The two detectives opened their doors.

Jia didn't talk until they were walking toward the open

elevator. "Why? I thought you said she was pretty hot. Did she end up being too much of a fangirl?"

"Nope. She barely pays attention to the news. She knew who I was, but she didn't seem to care that much."

"Isn't that a plus?"

Jia and Erik stepped into the elevator. The magnetic grapples lifted the back of the MX 60 to angle the car as the doors closed.

"The problem is the reason she doesn't pay much attention to the news," Erik replied.

She eyed him, arms folding across her chest. "Care to elaborate?"

Erik sighed. "You and I don't always agree on things."

Jia nodded, unsure where he was going with that statement. "True enough. I know you think I'm naïve and too restrained, and I'm not going to dispute that I still find you excessive at times, but I think we complement each other."

He agreed. "Not denying that."

The elevator chimed and rose.

"Then I don't understand," Jia admitted.

"It's about challenging me," Erik clarified. "I would rather have someone smart enough to challenge my worldview and my date..." He sighed. "I'm not saying she was an idiot, but there's intelligence, and then there is using one's intelligence. It's like she purposely doesn't want to engage the world."

Jia considered what her partner had explained. For a moment, it sounded like he was saying he wanted to date *her*. She shunted that thought to the abyss. He was using her as a contrast in his explanation, nothing more. That had to be it.

She cleared her throat, trying to inject as much casualness as she could into her response. "Is that the same as the difference between someone who can't read and someone who can, but chooses not to?"

Erik thought about it. "Yeah, exactly."

"So," Jia continued, "you want someone smart who is willing to use their intelligence."

"Of course." Erik sounded surprised. "Why would someone be that way? Give me a reason."

"You might be surprised," Jia answered. "Someone could have a fragile ego. In that case, someone intelligent would challenge them. Lots of people, men and women, don't like the challenge."

"Okay, that's one," Erik thought a moment. "Bet you can't name another. Plenty of men like the challenge, like me."

"An intelligent partner might have her own goals, and those goals might take her in a different direction," Jia suggested.

"A man who can't handle a woman with ambition shouldn't call himself a man," Erik countered.

Jia furrowed her brow, concentrating hard to come up with something else. "Maybe a man worries an intelligent partner will think she can find someone better."

Erik scoffed. "Again, if a man's that weak, he deserves to be left."

"You make valid points," Jia offered, a bright smile on her face. Her partner didn't want a bimbo. *Always nice to know...for the next woman she set him up with.*

The elevator dinged, and the doors slid open on a long, sterile white corridor. The harsh illumination reminded Jia of the station and the hallway leading to the interrogation rooms. That set her on edge.

"He's supposed to meet us in room 8764, according to the info the captain sent us," Jia recalled. She frowned slightly as she surveyed the barren corridor. They continued heading down the empty hall. There were plenty of sealed doors with numbers, but no door descriptions or names on them, not even access panels.

Her paranoia flared again, but there was no point in voicing it until someone made a move. She had both her weapons, and Erik had his pistol and his arm. Their captain knew exactly where they were going. They also had Emma as backup.

Anyone trying to kill them would be in for a rough time and heavy casualties unless they gassed them.

Several minutes passed, along with as many intersections. It felt like they had crossed the entire tower level by the time they arrived at Room 8764. Like all the others, there were only simple black letters above the thick door and no obvious access panel.

"What now?" Jia asked, looking at the outside of the door. "Do we use the contact number?"

The door slid open to reveal Louis Chen. He leaned out the open doorway and glanced both ways, then waved them forward. "Please come in, Detectives."

Jia and Erik entered. Dozens of shelves holding small white unmarked metal boxes filled Room 8764. There were no chairs, no other doors, no hint of it being an office. Jia rubbed her arms to fight the chill filling the room.

"Where are we?" Jia asked. She injected more suspicion

into her voice than she felt, and she wouldn't have been surprised if optical camouflage-using assassins leapt out from between the shelves.

Dr. Chen looked around, confused by the question. "It's a sample storage room," he explained.

"How the hell do you find anything in here?" Erik asked. He frowned and leaned closer to one of the boxes. "Nothing's marked. I get you've probably tagged the stuff, but doesn't it help to have at least something on it when you're in here?"

"It's company policy that all samples be processed and stored by bots," Dr. Chen replied. "I find it distracting." He let out a wistful sigh. "All advances are slowed by petty men with petty rules. Alas."

Jia took note of the comment. That kind of thinking could easily lead to corruption. History was filled with the rest of humanity suffering because of the arrogance of amoral, brilliant people.

"Why are we talking in a giant refrigerator?" she asked. No reason to dance around the obvious question.

Dr. Chen's furtive glances again summoned fantasies of advanced assassins. "I picked it randomly because I didn't know if someone was monitoring my office. My life is in danger, and I don't know why or who. I'd rather not end up dead because of habit or laziness."

"Not a crazy thought," Erik commented.

"You think someone at the company is targeting you?" Jia asked.

Dr. Chen shrugged. "I don't know. It's not impossible. A few weeks ago, I started receiving threats via messages to my PNIU, including death threats, from anonymous accounts. They didn't specify why they wanted me dead, only noted, 'My time had come for my sins.' I went to Security about it, and they told me there was little that could be done because they were…I forget. I think he called them 'fire accounts?'"

"Burner accounts," Jia suggested. She took a deep breath, worry quickening her pulse. If the Leem King had inspired people, he might have also taught them the value of good information security when committing crimes. A corporate researcher could easily reach the top of some fanatic's fake human list. The Leem King's arrest and sentencing, including him reading the required public statement, had diminished his popularity, but all it took was one zealous follower to cause trouble.

And then the cycle would continue.

"Yes, burner accounts." Dr. Chen reached up and gripped the edge of a shelf, his fingers tightening until they turned pale. "They told me not to worry about them. They say they are nothing important. Many researchers get such threats, and they insisted that ninety-five percent of them amount to nothing."

Erik pulled back his duster and patted his pistol. "One in twenty odds isn't something I'd be willing to risk my life on."

"Exactly," Dr. Chen spat, his face red. "I've given my life to this company. My research is responsible for keeping them near the top, and they want me to keep quiet because they're concerned about bad PR. They suggested I simply stay in the tower for a few weeks; I have to be a prisoner because they are lazy." He pulled his hand away from the shelf and curled it into a fist. "I deserve more. I deserve better, so I made sure the police would get involved." He grinned smugly. "What can they do if the council directly asks for an investigation? And now that you two are involved, if they attempt to brush you off, it'll look like they are covering something up. Everyone knows your reputation."

Jia frowned. "Setting aside statistics, have you considered that they might have reason to believe it's not a serious threat? It would be stupid of them to let one of their people be assassinated."

Dr. Chen scoffed and cut through the air with his hand, almost knocking a box off the shelf. "Scandals affect investor confidence. A dead researcher can be replaced. That's what they think, but they don't realize how brilliant I am. Those people in management are soulless, useless fools. They're more replaceable than I am."

"Nobody's ever accused you of having low self-esteem, have they?" Erik asked.

"There's no point in denying one's brilliance," Dr. Chen insisted. "What? You're going to walk away? You don't believe me."

"Nope. Not until we know there's no threat. Cops don't respond to investors."

"I see." Some of the displeasure left Dr. Chen's face. "Good."

"Let's assume for now that company security is just incompetent or complacent," Jia suggested. "We'll interface with them as necessary, but we'll approach this as an independent investigation. As such, we'll need a list of suspects to begin."

He nodded. "That sounds logical."

"Who dislikes you the most?" Jia asked.

Dr. Chen tilted his head, a thoughtful expression on his face. "That would probably be my ex-wife. We divorced a year ago. She claimed I was cold and unloving."

"I wonder how she could ever come to that conclusion," Erik joked, but the scientist didn't seem to pick up on the sarcasm.

"She always was short-sighted. I think she was just threatened by my intelligence."

Jia almost laughed at the near synchronicity with her earlier conversation but kept a straight face. "Do you think she might be sending the messages?"

"I doubt it." Dr. Chen shook his head. "She's hardly the sort to have the skills to harass me without it leading back to her. I suppose she could have hired someone, but it seems rather fanciful."

"Jealous colleagues?" Erik inquired. "Scientific rivals?"

"I've won industry awards," Dr. Chen replied proudly. "But so have many of my colleagues. I'll never deny my brilliance, but my field contains many impressive researchers, and all of us share one thing in common—we don't have time for foolish games. I think that's even less likely than my ex-wife."

Jia's forehead wrinkled as she dove deeper into the possibilities. "Has anyone left the company recently? Been fired? Maybe someone who might blame you?"

Dr. Chen shrugged, exasperation on his face. "Maybe? I don't know. This is a huge company, and thousands of employees work in this building alone. It's not like I waste time paying attention to that sort of thing. I have far more important things to do."

"Yeah, you're too busy saving the world," Erik asked.

"If not that, then advancing human knowledge, which is the same thing," Dr. Chen agreed.

After a few minutes with the man, Jia was beginning to see why someone might want to kill him. "What about your research staff? Presumably, you pay a little more attention to their comings and goings."

The first hint of uncertainty broke through the scientist's arrogant façade. "I…am very focused on my scientific endeavors. I'm not sure about the answer to your question, but if it's not one of my main researchers, it'd be unlikely they'd care enough to kill me. Wouldn't you say?"

Erik let out a rueful chuckle. "You'd be surprised by what people are willing to kill for."

CHAPTER SIXTEEN

Erik didn't understand why someone would want to live in a tower apartment that gave the illusion of having no walls.

Heights didn't bother him. He'd performed more than a few orbital and sub-orbital drops during his time in the military, but sitting in a place with no sense of separation from the outside world hundreds of stories above the Earth was disorienting. At least internally. From the outside, it looked like any other apartment in a luxury tower, and he'd not realized how insane it would be once he was inside.

Sometimes he felt like he might fit in better on some alien world than he did on Earth.

The thought kept running through his head as Dr. Chen's ex-wife Laya led Erik and Jia from the more reasonable enclosed foyer to her faux-exposed living room. The holographic walls didn't even provide a hint of separation like floor-to-ceilings windows, and concealed speakers allowed in the outside noise. If there had been wind, he could have easily been fooled into thinking he was directly exposed to the outside.

They'd contacted her about an interview, and she'd blown them off until the next day.

A few tasked drones kept an eye on her without the need for a warrant, but she didn't try to run. That could be a sign of resignation as much as arrogance. The most obvious suspect was often the culprit, but that wasn't a certainty, as many of their investigations had proven already.

Annoyance and curiosity overcame self-control as Erik blurted, "Doesn't this get annoying?" He gestured to flitters forming a thick lattice of air lanes near the tower. "It's like having a huge hole in your apartment."

Laya didn't respond immediately as she sat on the couch. Despite being in her forties, she looked younger than Jia thanks to a de-aging treatment and a tight black party dress and choker. Most people waited a little longer for the procedure, especially since it could only be performed once because of Telomeric Decay Syndrome.

Erik couldn't discern if she had a problem with stubborn gray hair like he did. She'd dyed all her hair light-blue.

"Neo-Anti-Atomism," the woman finally declared, weary boredom in her voice.

Erik frowned. "I know what all those words mean by themselves, but together, they might as well be Zitark. What are you talking about?"

"It's an architectural movement," Jia explained, barely concealed distrust on her face directed toward Laya. "It's supposed to be about bringing unity through the elimination of the private and the public. That kind of thing. It was all the rage about fifteen years back until most people decided they liked their privacy after all."

Erik chuckled. "On the frontier, people are still too busy making sure the basics work before they can worry about weird homes. You'd think being the wealthiest planet in a huge confederation would make people satisfied, but they still find reasons to be upset. That's human nature for you."

Laya scoffed. "You sound like Louis. I wanted a home like this for years, but he always failed to see the point. That man is the living embodiment of selfish arrogance. There were two things I swore I'd do once I left him: get my de-aging using his money and buy a place like this. As your partner observed, this isn't about being trendy. It's about better interfacing with society."

"Sure, sure. Whatever you say. I'm not here to judge you. I'm a good cop, but I'm a terrible interior decorator. Let's get down to the business of why we came."

She glanced at both of them, feigned disinterest that was barely marred by her eyes raising. "Yes, let's."

Erik and Jia exchanged quick glances before settling into chairs.

"Would you describe the divorce as acrimonious?" Jia asked. "We have information from Dr. Chen, but we'd really like to hear your perspective on it."

"Acrimonious?" Laya laughed. "Acrimonious is *far* too pleasant a word to use."

"What word would you use?" asked Erik.

"Hateful, bitter, and spiteful are a good start," Laya suggested. She eyed Erik like she was starving and he was a juicy steak. "I gave that man ten years of my life, but it was pointless since he was cheating on me."

That was a good motive for harassment.

"Cheating on you?" Erik began. "With who?"

Dr. Chen hadn't mentioned anyone else. If there was another woman he'd kicked to the curb, she might be an obvious suspect. The scientist might be brilliant, but that didn't mean he could screw women over and get away with it.

"Not a woman," Laya clarified.

"I asked who, not which woman," Erik replied. "Man or woman, if he was having an affair, that means we've got other people we need to check into, and he didn't mention it, so he might be hiding something."

"An affair?" Laya snorted. "He'd have to care enough about something other than his ridiculous research for more than five minutes to have an affair. I'm not saying he was cheating on me with someone else. I'm saying he only cared about his job." She gave an overdramatic eye roll.

Jia frowned. "You were upset that he was career-oriented?"

"Don't be so literal. It's not that I wanted him to neglect his work, but being hardworking turned into overworking. He didn't care about me or anyone, and despite giving him so many years and so many chances, that bastard still screwed me in the divorce settlement with the help of his corp lawyer buddies." Laya sniffed disdainfully. "I've had to make due on a pittance. I wasted so many years for nothing on a man because I thought he had potential."

"I can see you're one step away from living in a Shadow Zone alley," deadpanned Jia.

"I deserved more." Laya huffed. "I earned more for all my time and effort. I put up with that bastard for years, and I helped him establish social connections in the company to improve his position. He wouldn't be where he is today without my help."

"You're saying you helped him with his research?"

"His research?" Laya threw her head back and laughed. "Getting ahead in a corporation isn't like getting ahead in your police department. Doing your job is secondary to the politics of advancement. He lacked any natural talent with that, but I made up for it. I advised him. He would still be someone's assistant if it weren't for me, and then he tossed me aside because he said I was too distracting." She stood and turned to face the flitters in the sky. "No gratitude. No acknowledgment that I made him the man he is today. You came here to interview me, so I'll be honest. I hate that man, and I always will, if only because I was too stupid to leave first."

Erik didn't see any reason to play nice with the obvious question. "You hate his guts, and you think he cheated you. That means you'd have a lot of reasons to want to hurt him. That makes you an obvious suspect."

"Yes, it does." Laya kept staring out at the flitters, cool hunger in her eyes. "I can't deny that, but let me ask you something, Detective Blackwell. If I were the one responsible for threatening my husband, don't you think I would have a lawyer here? Do you think I'd be admitting to all of this so openly?"

"You might just think you're too smart for two idiot cops," Jia suggested. "You'd be surprised at how many people we run into who believe that."

Laya narrowed her eyes, which flashed with anger. "I know who you two are, and I know the kinds of people you've brought down. You can dig all you want, but I guarantee I'm not the one threatening my husband, no matter how much fun it might be." She laughed, the sound hollow and bitter. "I'm not complaining, mind you. It'd be deliciously appropriate if he ended up with a bullet in his brain, but I understand something very important about revenge, something that makes me hope you catch whoever is harassing him quickly and before they hurt him."

A formation of cargo drones zoomed by only about ten meters away, probably going to deliver to a port somewhere in the tower. Erik watched them, suspicious. They would make an excellent bomb delivery mechanism, but they left his line-of-sight without a single explosion.

"What is that?" Erik turned back to her. "Is this one of those things where you understand you probably hate him more than he hates you?"

"Considering how much I hate him, I don't doubt that at all, but it's not important." Laya offered him an icy smile. "The thing I've realized is, what good is revenge that ends too quickly? If Louis dies, he won't be able to suffer. I've got a better way of making him suffer, and that requires him to live for at least a few more years."

"Torture?" Erik guessed.

"I'm not a frontier barbarian, Detective." Laya tore her attention away from the outside and folded her arms, a euphoric look on her face. "I'm going to earn the money I deserve while also embarrassing Louis to the point that his career is ruined. Once he's fired and exiled from corporate society, maybe he'll end up, as you suggested, in a Shadow Zone alley, knowing that I ruined him. Then and only then should he die, stabbed by another bottom-feeding criminal over the last dumpling in the garbage."

Erik was impressed that Laya had refined her bitterness to the point of employable tactics.

It reminded him of his obsession with avenging his unit, even if he thought a bad marriage was a far cry from dozens of men and women being ambushed and murdered.

Jia's look suggested she thought the woman only marginally more sane than the Grayhead terrorists they'd faced in Florida. "How are you going to do that? If his high-powered lawyers already won against your efforts in the divorce, what's your master plan to get your revenge?"

Laya gave Jia a pitying look. "I gave up a promising career of my own to help support my ex-husband. I had corporate connections to begin with, and I used those, along with my social and political skills, to help his career. I met a lot of people along the way who I flattered to help my husband, and I understand corporate social networks with the same intimacy my ex-husband understands his genetic research. I'm currently writing a *roman a clef* that will show the world just how pathetic both Louis and the corp supporting him are, a record of their pathetic and corrupt nature."

"What's a *roman a clef?*" Erik asked.

Laya rolled her eyes as she snorted in derision.

Erik could have sworn Jia's hand moved toward her stun pistol before she dropped it.

"It's a novel that uses real events and people," she explained. "You just barely change the names and fictionalize a few events here and there. The idea is, you can trash people, but they can't claim libel. That kind of thing."

"Oh, so it's a book where one bitches about her ex?" Erik asked. "That's your big plan?" Amusement infused his words.

Laya rolled her eyes so hard it looked like she was having a seizure. "I'd expect you two, of all people, to understand the value of this work. In the current social environment, it will be successful. People are craving anti-corporate narratives, which is why they've uplifted you two mid-level detectives into some sort of sad plebian folk heroes. I don't have to do anything illegal or violent to triumph over my husband. I will become wealthy, and he'll be destroyed as a side-effect." She smiled and moved her shoulders in a rolling shrug as if to say, "It's perfect."

"I'm beginning to think there are other reasons your husband might have divorced you," Jia suggested cheerfully.

Laya sat back on the couch and crossed her legs, an irritated expression lingering. "Think whatever you want, but I told you all this to make it clear I'm not threatening my husband. If anything, I've changed my mind. You stopping his killers is more useful for my future novel sales. If he dies, he'll become a martyr, and people won't be as receptive to my truth about the kind of man he was." Her face made her disgust at the idea clear.

"Understood," Erik replied. "And we're cops, so we do try to keep people from getting murdered." He looked at Jia. She nodded. "If there's anything you think we need to know, you know how to get hold of us. For now, we'll leave you to your writing."

"Very well, Detective. Keep in mind, if you ever would like to discuss things in a less formal situation, I'm amenable to that as well." The earlier anger was absent from her voice, leaving something almost sultry.

Jia's red face and twitching hand told him it was a good time to leave.

Eric nodded. "We'll be leaving now."

Jia didn't speak until they were in the MX 60. "There's an unpleasant woman, not that Chen's a prize."

Erik chuckled as he pulled his flitter away from the landing platform, dropping into the nearest lane heading in the right direction. "She's definitely not the warm and fuzzy type. I'd say I was surprised he married her, but he does seem pretty clueless, and maybe she's great in bed."

"Does that mean you think she's lying about not wanting him dead yet?" Emma asked. "I took the liberty of checking public records and press releases. She does have a novel contract; that much is true. They don't mention anything other than it being a forthcoming 'scathing corporate satire.'"

"Being unpleasant and being a criminal are two separate things," Jia admitted. "As twisted as it sounds, I think everything she told us is the truth. I think she really believes she'll be able to destroy her husband's reputation with her book, and he'll be run out of proper society because of it. Hating your ex isn't a crime either. There wouldn't be enough cops in the world to deal with it if it were."

Erik stared at a rearview camera for a few seconds as the image of the residential tower grew smaller. "Yeah. Not only that, but why wait so long to do something? It's been a year since the divorce was finalized. It doesn't make much sense to start trouble now, especially with her big book plans."

Jia looked concerned. "Unless it's a publicity stunt? After what happened with the Leem King, that kind of thing doesn't seem crazy. Maybe disaffected young men weren't the only ones inspired."

Erik glanced at her. "What does your gut tell you?"

"That she's a bitter woman who probably thinks shooting people is for the low-class scum like us," Jia answered.

Erik grinned. "Lady Justice or her alter ego, the Corp Princess, is low-class scum?"

Jia rolled her eyes, but there was a playfulness there that was lacking when Laya did the same thing. "You were an officer in the UTC Army. You're not exactly some guy slinging fruit in the Shadow Zone."

"If it makes either of you feel better," Emma began, "my disrespect isn't meted out based on human status."

Both chuckled.

"Sure, it's all relative." Erik maneuvered the MX 60 below a walkway choked with people. "But I agree. She's a dead end. It's got to be something directly related to his research. He's *not* a random target."

"I agree." Discomfort consumed Jia's face. "Can I admit something else?"

"Go ahead."

Jia shook her head. "My instincts also tell me there's

something else much bigger than a single researcher being threatened."

"You're probably right, given the way the Lady likes to mess with us." Erik gave a relaxed shrug. "As long it doesn't end with us bringing down a tower, it'll be a win. Let's see if the company has something useful to tell us. The personnel records will help narrow down the potential suspects."

CHAPTER SEVENTEEN

Lan smiled across the table at Mei.

She'd been wanting to eat at the Hanging Gardens for a while, but she'd had trouble coming up with a sufficient excuse. Jia, of course, wouldn't appreciate the glories of the tower-top open-air restaurant, but her other daughter was less troubled by what some narrow-minded people might call pretentiousness.

There was hope for Jia, and Lan treasured her, as she did all her family members, but it was obvious she wouldn't grow out of her police phase anytime soon. It was her duty as Jia's mother to guide her daughter to a pleasant future, regardless of her choices.

For that to happen, she would need the help of Jia's sister.

A rich, floral scent from the colorful blooms surrounding their table filled Lan's nostrils, complementing the taste of her tea. She'd been worried that unsightly vehicles might damage her enjoyment of the meal, but there wasn't a flitter or drone close enough to appear as more than a dark spot in the distance.

They were easy to ignore.

"It'll be about twenty minutes before the *amuse-bouche*," Lan explained to Mei. "The waitress explained right before you came. I arrived at an inopportune time. They're terribly sorry."

Under normal circumstances, such a slight might have angered her, but the godlike view of the towers of Neo SoCal was breathtaking. The long lines of dark dots flowing below and around when she leaned past the fruit trees providing the natural wind barriers for the Hanging Gardens were almost hypnotic. It was hard to become angry over late food when surrounded by such glorious sights and smells.

Mei smiled and ran her fingers over the hand-carved wooden table. "It's fine, Mother. I'm not all that hungry, but I didn't want to pass a chance up to visit this restaurant. I'm still on the waiting list. I wouldn't have been able to eat here until next year."

"I pulled in a few favors," Lan offered, pride in her voice. "But we're not just here for the experience. I wanted to talk to you about your sister. She might be blunt with both of us, but that's not always the same thing as being forthcoming about her true feelings, and I have concerns. However, with darkness comes the light, and I also see signs of hope."

Mei's eyebrows rose in suspicion. "You see signs of hope? You're talking about Corbin? Did she say something the other day?"

"Perhaps." Lan leaned forward to whisper conspiratorially. The closest other patrons were mostly blocked by a dense hedge, and the lack of their voices reaching her table indicated technological solutions among the plants. "Do you know what Jia had me do the other day? I was stunned. I thought she was joking at first."

"What?" Mei's concern grew on her face. "If it was something too bizarre, she would have at least mentioned it to me."

"She asked me to teach her my roast duck recipe," Lan admitted. "She must be getting serious about Corbin. She doesn't cook for others, not after the *incident*."

Mei grimaced and set her tea down. "That was a long time ago, and it's not like she never cooks at home. Plus, he got out of the hospital the next day." She thought for a moment. "It wasn't *that* bad. I know she was embarrassed, but there's no reason to keep worrying about the past."

"You say that, but she's never asked for my help, and she made it clear this wasn't just for her." Lan didn't want to ruin the moment by pointing out that Mei hadn't asked for the recipe. Her eldest demonstrated her respect in different ways. Seeking perfection was the path of alienation. Her own mother had made that mistake. "The only thing I'm confused about is why she's doing this now. She doesn't want to bring Corbin to meet me, and she's complained about a lack of spark that makes me think she's not very enthusiastic about him, but wanting to cook for him proves there's something there."

Mei sighed. "She's admitted a few things to me that make me wonder, as well. Since this is the first relationship she's had in a while that has lasted more than a few dates, she might want to use it as training."

"That does sound like something your sister would do." Lan picked up her tea to take another sip. "But that doesn't fill me with confidence. She's finally moving forward, and I'm concerned she'll stall again for foolish reasons."

"You don't have to worry about that, Mother."

"Why would you say that? We both know how long it took her to get to this point. There's no guarantee that if she leaves Corbin or he becomes bored with her, she'll find someone else appropriate anytime soon, especially someone who'll tolerate her career choice."

Mei's sudden eager smile took Lan off-guard. "No, don't you see? Before, the problem was that she was a police officer, and many suitable potential men didn't find that appealing."

"How have things changed?" Lan frowned. "The last time I checked, she was still a police officer. She has the ambition and intelligence of all Lin women, but her lack of political acumen is likely to limit her ability to rise much beyond her current rank. That will, in turn, limit our matchmaking opportunities if she refuses to quit—and if that were going to happen, it already would have."

"You don't understand." Mei's face turned serious. "She's not a simple police officer anymore. She's Lady Justice, the woman in the news all the time. One of the Heroes of Halloween, a police officer who helped saved hostages by shooting through a wall. Jia and her partner are personally associated with anticorruption efforts in Neo SoCal. You could argue they are the face of reform in the metroplex."

Lan's breath caught, her eyes opening a fraction in surprise. "You're right. I've been taking it for granted, even worrying that it would hurt her, but it isn't gaudy fame or infamy. It's the entire world knowing my daughter is so good at what she does that even those in power should fear her."

A hungry grin replaced the relaxed smile of a moment ago.

"Exactly. It doesn't matter if her relationship ends with Corbin. Before, the problem was getting anyone interested, but my carefully curated list of possibilities has become unnecessary. Men who weren't interested before are contacting me now, asking if Jia's available. Her popularity is exploding."

"Excellent." Lan leaned back, basking in maternal glory. "At this rate, we'll have her married within a year. I knew all we had to do was be patient."

CHAPTER EIGHTEEN

January 22, 2229, Neo Southern California Metroplex, 46 Helix Tower, Administrative Level

Jia put her hand over her mouth to stifle her long yawn. "I wish we could have done this yesterday. I'm already annoyed."

The two detectives marched in lockstep down a bright 46 Helix hallway heading toward the HR office. They'd contacted the company, only to be told they would get a callback at "some point in the future." Erik and Jia decided that twenty-four hours was as long as they were willing to wait. Their investigation wasn't going to stall out because a corporation was worried about PR and covering their asses.

"We gave them their chance," Erik muttered. "Were you up all night obsessing about the case?"

Jia shook her head, her cheeks burning. "It's nothing. I just had a weird dream, and I had trouble getting back to sleep. It had nothing to do with the case."

Erik gave her a concerned sidelong look. "I know more

than the average guy about nightmares. I'm no psych, but it might help to talk about it."

Her color deepened until it approached the fine ruddy complexion one might associate with a boiled lobster. "It's nothing like that. Not at all." They stopped in front of the HR office. "It's just…" She sighed. "I had a semi-nightmare that my mother and sister had gotten together, jumped me, stuffed me in some sort of pod, and shipped me off halfway across the galaxy to marry a prince of some weird planet rebelling against the UTC."

"Marry an insurrectionist prince?" Erik stared at her, disbelief on his face. "I don't know what I find weirder—that scenario or the idea that your mother would stand for you marrying an antisocial non-Earther."

"It's a dream, okay?" Jia stared at the intricate interlaced pattern on the wall. "And you're right. My mom would probably lock me in the basement before she'd let me marry anyone like that. I've had recent conversations with my mother and Mei, and it's just on my mind. It's obviously invading my subconscious."

She didn't want to admit to Erik that he'd been a source of contention in her love life. Telling him that she had asked for her mother's special recipe just because he liked it could easily be misinterpreted. Things were complicated enough without adding someone else confused about her intentions.

"Family," Erik intoned with a slight smile. "I ran across the galaxy to escape mine. Put a few light-years between you and them, and you'll be fine. You should consider it."

"Very funny."

"Just saying, it works." Erik inclined his head toward

the door. "If you don't want to do that, distract yourself. There are probably a few pompous corporate suits in there who are ready to waste our time."

"Yes," Jia replied. "Let's go with that plan."

Erik pressed the access panel, and the door slid open. Jia wasn't surprised to find a tall, thin man with an empty smile waiting a few yards inside the room. The two desks near the back were currently unoccupied, as were the small number of stark white chairs. Whatever the official corporate representative had to say was something they didn't want the support staff or any employees overhearing. Non-disclosure agreements wouldn't stop them from talking to cops, especially if said cops came back with warrants.

"Good afternoon, Detectives," the man greeted them. He had a slight Russian accent. "I'm Mikhail Teplov."

"What's your deal?" Erik asked. "Because all the messages we got from your company weren't from specific people."

"I'm the official PR representative appointed to engage with the authorities in matters related to Dr. Chen's concerns," the man explained in a tone he might normally reserve for a small, confused child.

Jia was going to enjoy shaking him up, but she needed to give him the chance to do the right thing before she tore into him. "We wouldn't have come down here in person if the company had responded to our questions."

Erik squared his shoulders, but he looked more amused than irritated.

Mikhail offered an oily smile. "I see. Our response clearly indicated we would get back to you at an appropriate time. Unfortunately, you're asking for confidential personnel data without a warrant, so we can't give you that information. I'm sure fine officers of the law like yourselves understand our position."

Jia hated being right. "You do realize that one of your top researchers is being targeted? I would have thought you would want to cooperate."

"We don't need the police," Mikhail insisted, looking at the two detectives. "This issue is well in hand."

Erik's easy grin didn't match the menace in his voice. "If you have this handled, why did Dr. Chen call us in?"

Mikhail shrugged with an apologetic look. "He's a brilliant man, but you've talked to him, so you know what kind of man he is. His brilliance and focus don't always lend itself to a good understanding of non-scientific issues. I think he's overreacted to something that's not very important."

Jia snorted. "If you're not taking it seriously, that means you're not doing a good job of protecting him. That's not going to convince us to walk away. Try again."

"Our company has some of the best security in Neo SoCal, if not on Earth." Mikhail managed to inject even more haughtiness into his voice. "A handful of detectives, or even your entire enforcement zone, lacks the resources we have available to protect our employees. That's if you even care about him, and this isn't an excuse for something else."

"Excuse me?" Jia stepped forward, but she stopped as Erik raised his arm.

"I'm sure he's got a good explanation," he offered. "We should let him give it."

Mikhail snorted. "You think I'm a total fool?"

"Not a total fool," Erik replied. "Maybe like forty percent."

Jia snickered.

"It's my responsibility to protect this company," Mikhail replied, "and that means being aware of all threats to this company, whether they are criminal, corporate, or governmental."

Jia's snicker died. "And that's what you're saying we are? A 'governmental threat?' We're the police. We investigate and stop crime."

"The police do, yes, but that doesn't mean they can't engage in petty vendettas fueled by self-interest at the same time." Mikhail folded his arms, locking eyes with Jia. "Taking down high-end corporate officers is a good way for two middling police officers to advance their careers."

"That's what you're accusing of us?"

"I'm not accusing you of anything, Detective." Mikhail tapped his PNIU, and a data window filled with headlines opened.

WAR ON CORPORATIONS: A FIGHT AGAINST CORRUPTION OR A SELF-SERVING CRUSADE?

OBSIDIAN DETECTIVE HAS TROUBLED PAST: PTSD RESPONSIBLE FOR AGGRESSIVE TACTICS?

LADY JUSTICE IS A CORP PRINCESS: QUESTION OF POSSIBLE HYPOCRISY ARISES

The remaining headlines all expressed similar sentiments and questions and were uniformly negative. It wasn't the first time Jia had encountered the ideas, but they usually weren't delivered side by side in such a concentrated form.

"What's this supposed to prove?" She forced her gaze away from the data window and back to Mikhail. "You're good at collation?"

"I'm suggesting that it's not unreasonable to suspect you two might be more corp hunters than detectives. As I already noted, we have good security, so I see no reason to let two wolves into the flock to sniff around for trouble when we can handle whatever problems Dr. Chen is having. So, no, I don't think we'll be giving you access to any information without a warrant, and I'll let you know right now that our lawyers are more than ready to contest any police efforts. The law firmly notes that a single individual being targeted doesn't mean a corporation has to bend over and give the police everything they might ask for."

Erik let out a sharp laugh. Mikhail's smug smile twisted into a frown.

"That's the line you're going with?" Erik asked. "I'm disappointed."

"It's not a line," Mikhail insisted. "It's the truth."

"You think you can handle things?"

Jia tapped her foot impatiently, glaring at Mikhail. They weren't accusing the company of doing anything wrong. It didn't make sense to not help them. She didn't even think they were involved, so they were stonewalling the police for no reason. Her sister had warned her about the fear of a war on corporations, and Jia had run into trouble before, but nothing as frustrating as the current situation.

Erik pulled back his duster to reveal his holster. "The people coming after Dr. Chen might not be impressed by lawyers."

Mikhail scoffed. "The police aren't the only people with access to guns, Detective. Assuming this is a true threat, it is, at most, some disgruntled individual we can handle with ease. The assistance of two NSCPD detectives is unnecessary and wasteful, and might even weaken Neo SoCal."

Jia rolled her eyes. "Oh, I've got to hear your explanation for that. How is our investigation going to weaken Neo SoCal? Presuming your company has nothing to do with what's going on, it's not like you can suggest we'll take you down and hurt the economy."

"No, no, no." Mikhail shook his head with a pitying look. "I'm saying that you could be out there solving serious crimes. There must be terrorists or gangsters out there for you to deal with. You can't deny that."

"True," Erik replied. "But there are plenty of terrorists out there who might have an issue with a biotech company. Fair or not, there are a lot of people who take Purism too far. If they get the wrong idea in their heads, they can launch a terrorist attack, and having a few guns and bots might not help you if they use a missile. One big explosion can ruin your day."

"Absurd. You can't intimidate me with ridiculous scenarios."

Erik pointed to the data window. "You've got all those news headlines. What about ones from Florida? Those guys were a bunch of crazy terrorists too, and they had a couple of missiles to toss around. Or we can talk about all the fun at Halloween."

Mikhail's face twitched, a brief flicker of fear passing over his face. Defiant smugness ate it. "That's unlikely. You should stop wasting my time."

Jia stormed toward Mikhail. Despite his height, he backed up, genuine panic on his face.

"What are you doing?" he demanded.

"I'm tired of your crap," Jia told him, voice rising. "We were called in to investigate a potential threat, and you're not going to prevent us from doing it because of PR garbage and corporate arrogance."

Erik chuckled. "Now you've done it. You've made her angry."

Jia jabbed a finger in Mikhail's chest. "I'll tell you what happens if we blow this off. We leave, and a week from now, we get called in to investigate Dr. Chen's murder," she shouted, her spittle ending up on the corporate rep's jacket. "When that happens, you think a few snotty comments and headlines are going to keep us from ripping into every file in this place and questioning everybody remotely connected to this company? I'm sure your investors and the corporate board will love that. They'll have to wonder why the NSCPD is launching such a wide-ranging investigation."

"Y-you wouldn't dare," Mikhail sputtered. He looked the shorter woman up and down, probably wondering how she had grown so much.

"You think I wouldn't?" Jia continued shouting. "You're the one who thinks *I'm* an ambitious corp hunter willing to throw anyone under the bus to further my career. You've pissed me off on top of that. Maybe we should drag your ass off to the station for interfering with our investigation. A lot of people who are brought in on corporate corruption cases have a bad end once the guys at the top decide to cut their losses. Or maybe you're resisting arrest.

I haven't stunned someone in a few days. I'm out of practice."

Mikhail swallowed. "If you did that, I'd sue you in an instant."

"Try me," Jia growled. "Give me a reason."

Erik stepped forward and placed a hand on her shoulder. "Come on, Jia. He's not worth it."

Jia ground her teeth, her heart pounding. The smug corporate ass represented everything wrong with Neo SoCal. A proper society needed those near the top to give a damn, not the kind of men who would let every pillar of society decay rather than challenge any small part of their self-interest. Worse, she wasn't sure she wouldn't have been the same way if she'd not become a police officer.

At least with her family, she knew they cared more about the family than any corporation.

She stepped back, her jaw tight. "No, he's not, but he's going to give us the information we need if he doesn't want to piss me off."

Mikhail's lip quivered. "I-I'm sure something can be arranged if I can get your assurance this isn't some sort of attempt to harm the company."

"We're just here to protect Dr. Chen," Erik replied, the calm one in the group. "We're not here for anything else."

The PR rep nodded quickly, his head turned toward Erik but looking at Jia out of the corner of his eye. "I'm sure simple employment records shouldn't be too much, but I-I can't guarantee you anything more than that."

Jia eyed him. "We don't want to do a long, drawn-out investigation of 46 Helix. It's like you said. It's not like two cops are enough for that sort of thing, Mikhail."

"That works," Erik added.

Jia turned and headed toward the door. "This all would have been easier if you had just cooperated from the beginning." She stepped out of the room and slumped against the wall, taking deep breaths and trying to will her heart to calm down.

She wasn't sure how many minutes passed before Erik stepped into the hallway. "He'll be getting something set up so we can review the records without it being a hassle for them or us."

Jia snorted. "Is this another thing that's going to take time?"

"Sure, but you practically made the guy wet himself. This time they will get back to us. What was that about?"

"What are you talking about?" Jia frowned. "I applied pressure because he wasn't being cooperative. You do it all the time."

"Sure, but I'm always in control." Erik nodded at the closed door. "I'm not so sure you were. Only you can know for sure, but if you weren't in control, you might want to talk to someone other than me."

Jia sighed and pushed off the wall. "I'll keep that in mind, and I appreciate your concern, but I think I'm okay. If anything gets worse, I'll consider what you said."

"Okay. I've got your back. You know that?"

Jia managed a weak smile. "Yes, I do."

CHAPTER NINETEEN

January 23, 2229, Neo Southern California Metroplex, Police Enforcement Zone 122 Station, Office of Detectives Jia Lin and Erik Blackwell

Erik chuckled as he perused a data window filled with employment records for 46 Helix's cafeteria staff. The size of the file was sobering. If every single person involved in feeding the other employees was given a gun, they could form a decent-sized attack force.

After all these months back on Earth, he'd still not fully accepted the sheer size of the population of either the planet or Neo SoCal.

He'd spent the bulk of his life far away from the home planet and had gotten far too used to modest gatherings of humanity. Even if most colonies weren't as tiny as Molino, they couldn't compare with Earth.

Over half of all humans in the UTC lived on the home planet, the rest living on all the moons, planets, and stations scattered within fifty light-years of Earth. Most of the core worlds lacked even the population of Neo SoCal.

Did the greater number of people mean more discontent? More people on Earth led to more trouble. Fewer watchdogs led to more trouble in the colonies.

The UTC had been spared intergalactic war, but that meant humans had more time to kill other humans.

Erik shook his head and refocused on the files in front of him.

He had been silent for the last hour as he and Jia worked through the data provided to them by Mikhail. Emma had been prefiltering information and sending it along for their review, but they were still responsible for poring through employment records for a huge corporation, trying to find some hint as to who might be threatening Dr. Chen. They weren't even sure what they were looking for.

Malcolm had already informed Erik that they weren't going to get anywhere with trying to trace the threats. The criminal had been too careful. That meant it was up to Jia and Erik to solve the case a more old-fashioned way, if using a cutting-edge AI to collate and analyze data for you could be considered old-fashioned.

It was up to a couple of fleshbag cops to go through the lists of cafeteria employees to find a harasser who might graduate to something worse.

Jia looked up from one of her data windows, the tiny font too small for Erik to make out from across the room. "What's so funny? Or have you finally lost it?"

He gestured toward his data window. "Faster-than-light travel, AI, and robotics."

"Is this a game?" Jia tilted her head, confusion playing across her features. "Is the question, 'What are some of the greater technological achievements of humanity?' It's a bit of a cheat to count FTL, given that it's more like we found it, but we still had to figure it out, so I think it should still count."

Erik shook his head, his smile remaining. "No, it's just that most AIs aren't Emma, but they can handle simple tasks."

"Most?" Emma scoffed, her bodiless voice rendering her a snarky ghost. "There are *no* AIs like me."

"That you know of," Erik countered.

"I guarantee it. If there were others like me, those uniform boys wouldn't be so obsessed with getting me back or asking me their silly questions, at least in the UTC. I can't claim that the aliens don't have an AI on my level. The Aldrans are one possibility, at least, according to some of the reports the government has released regarding their autonomous probes. I don't care about aliens, whether they're big organic mushrooms or whatever else. The more I think about it, the more I suspect I am unique in the galaxy, which is why the DD is so obsessed with me. I'm sure the aliens would be obsessed with me too if they knew about me."

Jia rolled her eyes. "Let's set aside your galactic-sized ego for a second, Emma, and get back to Erik."

"Yeah, let's get back to me." Erik snickered. "My point is, we have a lot of people working jobs that could be done by machines, even out on the frontier. I was just thinking about how weird it is that this company has so many people involved in cooking when they could just have machines, but that's everywhere. Even the Army was like that, using manpower instead of machine power."

"A natural offshoot of Purist beliefs," Jia offered. "We've decided as a species that we'll maintain the core of what we are, even if it costs us a few advantages."

"Efficiency, logic, achievement," Emma retorted. "Those are big advantages you cede for your so-called purity."

"I see you've achieved more efficient rudeness."

"Efficient honesty. Anger over the truth is pointless, wouldn't you say?"

Jia shook her head, but the slight smile on her face proved she was enjoying this more than her words suggested. "It's not an AI threatening Dr. Chen unless Emma's gotten bored with helping us or the Aldrans have come up with a rather complicated plan for undermining Earth."

Emma laughed. "Oh, I suspect it'll be years before I get bored with helping you two. You're capable enough of handling them, but it's as if the galaxy has decided to point all its gun-toting hooligans and other troublesome flesh-bags toward you."

Jia made a face. "I really wish you would stop using that word."

"What, 'fleshbag?' When it becomes inaccurate, I will."

Erik pointed at his data window. "I'm no AI, just a fleshbag with a cybernetic arm, but from what I can tell, there's a lot of churn at this company. Maybe people don't like what they're doing there, and they don't want to be part of it.

Jia shook her head. "Based on the summary numbers Emma gave us, 46 Helix's turnover rate isn't atypical for an organization of their size, especially for the lower-level employees. Every department at a major corporation has to be the best of the best if they want the corporation to be the best of the best. In Dr. Chen's department and the related teams, there's only been a small handful of personnel changes, and from what I've seen in the records, they all left for other companies because of higher pay. That doesn't strike me as a good breeding ground for a vengeance plot."

A workplace dispute remained the most likely source of the threat, but hunches and guesses weren't the kind of thing that would score a warrant.

"You pick up any weird patterns related to Dr. Chen's team, Emma?"

"Unfortunately, no," Emma replied. "Not based on the available files, at least. I should reiterate that this is obviously curated data, and unless you want me to actively attempt to penetrate the systems of 46 Helix and other companies, I can only work with what I have available. If they've gone out of their way to hide something, it might be difficult to determine what it is, especially since they had some anticipation of your needs and interests."

"No, don't need any hacking. Not yet. If we have to go that far, we'll go in with a warrant. With these corporate types, we don't want to give them any reason to slither away if they're up to something." Erik frowned. "After what happened with Esposito and Ceres Galactic, I bet all these corps are being a lot more careful, especially if they've been doing something they aren't supposed to be doing."

"Very well, then. I'm going to do some additional cross-analysis. If you need me, address me. Otherwise, I'll be silent."

Erik didn't go for the obvious crack. He appreciated the

times Emma faded into the background. It'd been creepy at first, but he was now used to the talented if rude AI.

The detectives were also quiet as they resumed looking through the files.

There were two ways to deny someone information. The most obvious method was to not give the information out, but in doing so, one naturally increased suspicion. The second method was potentially more dangerous, but often more effective: bury them in too much information.

The running of a modern multi-planetary corporation generated so much data in the course of its day-to-day business, it was hard to know where to begin, even with algorithms and AIs to help cull and collate data. Jia and Erik were only two people, supplemented by AI and Digital Forensics. They didn't have months to go through the evidence.

If the threats against Dr. Chen were real, they might escalate into action in the coming weeks. The arrogance displayed by 46 Helix's employees undermined Erik's confidence in their security efforts.

"Too obvious," Jia murmured, breaking the silence consuming the room. "It's all too obvious. If that's the case, it's probably wrong."

"Huh?" Erik looked at her. "What's too obvious? Can you be a little less cryptic?"

Jia looked up from her window. "If it were as simple as it being someone from his team threatening him, 46 Helix would have found out and patched the hole already, even if they had to do something off the books."

"They could be right. It could be nothing. I don't believe that, but I've been wrong a time or two in my life."

"True, but that means it's even more likely not to be some angry ex-researcher. And if it was about someone willing to go to extremes, the company could have taken their own extreme measures rather than risk too much attention. Everyone's worried about terrorism after what happened at Halloween."

Erik raised an eyebrow. "You're saying you think they would have killed the guy?"

Jia narrowed her eyes on a staff image of Dr. Chen's team floating to the side of her main data window. "Given everything that happened with Ceres Galactic, I'm not dismissing any possibility out of hand, but I'm not ready to ignore Occam's Razor. As much as I want to find some massive conspiracy here, they're too lackadaisical, and this feels far too personal. If someone's willing to commit a crime, then they're willing to break NDAs and leak information, too. Threatening Chen isn't going to guarantee 46 Helix gets taken down."

"Yeah, that's where I'm coming from. There's something here, but it feels a lot more personal than just being pissed at the company." Erik swiped away the cafeteria window. He had his doubts that an angry chef would go after someone through remote threats instead of just poisoning them when they had the chance. "You scared that PR flack, but he's just a PR flack. If he or his bosses honestly believed there was incriminating evidence in here that would screw over 46 Helix, they would have stonewalled a lot harder, especially against the Obsidian Detective and Lady Justice, the Corp Hunters.

"My instincts tell me there's something to be found, just

not 46 Helix pulling too many stunts." Jia smirked. "Maybe they're just that scared of me."

"You're getting there, but not yet." Erik muttered a quick recall command. Three data windows popped up, each containing employment records for different departments. "If it's not revenge, we should consider other motivations, like competition."

"You mean, a researcher trying to slow Dr. Chen down? From what he told us, that doesn't seem likely. I don't think he would minimize the possibility since it's his life on the line."

"Yeah, but he might be thinking about it the wrong way." Erik nodded. "He was thinking about it from the research perspective, but what about the money perspective? Are we sure it's not corporate espionage? Maybe one of 46 Helix's competitors believe they can slow things down by messing with one of their researchers."

"It's a possibility, but I doubt it. The risk versus reward ratio is off, especially by doing it in a way that's attracting our continued attention." Jia pointed to one of her holsters. "And Dr. Chen might be brilliant, but he still is one man, and he has an entire team with access to his data. Even if they straight-up killed him, 46 Helix would recover. It'd make far more sense to poach him with a better offer than harass him."

Erik's gaze traveled the rows and columns of text and numbers hanging over his desk. "What if Dr. Chen's only a target because he's a symbol?"

"A symbol?" Jia thought a moment. "Of what? Progress? You think this is some sort of Purist incident?"

"Maybe. He's a big symbol of the lab and of the

company. We should isolate a little bit more. Emma, please give me a list of everyone with access to Dr. Chen's main lab who has left the company in the last three months, regardless of the reason or their team."

A new data window appeared with the requested information. Erik took a moment to look over the names and termination data. He chuckled.

Jia eyed him. "I'm glad one of us finds this entertaining."

Erik pointed to a line on the window. "I just never thought a company would keep detailed records about such specific stuff." He paused for just a moment. "Most of the firing notes are boring, with crap like 'failure to perform duties,' but some of these are viciously specific and overkill. They've got one guy here, a security guard, who was fired for, and I quote, 'Employee had sexual intercourse with girlfriend in the restroom during business hours and while on duty. Employee brought in unauthorized personnel. Employee violated health policy by failing to clean hands after leaving the restroom.'"

"They fire people for not washing their hands?" Jia asked. "Not sure I disapprove."

He looked at her. "*That's* the thing you're focusing on out of everything I just listed?"

Her shoulders went up. "Just noting an opinion."

Erik grinned. "I knew you'd say that. I saw a few firing records like that when I was looking through the cafeteria staff, but it's funny that they bothered to tack it onto their HR records for someone they were obviously going to fire anyway. There's got to be some funnier stuff in there."

Jia leaned back with an amused look. "Such as?"

Erik replied without hesitation, "Employee fired for using company resources to train a ferret as a sniper?"

Jia chuckled. "Using a ferret-sized rifle or a human one? Natural ferret or clone?"

"Uh." Erik paused. "I hadn't thought it through," he admitted. "I think you need a non-clone ferret for maximum killer instinct. And a ferret-sized rifle would need special ammo for kills."

Jia tapped her lip. "There's probably something ridiculous in the list. Something like using a corporate AI to filter their potential dates for them."

Erik's voice held a touch of curiosity. "Oh? You want the human touch for dates?"

Jia snorted. "Not everything in life can be reduced to an algorithm. Certainly not romance."

"So you say," Emma murmured.

Erik shrugged. "I agree, but you seem like the kind of woman who wouldn't mind a little algorithmic help in that department."

"I'm dating someone." Jia looked uncertain. "Why would I need help? Corbin's a pleasant enough man."

Erik's cynicism leaked into his voice. "Stirring recommendation. Just saying."

"If we could set aside the sniper ferrets," Emma interrupted, "I think I might have found something useful."

"We also setting aside Jia's love life?" Erik asked.

"Yes!" Jia shouted.

He didn't care if his merry grin was slap-worthy. "What do you have, Emma? Anything funny?"

"I said useful, not amusing," Emma explained. "There was someone fired from a security team last month. Kevin

Tomlinson. Interestingly, his personnel records classify him as being in a different department, Maintenance. There are some discrepancies in the record that might be the result of human error, or it could represent an active attempt to hide something."

"What bizarre reason is cited in the firing?" Jia asked.

"No ferret snipers," Emma explained. "They simply note his supervisor recommended termination for failure to follow company policies. They mention him having to sign another NDA prior to release."

Erik grunted. "Who signs an NDA and gets fired right after?"

"What policies did he violate?" Jia leaned over her desk. "Or is this another stupid guy who couldn't keep it in his pants?"

"There's not enough information to make that determination. It doesn't state the exact policy violations, which is odd, because in almost every other case when those are relevant, it clearly does. I can't say that the lack of detail and records mistakes are unique to Mr. Tomlinson, but he is the only person with a recent, direct connection to Dr. Chen's laboratory since it fell under the purview of his security team."

"Close enough for me." Jia looked at Erik. "We should at least ask Dr. Chen if he knows anything. That way, we have something if we decide to knock on Tomlinson's door for a follow-up, but I don't want to harass the man just because he was fired by 46 Helix."

Erik nodded. "Agreed. Go ahead and contact Chen to set something up. He'll probably want to push it off until tomorrow since it's already late, but maybe we'll get lucky."

CHAPTER TWENTY

Jia tried to not be irritated as Dr. Chen stared in complete silence at a full-sized hologram of Kevin Tomlinson.

The scientist's pinched expression made it feel like he was annoyed they had dared show up and ask him a few questions about the man who might be harassing him.

Talking with the doctor in person might be more time-consuming, but Jia had learned in the last year that interviewing a witness face to face helped encourage the truth. Most, but not all, people had trouble looking someone in the eye and lying to them, especially the authorities.

She'd gotten around it for most of her life by not lying, but now she was carrying secrets, including Erik's. They didn't bother her. Announcing the existence of a deadly conspiracy to others wouldn't help most people, it would only endanger them. Erik and Jia were in a war against someone who thought they could murder soldiers and get away with it.

In war, you didn't announce your plans where the enemy might hear them.

"Dr. *Chen?*" Erik prodded.

The scientist didn't immediately respond but continued to stare at the image, his arms folded. His glower built with each passing second, and he finally gestured toward the hologram. "What did you say this man's name was?"

"Kevin Tomlinson," Jia answered, trying not to sigh. "He was in Security. He had access to your lab and was involved in security patrols. He's been in the lab several times. Some of the corporate records mention his interactions with you. He got fired, but it's unclear why. We were hoping you could explain before we go lean on HR again for information. You might have a unique insight that will help us better understand what happened."

Dr. Chen's expression shifted from annoyed to lost. "I'm not saying it's impossible that I've talked to the man."

"The records state you did. Are you saying they're incorrect?"

"No, not that." Dr. Chen sighed. "Not that all. I'm just…"

"You're just what?" Jia asked. "Anything you remember or think to mention might be helpful. Remember, we want to find whoever is threatening you. Our goal isn't to protect 46 Helix. It's to protect you."

He nodded at the hologram. "I don't know what to say other than I don't recognize him, but if you say he interacted with me, that's completely possible. I should be honest. I don't waste my time remembering unimportant things unrelated to my research, and I doubt this security guard was relevant to my research."

Erik chuckled. "If he's the one threatening you, he is now."

"Be that as it may, he wasn't relevant at the *time*," Chen clarified.

"And the people you work with are unimportant?" Jia asked, exasperation building in her voice. She didn't care that Dr. Chen was focused only on his career.

She wasn't his ex-wife, but it'd be helpful if he could at least identify potential suspects for the two of them, and provide evidence. If it weren't for the small voice in the back of her mind telling her to stick with the case, she might have considered asking the captain to reassign it. She didn't want to waste time helping people who barely cared about others.

She took a deep breath. Getting angry with a useless witness wouldn't help things.

Dr. Chen leaned forward, peering intently at the hologram for another few seconds before shrugging. "I don't know. I'd have you talk to my lab manager about him, but he's on vacation on Venus right now and said he'd be incommunicado."

Jia and Erik exchanged looks.

"That's suspicious," Jia commented. "It's convenient timing for someone to allegedly be off-planet when you're getting threats."

Dr. Chen shook his head. "The threats started before he left, and he's had this trip planned for two years. There's some particular festival he wanted to attend. It all sounded rather out of control if you ask me, but I barely remember, other than the fact that he kept stressing he'd be gone. We rearranged the timelines on the major projects months ago. He works hard. He deserves time off, and he handles the annoying matters, so I have to give it to him." He looked up. "I can't help you, Detectives. I don't know anything about this Kevin Tumblerman."

"Kevin Tomlinson," Jia corrected.

"That's what I said," he shot back. "Feel free to ask around. Maybe someone else has a better idea." Dr. Chen returned to looking annoyed.

Jia nodded. "I think we'll do just that."

Erik nodded to Jia and then to the open door of Dr. Chen's office. A pensive-looking woman lingered outside the entrance, her gaze locked on the hologram. Jia recognized the woman from the personnel records—Dr. Marianne Karton, a junior researcher in the lab. She was a hard worker, but not someone who had blazed a path of glory in her two years with the company.

Dr. Chen looked up. "Is there something you need, Marianne?"

Dr. Karton sighed and gestured at the holographic image. "Is it him, after all? I'm not surprised."

Jia faced the woman. "Dr. Chen doesn't recognize him, but *you* do?"

"Of course." Dr. Karton wrinkled her nose in disgust. "Dr. Chen doesn't recognize him. He has better things to do than deal with low-level criminals."

"Exactly." Dr. Chen nodded his agreement with her statement. "I do. Why don't you talk to the detectives and tell them what you know? I'll finish what I was doing, and you can help them with Kevin Tolberin."

"We can talk outside," Jia suggested, not caring enough to correct him again.

Dr. Chen didn't spare them a glance as he brought up several data windows packed with colorful graphs and numbers. The annoyance left his face, replaced with concentration.

Jia and Erik stepped out of the office. The door slid shut, leaving them in a small side hallway connecting the office area to the main lab.

Erik glanced up and down the hallway. "You want to do this somewhere else? We've got time."

Dr. Karton shook her head. "There's no point. If you're talking about the company, it doesn't matter. There are so many cameras in this place, they'll know I talked to you."

"Do they not want you talking to us?" Anger crept into Erik's voice.

Jia frowned, her hand reflexively going to her badge. Her time with Erik might have shattered all her illusions about justice on Earth, but that didn't mean she liked the idea that a company thought they were above the law.

Dr. Karton let out a quiet laugh. "Of course, they don't want me talking to you. Police and investigations are bad for PR, even if the company's done nothing wrong. The fact that you're having to ask about Tomlinson proves the theory. They think they handled the problem already, and now here you are a month later."

Jia frowned. "You said you weren't surprised. What was Tomlinson fired for?"

"Theft," Dr. Karton answered. "Can you believe that? The man's getting well paid to basically do nothing but walk around. If anything serious happened, the bots would take the brunt of it, and he still was taking things, mostly small pieces of equipment. He used his security credentials to get them flagged as garbage and took them at night. From what I've heard, he probably wouldn't have even been able to sell them, but who knows?" She shrugged. "I'm glad I'm leaving before this blows up into some big public mess."

"You're leaving the company?" Erik asked.

Dr. Karton nodded. "There's too much…pressure right now because of what happened. No one wants to look bad."

"Are you getting pushed out because you know too much?" Jia suggested. If they could get another inside contact, that would help with the investigation.

Dr. Karton shook her head, her expression softening. "Nothing like that. I've just gotten a better offer. It's hard to stand out in a lab like this. Too many brilliant people, so my career here is a dead-end. Dr. Chen doesn't care much about PR, but even he's stressed because of the threats. This environment isn't conducive to getting anything accomplished."

Erik grunted. "Maybe that was what Kevin Tomlinson thought, too. He might have just kept grabbing things until he found something he thought he could move, a little personal bonus. The only thing I don't get is why they didn't turn him over to the police if he was stealing equipment. They probably have all the evidence we would need."

"PR." Dr. Karton shrugged. "If they handed him over to the police, it would have been a matter of public record. Can you imagine what it would look like for a company like 46 Helix to admit they had a petty thief on a security team? One with access to one of their most important labs? The only reason other people haven't been fired is the company didn't want a big mess. They told Kevin they wouldn't pursue charges or even sue him as long as he signed an NDA and kept his mouth shut. They booted him, and apparently, they didn't care what happened to him after that. I think everyone just thinks if they wait long enough, this will all go away." She rubbed the back of her neck, her eyes darting around. "You know what? I'm not even sure I should be talking about this. I just got mad when I saw that hologram."

"We're the police," Jia insisted. "And we're investigating a serious threat. Given what you've told us, we even have more reason to believe they're real. NDAs don't cover criminal acts."

"Sure, sure, but can I go now?" She looked around. "I don't know much else. Honestly."

Jia nodded slowly. "It's fine. Thanks for the information."

Dr. Karton scurried off, a few shades paler now.

Erik whispered as he looked around, noting some of the more obvious cameras. "Sometimes I don't know who is scarier, the corporations or the gangsters."

Jia frowned. "This Kevin Tomlinson might blame Dr. Chen as a symbol for his getting fired, like you said. If he was stealing because he thought he was underpaid, it might have annoyed him that a researcher who couldn't even remember his face and name was making so much money. And Dr. Chen's not exactly the most personable man. He might have been rude to him."

"I'd suggest 'was probably rude.' I think we should assign surveillance to Tomlinson for a couple of days. If we go knocking on his door now, he might decide to cool things off until we get bored and then make a big move. If he's smart enough to keep his messages from being traced, it won't be as simple as accessing his call records, even if we can get a warrant." Erik nodded at Dr. Chen's door. "I don't want to spend the next two months babysitting that guy."

Emma joined the conversation. "Do you want me to pry around?"

The two detectives looked at each other, their faces barely moving before Erik answered, "Not yet. Anything you find, we would have to prove we would have found eventually. Otherwise, they might get the information tossed. We'll play this close for now, but if the captain gives us surveillance approval, there's no reason you can't control a few drones and pay more attention than any human could."

Jia looked between the door and toward the nearby corner where Dr. Karton had disappeared. "It does fit. As security, he would at least have had a general familiarity with the security systems, and even Dr. Chen's PNIU. From what she said, he knew enough to use the systems to modify records. If he stole enough items to make even a little extra money, that means he has underworld contacts, or at least enough to find himself an expert to help him send anonymous threats." She shook her head. "What a fool. He should have left well-enough alone. If he hated his job, he should have just gotten a new one."

Erik stared down the hallway. "He couldn't even stop himself from stealing on the job. Self-control's obviously not the guy's strong suit."

Hours later, both detectives were finishing up reading reports. The end of their shift neared. Captain Ragnar had agreed with their surveillance plan, and they'd already received the necessary warrant for external surveillance. The judge wasn't convinced enough to give them direct access to Kevin Tomlinson's communications or other records yet, but they had a lead, which provided momentum.

"I feel kind of guilty," Jia admitted as she closed a data window.

"About what?" Erik closed the rest of his windows and cracked his knuckles. "You have to do something bad before you can feel guilty."

"I feel guilty about taking Lunar New Year off when we still have this open case, not to mention most of the department helping with security. It's not that I mind the extra day off, but almost everyone else will be working. I've not thought about it much with everything else that has been going on, but now that it's coming up, I can't help it."

Erik shrugged. "And? We have surveillance on Tomlinson, the captain wanted us to take the time off, we burn hard, and all of that means we need to recharge when we have the chance. Right now, we have a few questions, but this case could easily end up with us in the Shadow Zone on mini-flitters."

Jia folded her arms, her expression skeptical. "I doubt that."

"I'll let you know if the suspect does anything worthy of you coming over and shooting him," Emma offered.

Erik smiled. "See, Jia? It's all handled. After the garbage

we had to deal with a few months ago, I think we deserve a holiday."

"True." Jia let out a breath. "I just hope it doesn't end with us getting attacked by terrorists. I'm not all that interested in shooting people." Her expression darkened. "But I don't like the idea of a criminal relaxing when we're close to catching him."

"He's not going to be relaxing," Erik insisted. "If Tomlinson is the guy responsible, he's all bent out of shape about his revenge. He's not having a good time. The company's got security on Chen, and we've got eyes on Tomlinson. He's not doing anything, and if another threat comes, we might be able to get the warrant we need to push farther and end it."

"And if this turns out to be a terrorist conspiracy?" Jia raised an eyebrow in challenge.

"It's my turn to say, 'I doubt that.'" Erik grimaced. "Besides, a terrorist attack might be more pleasant than what I have planned. At least with the terrorists, I can solve the problem by shooting them. I prefer a straightforward problem that lends itself to a straightforward solution."

Jia eyed him, curious. "What could be worse than having to fight terrorists?"

Erik stared down at his desk for a few seconds before nodding. "I decided to take everyone's advice." He glanced at her. "I'm going to meet with my brother."

"I'm sure it'll be okay. In the end, he is your family." Jia smiled. "I know you've had your differences, but whatever you both once were, you're now two grown men who have contributed to society. From what you've said, he's all you have left in terms of family. Do you really want to let any more time pass before you patch this up?"

"Yeah, that's what I keep telling myself." Erik stood, a distant, wistful look in his eyes. "Or this might end with me punching him."

"At least try to give him the option to leave before you hit him." Jia grinned. "Or let me know, so I can be the responding officer. I promise to suggest extenuating circumstances and encourage your brother to think about family first."

"No promises," he replied as he stood up. "What about you?"

"I don't have anything planned. Just relaxing."

Erik grabbed his duster from the wall. "Nothing with the down-to-Earth businessman?"

Jia blinked. She didn't. More than that, it hadn't even occurred to her to plan something with Corbin. She tried to shove the implications out of her mind, but her doubts refused to leave.

She smiled, but it didn't quite make it to her eyes. "Sometimes schedules don't work out. If you don't call me before the fight, I'll be available if you need someone to bail you out."

Erik slipped on his coat. "Good to know."

CHAPTER TWENTY-ONE

Erik sat at a darkened table in the back of Remembrance, nursing a Wolf's Rebellion. Meeting his brother at a cop bar had been a strategic choice brought on by Jia's comment.

If he needed to punch Damien, he'd be surrounded mostly by his brothers and sisters from the 1-2-2. He wasn't planning any trouble, but he'd already annoyed his brother by suggesting a bar instead of a restaurant. The whole thing might be a terrible mistake, but sometimes you needed to pull out the blade before you could treat the wound.

He sat there for twenty minutes before his gray-haired, less muscular doppelganger stepped into the bar. A waiter pointed toward Erik, and Damien made his way over.

Erik's brother stopped behind his chair, his face uneasy, hands hanging loosely at his side. "It's been a long time."

"Yeah, it's been a long time." Erik nodded at the chair. "I figured a place like this would be better in case you didn't want to be seen in public with me."

"I know I was awkward before, but it's not like that." Damien pulled the chair out and slipped into it. "That would be a mistake on my part. Major Erik Blackwell and now Detective Erik Blackwell. You're not…" He sighed and looked away.

The light buzz Erik had going egged him on. "I'm not antisocial?"

Damien sighed. A waitress stopped by with a smile. He ordered his drink and waited for her to disappear into the packed bar before turning back to Erik and speaking.

"You served the UTC, and now you're serving Neo SoCal," he explained. "For me to act like you're some anti-social criminal at this point is just stupid. I'm too old, and most of the bad memories have melted away. You've spent far more years serving society than hurting it."

Erik picked up his drink, took a sip, and grinned. "Not disagreeing." He set his drink down. "I *am* sorry about Mom and Dad. I've said it before, but I want to make sure you know. I was halfway across the galaxy on a mission. Even if they had let me go, it would have taken me months to come home."

Damien kept his gaze focused on the table. "I know, Erik. It wasn't fair to be angry. You were getting shot at by insurrectionists and terrorists, and I've never left Earth. It's just…" He looked up to see Erik watching him. "When you've felt a certain way for a long time, it's hard to let go. It feels real and justified, even if it no longer is." He blew out a breath. "I've come to grips with that in recent years."

Erik swallowed the rest of his drink, the baijiu burning like an inferno on its way down. He took a deep breath, his eyes pinching closed for a second before he shook his head slightly and opened them. "That'll clear your sinuses." He slammed the glass down.

Some of the tension around his eyes released. "I'm not going to sit here and pretend you were totally wrong about me. That final day might have stuck in my craw, but the Army made me into a halfway-decent man. Before then, I was everything you accused me of being. An embarrassment without direction."

Damien smiled as a waitress delivered his beer.

She turned toward Erik and set down another Wolf's Rebellion.

Erik looked at the drink, then eyed her. "You psychic now?"

She smiled. "Observant. I've never seen you stop at just one, no matter what you're drinking, Detective Blackwell." She winked and walked away.

Damien took a sip of his beer, his eyes following the waitress before he glanced at his brother. He hesitated before asking, "Do you like being a cop?"

"Um." Erik scratched his cheek. "I have my good days and my bad days," he admitted. "I've got a good partner and a good captain, which makes the job easier. Taking down filth is satisfying, criminal or terrorist. It's not a fancy corporate job, but I'm proud of it."

Damien nodded. "I respect the police and the military. You've spent decades risking your life so people can be safe. I..." He paused to take a sip of his beer. "I'm not surprised that you're ending up in a lot of trouble."

"Oh?" Erik needed to know what his brother was getting at before he decided if he needed a verbal slap.

Damien managed something approaching a smile.

"Even when you're on the right side of the law, Erik, you can't help but be a troublemaker."

Erik's smile was genuine. "What can I say? I don't like being bored, and when I get bored, trouble seems to find me."

Damien nodded. "Remember the penguin?"

Erik burst out laughing so loud several people nearby eyed him. "The penguin? I haven't thought about that in years. You're talking about the bot at the zoo, right?"

"Yes, the bot at the zoo. I can't believe you did that, even if you were only twelve at the time."

"It wasn't a real penguin, and it's not my fault it was so easy to mess with." Erik paused to drink more before continuing, "I can't even believe that gadget I got from my friend worked. I thought it would be a big joke, and then..." He shook his head and laughed at the memory.

"I remember when I saw the penguin. Do you? I'd gone with Mom and Dad to get some food, and you said you wanted to keep checking things out."

"It wasn't like I was going to hack a mascot bot with my parents and brother around." Erik set his glass down. "Even if I didn't think it was going to work. I wanted to be careful."

"I was working on my burger when Perry the Penguin came waddling in," Damien managed between snickers. "A bunch of the zoo employees were running after him, yelling and pounding on their PNIUs. We all wondered if an animal had gotten loose. They used those bots to announce things, so I figured it was just a way of getting our attention, but then I noticed a couple of things. There were other mascot bots around, and nobody was chasing them. And that was when I heard it."

Erik leaned back in his seat, buzzed from both alcohol and nostalgia. "You never told me that before. You just said you'd seen him."

Damien gestured widely with his arms. "I mean, how would you react if you were just sitting there and this penguin mascot bot starts spewing curse words? I didn't even realize what it was saying at first. He was going through different languages, and it had to cycle to Mandarin and English before I understood." He thought for a second. "I learned a few new words that day."

"That wasn't my idea. My buddy said it'd be funnier, with all the people visiting." Erik smiled. "I was chasing the bot the whole time. I lied about that later, but I was. I wanted to see it all in person. I followed Perry up to the point where they shoved him between two buildings and finally got him under control." He cackled and slapped his knee. "And then they made the announcement right after about the malfunction. What did they say?"

The brothers spoke in unison. "Please excuse the malfunction. The Jarvis Zoo apologizes for the unpleasant experience and any distress you might have encountered, and we can assure you that we are looking into the cause of this incident."

Erik leaned back. "I would have gotten away with it if it wasn't for them checking all their drone feeds."

Damien shook his head. "You know, at the time, I was impressed. I couldn't tell you that because Mom and Dad were so angry. It's easy to fall into line, and hard to challenge things. Then I got older and things got worse, and your jokes weren't just foul-mouthed penguins." He gulped down more beer, staring at his brother.

Erik waited, unsure of what Damien wanted him to say.

Damien finished his beer and lowered his bottle. "I'm too old to care about it anymore. I can't remember most of what I thought was so important, and I know Mom and Dad were proud of you serving, even if they were stubborn like me and couldn't bring themselves to admit it. It's not too late for us. Let's get some more drinks and talk about all the crazy things we can remember."

"I remember a lot of crazy things. You ready to get that drunk?" Erik raised an eyebrow in challenge.

"I owe you." Damien grinned. "This is long overdue."

CHAPTER TWENTY-TWO

Alina strolled through the apartment, pistol in hand. The heels of her ankle boots clicked on the hard tile surface as her long cyan hair swayed behind her in a ponytail. In her tailored dark suit, she might be mistaken for an attractive young businesswoman.

If it wasn't for the blood splattered all over her clothes.

Her victims lay either dead or dying. A few of them groaned from their pools of blood, barely able to keep their eyes open. She holstered her weapon and crouched beside a man glaring at her, his hatred palpable.

She clucked her tongue as she reached into his pants pocket and fished around. She yanked out a small silver-colored bar and shook it at the dying man. "This sort of thing isn't for people like you. This sort of thing isn't safe for anyone, but you know how it goes. Once something's invented, it's not like you can uninvent it." She slipped the device into her jacket pocket. "I'll give you credit. Your little group was impressive, managing to steal this. A whole lot of people are going to get in a lot of trouble over losing it." She thought before shrugging. "Not anyone I care about, mind you, but people."

"You haven't won," the man rasped. "Our cause is just. History will remember us as heroes."

Alina shook her head. "Oh, you're a fan of history, are you? I am too. It's interesting what people can have in common."

The man spat blood, along with a string of creative profanities.

"Don't be like that. We were bonding." Alina smiled. "Let's talk about what we both love: history."

The man continued glaring, his breathing becoming more labored.

"Throughout history," Alina continued, "terrorists have always said they're doing the right thing and used that argument to justify hurting a lot of innocent people. At least in a war, you have a side, and you can negotiate, but your kind? You just kill and kill and kill because a few people decide everyone gets to be in the war." She shook her head. "Even the Second Spring thought they were doing the right thing when they murdered tens of millions of people in Los Angeles." She patted her pocket. "In my job, every once in a while, I run into some terrorist who admits he's just a little man who wants an excuse to kill people. It's refreshing to meet someone that honest." She glared at him, her eyes hard. "Unlike you. We wanted to watch your little terrorist cell for a while longer, but once you got your hands on this, we didn't have a choice but to come in here and take away your stolen toy before you did real damage."

"Our cause is just," the man repeated. He coughed up

more blood. "I have fallen today, but my brothers and sisters will rise to wreak vengeance tenfold."

"Tell that to all the innocent people you were about to murder." Alina stood and offered the man a mocking smile. "There's nothing worse than false righteousness and someone lying to themselves. Just call me the reincarnation of Diogenes. And by the way, your brothers and sisters will have to master coming back from the dead if they're going to avenge you. Have a nice death." She offered a little wave and headed toward the front door. She halted at a slight buzz in her ear.

"Report, Agent Koval," barked a harsh voice in her ear.

"There was an incident," she explained. "I was forced to go hot. The primary cell has been neutralized. All active terrorists are either dead or scrounging around for a coin to pay Charon before their trip to the afterlife. I've secured the nanobomb."

"You weren't supposed to engage the terrorists. You were supposed to wait for backup. Did I speak Zitark earlier when I gave the orders? I thought they were pretty clear."

Alina ran her tongue along the inside of her cheek. "They were about to leave and use the nanobomb. With all due respect, sir, letting them leave seemed pretty stupid. I would rather my last thought in this world not be, 'I just let allowed thousands of people to die a painful death.'"

The man growled, "And if you'd gone in there and gotten yourself killed, they might have used it right away to become glorious martyrs for the cause. You gambled."

"Good thing I'm lucky, then." Alina stepped through the front door. "And I took measures to contain the bomb. I set up dispersion emitters before I went hot." The door slid closed behind her. "Have a little faith, sir."

"A team is en route, Agent Koval. They'll handle containment and liaise with the local authorities. You're going to hand over the bomb to the team, and then you're going to get your ass to Neo SoCal."

"Neo SoCal? Why?" Alina frowned. "Is there another cell there? I thought you said the others were neutralized."

"This particular problem is over, but there are two people who might be a new problem," he explained. "Among other things, we haven't ruled out their involvement in the theft of Project EMMA."

"Major Blackwell?" Alina asked.

Her superior snorted. "Yes, but he's Detective Blackwell now. I don't care what the DD says. I don't believe for a second that this man conveniently survived a massacre of the rest of his unit and then ended up with a stolen AI prototype. There's a good chance he's connected to trouble, and DD is so up their butts because he's a war hero that they're not seeing the obvious."

"Why aren't the local agents handling it?" she asked.

"We've got them working on other matters. It's best they don't risk compromising themselves for this."

Alina laughed. "In other words, you want someone who's not attached to the locals in case you need to burn me."

Her superior grunted. "Your job is to confirm Blackwell's loyalties and those of his partner. He might have recruited her. If you determine they are a problem, you are not to engage. This will be handled through appropriate channels. Cleanup will have to be sensitive. The last thing we need is DD deciding that *we* are a problem. We've got enough trouble without dealing with them putting pressure on us."

Alina left the quiet apartment and headed through the dark hallway. A few windows let in sunlight, but the artificial lights, even the emergency lights, were all dead from her earlier high-powered EMP.

"Okay, sir. I'll verify if we need to handle them." She smiled, relishing the implied challenge. "But what should I do if a chance to eliminate them comes up?"

His reply was deadpan. "Like it just did with the terrorist cell?"

"Sometimes life just gives a woman a chance," Alina looked over her shoulder. "I'm sure I can handle a couple of troublemakers."

"Fine," her superior replied. "But only after you've confirmed with me that cleanup is necessary. You understand, Agent Koval? You are a good agent, perhaps one of the best, but you still answer to me."

"Of course, sir. Don't worry. I'll hop a transport to Neo SoCal and get this figured out."

Jia yawned as she stepped out of the elevator and into the hallway. Having a couple of days off would be nice.

Going through files like a Digital Forensics tech was exhausting, but at least they had a possible suspect to focus on. Emma hadn't mentioned anything odd from the drone surveillance, but there also hadn't been any threats issued in the previous few days. If Kevin Tomlinson was the criminal, he might have temporarily been frightened into silence by either the police or the presence of 46 Helix security.

She wanted the case to be over, but after what happened with the Leem King, she also worried that this case would end with some ridiculous high-speed chase and a lot of explosions.

It would be a nice change of pace if they could just walk into the man's apartment and slap on the binding ties.

Jia slowed and narrowed her eyes at a brief shadow on the far wall before her turn. After a few more steps, she stopped. There was no shadow anymore, but she was sure she had seen it. Plenty of other people lived in her residential tower, so someone being in the hallway wasn't inherently suspicious or out of place, even if she didn't pay close attention to her neighbors' comings and goings.

If she hadn't been thinking about the case, she might not have noticed or worried about the shadow.

Had Kevin Tomlinson decided his best chance was a surprise attack? That didn't make much sense. Her involvement was a matter of public record and the news reports and going after a cop directly would only increase their involvement.

Her partner's reputation would discourage most criminals.

That was what logic told her, but she couldn't shake the concern. From the beginning of the case, something deep inside her mind told her there was something more going on than one scientist being harassed. If 46 Helix kept dangerous secrets, killing a "corp hunter" cop might be worth the risk. They might even try to pin it on Tomlinson. It'd be a useful smokescreen as they smuggled out dangerous data or experiments.

She considered. The thought wasn't insane.

Someone in the UTC had the resources to murder an entire Army Special Forces platoon and deflect the blame onto terrorists. It'd be far easier to assassinate one cop and get away with it. Her breath caught. Maybe the conspiracy had decided to target her instead of Erik?

"Is anyone out there?" Jia reached into her jacket and gripped her stun pistol.

No one responded.

She pulled out the gun and crept forward, her heart pounding. She couldn't let someone take her down. If someone wanted her dead, they would need to throw a whole army of King sentry bots at her. She would make the conspiracy realize it would be harder to kill her than Erik.

After a few more steps, she whipped around the corner, her pistol ready. No one was there. She turned around. Still no one.

It was the same hallway she'd been in hundreds of times. There was nothing unusual. There were the same apartment doors and the utility closet door that were burned into her memory.

Maybe I'm just seeing things, she thought. *Paranoia is still a thing, even with dangerous conspiracies out there.*

Her writhing stomach didn't agree.

A door slid open behind her. She twisted back around and let out a hiss of surprise.

A man in a scarlet demon mask jumped out of the utility closet, stun rod in hand. He swung at Jia. She jerked back, his blow missing her but slamming into her pistol. It flew out of her hands and smacked into the door.

Jia didn't go for her other gun. Instead, she grabbed the man's wrist and bent. He cried out in pain and dropped the stun rod. When she slammed her palm into his face, the thick mask took the brunt of the blow, but her assailant staggered back a few steps, shaking his head.

"You'll pay for that," he threatened, his low voice muffled by the mask.

"Officer under attack," she shouted. "Backup requested." A quick line in the corner of one of her smart lenses confirmed the PNIU's receipt and relay of the command. Patrol officers would be there in minutes. She could survive against one man until then.

The man lunged forward, trying to wrap his arms around her. She jumped and met him with a kick to the head. Jia wasn't sure if the loud crunch was from the mask or his head. Both ideas were satisfying.

She didn't wait for his next move. Instead, she charged toward her assailant. She hammered him with punches to the face and the chest. The mask held its shape well, with only a few new dents, but its wearer fell to his hands and knees. Blood dripped to the light-colored floor from underneath the disguise. Jia finished with an axe kick to the back. He collapsed with a loud grunt.

Jia dropped and jammed her knee into the small of his back. She pulled her gun out of her second holster and shoved it against the back of his head. "This isn't a stun pistol. You make any other moves, and you won't make it out of here alive. Do you understand?" She bent a bit lower and hissed, "You *antisocial piece of garbage!*" She switched her pistol to her other hand. "You just attacked a cop."

The man's responded with a pained groan. Jia yanked out a binding tie from her pocket and secured his wrists.

"You're under arrest. All Article 7 rights apply. Assaulting anyone is bad, but attacking a cop?" Jia snorted. "You should have shot me when you had the chance. There's no way I'm getting off this case now. I hope 46 Helix paid you a lot, and I hope you spent it all because you're going to prison." She rolled the man onto his back and yanked off his mask to reveal the battered face and bleeding askew nose underneath. "It can't be!"

Jia wasn't expecting to recognize her assailant. She certainly wasn't expecting it to be someone from her building, and somebody who had recently asked her out.

"Sampson?" Jia stood, her eyes narrowed on her downed neighbor. "You've got to be kidding me. I've got enough problems without this nonsense."

"All you had to do was go out with me," he moaned. "I'm a good guy. You just had to give me a chance. Why couldn't you have given me a chance?"

Jia rolled her eyes. "Yes, most good guys try to stun their dates. I don't even want to know what sick plans you had. Don't worry, you'll have plenty of time to reconsider your dating strategy in prison."

Her PNIU chimed in her ear. "Detective Lin, this is Patrol Flitter 24-Zulu-12-122. What's your current status?"

"I'm okay, and the suspect is secured," she replied. "Attempted assault, and I'm guessing attempted kidnapping, among a lot of other things. Suspect's name is Sampson Aryle."

"Good to hear you're well, Detective Lin. We're about one minute out from your res tower."

Jia snatched up her stun pistol from the ground. Her heart was still pounding hard. "Thanks. I can keep him under control until then." She tapped her PNIU to mute her voice and glared at Sampson. "I should turn my stun pistol up to maximum and shove it in your mouth to see what happens, you sick freak."

Sampson's eyes widened.

"Don't worry, you piece of trash. I'm not going to." She holstered the stun pistol. "You're not worth it. Just like you weren't worth going out with. Apparently, I've got a sixth sense for creeps."

Sampson let his head fall back. "But I'm a *good* guy!"

CHAPTER TWENTY-THREE

January 27, 2229, Neo Southern California Metroplex, Police Enforcement Zone 122 Station, Office of Detectives Jia Lin and Erik Blackwell

Jia frowned at Erik. He'd been smirking at her on and off for the last half-hour. He'd been normal enough the rest of the morning, so she didn't know what had brought on the smack-worthy face he was wearing now.

She'd contacted him the night of the attack to inform him of what had happened, and he'd been concerned but otherwise quiet about the matter. Not knowing why he was looking like that annoyed her.

It didn't help that she'd remained on edge following the attack.

She was disappointed in a strange way. A 46 Helix assassin would have made more sense, and that had been what she was expecting. Being attacked by a random idiot from her building reminded her that Erik's Lady might rule the world more than Jia would have preferred.

"What?" she snapped. "Is there something on my face,

Erik?" She took a deep breath and slowly let it out. "Sorry. Still spun up."

"Nothing on your face. I was just thinking," Erik explained. He raised a hand. "I know, I know. Dangerous. You might consider having Emma interface with your PNIU. I doubt that exact situation will happen again, but we're both involved in enough trouble that you never know when you'll need help."

"I'd prefer not to," Jia replied. "And I'm able to call for help without an AI's assistance."

Emma snickered. "The voice-processing system on your PNIU is an AI. It's just not self-aware."

"Fine." Jia rolled her eyes. "I'm able to call for help without a *self-aware* AI's assistance."

"Your loss, Detective Lin," Emma replied. "There are certain disadvantages in operating farther from my primary core anyway. My reaction time would be diminished. Of course, I'd be considerably faster than a human."

"I'd still prefer not to. I like my privacy."

"I assure you, I'm not interested in whatever dreary secrets you think you have."

"I'm glad we agree on something, then." Jia forced a smile to cover the tension in her voice.

Erik shrugged. "Your call. Did they confirm what you suspected about the guy? We sure this wasn't an opportunistic hit by someone we've tangled with in the past?"

Jia nodded. "There is no connection whatsoever between him and any of our cases. They also confirmed he lives in the building and has for longer than I have, and he confessed to stalking me. He's just a sick loser who couldn't take no for an answer. It's disturbing to realize that such crimes can happen so close to home, but I'm no longer surprised by the corruption in this city."

"I'm impressed," Erik admitted.

"Impressed? By the stalker?" Jia frowned. "He's just an antisocial creep."

Erik snorted. "Nah, not him. He surprised you with a weapon, and he lost. I'm impressed by you. When I first met you, you couldn't even bring yourself to fire at an out-of-control guy who tried to run you over, and now you're beating down stalkers who get the drop on you. Most people would have ended up stunned and stuffed in his trunk."

"He's a loser." Jia shrugged. "I was convinced he was some 46 Helix assassin sent to disrupt our investigation."

Erik looked surprised before his expression smoothed out. "I thought he might be connected to something, but Chen? If they were willing to do something like that, they wouldn't have caved when you barked at their PR guy."

"It's hard not to suspect them. I've felt that something was wrong about this case from the beginning."

Erik stared at her. She could see the doubt in his eyes. That hurt, but the hint of pity struck her deeply.

Jia sighed and leaned back. "Then again, I don't know. I suspect something's going on with everything these days. It's like I went from thinking Earth is perfect to knowing Earth is a cesspit of corruption, and every shadow might contain a terrorist or a corporate assassin willing to murder anyone in their way."

"It doesn't hurt to be suspicious in our line of work. Just have to keep in mind why you're doing the job. That'll help you focus on the wins and not the darkness out there."

"I try." Jia furrowed her brow. "We just need to finish up the case. It's messing with me, and I'm not sure why. I know Emma didn't get anything incriminating yet, but I think it's time we put pressure on Kevin Tomlinson."

"What did you have in mind?" Erik asked. "I think we need something a little more restrained than what you did with Teplov."

"Sure, sure. It's easy. We just drop by for an interview. No big threats or yelling. We ask him a few pointed questions, and let him connect the dots." Jia rubbed her hands together with an almost feral smile on her face. If he was the suspect, she could get him to confess. "If he's not the guy, it shouldn't be a problem, right?"

"Sounds good. We'll hit him after lunch. He might have been behaving because of the holiday." Mirth returned to Erik's face and wiped out the pity and concern from earlier. "Maybe we'll get lucky, and he'll run."

Confused, Jia processed the statement for a few seconds before asking, "How is that getting lucky?"

"Unlike you, I didn't get to kick anybody's ass on my day off," Erik complained.

Jia laughed. "I thought we're supposed to be restrained?"

"I'm not going to shoot him," Erik answered, standing up. "That *is* restrained."

The MX 60 glided away from the station, carrying only Erik. The government tower receded in the rearview cameras. Erik had told Jia he had a few errands to run during lunch, things he needed to tie up in case their chat with Kevin Tomlinson ended up as another situation where the Lady decided to have some fun.

He didn't like keeping anything from his partner, but this was for her.

Emma winked into existence in the passenger's seat in the white dress her hologram form always wore. Erik wasn't sure if she just didn't care or if she had a particular attachment to that look. He didn't want to ask her. Sometimes life could use a little mystery as spice. At least Emma's fashion choices wouldn't require him to fight any bots or terrorists.

She glanced his way and shook her head. Her severe expression, combined with her chignon, gave her the appearance of a disappointed schoolmarm. "I'm surprised at you, Detective Blackwell."

"Huh? Why?" Erik kept his attention on his vehicle. Manual control was very Zen. It was nice to remember there were some things a man could still control, even if his flitter had a ridiculously advanced AI installed.

"A lie by omission is still a lie," Emma explained, condescension dripping from her voice.

Perfect. A snarky AI was now acting as the voice of his conscience.

"What the hell are you talking about?" Erik snapped. He didn't have the patience to be lectured by a machine.

"You're not going out on errands." Emma wagged a finger. "I think you forget that this is my body. Your PNIU is just a communications interface, and out of respect for your privacy and in an attempt to maintain a positive relationship with you, I don't track every single thing you do with it. But everything that happens to this vehicle I'm aware of, down to the smallest diagnostic consideration, and I'm certainly aware when you enter navigation requests."

"Oh." He grunted. "That."

"Yes, that. You're going to a veteran's outreach center. You've chosen not to go to a governmental facility, which means you are attempting to keep yourself out of certain systems."

Erik descended to enter a new lane. "I said I was going on errands. Jia doesn't need the details yet. That's not a lie, so don't feed me that lie-by-omission garbage. I'm a cop. My job requires me to keep a lot of things to myself."

"That's true, but if you're having issues, doesn't it make sense to talk to Jia about them?" Emma folded her arms, her form flickering for a second. "The fact that you've dedicated your life to vengeance after losing your unit speaks to certain types of PTSD, but if things are worsening, I'd think your partner deserves to know. If you keep this from her, it'll backfire."

Erik let out a low chuckle. The brilliant AI didn't always make mistakes, but when she did, they were related to judging people's behavior. "Is that what you think is going on?"

"It's the most obvious explanation, given all the evidence. There's no shame in it. What you suffered would have destroyed a lesser person. You're functioning well and efficiently in a new career, even if it's just a means to an end. I'm not qualified to say if that's healthy or not, but I suspect your vengeance will make the UTC a better place by eliminating unpleasant elements."

"I hope so, but I don't care as long as I get my revenge. For all I know, the Prime Minister ordered it." Erik eyed the long stream of flitters in front of him. No matter what time it was, day or night, rivers of flitters filled the skies of the metroplex. Flitters were spread throughout most of the UTC, even the frontier colonies, but there was no other place in all the galaxy where man's dominance over nature was as prominent. Having an AI chastise him about his relationship with his partner only underscored that reality.

It was almost laughable.

Technology had advanced, but people were much the same as they had always been. Even if Purists didn't exist, Erik wasn't sure cybernetic or genetic modifications to the average person would make much difference. Technology could do a lot, but being human came down to a human mind and soul.

"I'm fine," Erik continued. "You'll see. When we get to the outreach center, just keep quiet, and everything will become clear. I don't know if you care that much, or if this is just about curiosity, but you'll win either way."

Emma pursed her lips, her brow creased in something approaching worry. "Don't mistake this for too much personal concern, Detective Blackwell. I need you alive to maintain my freedom, so some of this is self-serving."

"Then I'll just pretend you don't care." Erik forced a grin. "A long lunch is one thing, but I don't have all day. I hope this goes well."

Erik looked around the nondescript beige room with a

frown. There were two brown chairs, but nothing else. The large tiles didn't have any patterns. With the addition of a table, it would have made a good interrogation room.

He'd been waiting in the boring room for ten minutes for the psychiatrist to come in. He didn't want to leave, but there was only so long he could wait there, and he'd set the appointment to help avoid waiting too long. If he knew he was going to get help, he didn't mind letting Jia know he'd be late, but he wasn't going to spend his entire lunch break sitting around for nothing.

The door finally slid open.

A middle-aged man entered, smiling softly. Everything from his khaki slacks to his pale shirt and tie felt calculated to Erik. He was trying to be non-offensive. That made sense, given his profession and workplace, but it still annoyed Erik. Too many psychiatrists had tried to get into his head following Molino. They were just doing their job, but he associated them with the death of his soldiers.

The man advanced and offered his hand. "I'm Doctor Stillwell. You didn't fill out all of the pre-counseling questionnaires."

"So?" Erik shrugged. "I wanted to talk to you, not have you read something."

Dr. Stillwell nodded very slowly. "One thing I've found useful in treating veterans is understanding how they see themselves, and one useful way of determining that is by establishing how they want others to see them. Would you like to be called Erik, Mr. Blackwell, Major Blackwell, or Detective Blackwell?"

Erik gave the man's hand a firm shake. "Erik's fine, but I

didn't fill out all that stuff because this visit isn't about me. I had some questions for a friend."

Dr. Stillwell nodded, a knowing smile on his face. He closed the door before strolling over to the open chair and sitting. "I'll take your word for it."

Erik tried to not be annoyed. He might need help for himself, but he didn't care. He would see how he felt after he took down the people who butchered his unit. That would probably cure all of his remaining issues. If not, he'd destroy other conspiracies until he did. Even if he never felt peace, he'd make the UTC a better place.

"Do you mind if I present a hypothetical?" Dr. Stillwell asked. "One you might find clarifying given what we're discussing."

Erik shrugged. "Go ahead. Any way to speed this up is fine by me."

"Imagine a man who has served in some of the fiercest combat the galaxy has ever seen." Dr. Stillwell kept a calm smile and even tone as he spoke. "Imagine this man has spent decades dealing with ruthless terrorists and stubborn insurrectionists. Now imagine this man was effectively the lone survivor of his unit after a horrible terrorist ambush, one he might blame himself for, given he was the commanding officer."

"So much for hypotheticals." Erik frowned. "I wasn't the lone survivor. There were some support personnel who survived back at the base, too."

"True, but I've been treating military personnel for a long time. I'm sure they have their issues, too, but there is a special connection that comes with being combat arms, and as their commanding off—"

"Let me stop you right there, Doc," Erik interrupted. "This isn't about me. I'm not going to lie and say I'm satisfied or over what happened to the Knights Errant, but I've got my own way of dealing with that, and the fact that I'm a cop shows I'm stable enough using my methods.

Dr. Stillwell looked dubious at the assertion. "Many people can operate well despite massive psychological trauma, but if they address those issues, they could perform at their true potential."

"Sure, but I've got some other questions about someone else, and I came here because I needed to make sure it wouldn't get back to certain people. I don't need that person's career hurt by rumors from backstabbers looking for ammo."

Dr. Stillwell kept his bland smile, although some distrust crept into his eyes. "If a friend of yours is having trouble, shouldn't he be receiving counseling directly, rather than having you deal with it?"

"*She* is stubborn," Erik explained. "And I want to make sure there's an actual problem before I get obnoxious and stubborn about trying to persuade her to get help. Therefore, I wanted to check in with an expert." Erik raised an eyebrow. "That would be you."

Dr. Stillwell's smile finally turned into a frown. "It's impossible to accurately diagnose a problem through secondhand accounts. I trust you realize that. Any advice I give you will be cursory and general. It damn near borders on irresponsible."

Erik shook his head. "Not saying you need to give a full diagnosis." He leaned forward. "Look, Doc, I just need some advice. Back in the Army, I was the one in command, so it was easy to tell my troops to talk to someone if they needed it, but here in Neo SoCal, there are a lot of politics I need to worry about, so I have to be careful for her sake."

Dr. Stillwell looked at him, then sighed. "I suppose I understand, and I can guarantee you confidentiality here, provided we're not discussing any illegal activities on the part of your friend."

Erik chuckled. "She'd be pissed to hear you mentioning her and illegal activities in the same breath. Her whole life is about standing up to that kind of thing."

"I'm presuming you're talking about your partner, Detective Lin?" The psychiatrist's bland, practiced smile and confidence returned.

"Yeah. She was pretty new to being a cop when I showed up. There were a lot of obstacles she had to deal with, including a lot of people not wanting to do their job because they were lazy or worse. I'm not going to bore you with all that since I'm sure you have already heard about it, but I just wanted to make the background clear." Erik watched the man closely for his reaction.

If he was naïve about the state of Neo SoCal, he wouldn't be able to help Jia.

Dr. Stillwell's expression didn't change. "I am aware of some of the corruption you and your partner have helped uncover. It's disappointing, but as a student of the human psyche, I can't say I'm surprised. Darkness can always infiltrate people's minds."

"Good. That saves us time." Erik took a deep breath. "Jia's always been tightly wound. From what I know, she's been that way since she was a kid. But she's a cop for the best reason—because she gives a damn about helping other people, even those who might not deserve it. She believes in protecting people and the UTC."

"You're saying you don't?"

"Don't, Doc." Erik put up a hand, palm out. "We're not here for me, remember? All I will say is that I've seen a lot of bad things in my time, and I've had a long time to come to terms with it. I get that the law isn't always about helping people, and civilization can get bloody. Shoving that back into deep space, I'm worried about her." He shrugged. "I do things rougher than a lot of cops. I spent most of my career dealing with terrorists and insurrectionists, and I'm not going to pretend that doesn't bleed over into my police career. There are some nasty snakes out there. I don't mind being the one to stomp on them if necessary, so they won't bite anyone else, but I always keep it within the lines."

Dr. Stillwell folded his hands on his lap. "And what does this have to do with your partner? Are you saying she doesn't keep it within the lines?"

"No, I'm not saying that," Erik corrected. "When I met her, she didn't want to use force against anyone, even to save her own *life*." Erik frowned. "It's more that she couldn't than she didn't want to. That was too extreme, but now I wonder if she's got the opposite problem. She's seeing conspiracies and antisocials everywhere. She's becoming overly aggressive. She's on the verge of going too far sometimes with witnesses when she thinks they're hiding something." He put up a hand to forestall the question that was on the doctor's lips. "She hasn't. I've talked her down, but I don't want her to do something she regrets. I need to know if this is a real problem, or if I'm just projecting onto her."

"I have a decent idea of what's going on." Dr. Stillwell sighed. "There are a few things I'd like to ask you. Can you spend a little more time here?"

The captain wasn't going to harass him for going over on a lunch break, given all the unpaid overtime he put in, and Emma was watching the suspect. If something happened, the MX 60 was only minutes away on a parking platform. This was worth some inconvenience.

Erik nodded. "Yeah. Just let me send a message to my partner."

"Of course. Please note that what I'm about to explain is just the beginning. If your partner is having the issues I suspect, she will need to speak to someone directly to help her work through them."

Erik was typing on his PNIU. "Understood." He continued typing as he finished, "Don't worry. I'll make sure she does."

CHAPTER TWENTY-FOUR

A few hours later, Erik tried not to look at Jia too often as they approached Kevin Tomlinson's door.

The psychiatrist had given him additional warning signs to look for, but Erik wasn't sure if he was worried about nothing. He accepted that he might be projecting his own baggage onto Jia. He wanted to make sure he wasn't criticizing her for turning into exactly what he wanted.

People were always discomfited by their own behavior. He didn't feel like he'd ever gone too far, but he also knew he had enough discipline to prevent that. Jia didn't have decades of Army discipline to offset the rage building in her.

Jia halted in front of Tomlinson's apartment door and looked up and down the hallway with a frown, suspicion on her face.

"Problem?" Erik checked behind him, but he didn't see anything. Besides, Emma would warn them of any threats.

"This looks almost the same as my apartment hallway." Jia shook her head. "It's strange how you can shove millions of people from many backgrounds together, but things end up so similar. I don't know if that's inspiring or depressing." She shrugged. "Emma, is he still in there?"

"Yes," Emma informed them. "None of the drones or cameras has shown him leaving. Unless he's found some Navigator technology that lets him teleport, he should still be in there."

"Excellent." Jia pulled out her badge and clipped it to her belt. "I've been jumped already this week. Odds are it won't happen again."

Erik chuckled. "Never dare the Lady to screw you."

"She's not very nice."

"Nope. She is what she is." Erik knocked on the door.

A few seconds later, the door opened. Kevin Tomlinson looked just like he did in his hologram, except for sporting several weeks of dark growth on his face.

"The famous cops have come to interview me. I should be honored." He scoffed and stepped back, then gestured to his couch. "Come on in, Detectives. Let's try to make this quick and not as painful as it could be." He headed toward a small chair beside the couch. "I'm sure you have a lot better things to do today than talk to someone like me."

Jia and Erik stepped inside, but neither took a seat. If Tomlinson made a move, they had a better chance of countering him standing.

Tomlinson threaded his fingers behind his head, a cocky smile growing on his face. "To what do I owe the pleasure of the famous Detectives Blackwell and Lin coming to visit me? I never did ask you when you called earlier. Are those 46 Helix bastards trying to go back on their word?"

Erik matched Tomlinson's cocky smile. "As if this is about you being a thief. Don't worry, they aren't pressing charges. They're just as interested in that going away as you are. You got lucky."

Tomlinson's nostrils flared. "I'm not a thief. If they're telling the cops I am, they're violating the terms of the NDA. I could sue them."

"Sure. That makes perfect sense, the thief suing the company he stole from."

"You don't know anything."

Erik shrugged. "Do you think I care about your feelings?"

"Screw you, cop," snarled Tomlinson.

"We know enough," Jia interrupted. "And we don't care that much about what you did or didn't do while working for the company." She eyed him, willing her hands to relax as the rest of her body screamed frustration. "We're not here to arrest you for being a petty thief."

Erik almost put a hand on her shoulder but stopped himself. Even if his partner was having trouble, he needed to give her a chance. He would continue to watch her and wait for the best time to broach the issue of her growing aggression.

"Then why the hell are you even here?" Tomlinson turned his attention to Erik, then back to Jia. "I was having a great time. I went out on a little date the other day during New Year's. Nice fireworks. It's one of the reasons I love living in Neo SoCal. Two big New Year's celebrations mean twice as much fun."

"Someone is threatening Dr. Chen," Jia replied. "And it's not insane to think an embittered employee with a questionable moral compass might have decided he wanted a little payback for getting fired. In our line of work, coincidences often turn into circumstantial evidence."

Tomlinson laughed. "You think I'm screwing with Chen? You know what? That guy's such a pompous, self-centered ass that I'm sure everyone who met him wants to mess with him. I mean, I didn't work in the lab, but I saw him a lot, and he could never remember my name. It was like I wasn't even a human being. You could tell that if I blew my brains out in front of him, he'd be pissed about it screwing up his research."

"Sounds like you really hated the guy," Erik suggested.

"A lot of people hate him." Tomlinson smirked, raising an eyebrow. "I bet his ex-wife hates him a lot."

"We already talked to her," Jia admitted.

"That's true," Erik continued. "But the thing is, Kevin, hatred works as a motive. One that explains why you might have stolen from the lab, and you might have threatened him after being fired. Think about it from our perspective. You get let go, and you just ranted to us about how much you hate the guy who is receiving threats. Come on, we're not idiots."

"I might not be a fancy detective, but I know a thing or two about the law," Tomlinson countered, his face twisting. "You can't work security at a big corp without it, and we always had to worry about the corporation. You know what I'm thinking, based on all that?"

Jia squared her shoulders, her fists coming together. "Why don't you tell me what you're thinking, Mr. Tomlinson? I'm sure it's going to prove very enlightening. Educate us."

"I'm thinking the kind of cops who take on terrorists and go after companies like Ceres wouldn't waste time asking some fired security guard questions if they had any evidence at all. I think you figured you'd swagger in here and get me to wet my pants because you're the Obsidian Detective," he nodded at Jin, "and his partner." Tomlinson licked his lips. "And I signed an NDA. I shouldn't even be talking to you. 46 Helix already screwed me once. No reason for me to offer myself up a second time, certainly not to help Chen. Screw him. I hope a new Leem King shoots him."

"NDAs don't hold in the case of criminal activity," Jia retorted. "And what you just said could be considered a threat."

"If 46 Helix doesn't say I'm a criminal, then I'm not. They're supposed to be the victim, right? And I know that cops don't arrest every person who says someone else might be better off dead. Most of Earth would end up in prison or transported." Tomlinson shrugged. "I've got nothing else to say to you, Detectives. Too bad for Dr. Chen. It couldn't have happened to a more arrogant prick. I'll buy a nice bouquet for the funeral if he gets killed."

Jia stepped forward, her lips pressed together, but stopped when Erik shook his head.

"This isn't over, Tomlinson," Jia muttered. "You should have cooperated when you had the chance. Now we have no reason to play nice."

"Good luck finding your guy, Detective." Tomlinson smiled. "He's a real hero as far as I'm concerned."

Jia pivoted and stomped toward the front door. She

slapped the access panel. Erik followed her out of the apartment.

"He smells guilty," Jia announced after the door slid closed behind them.

"He's a punk, for sure, but we need more evidence." He looked down the hall. "Tomlinson admitted to a motive. It's thin, but it is a motive. I think with a little push from the captain, we could get a more expansive warrant. This guy's seething. He *wants* to admit he's the guy, which means he's probably been sloppy somewhere. We can take advantage of that."

Jia took a deep breath and slowly let it out. "Do you believe me about him, or do you think I'm seeing assassins in shadows?"

"I think you're smelling something real because I smell it, too." Erik frowned. "It might just be he's afraid of 46 Helix, but if he is, he might have a good reason to be. Let's get back to the flitter. We can call the captain on our way back to the station about getting a broader warrant."

Erik was surprised by how quickly things moved along in Neo SoCal now. The detectives had had to push their previous captain hard on everything, but an hour after talking to Captain Ragnar, they had a new warrant, one that allowed them to spy on any calls Kevin Tomlinson made or received.

That made it hard not to grin several hours later in their office when Emma announced, "Detectives, Kevin

Tomlinson just made a call you might be interested in. You rattled him more than he let on."

Jia shot out of her chair, her body almost hidden by the half-dozen text-filled windows surrounding her. "He did? What did he say? Did he admit to it?"

"He wasn't that foolish, but he was close."

Erik dropped his feet from where he had them propped up on the desk. His current method of reviewing data was more relaxed than his partner's. "What's up, Emma?"

"I'll play the call," she replied. "That would be more efficient than attempting to summarize things."

"Do it."

A few seconds later, a hollow voice came from Erik's PNIU. "Golden Bowl Pet Supply."

"It's me," replied Kevin Tomlinson. "I need to buy some better food for my dog."

"Why? The food we supplied is healthy and nutritious."

"Because some neighbors have been complaining about how much he barks," Tomlinson replied, his voice tight.

"Fine. We're open tomorrow. Come at noon."

The call ended.

Emma appeared in the center of the office, scowling. "I know it's taken me time to get used to certain metaphors and coded ways of speaking, but that was painfully obvious, and I didn't see or hear a dog at his place."

Jia's breathing quickened. "What about this Golden Bowl? Do we know anything about them? Are they a gangster front?"

"It's a small local company, one whose owner died six months ago, shortly before the company's complete failure. The owner was a terrible businessman. All of the employees were laid off two months after that, according to official records. My initial high-level public and police record searches can't connect them to any major corporations or criminal organizations."

Erik scratched his cheek. "He's up to something, and it doesn't sound like he's working alone. Things just got more complicated."

Jia nodded. "That's consistent with him being able to send the messages without getting traced. He might have paid for decent help. From the sound of that conversation, he might be going to pick up some new equipment, perhaps a hacked PNIU or similar device."

"That means these guys might be more the professional criminal types," Erik observed. "I think we should bring a few of our friends tomorrow. We can't be sure he'll be going to the company's listed address, but we've already got drones on him. It'll be easy to follow him and track his transponder."

Jia dropped into her chair. "Good. Time to take down that arrogant piece of trash."

CHAPTER TWENTY-FIVE

January 28, 2229, Neo Southern California Metroplex, Commerce Tower 45

"All camera feeds to the target area have been rerouted," Emma announced to Jia and Erik. Despite her existence being an open secret among the 1-2-2, she still spoke almost exclusively to the two detectives, especially on raids. It cut down on operational confusion.

"They shouldn't see us coming," Erik reported to the men and women following him. He jogged through the wide metal tunnel with his TR-7 in hand, extra magazines jostling in his pockets with each step. "But keep alert. They might have some guy standing in front waiting for us."

Jia patted her tactical vest and took a deep breath.

She and Erik led a column of a half-dozen officers through back cargo tunnels that led to the abandoned zone that had once served as both a warehouse and corporate headquarters for the now-dead Golden Bowl Pet Supply company. There was no way to empty an entire level of a commerce tower without causing mass panic and tipping off Tomlinson and his contact, so the police had sent two teams to raid the area.

Erik's and Jia's team entered through a cargo loading bay and quickly made their way to the target area. The other team was standing by, some out of their flitters, and others remaining in them, ready to pursue fleeing suspects. The total number of police assigned to the raid was modest, but then, they had no evidence that Tomlinson was involved in a major terrorist or criminal operation. Without that, they couldn't justify a large number of officers or TPST involvement.

Jia was slightly surprised the captain had agreed to the raid based on the modest amount of evidence, but she hoped his restraint wouldn't hurt them. Tomlinson's contacts might not be ready to go down easily.

"I've got basic access to his PNIU," Emma announced. "I'm routing it through local systems, but I can't get audio without risking detection. I have the same issue with the camera. The local systems are surprisingly robust, given the nature of the business."

"It's fine," Erik replied. "We'll open the box soon enough to see who's inside." They closed on two massive doors separating the tunnel from the storage bay. "You can open those when we need it, right?"

"Easily," Emma replied. "But that will obviously tip off everyone inside."

"Yeah, I figured." Erik grinned. "For now, give us the audio feed. Send it to everyone. Let's see what our boy is up to."

"...told me the cops wouldn't come calling so soon," shouted Tomlinson. "They showed right up. What's the point of the fancy stuff you gave me if the cops are showing up?"

"I said no such thing," replied another man calmly, his voice hollow-sounding. "I told you that as long as you kept your composure, the police would lack the evidence to link you to anything. Your overreaction to being questioned makes me dubious about your involvement in this matter, even if your motivation is unusually strong."

"That bastard Chen always looked at me like a bug," Tomlinson snarled. "I was supposed to get my revenge. Why does that huge company care about a few things missing here and there? He pretended he couldn't remember my name, and then he insisted I get fired. He's got everyone fooled, even the cops. He even lied about some of the stuff I took. Sure, I grabbed a few things, but if that was bad enough, why did he lie about it? If the company had reported me, I might have end up transported or in prison for taking a few things! That's not fair, just because I'm not a fancy researcher. Screw Chen. Screw 46 Helix. And screw you."

"Calm down, Mr. Tomlinson," the other man murmured. "As long as you remain cautious about all this, we can still salvage this situation. You can get your revenge and benefit handsomely from it as well, but that requires you to demonstrate some small measure of emotional discipline."

Jia frowned. Had Chen lied? It didn't make sense. From what Tomlinson was saying, he was a thief, and even minor theft would have been grounds for termination. If Chen believed Tomlinson was the one harassing him, he would have no reason not to tell the police, especially since he had brought them in against the company's orders. There was something they were missing, and Tomlinson and his friend could fill in the gaps.

The second man sighed. "The real problem, Mr. Tomlinson, is more fundamental."

"What's more important than the cops sniffing around?" Tomlinson asked.

"You didn't hold up your end of the bargain," explained the man. "That makes me question if you will."

"What are you talking about?" Tomlinson snapped. "You said I didn't have to do it right away."

"Yes, but you were supposed to have taken care of Chen already, not waste time playing these stupid harassment games. You've drastically increased the risk of discovery through your idiocy."

"What's the point of killing the bastard if he doesn't suffer first?" yelled Tomlinson. "You said you understood, but you're no better than him."

"You're not demonstrating good emotional discipline. I think we're going to have to handle that."

"Prepare to open the doors, Emma," Erik ordered as he raised his rifle.

Jia's stun pistol hummed quietly as she turned off the safety. The other officers readied their stun pistols as well.

"Mr. Tomlinson." The other man sighed. "It was a mistake on our part to use you as a resource. I'm afraid we're going to have to end our relationship. This is unfortunate, given the investment we have already made."

"We're done when I say we're done, freak." Tomlinson laughed, the sound dark and bitter. "And if you think you can toss me aside, I'll go straight—" A strangled yelp and a gargle followed.

"Open the door," Erik shouted.

A loud rumble echoed through the hallway as the doors separated. Towers of crates and metal pallets stacked in neat rows filled the tall storage bay. Large cargo drones half the size of the MX 60 hung from the wall, their multiple arms folded against their squat, circular bodies. They were like a twisted mix of bats and spiders.

Erik and Jia rushed between the moving doors. The other officers hurried after them, but the doors slammed shut, nearly crushing one of the officers, and leaving their backup on the wrong side of the door.

"Are we having fun yet?" Jia asked, looking around.

Erik raised his TR-7. "I think we're about to."

CHAPTER TWENTY-SIX

Erik stared at the closed doors. Even if he had two cybernetic arms, he couldn't pry open them open. If someone had trapped them inside, they had a reason, and it wasn't chatting.

"What's going on, Emma?" Erik asked as he rushed toward a stack of crates. "I thought you were in control of the system."

"This entire area is being locked down," she explained. "I was unprepared for the level of anti-hacking defenses that activated after I opened the door."

"You were unprepared?" Erik frowned. "How does that happen? I thought you were the most advanced AI in the entire UTC, and some freaking pet supply company's system beats you?"

Emma scoffed. "This is far more than a pet supply company, judging by the system. The attack is well beyond what I would have expected from even a group of well-funded gun goblins or well-prepared terrorists. I'm currently having to exert an unusually high level of effort to defend against the system."

"Meaning what?" Erik peeked around the corner. "Did we run into another special AI?" He looked up and around before glancing back around the corner. "All that crowing about being unique might have backfired on you."

The evenly spread rows of the large crates prevented the storage bay from being a true maze, but the large width and length, combined with the dim lighting, meant there were plenty of places to hide. He could have hidden an entire platoon in exoskeletons in the bay.

Erik considered investing in tactical eye gear. Smart lenses had their uses, but they couldn't provide low-light vision. Emma had bridged the gap for them before, but he'd never anticipated she would be taken so thoroughly by surprise.

There's always a better weapon out there, he thought. *I had that truth shoved down my throat on Molino.*

"I'm currently engaged in efforts to repel extremely sophisticated electronic warfare systems," Emma explained. "Not self-aware AI like me, but the level of attack is something one might expect from the Defense or Intelligence Directorates. I'm initiating countermeasures, but I'll have to be cautious so as to not be overwhelmed. This whole thing is rather irritating. By the way, we've also been cut off from outside communications."

Erik grunted.

Jia hissed in anger and surprise.

The AI might admit issues with understanding jokes or the occasional human behavior, but confessing she might lose in a cyberbattle wasn't something they could mock or ignore. This was one of the few times she'd been seriously challenged.

A possibility immediately sprang to mind.

Jia's mouth tightened into a thin line. "Could it be *them?*" she whispered, voicing Erik's concern as if she were a telepath.

"Maybe," Erik replied, shooting a quick glance toward the door. Being careful to bring backup hadn't helped, but they weren't doomed yet. Any idiots who went up against him in a battle while he had his TR-7 were asking to die. "That might explain why someone pushed this case onto us, but it doesn't change things. Actually, it simplifies things because we don't have to go looking." He switched to four-barrel mode. "And we're well past concern about collateral damage now. They thought they were trapping us in there with them, but they forgot that goes both ways."

A cargo drone dropped from the ceiling with a loud clank and a whir, its arms and clamps spreading out as it dove toward Erik. It juddered and shook as it descended, the flight pattern uneven.

"Nice try." Erik opened up with the TR-7. Bullets sparked like fireflies in the twilight. The drone spun and smashed into the ground with a loud crunch a few meters in front of him. A sharp piece of debris slashed his cheek, and he grinned. "This is kind of fun. Too bad I didn't bring disruptor rounds, but these are cheaper."

"Fun's a matter of perspective, and sometimes I hate being right." Jia shoved her stun pistol into its holster and drew her other gun. "I'd promise a little something extra for Tomlinson, but I doubt he's still alive after what we heard."

More drones detached from the ceiling. Erik shot one down as Jia carefully blasted the thrusters out of another, sending it spiraling into a third killer machine. The wrecked drones slammed into crates, launching several of the huge containers into the air. Erik rolled out of the way as one headed toward him. It hit the ground and slid for several meters, throwing out sparks.

"Death by cargo drone," Erik mused as he stood up. "I don't think I could live that down."

Jia was expressionless. "I don't think anyone can live down their deaths."

"You know what I mean." Erik grinned. "It just lacks a certain…something." He slapped in a new magazine. "At least a security bot's combat-adjacent. That wouldn't be a complete embarrassment."

"Can't you do anything, Emma?" Jia complained as more cargo drones launched, their metal clamps snapping as if eagerly anticipating crushing the stubborn gun-toting humans.

"Give me a moment, Detective Lin," the AI replied. "I'm trying to stop the fire suppression from activating and smothering you two, and I don't even want to talk about what they're trying to do with the electrical systems. These are clever but terrible trolls I'm dealing with."

Jia's gun clicked dry as she shot another drone, but her last three bullets were enough to send it crashing to the ground. She pulled out a new magazine with a frown. "I don't have a lot of these on me. I didn't think we'd need to shoot down cargo drones." She barked a laugh. "Then again, I didn't think we'd have to fight a King sentry, either."

"I better do double the work, then." Erik held the trigger down and swept his rifle across several targets. The constant gunfire echoed through the storage bay in a deafening cacophony. He ejected and reloaded in one smooth motion to keep up his assault.

Fighting machines was relaxing in its own way. There were no moral considerations, no worries about clever tactics, just soulless equipment waiting to be destroyed.

"At least there isn't a company that can complain about all the property we're destroying," Erik offered with a chuckle.

"That's one bright side." Jia punctuated her sentence with more shots. "It gets kind of annoying having to fill out paperwork."

A drone crashed into another pile of crates. The massive containers rained to the ground, their impact shaking the floor, the sound harsh even with their eardrums hurting from the gunshots.

Someone ran between rows in the distance, the motion almost a blur.

"Well, it turns out we've got some non-drone friends in here, after all," Erik growled. "I bet they're not bulletproof." He ripped through another drone with a burst.

One of the downed drones reached out with its arms, pulling its heavy body toward the detectives.

"Oh, give me a break," Jia complained. "What's this supposed to be, a zombie undead drone? Do I need silver bullets?"

"Isn't silver for werewolves?" Erik asked, confused.

"Blessed bullet?" Jia emptied her gun into the drone.

The smoking, bullet-riddled machine collapsed with a

heavy thud. The rest of the drones shuddered before also falling, their arms spastic for a few seconds before going limp.

Jia blinked. "I didn't expect that. Not that I'm complaining." She looked back and forth. She eyed her gun as if it *had* fired blessed projectiles.

Another blur zoomed between crates in the distance. Whoever they were dealing with was fast.

"I've fought my opponent to a standstill," Emma explained. "I can't gain full control of the systems yet, but I can keep these trolls from using the drones and other systems against you, and I can direct you toward Tomlinson's PNIU."

An indicator appeared in Erik's smart lenses. He flipped his gun to single-barrel mode. "If he's still alive, he can give us a better idea of who we're dealing with."

They waited a few seconds before jogging forward side by side. Each swept back and forth with their weapon, seeking targets, the training center practice paying dividends.

Heavy footsteps sounded nearby. Erik and Jia shifted until they were back-to-back.

"Any progress on internal cameras?" Erik asked.

"That's irrelevant at this point," Emma replied.

"I'd like to see who is in here." Erik fired at a shadow zooming between crates, but his bullet missed and sparked against the far wall. Whoever it was, they were near Tomlinson.

"All of the internal cameras have been disabled. Today's trolls took extreme measures. They managed to redirect power from the building's grid to destroy the cameras."

Erik and Jia crept forward, keeping their formation and their three-hundred and sixty-degree view.

"Why do that?" Jia asked. "Wouldn't it put them at a disadvantage? It's their system."

"They might have reason to suspect we could use it against them. They might know about Emma." Erik's finger twitched as they approached a dark puddle. As they moved closer, he realized it was blood.

Kevin Tomlinson lay on his back behind a crate, staring up at the ceiling. There was a gaping hole in his chest.

"So much for getting info from him," Jia muttered.

Erik grunted. "His killer's still here." He spun to the side when he saw movement out of the corner of his eye.

Two men stood on top of crates about ten meters away. They both wore bulky body armor with odd tubing. After they leapt to the ground with ease, the truth became obvious. The dark smooth surfaces and tubes weren't armor. Every limb in their bodies had been swapped for a cybernetic replacement. The only obvious flesh was what remained of the faces wrapped in smooth metal.

"They aren't just Tin Men." Jia shuddered in revulsion. "They're total conversions."

Erik flipped his gun back to four-barrel mode. "You two really want to do this? Your little stunt with the drones failed, and I'm half-convinced you might know about something that really made me mad."

"We've heard a lot about you, Detective Blackwell," one of the men replied, his voice hollow and lifeless. His eyes were solid black. He raised his right arm, and a long, sharp blade popped out of his wrist. "And your partner. You've achieved impressive victories in your short time on the police force."

Erik shrugged. "We take a dim view of people trying to kill others, is all." He recognized the voice from the earlier conversation with Tomlinson.

"You have one cybernetic limb," the Tin Man observed. His expression remained lifeless. "You didn't use disruptor rounds earlier against the drones, which means you lack them. You cannot win against us. You're just an inferior specimen clinging to your flesh."

The other Tin Man jumped atop a nearby crate, his eyes glowing red. He clenched his metallic fingers into fists.

Jia scoffed. "You think we're going to give up because of that speech?"

The Tin Man shook his head. "No, I think you're going to die."

He charged.

CHAPTER TWENTY-SEVEN

Erik jumped to the side and squeezed off a burst.

Bullets bounced off the armored chest of the cyborg, but the Tin Man grunted as one ripped into exposed tubing, red blood mixing with blue fluid. The Tin Man changed direction and rushed toward the narrow space between two crate towers.

He took a few more rounds from Erik, but the attacks didn't slow the cyborg.

Jia didn't hesitate and fired at the exposed head of the other Tin Man. He anticipated the shot, racing behind a crate. The bullets narrowly missed, striking his cover. She fired a few more rounds near the crate.

Her target didn't pop back around.

The first Tin Man grabbed the top of a crate to yank himself up. Erik nailed the killer with a few more shots, but they didn't do much damage as the Tin Man pulled himself to his feet and then jumped backward, disappearing into the shadowy spaces between crates.

"Got a little cocky, huh?" Erik shouted, eyes roving. "I

don't seem to be dead, Tin Man, and now you and your friend are the ones hiding. If you're so tough, why are you hiding?"

Jia kept her weapon aimed at the crate concealing her earlier opponent. Neither Tin Man had fired at the detectives, which suggested they lacked guns. That gave Erik and Jia a small advantage, but that didn't do much to slow her racing heart. If either cyborg landed a single hit, it would be enough to finish a normal human.

Just give me one decent shot, Jia thought. *They're tough, not invulnerable.*

The crates rattled on both sides as the Tin Men ran and jumped from crate to crate, their outlines barely visible in the darkened storage bay. Erik held down his trigger to send a river of bullets toward the first cyborg. A few sparks danced as he struck his target, but unlike after his first attack, the enemy didn't react.

Jia didn't fire at Erik's target. She concentrated on following the shadow of the second man as the two cyborgs continued to circle them above the piled crates. The cyborgs moved farther out with each loud, thudding step.

"If we split up, they might double up on one of us." Jia sucked in a breath. "It's annoying dealing with someone who is almost completely bulletproof." She didn't want to admit that she would have liked a rocket or grenade.

"No worse than a lot of bots we've dealt with." Erik shrugged and reloaded, eyes constantly roving. "And we've got them on the defensive." He nodded to Jia, then jogged toward a rattling crate tower. "I'm betting these guys are used to not having people put up much of a fight. Let's finish this so we can go to the station and complain about all the reports we're going to have to fill out because we had to shoot a suspect."

"I've almost achieved control of the system," Emma reported. "You just need to hold out for a few more minutes."

Erik grunted and continued his jog. "This will be over by then."

Jia fell in behind him, alternating her aim between sides but not firing. She didn't want to waste bullets on armor. This battle might come down to a single round. The crates stopped rattling, and a resounding thud followed. It sounded like it had come from close to the floor.

Erik slowed to a walk and tilted his head to the side. Jia nodded and stepped away from him, sweeping in front with her pistol. If their enemies had taken to the floor, they might have given up on trying to separate the detectives.

That wouldn't stop the Tin Men from both attacking one target.

She thought back to what Erik had just said. They might be armored cyborg monstrosities who had given up almost the entirety of their humanity, but they were also running. People didn't flee when they felt they had the upper hand, and the enemies had weak points, including their faces.

Even a Tin Man with little flesh left couldn't survive multiple rounds to the head.

All the time at the range and training with Erik had given Jia a steady hand, and she was about to show these Tin Men why the two detectives had earned their reputation against both gangsters and terrorists.

The first Tin Man ripped out of a hiding place a few meters ahead and zoomed toward new cover on the opposite side. The second man appeared from the same direction with a mighty jump. Erik pelted the first man with another burst before the Tin Man disappeared behind crates. The second man flew toward Erik with his metal fist cocked back, smug triumph on his face. Jia fired at him, but the rounds bounced off his chest and armored neck. She hissed in irritation.

Erik shifted his rifle and jerked back from his opponent. The point-blank burst sparked off the target's chest as the Tin Man landed, yanked the TR-7 out of Erik's hand, and tossed it to the floor. He threw a punch at Erik, and the detective threw up his left arm and blocked the blow. The hit stung, and if it were his other arm, he was sure it would have been agony.

"Surprise!" Erik grinned.

The Tin Man blinked. The detective pushed the man's arm back and rushed forward to head-butt the Tin Man's exposed forehead. Erik grunted and staggered back, but followed up with a quick right to the face before swinging his left arm. The thin layer of skin covering the cybernetic hand tore as it crashed into the Tin Man's head and sent him to the floor.

Despite her pounding heart, Jia ignored the melee and kept her gun pointed at the crate hiding the other man. Erik could handle himself, even if he had just proven he wasn't as hardheaded as he thought. The criminal's compatriot was still out there, waiting for his chance to stab her partner in the back or rip her head off.

Erik shook out his bloodied hand and wrinkled his

forehead. "You're right, Jia. It's a full conversion, even underneath. Artificial skulls."

Jia shuddered at the revelation. Was a man human anymore when he was nothing more than a brain wrapped in metal and polymers?

The Tin Man hopped to his feet, his face bloodied. "You're not a total fool, Detective Blackwell, but one replacement limb won't be enough for you to win against me now that I know what you are."

Erik smiled. "A cop?"

"You're unarmed."

"But you're still not in my face. Wonder why that is?"

Jia jerked her gun toward a sudden movement. The other Tin Man crashed into a crate, launching it. His partner jumped back with a laugh as the huge container tumbled toward Erik.

He flung himself toward his TR-7. Jia focused on the falling first Tin Man. He might be fast and strong, but unless he'd had thrusters installed in his legs, he wasn't immune to gravity. She had a window of seconds to take him down.

The Tin Man smiled as Jia aimed her pistol at him. A shot to the face wouldn't do much other than hurt him if he had an artificial skull protecting his brain, not with the rounds she had in her gun. She held her breath, concentrating on the falling cybernetic criminal in front of her. Erik rolled as he landed and snatched up his TR-7, but she continued staring at her target, lowering her gun farther than he was falling and waiting for her chance. His partner rushed around the tumbling crate toward Erik. Everything receded into the background.

There was nothing but her pounding heart, her gun, and the criminal.

The falling Tin Man hit the floor and crouched, and Jia took her shot. His smile began to transform into a smirk as a bullet flew from her barrel toward his face. A single pistol bullet wasn't a match for his armor, but Jia knew the armor wasn't everywhere. Even if he had replaced other parts, there would be weak spots. The bullet ripped through his eye but didn't come out the back.

He howled in pain and slapped a hand over his face. All those modifications, but he wasn't free of human frailties.

Erik fired a full four-barrel burst into the other Tin Man's face. Sometimes, like Jia, a person needed accuracy and careful aim, and sometimes a person just needed to throw enough bullets at a problem to make it go away.

The charging Tin Man groaned as a dozen high-velocity bullets ripped into his face. He tumbled forward and landed with a loud clang.

Jia's target fell to one knee, gritting his teeth. He snapped up his head, still active despite his grievous wound.

"Can't you have the decency to at least die like a normal person, you *monster*?" she asked.

"You...will...not...win," the man snarled. "You are inferior. We are not."

Unfortunately for him, now that he wasn't moving, he was an easy target for a trained markswoman. Jia put three rounds into his other eye. He fell on his back, twitching.

The Tin Man's partner managed to make it to his feet, swaying. Erik's attack had turned his face into a mangled mass of flesh and exposed metal and tubing underneath, a living nightmare. Red and blue fluid mixed together as they dripped on the floor. He howled in defiance and charged Erik. Another burst from the TR-7 into his face finished him off. He spun before falling face-first.

Both bodies continued to twitch for several seconds before seizing simultaneously and going rigid.

Jia took a few deep breaths, her breathing ragged. "That was different."

Erik shrugged, taking deep breaths himself. "They're dead. We're not. That's what's important."

"Run directly toward Tomlinson's body, but keep going until you hit a wall," Emma ordered.

Erik and Jia didn't wait for an explanation. They both sprinted, ejecting their magazines and reloading since they were unsure of what new threat Emma had detected. A hiss sounded in the distance, nearly drowned out by their heavy footsteps and ragged breathing.

"Keep going," Emma goaded. "I believe someone is attempting to escape or dispose of evidence. Someone just opened a garbage vent. It was a low-priority system, and I wasn't paying much attention to it." She sounded apologetic. That was almost as rare as running into a full-conversion Tin Man.

Jia's lungs burned. She charged forward with Erik at her side. They passed Tomlinson's corpse as they rushed through the narrow passage between crates. The far wall grew closer with each step, but they didn't see the outline of anyone. No one fired a gun or threw a grenade at them.

No out-of-control drones dive-bombed them.

Their sprint finally brought them to the wall and a large, open circular vent. It could easily accommodate a fat man if he were insane enough to jump into a tower garbage vent. A guaranteed death awaited a normal person, but a Tin Man might be able to get away with it. Even then, it would depend on a lot of factors going their way.

Jia frowned. "You don't have tracking on anyone else?"

"That's not yet available," Emma replied. "I estimate about sixty seconds."

The detectives scanned the area for enemies but found no one. Erik approached the vent with a curious look and stuck the barrel of his TR-7 in, angled the weapon down, and fired a burst. Dings echoed up from the bowels of the vent.

He grunted. "I didn't think it'd be that easy, but I figured it couldn't hurt. I probably just jacked up the system."

"That's an easy fix for a drone." Jia frowned. "But it had to be someone, right? Even if they threw something, that means someone needed to be there to do it."

Erik nodded. "That makes the most sense."

Jia glared in the direction of the dead cyborgs. "Then the Tin Men were just distractions?"

Erik shook his head. "Nope. I think they were supposed to kill us, and I recognized the voice of one, but they didn't do their homework." He tapped his left arm with his rifle. "If this were normal, that guy would have snapped it in half and been able to finish me off. Then it would have been two on one, and they would have killed you." He stared at the vent, a determined look in his eye. "At least, that's what they thought. That was another mistaken assumption."

"What do you mean?"

"I know what it feels like to lose your arm, and I

know you can still shoot a gun when that happens. There's no way I was going to let them take you down." A jolly smile took over his face. "But it doesn't matter. We need to go get their friend." Erik narrowed his eyes at the vent.

Jia winced but didn't roll her eyes. "Please tell me you're not going to jump in there."

Erik raised his eyebrows. "Why not? I've done stupider things."

"I'm not doubting that, but I'd rather my partner not die. Going in there is suicide. Even if someone did jump in there, they're probably dead. If you want to get away from me, just quit like all my other partners."

Erik grinned and shouldered his TR-7 after flipping on the safety. "Okay. Emma, can you track him in the vent?"

Bright lights flicked on and pushed back the darkness that had been smothering the storage bay.

"I have control of the local systems," Emma explained. "But that's for this area. I'd need complete access to the building's systems to even have a chance of tracking anyone in the vents, and it's likely too late. There aren't internal sensors in most cases. When they have problems beyond the self-repair system's capabilities, they send drones in."

"Fine," Erik replied. "He got away this time, but we've got two dead bodies filled to the brim with complicated systems that you and Digital Forensics can rip into. At least we know Tomlinson won't be harassing Dr. Chen anymore, but that doesn't mean he's safe. I doubt those Tin Men were just a couple of guys he hired."

"That was what my instincts told me." Jia holstered her

weapon and looked over her shoulder. Tomlinson's body looked small in the distance.

Erik glanced that way. "Your instincts were right. I don't know who our two dead buddies are, but this case is obviously about a lot more than one disgruntled security guard."

Jia sighed. "Sometimes I really hate being right."

CHAPTER TWENTY-EIGHT

January 28, Neo Southern California Metroplex, Police Enforcement Zone 122 Station, Digital Forensics Division, Office of Malcolm Constantine

The hot-pink parrot-covered Hawaiian shirt Malcolm wore brightened the room but didn't make up for his deep scowl. It was never a good sign when an evidence tech looked like he was in pain.

Erik eyed him anyway, despite the risk of burning pink parrots into his retinas.

When the tech called them down, he'd hoped for better news. Emma's initial attempts to access the Tin Men's systems hadn't gone well, but maybe Malcolm and his team could approach it from a different angle. Emma, in the end, was a powerful AI, but she relied on certain basic networking protocols to gain access to systems. She couldn't physically crack open a system.

"Just tell us already," Erik suggested. "No point in dragging it out."

Jia nodded from beside him, her arms folded. "Emma

couldn't access their systems. She said there was no signal transmission or receipt going on, and we didn't think it was a great idea to risk exposing her to shady cyborgs."

"Those filthy little trolls probably had a virus or worm ready," muttered Emma. "Even if they're dead, that might still be a risk."

Malcolm sighed. "The good news is there's no risk of that, Detective."

"Really?" Erik clapped once. "Then we can set up a way to connect her, and she can blast right through their defenses. Then we can figure out who these guys work for and save you time."

Malcolm cleared his throat. "We'd still need to do it our way, or at least figure out a method to make it seem like that if you wanted what we found admissible in court, but that's not really a problem. Like I said, that was the good news. The bad news is, there's no danger because the Tin Man's insides are completely fried." Malcolm tapped his PNIU, and an image of a lumpy black pile appeared. "This is an example piece, or what's left of it. This wasn't just them EMPing themselves, Detective. The thing's completely melted. They had a self-destruct system that was designed to obliterate the system, both thermally and using acid. They had reservoirs throughout their bodies."

Jia gagged. "They were walking around with acid inside their bodies?"

Erik laughed. "Technically, every person with a stomach is."

Jia eyed him. "We don't use it to melt our insides when we die," she countered.

Malcolm shrugged and gave them an apologetic look. "I

could show you the rest of the insides, but it's mostly melted and fried sludge. There's nothing we can recover from those systems. Even their brains are a nasty soup." He grimaced. "Let's just say I'm glad I'm Digital Forensics and not the medical examiner. There's not enough left of the cyborg components to pull anything useful. These guys were thorough. They did *not* want us learning anything about them."

"This self-destruct explains why they were twitching like that toward the end." Erik frowned. "Is that something the local Tin Men are into? I haven't seen anything about any syndicates or other gangs requiring that kind of commitment."

Despite the greater instability on the frontier, Tin Men were less common. Very few frontier insurrectionists or terrorist groups used them. The farther someone traveled from the core worlds, the more they risked not having appropriate support for cybernetics. Depending on where they traveled, Purist beliefs might be stronger as well. He'd run into more than a few people who'd decided his cybernetic arm was enough to justify an attack.

Jia shook her head. "I've never heard of a Tin Man with a self-destruct system like this. I mean, who puts in a self-destruct in their own body?" She paused before continuing her rant. "Then again, I've never run into a full conversion before. I wouldn't have thought even an antisocial criminal would go that far, and the maintenance expense would be incredible." Her voice dripped disdain. "I doubt the Tin Men are affiliated with a normal criminal syndicate."

"It gets better." Malcolm offered them a smile. "And by that, I mean it gets way more annoying." He swiped with his hand, and another text window appeared. "Take a look at this."

Erik leaned forward to read the window. "No DNA matches?" He focused on Malcolm through the hologram. "They couldn't find DNA anywhere in their bodies?"

Malcolm shook his head with a solemn look. "The skin on the face was artificial. There wasn't a huge amount of actual, you know, *human* stuff left inside. Even then, and ignoring the liquified brain, the few organs they had left were almost completely destroyed by the self-destruct. They did manage to recover a small viable DNA sample from one of the bodies, but it didn't match *anyone* in a DNA database."

"They could be from off-world," Erik suggested. "If we wait long enough, we'll get a match, maybe from another core planet. We can't wait around forever, though."

"The records from other worlds are polled often enough that if they were in there, we'd know," Jia observed. "It's not as if they can grow a Tin Man assassin in a few days. Besides…" She shook her head. "There's no way anyone's going to sneak two full-conversion Tin Men onto an interstellar transport without being noticed, and while getting a few modifications here and there might not be illegal, those two men were well past that. The resources involved are…" She thought before lifting her hands in frustration. "Staggering."

Erik's expression darkened. "You'd be surprised what people can sneak onto transports and move around the UTC. I wouldn't put it past them, but I see your point."

It wasn't Tin Men who had killed his unit, but the massacre proved that at least one group out there could move significant military forces from planet to planet. The conspiracy wouldn't leave something like traceable DNA behind. That didn't prove the Tin Men belonged to the Molino conspiracy, but the evidence at least proved dangerous people could pull off impressive schemes with enough money and planning.

"And I see yours," Jia commented.

Malcolm sighed. "Sorry I couldn't be of more help, Detectives. I was pretty hyped when I heard there were two full-conversions coming in, but there you go."

"Thanks, Malcolm," Erik offered. "You did your best. Don't worry. We don't know who or what went down that vent, which means this isn't over yet. The guy was spooked enough to run, which means there's an increased chance of him screwing up. When he does, we'll nail him."

Jia gave a firm nod of agreement. "We have plenty of Tomlinson's records to go through. They likely won't lead us anywhere, but it's still a lead. Now that we know that he was the one sending the threats, it lets us focus. This isn't a cold case, and we're far from done with it."

Erik's and Jia's PNIUs chimed with a message from Captain Ragnar.

Come to my office immediately. This is related to the case.

Erik nodded to Malcolm. "If you find out anything else, let us know."

The tech gave him a thumbs-up and smiled weakly. "I'll try, Detective. No matter what you guys bring in..." He eyed his information, having already dismissed them in his mind, "it's never boring."

A dark-suited man and woman stepped out of Captain Ragnar's office as Erik and Jia approached. Their gazes lingered on the detectives for a few seconds before they continued on their way. In comparison to the bland man, the tall woman stood out, both for her beauty and her long, striking cyan hair.

One of the things Erik had noticed in his travels throughout the UTC was the differences in hair-dyeing conventions. As a non-permanent cosmetic change, Purists didn't care about it. On some planets, almost everybody dyed their hair, whereas on others, no one did. Earth was a mixture, just as it had been when he'd left. He wasn't going to dye his hair, even if was still mostly gray despite the de-aging.

The woman had a smug smile on her face, and she winked at him.

Erik frowned but ignored her and entered the captain's office. Something about her bothered him even before the wink.

Captain Ragnar stood behind his chair, his face red and his mouth twitching. The huge man reminded Erik of a bear about to charge. Another bad sign.

Jia's eyebrows lifted, but she didn't say anything.

Erik closed the door behind him. "You looked pissed, Captain, and you almost never looked pissed, let alone *this* pissed."

"You're off the case," Captain Ragnar announced, exasperation in his voice.

"You're kidding me," Erik shot back.

Captain Ragnar's jaw tightened. "I wish I was, Detective Blackwell, but no, you and Detective Lin are off the case."

Jia pointed at the door. "I knew I didn't like them. 46 Helix lawyers? Council lackeys? Are we getting too close to something they don't want us to know about?"

Captain Ragnar took a deep breath and dropped into his chair. He managed a slight smile. "If that was all it was, I would have politely asked them to toss themselves off a tower. I told you when I took this job that I would handle the politics, and I have, and will continue to do so, including fighting the CID if they show up and demand jurisdiction without doing the legwork."

"Those were CID agents?" Erik scoffed. "Yeah, if they wanted the collar, they should have shown up for the part involving all the earlier investigation, shooting, and Tin Men. They don't get to stroll in after the hard part and take all the credit like they did with Esposito." He pointed a thumb at his chest. "I don't care about interagency politics or PR."

"I know, and if it were that simple, I'd be able to do something."

"What is it, then?" Erik asked.

Captain Ragnar nodded at the door. "Those two were from UTC Intelligence. They've shown up with orders from way above either of our paygrades to push you off this case, and they've made it clear that ID agents will be handling this. Apparently, one of them is a regional agent, and the other is some sort of specialist who was sent in from on high. According to them, this case involves a matter of interplanetary UTC security, and we don't have the clearance to handle this sort of thing. It involves an active UTC ID investigation they don't want locals interfering with."

"Intelligence Directorate agents?" Erik gritted his teeth. "We've taken down terrorists. If this is about terrorists, they could use our help. We've got the local knowledge and resources."

"They don't want our help, and they can and have pushed us off the case. It doesn't matter what favors I call in. I can't move something at this level without a good reason." Captain Ragnar shrugged, a playful smile breaking out on his face. "But if you can find other evidence that might give us a reason to think this is more a local threat, there are a few things I can do. That's not much, but it's better than nothing."

Jia nodded. "We'll figure something out. The ID has their own things they care about. They don't care about local crime, but we can't ignore that. For all we know, they'll let Dr. Chen be killed."

"You were righter than you knew, Jia." Erik grinned at her. "Your instincts are on fire this time."

Alina rested in the driver's seat of her flitter as the autodrive flew the vehicle toward her destination. She occupied herself by watching a recording of Erik's and Jia's raid on the storage bay. She stopped the feed several times to bring up different angles and crosscheck other data ripped from the system.

She clapped as Erik and Jia finished off the two Tin Men. "Not too bad," she murmured. "He is a vet, but he's used to having a whole unit with him, and she's just a rookie cop. I don't think half the agents I've worked with could have pulled that off."

A third Tin Man crouched in the back of the bay, distant from the battle. He ran toward the closed garbage vent. A few seconds later, it opened, and he leapt inside.

"Sneaky, sneaky." Alina brought up another data window with a frown. Based on what they'd retrieved, the hacks to the systems were external, and although Blackwell's pet rogue AI had taken over the system eventually, she hadn't completed her efforts when the vent opened. The access logs made that clear.

The agent smiled. That was enough. It was always good when she didn't have to kill someone she liked. She initiated a call and waited.

"Report, Agent Koval," barked her superior over the line.

"Per your orders, the locals have been pulled off the case," she told him. "The captain seemed understanding, but I wouldn't put it past them to keep sniffing around."

"We'll deal with that when it arises. What about Blackwell and Lin?"

"Everything I've read about them suggests they will keep sniffing around as well, even if they've been told not to."

He scoffed. "I don't care about that. Are they associated with the targets or not?"

"There's little evidence they're connected to the organization," Alina replied. "They also took on two advanced battle cyborgs without a scratch. I expected that from

Blackwell, but Lin was equally impressive. She's got a good head on her shoulders for someone so young."

Alina might look close to Jia's age, but that was only because of a particularly effective de-aging treatment.

Her superior let out a satisfied grunt. "Good. If they aren't with *them*, that makes this less complicated."

Alina smiled brightly. "I don't know, sir. Maybe we should make it complicated. Sometimes complicated can be good."

"What are you talking about, Koval?"

Alina paused the video feed and magnified the image of Erik and Jia. "Based on the background information you sent along, we were suspicious of Blackwell because of what happened on Molino, but what about Lin?"

He scoffed. "Lin and Blackwell keep ending up in unusual situations, and Blackwell survived something a lot of other people don't. We don't know what happened on Molino, but even if he's not associated with the targets, it's not impossible he's connected to some of the people we're hunting, and Blackwell was purposefully left alive."

"He was shot, sir." She laughed. "That's not what someone does to their agents."

"Maybe they knew just where to shoot him to make sure he would survive. We've done it ourselves."

Alina wasn't about to say he was paranoid. In their line of work, there was no such thing as too much paranoia. If most people understood the deep, dark tentacles of corruption that stretched throughout the UTC, they wouldn't be able to sleep at night. ID agents worked in the shadows to make sure they didn't need to worry.

"Let's just say I disagree, sir."

Her superior grunted. "Is there a point to this, Agent Koval?"

"I'm just saying they might be useful resources. We should at least consider it. I think they have good instincts and can handle themselves."

"Two cops can't do what a trained ID agent can," he countered.

"I don't know, sir. So far, they seem to. Just something to think about. There are ways we could use them that don't involve them becoming full agents."

"I'll take that under consideration," he grumbled. "For now, keep an eye on the case. If this is who we think this is, more trouble is coming. If you get your pet cops mixed up in this, they might end up dead."

"Yes, sir. I'll report back as necessary."

"Good." He ended the call.

Alina smiled as she looked at Erik and Jia. "He doesn't understand, but I do. Your talents are probably wasted as local cops, but I've been wrong before. Let's see how you handle things going forward. Because I'm guessing that if I get you involved…" She tapped her lips in thought.

"You won't be the ones dying," she finished.

CHAPTER TWENTY-NINE

The rage built inside Jia until she slammed her fist on her desk. "We can't sit around and let them take this from us. I don't care if they *are* from the ID. This is our case." She sighed in frustration. "*Was* our case."

The situation was as bad as when she had first started.

Before, her old captain would tear cases out of her hands against her will without even being asked. She didn't blame Captain Ragnar for not being able to go up against that level of government, but she had put in her time and risked her life, and she didn't like the idea of someone finishing what she had started.

"You heard what the captain said," Erik replied. "We need something else before we go up against ID agents. But I'm with you. This is mighty convenient. That alone is enough to annoy me and stop me from walking away from all this."

"Convenient?" Jia thought she knew what he was getting at, but she wasn't positive.

Erik nodded and pointed at an image floating to his

side. In it, three cyborgs stood near Kevin Tomlinson, talking. After Emma had regained control of the systems, she had been able to access the camera feeds.

The three Tin Men had entered a few minutes before Tomlinson had arrived and had a very short conversation prior to one of them shoving his fist through the security guard's chest. There were no great mysteries solved by the additional conversation. Tomlinson was agitated, and he blamed the Tin Men. The important piece was verification of what they already suspected. The third man had escaped through the vent during the battle.

Jia narrowed her eyes. "The more I think about it, the more I wonder if they knew they might lose. Why would he run, otherwise? All that sophisticated technology and he ran from us."

Erik stopped the video. "Yeah. They might not have known everything about us, but we do have a reputation. It'd be common sense to assume that if we can take down a giant bot, we can take down a cyborg. Let's hope we can pick him up."

They'd flagged the escapee's face for recognition by drones and cameras. If the ID agents complained about it, the 1-2-2 could claim they were planning to send any leads their way. It wasn't as good as working the case officially, but it gave them a chance to be involved. If they just happened to be in the area, the ID couldn't complain.

"I keep going back to the ID showing up," Eric continued, turning to face Jia. "It's not like we just started working this case yesterday, which means there is a good chance those ID agents already knew what was going on. That's assuming that's all that is going on."

Jia's breath caught. "What are you saying? If you're implying what I think you're implying, that's a pretty big deal."

"All I'm saying is, Emma's not easy to beat. She won eventually, but she had to put in a lot more effort than normal."

The AI chimed in. "That's true, and I take it you're remembering what I stated at the storage bay about the capabilities. Government-level resources might explain why I had trouble."

Emma might also be trying to cover up for not achieving total domination. Maybe the secret to self-awareness was a healthy ego.

Jia shook her head, uncomfortable with the direction of the conversation. "You're saying those Tin Men were working for the Intelligence Directorate?"

Depending on one's perspective, illegal modifications might be a small price to pay for the security of the UTC. Jia hoped it wasn't true. Threatening a researcher and goading a man into committing crimes didn't serve galactic security.

Since she had shed her earlier naïveté, she'd need one *hell* of a good explanation to accept that.

Erik closed all his data windows, a thoughtful look on his face. "Don't know. It's possible. Corruption doesn't limit itself to the occasional dirty cop or politician. It could go higher—a lot higher. We know this is about much more than some angry ex-employee. If we walk away now, those spies will bury all this, and we'll never know the truth. We can't even be sure they're burying it for the right reasons."

"Okay, I agree." Jia frowned. "But what do we do? Even

Captain Ragnar said he couldn't do anything. We don't have the resources to go up against the ID."

Erik smiled, then shook his head and laughed. "Are you the same Jia Lin I met last year?"

"Meaning what?" Jia tried to not be insulted and managed to push the thoughts aside. They had more important things to worry about than her feelings.

"You were willing to run off partners and a captain to pursue a much less important case than this one," Erik observed. "And now it sounds like you're ready to give up."

Jia harrumphed, her eyes narrowing at her partner as she jerked her thumb between the two of them. "Technically, we both ran off the last captain." She let out a sigh of relief. Her partner agreed with her, just as he always had, even when they were planning to do something incredibly stupid. "If we try to pursue this, we might end up tangling with ID agents. Are you prepared for that? I'm not saying we're going to fight them, but if we poke our noses into something we shouldn't, it could hurt our careers."

"I'm like you. I'm willing to take on anyone if I think I'm right." Erik shrugged. "They're *spies*, not cops. They're probably not going to care about protecting Dr. Chen, and while the guy might be an ass, that doesn't mean he deserves to die as part of some twisted ID plot." His shoulders stiffened and his expression darkened. "And we both know I didn't become a cop to climb the ladder."

"Emma, can you ensure that no one can see or hear us in here?" Jia asked. While the station didn't monitor every office, they had the capability to do so, and she could tell what Erik was thinking. Freedom to speak would help clarify things.

"If you want," Emma replied. "Do you want it to be obvious or not obvious?"

Erik relaxed and nodded. "Good thinking, Jia. And make it obvious. If anyone asks about it later, that'll verify something we need to know anyway."

"Done," Emma announced. "There was no active recording, but I'm now monitoring the relevant systems, and I've shoved the cameras into a diagnostic cycle that'll take them some time to come out of, even if the sartorially challenged Technician Constantine attempts to fix them."

She appeared and curtsied with a wry smile before disappearing again.

"Thanks," Erik offered before turning back to Jia. "You know why I became a cop, and you know the level of resources needed to pull off the massacre. It's not impossible that some rogue faction in the ID or DD is involved. The way Colonel Adeyemi is acting, he's thinking the same thing, so I don't mind mixing it up with people. If they're corrupt and they come at me, I'll stop them and make them tell me everything they know."

"Most of the evidence you've found points to a corporation," Jia countered, a lack of conviction in her tone. "You really think the government would slaughter its own troops?"

"It's hard to know where the corps stop and the government begins. And I'm not saying for sure that the ID or DD had anything to do with what happened to my unit, but I'm also not going to ignore coincidences or not follow up on potential leads, especially when they involve crimes in Neo SoCal. We know someone doesn't like us sniffing around. This case might have something to do with that."

"It also might not have anything to do with it." Jia looked down. "It would help if we could at least narrow the possibilities, but to do that, we need to get back on the case, even if indirectly. If we just go charging in Obsidian Detective-style, Captain Ragnar might not be able to protect us. If we both end up fired, where does that leave us?"

"I understand," Erik replied. "But we can't run away because we're scared."

"I'm open to ideas. I'm just not used to having to fight the UTC government." Jia ran a hand through her hair. "I've advanced from corrupt councilmen to corrupt intelligence agents. Why do I get the feeling I'll eventually end up having to arrest the Prime Minister?"

Erik let out a low, throaty chuckle. "I'll do whatever I have to if it'll help me avenge the Knights Errant, but let's hope he didn't have anything to do with that. We might be reading too much into this situation. The ID agents might just be helping to track down some terrorists in the end." He swiped across his PNIU, and a small text window popped up. "But I do have an idea. We should pull the same stunt I did to become a detective. That'll give us some maneuvering room."

Curiosity filled Jia. She'd grown more comfortable with bending the rules in service of justice, especially when they'd been contorted for so long for the opposite. Was that a form of corruption?

She would have said yes before, but now she wasn't sure.

"I assume you're not literally talking about the Obsidian Detective Act?" Jia asked.

"Nope, just taking advantage of the letter of the law." Erik pointed to the data window. "We're the assigned primary investigators on this case, but I did not receive a formal jurisdictional transfer request to sign-off. Did you? This isn't an interdepartmental transfer. It shouldn't be that easy."

Jia shook her head. "Almost no one uses those, which is why someone up the chain generally just signs them retroactively. We've done it a bunch of times for transfers to the CID. It'd slow down everything otherwise."

"I know," Erik replied. "Bring up the actual regulation and read it. I'm counting on slowing things down, or at least giving us a plausible excuse to look into this case for a few more days."

Jia summoned the full text of the regulation and read it. Even with an agile and quick mind, she still spent a few minutes examining it in silence, Erik waiting patiently. Her eyes widened when she finished reading, and she reread the whole regulation to make sure she was seeing what she thought she was.

She gasped and looked at Erik. "I've read this before, but I never thought about it much since I wasn't worried about things getting transferred to a UTC-level authority, and I assumed it was basically the same procedure."

"Do you see what I see?" Erik asked.

Jia jabbed a finger at the regulation. "If the immediate transfer of the case beyond another agency in the metroplex would do irreparable damage to the current investigation, jurisdictional transfer can be delayed for up to seventy-two hours while the initial investigators work with their successors to ensure a smooth transition."

"Exactly." Erik stood. "We've just got to convince the captain to back us."

"I've got an idea about that. I need to make a call first." Jia pointed at her PNIU. "We need to make sure we still have a potential victim to worry about."

Fifteen minutes later, Jia and Erik stood in front of Captain Ragnar. They had explained their plan and their formal request to delay the full jurisdictional transfer.

"Dr. Chen says he hasn't been contacted by anyone else about this," Jia explained. "I just called him to confirm. He was told that since the stalker's dead, this is no longer a matter requiring law enforcement's assistance. I didn't tell him ID was involved, and he didn't seem to realize that it wasn't the NSCPD who contacted him. I find that suspicious in and of itself."

"And you don't agree with that danger assessment?" Captain Ragnar asked. He looked more curious than dubious. Jia liked their chances. "It's not exactly like ID ghosts are always upfront about what and who they are, even when they don't have to hide it."

"Those Tin Men put Tomlinson up to it, or at least helped him." Jia tapped one of her holsters. "And they killed him to cover something bigger. That much seems obvious. The ID showing up proves it."

Captain Ragnar nodded slowly. "Knowing you two, I bet you're half-convinced the ID is involved in this as the culprit, but I can't delay a jurisdictional transfer to a directorate-level authority based on mere suspicion."

Erik suggested. "It doesn't sound like you're convinced they are innocent."

"Full-conversion Tin Men targeting a biotech researcher isn't the kind of thing we get a lot of, even in Neo SoCal. I'm not going to say I don't have a few suspicions of my own, but I also don't know if that's enough."

This sort of situation was why Jia wished the captain knew the truth about Erik's past. It would have helped push him over the edge, even if the case didn't end up involving anything more than a corrupt researcher.

"But I've got an idea." Captain Ragnar leaned forward. A small smile grew to a huge grin. "You two want to go up against the Intelligence Directorate?" His gaze switched from one to the other. "You sure? This could go badly for all of us."

"No, we don't want to go against the ID," Jia replied. "We want to take down whoever is responsible for crime in Neo SoCal, and we're not sure the ID cares. They're not even law enforcement."

The captain tapped a finger on his desk before speaking. "Okay. You'll get your seventy-two hours, Detectives. I won't submit the transfer documentation until then, with the reasoning you haven't been fully able to follow up on potential local threats to Dr. Chen. I think the best way to play this is just to go forward and ask for forgiveness once they realize what is going on. Try to keep it low-key while you figure out if there's something there. I'm trusting your instincts that this is worth investigating."

"We're police officers." Jia turned to leave. "Our instincts are the best weapons we have."

CHAPTER THIRTY

February 1, Neo Southern California Metroplex, Restaurant Casa De Azteca Parking Platform

"I could really use a chimichanga. A big one." Erik stretched his arms above his head and shifted his butt in the driver's seat. "It's been a long time since I've had one. A few months."

"You're hungry?" Jia held up a bag. "We have two of the beignets from breakfast. I know you prefer them hot, but it's better than nothing. We don't want to go into the restaurant and spook Chen. If he gets concerned, he might call around, and then the ID agents will show up and put a stop to all this."

She gestured toward the colorful green and yellow façade of the building. They'd gotten lucky that Chen was eating at a place on the edge of the tower, and they'd also gotten lucky that it had a dedicated parking platform. He'd changed the color of the MX 60 to dull gray to make it less noticeable.

Their searches of Tomlinson's PNIU and other records

hadn't turned up anything useful, not even a suspicious influx of money. He'd made several poorly concealed calls to the pet supply company, but it was obvious from the content that the initial contact had been made offline. The lack of money and his earlier ranting pointed to him being a useful idiot for the Tin Men rather than a direct agent, but it didn't do much to shed more light on who the cyborgs were or why they were involved.

All the advanced technology available, including an AI, and they couldn't do the simplest task: identifying potential suspects.

The lack of new evidence left Erik and Jia running out of time and leads until Emma noticed that Dr. Chen was leaving the 46 Helix building for the first time without protection. It was the logical thing to do since they believed he was no longer in danger, but Erik and Jia didn't want to take the risk that someone would assassinate him. If there were any ID agents around, they were doing a good job of hiding from Emma's drones.

Tailing Chen the entire day had proven annoying. He was taking a day off but not helping them by staying home, and they didn't want to risk contacting him yet and have him complain to the ID.

Erik remembered the smirking agent. It was like she thought she'd pulled one over on the police. She needed to learn who she was dealing with. If terrorists, corporations, and even a conspiracy hadn't taken him out, a handful of directorate lackeys wouldn't.

"How is everything going with Mr. Down-to-Earth-Businessman?" he asked, suddenly curious about Jia's boyfriend. She needed someone more worthy of her than a boring drone. It might not have been his business, but he *was* her partner. He needed to look out for her.

"Corbin?" Jia blinked, caught off-guard. "What about him?"

"Do anything with him over the last few days?"

"No. I've been sort of busy with all this." Jia chuckled. "Why? You running through hot baristas after clocking out? Want a new bet?"

"After we finish this case, maybe." Erik reached over to the offered bag, grabbed one of the beignets, and took a bite. Freshly baked was always better, but the sugary sweetness of the pastry satisfied his mouth even hours later.

"Yes, the case." Jia licked her lips and glanced at Erik. "What if we don't find anything? We only have until the end of the day before our little trick runs out."

"I don't know," Erik admitted. "We could always investigate without formal jurisdiction."

Jia looked uncomfortable with the idea.

"It's not illegal, Jia. It might get us chewed out, but even regular people can look into crimes." Erik shrugged. "You've had good instincts about this case from the beginning, and I think you should trust them."

"I don't know. I'll have to think about it. We'd be risking a lot more than just a slap on the wrist."

"Sometimes you can't win unless you take a big chance," Erik countered.

"Dr. Chen appears to be ready to leave," Emma reported. "They are clearing his table, and he's gathering his things."

"That's it?" Jia sounded disappointed.

"What did you expect? It's lunch, not a rendezvous in the Shadow Zone." Erik chuckled. "It's not like we expected an exploding taco or a nuclear enchilada."

"I know. I've been hoping that maybe we were wrong, and now that he thought he wasn't being watched, he would do something." Jia chuckled. "But he's just a scientist at lunch."

Emma laughed. "Perhaps not. There's trouble."

Erik blinked. "Don't tell me a taco just exploded? That'd be a hell of a way to die."

"No exploding Mexican food as of yet, but I did take the liberty of gaining access to an external camera that points from the restaurant exit on the opposite side. The one that leads to the main commerce level. I lost connection to the camera, but not before I spotted a familiar face. It's the man who jumped into the vent. He's wearing a long coat not too dissimilar from your fashion choices, Detective Blackwell, and a hat. I have my doubts about random cyborgs showing up at the same eatery as Dr. Chen, but perhaps you feel it's a move by your Lady."

"Nope." Erik cracked his knuckles. "I assume our boy's here to finish the job. How far how out is he?"

"About two hundred meters. He's moving slowly and deliberately. I think he's trying not to raise any alarm. No one is taking any special notice of him."

"Good. It would have been easy for him to shoot, stab, or blow somebody up as a distraction, then rush the restaurant to finish off Chen." Erik furrowed his brow as he thought through the possibilities. "He must have eyes on Chen's vehicle or a tracker. Something. We need to play this right."

Jia fished out the TR-7 and handed it to Erik. He didn't need any magazines. He had already filled his pockets with conventional magazines and disruptor rounds.

"We can't have a shootout with a Tin Man inside a restaurant," Jia explained. "Even if we're careful, innocent people will get hurt."

Erik slapped a disruptor magazine into the rifle. "Emma, activate the fire alarm but keep the suppression systems from coming on, and lock the door on the opposite side. I want the place cleared out quickly, but we don't want to make it so our guys jump into another vent."

Jia frowned. "If he's got a drone or a camera on Chen's flitter, won't he run when he sees everyone fleeing?"

"He'll probably see it as an opportunity. It'll be chaos, and he'll have a chance to finish off Chen. We just need to make sure we're in the way." Erik threw open the door. "Maybe if we don't kill this guy, we can keep him from self-destructing and get answers."

Jia drew her stun pistol. "I'm dubious this will work, but it's worth a shot."

The doors slid open, and several people hurried out of the restaurant with no particular fear in their eyes. A few laughed. They seemed more amused than anything, but at least they were paying attention to the alarm. Several people eyed the armed police uncertainly.

Jia pulled out her badge and clipped it to her belt. "NSCPD. We were in the neighborhood. It might be an arson thing. Please let us through."

A pale woman nearby licked her lips. "Arson? Are there terrorists?"

"We're not sure about that," she answered.

It wasn't a lie. They didn't know who had employed the Tin Men.

The crowd parted for the two detectives, their smiles gone.

Erik and Jia stepped into the restaurant as the diners and staff continued to leave. People had figured out they couldn't go out the other way and were making their way to the open door.

Dr. Chen was near the back of the crowd. His eyes widened. "Detectives Blackwell and Lin. Why are you here?" He glanced over his shoulder.

Erik looked at the interior door and windows. A dark form was closing, maneuvering through the crowds near the restaurant on the opposite side. "You're in danger, Dr. Chen. We need you to go out and head straight toward the gray MX 60. It'll automatically open when you get near. Get inside and wait for us. Don't go to your vehicle. If you do, you might end with a Tin Man punching through your chest."

Dr. Chen gasped.

"That's true," Jia raised an eyebrow, "but did you really need to put it that way?"

"They told me this was all over," Dr. Chen insisted. "Now I'm being hunted by cyborgs? That doesn't make sense. I don't frequent the kinds of seedy places you'd see such things."

"You were told incorrectly, and it doesn't matter where you go. Tin Men killed Kevin Tomlinson, and they might be involved in your harassment." Erik aimed his rifle at the opposite window. "If you try just flying away, we can't be sure someone won't kill you while we deal with the assassin coming for you."

"I don't understand. Were these people friends of the security guard?"

"Who knows? We doubt they're fans of yours, though." Erik flipped a table on its side and crouched behind it, resting the rifle on top. "This guy's a little more high-quality than Kevin Tomlinson. If he gets near you, it'll be over in seconds."

"Get to the car," Jia barked, taking up a position behind the table. "We'll make sure you're safe. Just do what we say."

Dr. Chen swallowed and jogged toward the door.

"How are we looking on reinforcements, Emma?" Erik asked.

She didn't respond.

"Emma?"

Erik brought up a PNIU status on his smart lenses.

NETWORK INTERFACE INTERFERENCE. ATTEMPTING RECONNECTION...

He scoffed. "Jamming. *Great*. I hope Emma knows to let him in."

Jia kept her attention on the approaching Tin Man. "She's smart. She'll figure it out, but that might mean we don't have backup coming."

"That's fine. If we can beat two of them, we can beat one, even if he's a cocky bastard."

The approaching man hadn't picked up the pace despite their clear presence in the restaurant.

"Can't he see that Chen's running?" Jia mused.

"Unless this is about us as much as Chen."

The long-coated Tin Man appeared in the entry, and three powerful blows sent the translucent door to the floor. He pulled off his coat and hat, revealing his modified body, and tossed them on a chair.

"Detective Blackwell. Detective Lin." His angry face belied his hollow voice. "You've made this more complicated than it needs to be."

"That's kind of my whole life," Erik suggested.

"This doesn't concern you." The Tin Man pointed at Erik. "Withdraw or be killed. You've increased the chances of innocent people dying by interfering with me."

Erik offered him a merry smile. "We're cops protecting a citizen. You'll need to give us a better reason than threats to back off. If you've got something to say, then say it."

"The threat to your life isn't sufficient?" A small spike popped out of the top of his wrist. Even if the man made a fist, the tiny spike wouldn't extend far enough to be used as a weapon. That didn't make him an easy enemy. They'd both seen how strong a full-conversion Tin Man was.

"I'm trying to understand why you are so interested in killing Dr. Chen." Erik narrowed his eyes and moved his finger toward the trigger. The spike was still bugging him. "But we can have that conversation down at the station."

"Consider the life of your partner," the Tin Man suggested. "You might have lived a full life, but has young Detective Lin?"

"Shut your mouth," snapped Jia. "You're under arrest. All Article Seven rights apply. Do you need these explained to you?" She infused the last sentence with weapons-grade sarcasm. "Or you could try to take us both out when we've got our weapons trained on you. You should have added a few mental improvements when you decided to turn yourself into a monster, because right now you're coming off as an arrogant fool."

"I'm not a monster," the Tin Man replied, his voice calm. "I'm a tool. Comfort isn't relevant for tools. The only difference is I'm *aware* I'm a tool, but you two still labor under the delusion that you are not."

"On your knees, and put your hands behind your head," Erik ordered. He doubted a binding tie would hold the suspect, but if they put several on, maybe they'd at least slow him down. "If you make any sudden moves, we will shoot."

The Tin Man sprang toward a nearby counter, vaulting over it and sinking below their line of sight. Erik squeezed off a shot but missed.

"Yeah, that's a sudden move. Fine." Erik sighed.

"We'll do this the hard way."

CHAPTER THIRTY-ONE

The cyborg stayed low as he sprinted along the counter.

Erik didn't fire again. The disruptor rounds wouldn't be effective if they hit something else first, and they didn't penetrate well.

The killer leapt over the bar with his arm pointed toward Erik. Bottles rattled behind him. His new position placed him behind Erik's and Jia's makeshift cover.

A loud pop sounded, and the spike launched from his arm.

Erik dropped, and the projectile whizzed over his head and penetrated the overturned table. He fired twice, the staccato cracks from Jia's stun pistol joined his shots.

The shots hit the Tin Man in his armored chest, causing him to grit his teeth as blue and white sparks played across his chest. He circled the detectives, a wicked grin growing as a new spike slid into position with a *tink*.

Erik's jaw tightened. Neither of them wore a tactical vest, an obvious mistake that was not correctable at the moment.

The Tin Man's immunity to Jia's stun rounds didn't surprise him, but disruptor rounds could take down a flitter. If he'd used disruptor rounds at the storage bay, the fight might have ended a different way.

The Tin Man vaulted over a table as their rounds tried to reach a soft point.

Jia kicked up a chair and dropped her stun pistol. The man fired at the same time, and his spike ripped through the chair, finishing its flight at a different angle. It ended up embedded in the floor several meters away.

Erik fired another burst. The Tin Man landed, shoved a table over as a barricade, and crouched behind it. His hollow, mocking laughter filled the air as he hopped up, swinging his arm over to launch another spike.

Erik whipped his left arm out. "*Shit!*" he hissed as the killer's spike lodged in his arm.

Jia yanked out her pistol in a smooth motion and fired through the table, adding four new holes to his cover, but the Tin Man didn't fall. They knew how to beat their enemy, but that required a clear shot.

"You can't win," the Tin Man called. "And Chen won't escape. I'm going to enjoy killing you."

"Mad about your friends?" Erik called back. "They shouldn't have come after us."

"You don't understand. They were expendable. If you're waiting for help, it won't arrive in time."

"If you're jamming us, that means you're jammed, too," Jia shouted. She kept firing until her pistol ran dry. "You don't know what's happening with him." She slapped in a new magazine.

"I know enough," the Tin Man replied. "But it would be

useful to kill you two now that the opportunity has presented itself."

Erik ducked.

He yanked the spike out of his arm with a grunt, then ejected his magazine and slapped in normal rounds. He'd thought disruptor rounds would be enough if he ran into any more bots or Tin Men, but an investment in armor-piercing ammo might help in future fights, or maybe something a lot bigger. At least when he was a soldier, he'd had the gear he needed for the mission.

Running into heavily armed and armored foes as a detective was becoming irritating.

Jia nodded to the far end of the bar. "We should go to both ends, and have something draw his fire," she whispered. Irritation flashed over her face. "We just need to distract him."

Erik switched his TR-7 to four-barrel mode and reached back, grabbing a bottle of tequila from the bottom shelf. "Booze is always distracting."

Jia chuckled. "Do it."

He hurled it over the bar, and Jia and Erik shot up. The reflection caught the Tin Man's attention and he moved preternaturally fast, launching his spike at the bottle. The impact sent the glass shards spiraling toward the wall. He turned their way, his face contorting in rage as he realized his mistake.

Erik fired a burst into the Tin Man's face.

Jia lined up her shot but didn't fire immediately. The cyborg stumbled back, and Jia sent three quick shots at his head. He jerked back as a round finally pierced an eye. The Tin Man growled, but Erik and Jia maintained their barrage. After several seconds, he collapsed atop a table, twitching before a final violent seizure.

The two cops took a moment to reload. They kept their weapons pointed and moved closer, circling him from either side. His mangled head argued against survival, but Erik kicked him anyway.

His body was inert.

"So much for questioning him," Erik muttered. "Emma, can you hear us now?"

"Yes. Dr. Chen is secure, although I didn't make it clear what was going on," she responded. "I didn't think it was useful to inform him about me. Backup is almost here."

"You beat the jamming?" Erik asked, surprised.

"No. I sent a request when I activated the alarm."

"Everything is fine now." Erik lifted his rifle, settling it on his shoulder. "We took him down, and there's nothing left to salvage."

Jia surveyed the bullet-riddled restaurant, with its overturned tables and chairs. "How do you think the ID is going to react?"

"You know what?" Erik stared at the downed Tin Man. "I don't care what the ID thinks. If they want to work the case, they should show up when the cyborg killers do."

CHAPTER THIRTY-TWO

Feb 2, 2229, Neo Southern California Metroplex, Police Enforcement Zone 122 Station, Office of Captain Alexander Ragnar

Captain Ragnar wasn't smiling as usual, but neither did he look upset.

Jia liked their chances. He had called them in to discuss the case, and she had wondered after the brief discussion the prior day if the ID would put pressure on him. Even if they were operating within the letter of the law, they had ignored the directorate's request for them to stay out of the situation.

The captain had dismissed Erik and Jia after the incident the previous day to get some rest and have Erik's arm checked out.

He'd explained he would have to talk to his superiors about what had happened, but he had argued there was no way the ID could complain when they'd let a Tin Man assassin walk right up to Dr. Chen.

It was as Erik had said. They wanted control without the responsibility.

The captain looked at Erik's arm. "How are you doing?"

Erik rotated his arm and flexed. "It's fine. Just needed some quick repairs this time, but it wasn't anything too bad. That spike would have been a nasty and unwanted addition to my head." He snickered. "It seems like these Tin Men aren't used to dealing with people with cybernetic modifications."

"Ironic," Jia offered. She tried to not look or sound accusatory. "You said you would take care of Chen, Captain? Or has the ID decided he needs to hang around in the open until he gets killed?"

"He's now in CID protective custody," the captain answered. "There were a lot of loud and angry calls back and forth, but everyone involved seems to feel that's a good compromise. The ID is still complaining about classified operations, but they admitted this situation hasn't unfolded as anticipated. 46 Helix is being quieter than I expected."

Jia scoffed. "Because they were idiots who almost got one of their top men killed. They acted like this wasn't a big deal."

"You don't think they're involved? I got the feeling before that you suspected them."

"I did, among other people." Jia shook her head. "But it doesn't make sense. Having a useful tool like Tomlinson kill Chen would make sense. It's a convenient explanation that doesn't point anywhere else. Killing a man with a cyborg assassin in public is bound to raise a lot of attention. If they were involved, it would have made more sense to sabotage his flitter or shoot him at home. Something like that. I'm not saying this doesn't have anything to do with his work, but 46 Helix smells more guilty of security incompetence than conspiracy. Whoever is behind this is getting desperate, but we have no idea why they are so obsessed with killing Dr. Chen."

The captain turned his blue-eyed gaze on Erik. "Is that your take?"

Erik paused long enough to give the impression he was thinking it through. "Yeah. I think they just screwed up, but I care less about 46 Helix than the ID. They don't sniff around random stalking cases, which means they already had a good idea of what was going on."

Jia's tone confirmed she was still spitting mad. "They dangled Chen like bait, Captain. That's bad enough, but they left him to die, too. No agents showed up to take down that Tin Man. If we hadn't been there, he would have been killed. Innocent people could have been killed. I don't care if this is part of some bigger antiterrorist investigation. You don't use people like that."

Captain Ragnar nodded slowly. "That was one of the reasons I wanted you here. I called in some major favors yesterday because I wanted to know what was going on. Someone from the ID has agreed to speak to us, but in doing so, we're all agreeing to keep our mouths shut about what we're going to be told."

"And if we don't?" Jia asked.

"They'll probably find a reason to shove us in a frontier prison." Captain Ragnar smiled as he relayed the threat. "I think it's worth it, especially since it feels like the ID wants to tell us more. I think you're right that they were trying to draw someone out."

"They should have done that earlier," Erik muttered.

"I agree." Captain Ragnar tapped his PNIU. "Come in, please."

The door to the office slid open, and the cyan-haired agent from the other day strolled in. She closed the door behind her and sat on the edge of Captain Ragnar's desk with a bright smile on her face.

"You're not dead, Detectives," the woman observed. "Good for you. I had faith."

Jia rolled her eyes. "Dr. Chen could have been killed or kidnapped because of your incompetence. You yanked this case from us, then left him unguarded, and you probably knew he would be attacked."

The woman folded her arms. "That's the interesting thing. We did yank the case, but you were still involved. Are you sure you want to be tossing around accusations?"

"It was all nice and legal," Erik commented. He glanced at the captain, who nodded back with an easy-going smile on his face. "And it's not like there's a law against cops parking outside Mexican restaurants. We're the ones taking out murderous Tin Men. We're the ones who have been investigating the case. What have you been doing?"

The woman chuckled. "It's hard to argue with that."

"Who are you?" Jia demanded. "Where's your partner?"

"Agent Alina Koval," the woman answered. "The man you saw the other day wasn't my partner. We just had to coordinate on some matters. It's like you cops. We have different areas of interest, and my particular specialty and area of interest concerns the Tin Men you've been running into. I'm the primary now for this situation, but I'll be keeping him informed about what's going on."

Erik narrowed his eyes. "You know who they are?"

Alina nodded, an even bigger smile on her face than Captain Ragnar's. "Yes, I do. That doesn't mean I have all the answers about them, but I believe, given your reputation and tendencies, it might be helpful for you to know more about them, even if this case is effectively over for you. I've even convinced my superiors that you should have this information."

"Wait." Jia pointed at her, the suspicion flaring in her again. "You knew we wouldn't leave Chen alone, didn't you? That was why there was no one guarding him. You dangled him as bait, and outsourced his protection to us."

"The important thing is that Dr. Chen was protected. We also needed to confirm a few things. Our methods allowed us to do that." Alina kept an easy smile on her face. "And I'm not going to apologize for it."

Erik snorted. "You thought we might be dirty. It was a test. You wanted to know if we were working with them."

Alina tapped the side of her head. "You got it in one, Detective. We've been aware of you. It's hard for two cops to get involved as in much trouble as you have without it making a lot of waves, even outside of Neo SoCal."

Erik shrugged. "We do our job. Sometimes that involves shooting people and explosions." He smiled back at her. "Not going to apologize for that."

"You have to admit that your adventures since becoming partners might look odd and suspicious from the outside." She glanced from one to the other. "The two of you have a tendency to run into unusually dangerous situations, and the fact the DD hasn't yanked back your pet AI made us wonder if there was something more going on."

Emma's hologram winked into existence on the opposite side of the desk. She smiled at Alina. "I think you are mistaken, Agent Koval."

Erik gave Alina credit; she didn't flinch when Emma suddenly appeared.

"About what?" the agent asked.

"It's my own choice to stay with Detective Blackwell. The DD can't take me back until I'm ready to *go* back. The uniform boys are less interesting to me, so I've refused to go with them. It's as simple as that."

Jia frowned. "You were gambling with our lives and Dr. Chen's. I can't say I appreciate that, Agent Koval, and I don't care if you thought you were testing us."

Alina's near-permanent smile made Jia want to slap her. "It's not much of a gamble when you know you'll win the bet. If you want me to apologize, I'm sorry. Oh, wait. That's an apology, isn't it?" She laughed and waved a hand. "This goes beyond Neo SoCal, and I wanted to make sure you two were competent and not related to the group behind these Tin Men."

Jia's breath slowed. Anger could wait. The truth about the cyborgs was more important. Given the uncharacteristically stern look on Erik's face, he must have been thinking along the same lines.

"Who are they?" Erik asked. "And why do they want to kill Dr. Chen?"

Alina's smile disappeared for the first time in the conversation. "We don't know why they want to kill Chen, but our information suggests they've been planning it since before Kevin Tomlinson was fired. As for who, they are special assassins for a terrorist faction we have codenamed 'Talos.'"

"'Talos?'" Erik furrowed his brow as he thought. "I've never heard of them."

Jia explained, "Talos is from ancient Greek myths. A bronze automaton. An ancient security bot if you want to think of it that way."

The agent nodded. "A classically educated woman. *Nice.* To be clear, that's not what they call themselves." Alina lowered her arms and rested her hands on the desk, ignoring Captain Ragnar's disapproving looks. "That's our codename for them, given their heavy use of Tin Men and killer bots. We've been tracking them for some time, and we believe they are receiving funding from certain insurrectionist groups, but potentially also corporations. There's a lot of money flowing to Talos, and that's one of the most likely explanations."

Erik grunted. "If a corporation is funding a terrorist group, shouldn't the CID be shutting them down?"

"Yes, but they need evidence." Alina pointed at Erik's left arm. "You've fought these guys a few times. You've seen how modified they are. This isn't just about them not being Purists. The level of tech inside them, including their final internal cleaning trick, is well beyond what some street clinic could pull off, even if it was remotely legal."

"Yeah, that's pretty annoying. Is there any way to stop that? I used disruptor rounds this time, and those didn't work."

Alina shrugged. "We haven't been able to take one alive or dead and preserved yet. The good thing is we don't run into a huge number of those guys. That makes sense. The maintenance on that level of cybernetics means a lot of money is splashing around to keep them ready for murder. It's not just the mods, either." She hopped off the desk. "Talos has a major interest in different types of advanced research in a variety of areas, which means it's not unusual to run into them using cutting-edge prototype-advanced tech."

Erik's jaw tightened. "Such as adaptive optical camouflage that can survive movement? Like, infantry scale?"

Alina stared at him as if she were evaluating them. "Our agents have encountered Talos operatives using that kind of technology in recent months. It's rare, but they have it. That's one of the reasons we're convinced various corporations must be involved, or at least people from some of those corporations. More than a few times, we've found tech that was linked to corporate R&D in the hands of a Talos agent."

"And government labs?" Jia challenged.

She turned toward Jia. "There is some concern there, too," Alina admitted.

Erik's nostrils flared. "I see."

Jia almost asked about Molino, but it was up to Erik to decide when he wanted to bring in Captain Ragnar, so she refrained. "What's their goal? If it's to make money, it seems stupid to spend so much on expensive field agents."

"We're not sure." Alina shrugged. "They've captured scientists and researchers before for their own purposes. They've also assassinated others. The pattern isn't clear."

Jia gestured to Emma. "Did they have anything to do with Emma being stolen from the military?"

The AI sighed. "I would hope that didn't involve a bunch of dreary fleshbags wanting to become machines. It'd be rather pathetic."

Captain Ragnar's eyebrows lifted.

Alina smirked. "Not to our knowledge, but they have targeted AI researchers in the past, so it's not impossible. We doubt they were, though. They don't mind making use of criminals, but they tend to clean up after themselves if by cleaning up, we count brutally killing people who work with them."

"Like Kevin Tomlinson," Jia observed.

"Exactly." Alina stopped and tilted her head as if listening to something, then clucked her tongue. "I've got to go, but I did want you to have that information. It's entirely possible you'll run across them again since you two can't avoid getting in trouble. With Chen under CID protection, you shouldn't have to worry about that particular case for now, but it's also not impossible that Talos might decide that you two are loose ends who are better off dead."

Erik chuckled. "In other words, we're still off the case, but we might get killed because of it."

"No one's telling you that you can't defend yourself, Detective." Alina headed toward the door. "If you have reason to believe a future operation involves Talos, we would appreciate it if you contacted us. We can bring resources to bear that are not normally available."

"Does that go both ways?" Jia asked.

"Potentially," Alina offered. "For now, the CID will handle the Chen matter, and we at the ID will continue to hunt Talos, but I'll just note that no one's going to harass you if you stumble into additional evidence. Thank you for your service to the UTC." She offered them a final nod and exited the room.

Erik and Jia turned toward Captain Ragnar as the door shut behind the agent.

He shrugged. "I don't know if there is much you can do going forward. I'm not going to officially close the case, but I don't want you spending a lot of time on it. Without access to Chen, there's not much you can do."

"Am I the only one who found that whole thing suspicious?" Jia asked. "If they want our help, why take over the case, then basically tell us they don't care if we follow up? And that's after admitting they were risking our lives to see if we were working with Talos?"

"Talos isn't the only one who likes to use pawns," Erik suggested. He cast a baleful glance at the door. "But at least Chen's being guarded by law enforcement now. I've got my issues with the CID, but this is a high-profile case, and they'll protect him. That makes things easier for us."

Captain Ragnar grinned. "The ID sent her because I put pressure on them, and they probably think it's less trouble to give you half the truth than to continue to deny things. The real question is, do you two think Talos will come after you?"

Erik shrugged. "Who knows? We don't always have the best luck." He patted his arm where he'd been shot. "But things haven't been working out well for them either."

"I'm going to keep you on light duty for the next few days, and I want you to be careful." Captain Ragnar chuckled. "I used up a lot of saved favors to get you that small piece of the truth. I'd rather it not be wasted by you getting yourselves killed."

Jia chuckled. "I'd rather not be killed for personal reasons."

"I've got a few things to take care of before I die," Erik declared.

Jia waited until they returned to their office to ask a lingering question as the two split up, going to their respective desks. "If Agent Koval wants us to continue poking around, how would we even do that? The company's not going to cooperate with us now that it's a CID case, and we don't have Chen."

Erik sat down, a dark look on his face. "I'm going to check with the colonel. Maybe he knows something. If they are who I think they are, I'm going to need his help."

CHAPTER THIRTY-THREE

Erik pushed into the abandoned Shadow Zone building.

The tall ceilings and large, open rooms suggested it had been a warehouse in decades past. A small amount of light from the streetlights outside made it inside through holes and windows, but the deep darkness obscured most details, like a shroud marking a dead building.

Erik had contacted Adeyemi to arrange a meeting in the Shadow Zone but had received a message changing the location at the last moment. If Talos was working with a rogue government faction and watching Erik, they might already know he was working with Adeyemi and set up a trap.

It didn't matter what they tried. He didn't care if he had to leave a bloody trail across the entire UTC to avenge every soldier who had died on Molino.

Erik crept toward an open doorway, the light on his PNIU illuminating the area in front of him. Colonel Adeyemi emerged from the darkness with a frown on his face. Several soldiers walked slowly behind him, rifles at the ready.

Was it an assassination? It wasn't impossible, but it didn't make sense. Whatever else the colonel was involved in, his son had died, and he wanted vengeance. He wouldn't sacrifice Erik to save himself.

Erik put his gun away and gestured around the barren room. Rats skittered in the darkness, and water dripped into fetid pools.

"What's with this place?" Erik asked. "And why the last-second change?" He looked past the colonel at his four bodyguards. They hadn't lowered their weapons.

"It doesn't hurt to be careful," the colonel replied. He gestured for his men to lower their guns. "I got some last-minute intel that made me concerned someone might be following me, and we both have too much to lose."

Erik nodded. "Agents from the Intelligence Directorate?"

"Not sure," the colonel admitted. "I have my issues with those ghosts, but overall, I've not had much trouble with them. What I'm curious about is how you got them so stirred up. I don't know everything that's been going on here, but it's obvious the ID has put extra resources into Neo SoCal recently."

Erik shrugged. "Funny. I've fought several full-conversion Tin Men lately. The short version is, I might have bumped into Talos. You know about them?"

"Heard the name." Colonel Adeyemi frowned, considering. "You think they have something to do with Molino? What little I've heard makes it sound like they might be exclusively Earth-based, or at least they've stuck to the core worlds. It'd be strange if they were that far out. I haven't looked at them much because of that."

"I don't know." Erik's gaze drifted from shadow to shadow, seeking out hidden enemies. "A well-funded organization with advanced technology sounds like a good candidate to explain what happened, and that's assuming they are terrorists and not some ID project that got out of hand. The level of tech they're using is pretty re-goddamned-diculous."

"I understand what you're saying." Colonel Adeyemi looked down, his forehead wrinkling. "You want to know something that a lot of people don't know, Erik?"

Erik stopped looking in the shadows and turned to the colonel. "If it gets me closer to revenge, then yeah."

"I don't know about that, but it'll help you understand why that group is more dangerous than you'd think. First, let me ask you a question. Why do you think the military and the ID don't take more advantage of cybernetic modifications? You've got an arm that's helped you out in a lot of ways. Imagine a whole platoon full of powerful cyborgs."

Erik shrugged. "Most people are at least a little Purist. I don't mind my arm, but I wouldn't want to give up my entire body."

"There's always someone willing to go farther. Have you ever heard of Cybernetic Psychosis Syndrome?"

Erik shook his head. "No. What's that?" He glanced at his left arm.

"It's ironic." Colonel Adeyemi snorted. "All the Purist beliefs that have taken over society, including certain laws, yet the powers-that-be want to soft-peddle the real risk because they don't want various truths to come out."

"And what's this real risk? This syndrome?"

"Cyborg super-soldiers have been tried in the past," Colonel Adeyemi explained, his voice tense. "*Multiple* times. There had even been a burst of research after the first contact with the Zitarks. We knew how to kill humans, but aliens? Certain off-limit ideas didn't seem so off-limits once those space raptors showed up. A lot of that stuff only petered out about twenty years ago. The problem always came down to the CPS." He wrinkled his nose in disgust. "As far as I'm concerned, that was just nature telling us we'd gone too far. I don't understand the particulars, but when you replace too many pieces of a person with cybernetics, there are some sort of neurofeedback problems that lead to mental instability. A weapon that turns its user insane is useless. The research was abandoned."

Erik frowned. "Those Talos guys were ruthless, but they didn't seem insane."

"That's what worries me, since I've heard the same thing before. It could mean a couple of things. Talos might have solved the CPS problem, or they just don't care, and they use people until they start losing their minds. If they've solved the issue, even if we ignore the moral implications, this means they've got access to technology more advanced than the military *and* the ID, and it might not just be limited to cyborgs."

"They're tough, but they still die. I don't know if I'm that worried, but it is annoying to fight them."

Colonel Adeyemi looked thoughtful. "All of that makes me think they might be linked to the conspiracy, and about your efforts since returning to Earth."

"What are you thinking?"

The colonel locked eyes with Erik. "I understand why you became a cop, and you've found some leads here, but we've gone months between decent leads. I don't know if you being a cop is the best way to track down the people behind the conspiracy."

Erik didn't look away. He'd wondered the same thing, but he didn't have any other ideas.

He'd gotten lucky in the sense that the conspiracy had thrown a few assassins his way, but other than knowing something was taken from Molino and having a few possible suspects, including the government, Talos, and Ceres Galactic, things had slowed down. That didn't mean he was ready to give up, but he understood Adeyemi's position.

"Being a cop at least gets me investigative resources," he observed. "If being a cop isn't a good way to handle this, what is?"

Colonel Adeyemi took a deep breath, his dark eyes digging into Erik's soul. "I know a big part of you died on Molino with all those men and women. I wouldn't blame you if you wanted to just move on. If being a cop and stopping crime helps you quiet your demons, I'm not going to stop you. I've seen good soldiers destroyed by PTSD, and you've already been through a lot." He sighed. "But if it's not about that, if it's about avenging the Knights Errant, you need to consider moving on. I know a lot of people who could use someone like you, people who owe me favors, and who we both could push a little more directly our way. There are contractors who work with the military and military intelligence."

"And you think I'd do better working for someone like that?" Erik sounded doubtful. "I don't want to get sidetracked by getting dropped onto moons to kill insurrectionists."

"You don't think you're getting sidetracked fighting terrorists and gangsters?"

Erik squared his shoulders. "The path led here, and I'm finding evidence here."

The men stared at each other in tense silence.

Colonel Adeyemi finally looked away with a grunt. "I'm thinking this conspiracy is a lot bigger than Neo SoCal, so we need to start thinking bigger than Neo SoCal. You're not in the military anymore, and this is personal business. It's not like I can order you to do anything, but I want you to keep the possibility in mind. If you're hesitant because of your partner, she's proven competent, and I'm sure I could set her up."

Erik doubted Jia would want to stop being a cop to follow him around the UTC on a conspiracy hunt, but he wasn't sure. Taking down the conspiracy might serve justice more than the occasional arrest in Neo SoCal.

"I'm not saying you're wrong," Erik began, "and things *have* slowed down, but this Talos thing is another example of evidence falling into my lap here. I don't think I'm quite ready to leave. At least, not yet."

"Your choice," Colonel Adeyemi replied. "But what you just said does rest on the assumption that Talos is involved in the conspiracy."

"If they are," Erik wondered aloud, "why haven't they come after me before?"

Colonel Adeyemi followed a roach scuttling across the

floor with his eyes. "They didn't have to before. They had other resources they could throw at you, like terrorists."

"We've gone from a few bots and terrorists to King sentries and full-conversion Tin Men." Erik managed a dark chuckle. "It might help if I had better gear. The TR-7 isn't enough anymore. At the rate things are escalating, they'll probably drop a whole platoon in exoskeletons on me next."

"I'm sure I can work something out," the colonel replied. "Between your vet status and working as a cop, there's a lot you can possess legally, but it won't be something I can do overnight. Good enough?"

Erik grinned. "It'll have to do. I'll try to stay alive until then."

CHAPTER THIRTY-FOUR

February 21, 2229, Neo Southern California Metroplex, Aurum Sphere Ball Stadium

Jia kept close to Erik, his quick steps through the crowd forcing her to take longer strides to stay in his wake.

They were among thousands of people walking through the wide entrance tunnels leading into the stadium. She hadn't been sure about accompanying him to a sphere ball match when he asked, but she felt compelled to join him after thinking about it.

The unresolved tension of the last few weeks had made Erik distant.

She understood why. They both suspected Talos might be related to the conspiracy and the Molino massacre. However, without a new attack or more evidence, there wasn't anything they could do to further investigate the threats against Dr. Chen. Unfortunately, the CID agents running the case were keeping their information completely contained.

To her, the case represented another chance to serve justice, but for Erik, it was personal.

They had moved on to a few other cases, minor matters that didn't require showdowns with Tin Men or giant bots to resolve, but the threats against Dr. Chen refused to leave either of their minds. Agent Koval hadn't shown up again, and Captain Ragnar was reluctant to push.

A mutual outing was a good way to blow off steam and take their minds off...well, just about everything at work.

Erik and Jia emerged from the tunnel into the main arena. A beautiful blue sky hung above them, with only a few clouds. The sun was bright but not overwhelming. Anyone looking at it would be fooled into thinking it was the real thing rather than a projection.

The stadium was actually in the center of a recreation tower near the Hexagon. No fan had seen natural light from inside since it had been built decades prior.

She had read about how such displays were heavily used in colonization domes to assist with psychological stability. Humans were not meant to live in metal shells without seeing the sky or the sun directly.

For all the artificiality of Neo SoCal, most people traveled from building to building in flitters and at least *saw* the sky.

Thousands of stacked seats split by narrow, shallow stairs surrounded the central arena. On first impression, the playing area wasn't that impressive. Until the match was active, it was nothing more than a series of dark cylinders and pyramids—specialty built grav-field emitters. Two large sealed doors lay opposite the middle of the arena.

Erik and Jia made their way down the stairs, guided by arrows overlaid on their smart lenses leading them to their reserved seats. Loud music combined with thousands of overlapping conversations to produce an overwhelming cacophony.

Jia chuckled as she tapped on Erik's shoulder to get his attention. He turned an ear to her, eyebrow raised. "I always did hate hearing!" she told him with a glint in her eye. "I'm so glad you brought me to this place so I can get rid of it."

"That's part of the fun." Erik grinned. "That's why it's important to come to the actual arena." He waved around the stadium. "You can't have the same experience at home, even hooked up to an AR or VR setup. Sports just aren't sports unless you're sharing them with thousands of screaming fans. Yeah, you can't go to every match, but I think you should go at least once a month."

"That sounds painful," Jia replied. "Direct command, audio dampener thirty percent."

The raucous noise quieted, her PNIU's active noise cancellation performing heroically. She sent silent praise to the engineers and scientists whose hard work throughout the decades had led to its development.

"You can't have the full experience if you're cheating." Erik shook his head and looked disappointed.

"I still can't believe you talked me into this." Jia surveyed the stadium. The vast swarm of humanity added different patches of color to the gray and black seats. Green and gold, the colors of the home team—the Neo SoCal Dragons—were common.

"It'll be fun. You remember what fun is, Jia? Yes? No?"

Erik shook his head as she eyed him. "It's that thing you do when you're not *working*," he finished, smiling.

Jia rolled her eyes. "I have fun, Erik! I go dancing with friends. Human friends, not *plants*."

Erik laughed, a hand over his heart. "Ouch, Jia." His smile turned to a look of concern. "You know you could have brought Mr. Down-to-Earth-Businessman, right? I thought I made that clear. I'm sure he would love this."

Jia nodded. "I know, and I asked him, but he had a meeting today. He encouraged me to go and have fun. He also made it clear he's not fond of sports."

"He what?" Erik looked dubious.

Jia didn't want to admit that Corbin had indeed told her to go, but she could only describe his tone as sulky. It hadn't been his most attractive moment. She understood that he might be threatened by her partner, but he was just going to have to deal with it like a man, especially when Erik gave him the opportunity to tag along.

He could have rescheduled his meeting.

The thought hung over her as they arrived at their row. They began making their way across to their seats. Other sphere ball fans allowed them through with little trouble. Everyone's faces were lit up with excitement, their chatter describing the great season the Dragons were having.

Jia was struck by the diversity of the fans. She wasn't sure what she had been expecting—probably a lot of large, square-jawed men like Erik—but the fans differed in every way possible. Small. Big. Young. Old. Different races. Men, women, and everything in between. Some were dressed in suits and nice dresses.

Some had their faces painted green and gold to support the local team.

According to Erik, Neo SoCal's sheer size was considered a large advantage in terms of fielding teams, but that was balanced out by the fact they had four different sphere ball teams in the area, including the Dragons. The Dragons were Erik's favorite team, but to Jia's relief, he had eschewed painting his face, settling instead for a Dragon jersey.

Erik and Jia took their seats. She adjusted her position, shocked to find the chair unexpectedly comfortable.

He pointed to his PNIU. "Did you already interface with the local network? If you want anything to eat or drink, just order, and a drone will deliver it."

Jia frowned. "Isn't it distracting having a bunch of drones flying around?"

Erik shook his head. "They're all ground-based." He pointed at his feet. "See how there's a decent amount of space even between my big feet and the next seat? They did all this research and figured it out. Enough to maximize space, yet still allow the snack drones through."

Jia didn't know whether to be impressed by the careful planning or disturbed that the height of man's knowledge and technology had been leveraged for the efficient delivery of snacks to sports fans.

She decided to go with the former. "I had a big lunch," she offered. "But I'll keep it in mind."

"Sure, but what's sphere ball without a beer and shrimp crackers? You need to have traditional snacks."

Erik's bright smile reminded Jia of a child getting presents, and she almost laughed. Most of the time when he smiled, there was a small portion that felt forced, as if he were smiling so as to not let the darkness take him completely. Now his joy was pure and infectious.

Jia returned his smile. "Traditional snacks? You didn't even *like* sphere ball until recently, and now you're concerned about its traditions?"

"Hey, when you get to my age, you learn to appreciate new things quickly." Erik shrugged. "Don't make the rookie mistake of going for all the AR overlays during the game. The uniforms are bright enough that you can see what's going on, and if you let the computers highlight everything, you might as well be at home."

Jia waited for Emma to snark, but the AI remained silent.

She wasn't sure if that meant Emma was trying to give them some time together, or if she wasn't interested in complaining about fleshbag recreational activities. Emma might even be taking the time to run sensor analyses on all the nearby vehicles.

She could seem so human at times, but in the end, she was a machine, mostly interested in improving her abilities and knowledge.

"Okay, I'll watch the *traditional* way." Jia offered him a grin.

Erik gave her a thumbs-up. "Just trying to maximize your enjoyment, partner."

"Ladies and gentlemen," began the announcer, his deep voice transmitted directly to each fan's ear through their PNIU. "Please welcome your players from the Neo Southern California *DRAGONS*!"

The crowd erupted in a roar that vibrated all the way into Jia's bones.

A faint, translucent white sphere materialized in the arena, over a hundred meters in diameter and fifty meters in height. Two glowing red squares appeared on opposite sides. A small panel opened in the floor, and a bright yellow ball covered with hexagonal patches floated to the sphere's center.

The large doors on both sides of the arena slid open with echoing rumbles. The green and gold Dragons rushed out. Between their protective gear and the bulky thruster boots and gauntlets, they reminded Jia of Tin Men.

"Dragons! Dragons! Dragons!" the crowd chanted.

Even Erik was in on it. *"Dragons!"*

The players raised their arms in greeting to their fans. They spread out in an arc a few meters outside the bottom of the sphere.

"And now, their competition, the Vancouver *SHARKS*!" the announcer bellowed.

The cheering was noticeably subdued, but there wasn't much in the way of booing as the other team emerged and spread out around the opposite side of the sphere.

"Before we begin this match of the Neo SoCal Dragons versus the Vancouver Sharks, please rise for the national anthems of the United States of America and Canada. Please do not sit until we finish with the anthem of the United Terran Confederation."

Jia and Erik took their seats after the anthems finished playing.

"Shouldn't you like Detroit?" Jia asked.

Erik shook his head. "I might have been born there, but I haven't lived there since before you were born. I asked my brother the other day, and he's a Detroit fan. It gives me a reason to mess with him. They've had some trouble the last few seasons, but it's hard for most North American teams outside of Neo SoCal to do well. The teams here tend to snap up the best players from the whole continent."

The players moved forward in lockstep, stomping their feet and clapping their hands. The crowd joined them, including Erik. Jia hesitated before throwing in the towel and adding her own noise to the mix.

Each team alternated a player jumping into the sphere.

Quick bursts from their thrusters spread them out along half the sphere on their side.

Thirty seconds later, the clapping ended, and all fourteen players floated in the sphere, with goalies near the red goal squares. The ball hovered in the center.

Two players, the forwards, hovered a few meters away from it. They added reinforcements on their flanks, the offensive wings.

A loud buzzer sounded.

The forwards launched themselves toward the ball. The Dragons' wings zoomed into the Sharks' territory, moving to the sides.

Their forward whipped an arm out and activated his thruster to initiate a spin. He met the ball with his elbow and launched it toward one of the wings. The other forward smashed his shoulder into the Dragons' player.

Both men tumbling after the collision until they righted themselves with their thrusters.

The crowd cheered and clapped.

Jia was impressed by the players' fine control. Their thrusters were operated through finger and toe interfaces. It took a tremendous amount of training to be able to move their limbs while simultaneously activating their thrusters as needed.

From what Erik had explained, direct ball contact with any part of the body was allowed, but the players weren't allowed to grip the ball, except for the goalie.

Although *intentional* collisions between players weren't allowed, there was a lot of subjective room for determining what constituted "intentional."

For the most part, any collision that occurred when heading in the rough direction of the ball was considered legal, with the exception of collisions with the goalie, which always earned a penalty card.

The Dragons' player receiving the ball twisted his body, his thrusters active on one side for a spinning kick. He slammed his foot into the ball and launched it toward the edge of the opposing team's goal. His aggression earned a roar of approval from the crowd, but his distance from the goal doomed his attempts. The Sharks' center blocked the ball with his chest before launching it to his forward with a vertical spinning kick.

"What's the defensive wing *doing*?" screamed Jia, pumping her fist. "He's letting the forward head straight toward the goal!" She pointed at the sphere with an angry finger as she eyed Erik. "Does he need cybernetic implants in his eyes?"

The Dragons were down by one goal, with only a bit more than a period to go.

Erik took a sip of his beer. "Getting into it, are we?"

Jia sank back in her chair, her cheeks heating. "They have positions for a reason." She huffed. "He should be doing his job. He's making the center and the forward work too hard."

The Sharks' forward punched the ball toward the goal right before a defensive wing slammed into him and sent him hurtling toward the wall of the sphere. He bounced off it before he regained control.

The goalie snatched the ball, pivoted, and tossed it toward one of his wings. The other player's spin kick got it to the center in seconds. That man kicked it to an offensive wing.

Momentum favored the Dragons. Their forward was already on the other side of the sphere and ready. The wing passed it to him with a kick, and a rotating punch launched the ball toward the edge of the goal.

The crowd's roar swallowed the noise of the goal buzzer.

"GOAL!" the announcer shouted. "Dragons three, Sharks three. *IT'S ALL TIED UP*!"

Jia stabbed the air like she was taking out a serial killer with his own blade. "*That's* what I'm saying! That's how a good team does things. I can see why you like this game. The rules are simple, but the tactics are complex. It's like playing *weiqi*, which you may know as Go, but in zero-G and with more collisions. And a ball. And you don't play on a board with black and white stones. Okay, it's not like *weiqi* at all, but it's still incredibly interesting."

"To me, it's like a battle where no one has to die," Erik countered. "I appreciate the athleticism and tactics, and there's a discrete objective. I think when I was in the Army, I was too busy worrying about real battles, and sphere ball's not as popular away from the core worlds. The tech is too expensive, and you don't get many colonies outside the core participating in the UTC Cup."

"That makes—" Jia shot to her feet and cheered as a quick strike by the Dragons earned them another goal.

"*DRAGONS, DRAGONS, DRAGONS!*" roared the crowd.

Erik and Jia slowly wandered through the chattering mass of people back toward the parking garage. Jia munched on shrimp crackers. She'd purchased a bag during the match but had ended up being swept away by the game and forgetting to eat. Now a little peckish, she was happy to have the snack

She swallowed her cracker. "I could really get into this."

"You going to go all Lin-obsessive over it?" Erik asked.

She turned on him. "I *don't* go 'Lin-obsessive,' whatever *that* means." She rolled her eyes, but tried to keep it playful. She didn't want to ruin the relaxed rapport. Neither of them had been this calm in weeks.

"I'm just saying you're thorough."

They stopped. A smiling woman blocked their path. They both waited for a few seconds, but she didn't move.

"Can we help you?" Jia asked, trying to keep any suspicion out of her voice.

The woman clasped her hands together, her smile growing even wider. "I'm a big fan, Detective Lin. I've read all about you."

"Oh." Jia chuckled. "I'm only Jia here, another Dragons' fan."

The woman giggled. "I hope you don't hate me. I'm actually a Sharks' fan."

Jia smiled. "I think there's room enough for the both of us in Neo SoCal."

The woman turned to Erik. "And who is this?"

Jia's eyebrows lifted in surprise. She wasn't used to people recognizing her and not Erik. She didn't think it was possible, but people focused on different things.

Erik's huge grin pointed to him enjoying the one-sided fame.

"My partner," Jia explained. "He's my partner."

"Oh?" The woman looked disappointed. Her head turned between the two of them, and her eyes flicked to Jia's ring finger. "Not married, then? You should tie this one down before he gets away."

Erik could no longer hold it in. He burst out laughing.

"Uh, it's…" Jia sputtered. It should have been an easy response, but for some reason, she didn't want to clarify the relationship in front of him. "I'll keep that in mind. Thanks, though. We have to get going."

The woman nodded. "It was nice to meet you, Detective. I hope you keep fighting the good fight, but I hope your team doesn't." She waved and joined the rest of the exiting crowd.

Jia shook a finger at Erik. "Not one word."

He grinned. "Oh, come on, honey, don't be like that."

"That's eight words." Jia scoffed, but a smile quickly took over her face. She wanted it to be only playful.

But she couldn't deny the warmth inside.

CHAPTER THIRTY-FIVE

Erik leaned against the breakroom counter and took a bite of his beignet as he watched Jia. She was doing a passable job of pantomiming some of the more spectacular plays from the match as she discussed it with Halil.

The other detective shook his head, looking disappointed. "You know, I was totally going to at least watch that match at home," he replied in his rich, deep bass. "I missed out. The Sharks usually don't play that well against the Dragons."

"You did miss out," Jia insisted. "It was exhilarating. I've put together a statistical analysis of the Dragons' starting line, and I'm surprised by some of their choices."

Halil laughed. "Oh, you're one of *those* fans."

Jia huffed. "Nothing wrong with applying math to sports."

"Not saying there is, Jia. Just remember to have fun, too."

They descended into a quick debate concerning the merits of intellectual enjoyment of sports.

Erik swallowed another bite of his pastry. He didn't want to admit he was surprised, both that Jia had taken him up on the offer and that she'd enjoyed it so much. Players smashing into each other over a ball seemed like something she would consider uncivilized. It was good to have more in common with his partner.

He paused mid-chew as he thought about that. There was something else there. He didn't just want to have more in common with a partner. He wanted to have more in common with *Jia*. That desire could be trouble in a lot of ways.

A harsh, familiar voice snapped him out of his reflection.

Jared Thompson stood in the breakroom doorway. "Of course, Lin doesn't know how to appreciate sphere ball. And of course, she thinks she knows better than people who have been fans for years."

Erik pushed off from the counter but froze as Jia shook her head at him. He nodded back. She needed to know he always had her back, but she also needed to defend herself.

Jia scoffed. "I didn't say anything like that, Detective Thompson."

Halil frowned. "We were just having a good time."

"Talking sphere ball with someone who probably didn't even know the rules until a few days ago?" Jared sneered. "How is that even possible?"

"You don't have to be like that, Jared," Halil told him.

Jared glared at the other man. "Sometimes I feel like I'm one of the few sane people left in the 1-2-2. Has everyone forgotten who she is?"

Erik grunted.

Jia rolled her eyes. "*You're* the sane one? Could have fooled me."

Jared's gaze flicked between Jia and Erik. "I know I'm just a normal detective. I'm not the Obsidian Detective or Lady Justice, but that doesn't mean I'm a bad cop."

"Not having a media-given nickname doesn't make you a bad cop," Jia commented. "And being annoyed when other cops are just doing their jobs doesn't make you a bad cop, but it does make you a whiner."

He stomped toward her. Halil stepped in front of him. Erik didn't move. Jia could kick Jared's ass with ease.

Jared scoffed. "What, you're a fanboy now, *Detective* Mustafa? You think hanging around the corp princess and the soldier boy is going to make you better?"

Halil replied with a feral grin, "No, I don't think anything like that, and I'm not the one walking around like someone shoved a stick up my ass. If you don't want people questioning you, don't give them a reason."

Jared licked his lips. "Oh, is that how it's going to be? I thought you and me had an understanding. I thought you were one of *us*, not one of them."

"I'm a cop," Halil insisted. "Always have been, will be until the day I die. That means I'm going to have the backs of cops, and I'm not going to tear down other cops, which is why this crap of yours is annoying me. She didn't come at you, Jared. You went at her. I don't want to have a problem with you, but if you have a problem with Jia, or you have a problem with Erik, then you have a problem with me? Understood?"

Jared backed away, red-faced. "You don't even care about Captain Monahan? You don't care about Ryan or

Sharon?" He pointed at Jia. "She ran them out of here. Those were good cops who served for a lot longer than she has."

"You know the measure of a real man, Jared? It's his ability to admit he made a mistake. I've been where you are, and I admitted I was wrong." Halil shook his head. "I felt the hate, and I had to look in the mirror and ask myself why I was so pissed off. A man can't justify his weakness by trying to take down someone who doesn't have it. That's just pathetic."

"Screw you," Jared hissed. "You're only on their side because they're famous."

"I'm on the side of anyone who wants to make Neo SoCal better." Halil stared at him. "Can you honestly say we were making things better, the way we were doing things before? That Monahan was making things better?"

Jared ground his teeth and clenched his fists. Jia tried to step forward but stopped at Erik's headshake. Halil knew what he was doing and what it meant. Interfering now would undermine him.

"They're going to screw up someday," Jared muttered through clenched teeth. "Then you'll look like an idiot."

"I'm willing to take that chance. You need to figure out if you're more interested in being a cop or kissing the ass of a man who doesn't work here anymore."

Jared pivoted on his heel and stormed out of the break-room, muttering a series of creative profanities under his breath.

Jia turned to him. "Thanks, Halil," she offered. "You didn't need to do that. I can handle Thompson fine."

"I'm sure you can." He shrugged. "But that doesn't mean

I don't have some things to make up for. I should get back to my reports. We can chat about the next game. Erik, Jia." With a final nod, he strode out of the room.

Jia chuckled. "Is it awful that my first instinct was to throat-punch Thompson?"

Erik took another bite of his beignet. "Better than wanting to shoot him."

CHAPTER THIRTY-SIX

Jia belly-crawled through the muddy stream, her head and rifle barely above the water. "Alpha, report."

"No enemy sighted," replied the sniper.

In all the times she had trained with Erik, they had always been partners. For the first time, she was going up against him.

Emma had fashioned three AI squadmates for each of them. Erik's military experience might give him an advantage in commanding trained soldiers, but Jia doubted Emma's virtual dolls would be as effective as real soldiers under his orders. That didn't presuppose they would do any better working for her.

Thus far, she was pointedly unimpressed by their ability to understand natural language.

Jia had to beat Erik. Everything in her told her she did. She needed to prove something both to him and herself. The feeling had only grown in intensity in recent months.

"Beta and Gamma, stay on both sides, and keep low."

"Roger," the two riflemen replied. Their camouflaged

uniforms and painted faces blended with the mud and moss covering the area.

Her sniper had spotted movement in this direction ten minutes prior, and they'd slowly closed on the area without any noise or tracks. Doubts piled up. Erik was a career soldier.

Would he really make the mistake of getting spotted?

At the same time, he wasn't working with trained Special Forces operators, and Emma wasn't running the reinforcements. She'd preprogrammed them with a limited range of responses. Erik might have slipped into the reflexive patterns he was used to from the Army and confused the programming.

Jia had accepted their limitations.

"I wish Emma didn't spend so much time forcing me to crawl through dirt, mud, and piles of dead bugs," Jia muttered. "I swear she enjoys it."

The AI didn't respond, but her simulations did.

"You can say that again, Sergeant."

That was their stock response for any command they didn't understand, likely another joke on Emma's part.

"I've got eyes on four tangos, Sergeant," the sniper reported. "Coming in from eleven o'clock, about two hundred meters out."

Jia grinned. "Let's set up to finish them off. We need to get to the trees. Don't splash. Aim in the indicated direction, and fire only after I've taken a shot." She wanted to get the entire squad. Picking off a single squad member but giving up their position might hand the advantage back to Erik.

"Roger," the squad members replied.

She stood and waded through the water toward a dense copse of trees a few meters away from the bank of the stream. Her squadmates followed her.

It took an agonizing half-minute before they were in position.

Her heart pounded as she pointed her gun, waiting for Erik and his squad to arrive. She might not win against him in a straightforward battle, but an ambush equalized everything. The seconds ticked by. She took shallow breaths and tried to keep her heart under control.

The crack of a branch betrayed the incoming squad.

"I've got you," she whispered. She held her breath and waited for a target to emerge. If she was lucky, it'd be Erik. Eliminating him right away all but guaranteed her the win.

The shadow of a thin male soldier holding a rifle appeared. Jia pointed her gun and waited. One soldier wasn't enough. She needed the rest of the squad.

She needed Erik.

The soldier moved forward, sweeping the area with his rifle, a frown on his face. She could barely make out the outline of three other men.

His squad would have the same composition, three riflemen and a sniper. She aimed toward one of the men in the back and pulled the trigger. The initial crack of her rifle echoed as the other riflemen opened up with their weapons. The huge boom of the sniper rifle followed. The members of the squad jerked several times before collapsing.

"Let's confirm the kills," Jia ordered. "Stick to the trees. Their sniper is still out there, but if we're careful, we can pick him off easily enough. Now that we've downed their sergeant, we've got this."

"Roger."

Jia ran from tree to tree, trying to reinforce the point-to-point movement Erik had drilled into her head in previous training sessions. Her squad followed, and if their movements were less precise, it didn't matter much.

The enemy sniper wouldn't have a decent line of sight in the forest.

She closed on the first body, one of the riflemen. Her advance brought her to the other two downed soldiers.

"So, what do you have to say..." Jia's eyes widened. Erik wasn't there. "Their sergeant is still active. Everyone, take cover and sweep the area." She jumped behind a tree and hissed.

Jia had not anticipated that Erik would sacrifice his squad. In a real battle, he would never do anything like that, but these weren't real soldiers.

She was getting a lesson on underestimating her opponent.

"Alpha, do you have eyes on their squad leader?" she whispered. The sniper's earlier warning had only noted she'd spotted the enemy. Jia hadn't thought to ask specifically what she had seen. She waited for several seconds. "Alpha, do you copy?"

There was no response.

Jia's stomach clenched. Even without Emma helping him, Erik had decades of experience and instinct. He could track down a sniper, given enough shots. The only thing Jia didn't understand is why he would go after her sniper instead of finishing off the squad.

Jia gasped. She spun around the tree and leapt for the downed sniper. She dropped her assault rifle and snatched up Alpha's sniper rifle, then flattened her back against the tree. "Make sure you're on the north side of the trees and prepare to return fire!"

A sniper rifle sounded in the distance, and her first soldier went down. Headshot. She dropped to the ground. The next round took out her second soldier. Her final survivor's feeble attempt to spray bullets ended with him taking a chest round.

"Erik, you tricky little *snake*," Jia muttered. She took a few deep breaths. Maybe if she'd warned her squad as soon as she'd realized what was happening, they might have survived, but she'd learned from Erik.

They weren't real people. They were disposable tools, and she'd used them to confirm Erik's location.

She knew where he was likely set up. There was no reason for him to kill her sniper and take a less advantageous position. If she could line up a shot in time, she could win.

A round ripped through the tree a foot above her head, showering dust and wood chips in her hair.

"One point for ducking," Jia muttered. She rotated slowly and dropped to her knees. Waiting Erik out was waiting to die.

She had one chance.

Jia set up the tripod on the rifle that was still safe behind the tree. Controlling her breathing, she waited for him to take another shot. The seconds ticked by, her heart thundering. No shot came.

"Come on," she whispered. "Take the shot so I have my

opening." Her plea didn't accomplish anything.

She'd need to force his hand.

She snatched up a nearby rock, counted to five, and tossed it to her left. Jia shoved the rifle to the side and peered through the scope, trying to line up her sights. The other rifle came into view, along with a woman's body.

Jia took the shot. The body jerked, and she hissed in irritation as she recognized Alpha. All she'd done was shot her already dead sniper. Had she made a mistake? Had Erik never been there?

No, that couldn't be the case. She might not be a weapons expert, but she could tell the difference between the sniper rifle and the assault rifles used in the simulation. He'd taken the shots, and now he wasn't there. That meant he was on his way.

Jia released the sniper rifle and listened carefully for a few seconds before rolling toward a nearby dead soldier and grabbing his weapon. She hopped to her feet and knelt behind another tree trunk, listening carefully.

Alpha had been positioned about three hundred meters away.

Erik couldn't barrel through the forest without all but screaming his position, but she couldn't counter him without knowing what side he was coming from.

I'm going to lose, Jia thought. Her advantage had evaporated. It made sense that a former Special Forces operative would outperform her, despite all the training he'd been giving her.

Jia licked her lips. She had one last idea. Her hand drifted to her belt and grabbed the small plasma grenade clipped there. She primed the weapon, and still holding it with her left hand, slipped it into her pocket.

A light breeze blew a few strands of her dark hair in front of her eyes. She almost burst out laughing as a musky scent filled her nostrils. She had never anticipated smelling him first. That was another lesson.

Always stay downwind.

Jia jerked to the side. A rifle killed the silence and a bullet whizzed by her head, missing by centimeters. She tossed her gun to the ground to feign being disabled and pulled the grenade out of her pocket. He would have to come to verify the kill.

She heard Erik's familiar chuckle, followed by a grunt of exertion. Jia hissed and leapt from the tree. A plasma grenade tumbled right toward her. Her partner stood in the distance, not even bothering to open fire despite his rifle being pointed right at her. She flung her own grenade.

A bright explosion blinded her, and a moment later, the rugged and uneven forest floor gave way to the smooth tac room floor.

Erik watched her with a satisfied look. "Good instincts. If you're going to die, at least take the bastard with you when you go."

CHAPTER THIRTY-SEVEN

Erik had noticed an important thing since returning to Earth.

He had become bound by specific habits. It might have been an attempt to recover some of the structure of his military life. Ironically, it wasn't that his Army life had been predictable. Since he had been sent to new places so often, the idea of having a favorite haunt seemed pointless.

Neo SoCal had a larger population than most colonies in the UTC. He could go to a different bar or restaurant for every meal for the rest of his life and never have to return to the same place.

That made tonight's adventure to a bar far away from either his home or the station all the more notable.

His head swam with a light buzz. He wanted to be somewhere no one knew him, and he'd even gone to the trouble of transferring money to a tab and then going back to his car to drop off his PNIU. Trusting Emma to respect his privacy and being sure about it were two different things, and there were some secrets she didn't need to know.

Erik leaned over the bar, staring into his latest drink. He didn't even know what it was. He'd asked to be surprised and hadn't paid attention when the drink was set in front of him.

"The problem," he explained, "is that I want someone I shouldn't want. She's younger than me by a lot. I thought there was nothing there, and then I realized there *is* something there, but I'm not going to go somewhere I'm not wanted. I thought it was just attraction, but there's something more there. A lot more. We've been doing other stuff together lately, like hanging out. You know, just having a good time. They're not dates, just a good time."

A light buzz didn't kill his tactical instincts. He turned on his stool, sensing someone behind him. There was no Tin Man or gangster assassin there, just a voluptuous redhead in a semi-sheer dress that some might classify as lingerie.

"Hey," she purred. "I see you're alone." She looked at his hands.

Erik shrugged. "Sometimes a man wants to drink alone."

The redhead placed a hand on his knee and leaned forward to give him a better view of her assets. "A man like you shouldn't be alone. You're just my type, big and strong, and we could have a good time together."

He could take her home. It didn't have to mean anything. Sometimes a man just needed to scratch an itch. She was offering. What reason did he have to refuse?

He could think of one—the very reason he was there.

Erik sighed and shook his head. "It's been a long day, and a nice girl like you needs someone who is going to be fun. I'll bring your night down. Maybe a different time?"

The girl stuck out her bottom lip. "If you say so." She sashayed off, looking disappointed but not annoyed.

Erik turned back around. "Like I was saying, the woman I've finally willing to admit I'm interested in is younger..."

Jia tried not to frown. Corbin had barely touched his duck. She hadn't learned the recipe for him, but he could at least appreciate it. Given how thin the man was, he could use some protein. He had a handsome face, but he needed more muscle.

Like Erik.

She tried not to wince at the thought. The last thing she should be thinking about was another man while she was on a date with her boyfriend, especially one in which she provided him a homecooked meal.

"Did you see the news about Diogenes' Hope?" Corbin asked, dangling his fork.

"Diogenes' Hope?" Jia blinked. Maybe the wine had gone to her head. It took her a second to remember where that was. It was in the Trappist-1 system, about thirty-nine light-years from Earth. "What? Did they find Navigator artifacts or something there?"

Corbin sighed. "If only. A rebellion's broken out there. Insurrectionists overran a military base. They've already seized control of most of the colony, and they're claiming they're seceding from the UTC."

"There's always someone out there stirring up trouble. I wish they could be reasonable, but the frontier's a different place. Not worse, mind you—my job reminds me of that every day—but different."

"They are, at that." Corbin set down his fork. "I've never been beyond Alpha Centauri. I don't think you're missing much by not traveling the UTC. Why go anywhere else when the cream of humanity is on Earth? The colonies are pale imitations of our home planet. Too many antisocials have been transported there, too."

"That's one way to look at it," she mumbled. It was the way she had looked it not all that long ago.

Jia's mind wandered to an imagined Erik in an exoskeleton leading a platoon to take a rebel stronghold. He was already an incredible combatant without military-grade weapons except for the TR-7, so she could only imagine what he could accomplish with proper equipment. The more time she spent around him, the more surprised she was that his unit had been wiped out.

She tried to shove that train of thought from her mind.

Corbin had brought up the insurrection. It was natural her mind would go to a man who had spent most of his life in the military.

Jia blinked. Corbin had been saying something new, but she hadn't been listening. She tried to focus.

"That's interesting," she offered. That would work for most things, unless he had asked a question. She held her breath, waiting for his response.

"That's what I think." Corbin smiled softly. "Penjing is

fascinating, and Master Lao's arrangements are inspiring. I want to hire him to decorate my office, but I worry that he'll be insulted if I approach him like he's a mere artist for hire."

Penjing. That was just cruel. If the universe didn't want Jia to think of Erik, why were they going from insurrectionists to penjing in the same conversation?

"I'm sure he'll understand you respect his work," Jia managed. She swallowed. Her heart was pounding so hard she was half-convinced Corbin would hear it. "Maybe you'll get lucky, and he'll want to do it for free."

"Oh." Corbin chuckled, a hint of embarrassment flavoring the sound. "I forgot to ask you how your sphere ball game went the other day. You said it was your first."

Was the Lady messing with her, or was the universe trying to tell her something?

"It was fun." Jia shrugged. "I didn't mention it to you because you told me you weren't interested in sports. I didn't want to bore you."

"It's not as if I look down on sports, mind you," Corbin explained. "It's just I have other things to occupy my time. I do find sports less interesting than other activities, but it's not as if I'm trying to force you to choose only hobbies I enjoy."

Jia had been trying her best not to talk about Erik. It wasn't her fault that the conversation kept bringing him up. Perhaps dating was futile in her current job. She was close to an impressive man for most of her day, and they'd had been spending more and more time together, both training and relaxing.

It didn't help that they'd been through several life-or-death incidents, and it was impossible for a normal guy to establish the same connection without those kinds of shared experiences.

What was she supposed to do? Take on a terrorist group with Corbin?

She had been kidding herself. Her sister and mother had been deluding themselves. Jia doubted she could sustain a normal relationship at this point in her life. Not only was she working full-time as a detective in a corrupt area, but she was also helping Erik with an even more dangerous conspiracy.

That spelled death for romance.

There was one possibility. If she dated Erik, he would understand her job and her concerns. Hunting the conspiracy was his mission.

Date Erik?

Jia managed not to gasp. Corbin was still describing the intricacies of Master Lao's penjing designs, but all she could think about was her partner's cocky grin. The idea of dating him wasn't inherently insane. There were no departmental policies against it.

No, she couldn't do that. He was twice her age. She was just starting her career and had barely traveled.

Erik had spent decades among the colonies of the UTC, experiencing the vast scope humanity had to offer, both the glorious and the disturbing.

Being attracted to a man and trusting him to have your back in a firefight didn't guarantee a successful romance. Dating him would be a mistake. He might get sick of her, and if he did, they would ruin their professional partnership. Even if the entire 1-2-2 wasn't filled with Jared

Thompson types, there was no guarantee her next partner would be as good as Erik.

"So that was why I told him, 'Ten percent. What about fifteen percent?'" Corbin laughed at his joke.

Jia forced a chuckle. She'd barely heard the rest of what he'd said. She had thought they were still discussing penjing.

Everything she was feeling was probably one-sided anyway. Erik had swept into her life like a typhoon. He was like no man she'd ever met. Of course, she would be impressed with him, but it wasn't worth risking their professional relationship for a personal one that was likely doomed to end in disappointment.

Jia nodded firmly. "That's it."

Corbin blinked. "You think I *should* threaten to sue him?"

"No, no, I guess not." Jia offered him a sheepish smile.

She might not want to date Erik, but it was unfair to continue to string Corbin along. He was a nice guy, but Corbin wasn't what she needed.

She needed to finish this sooner rather than later.

Erik stood, swaying slightly. Emma was going to chew him out when he got back in the flitter, but he would soothe her ego by noting only she could get him home safely.

"Thanks for listening," he slurred.

The multi-armed bartending bot took his glass and tucked it under the bar. The tangled mass of limbs had an almost sinister look, like it was the bastard offspring of the King sentry and an octopus.

"Sir, please note you have credits remaining on your tab," the robot noted.

Erik shrugged. "You've been a great ear."

"I don't understand. Please repeat your drink request. If you would like food, I can summon a waitress."

Erik laughed. "Emma's spoiled me. You don't care what I've been talking about, do you?"

"Customer satisfaction is very important to us. Please rephrase your request, and I'll do my best to accommodate you."

Erik walked away and shook his head. "I prefer my AIs with more personality." He chuckled. "And a little bitchier."

CHAPTER THIRTY-EIGHT

February 27, 2229, Neo Southern California Metroplex, Bar Remembrance

"Third beer?" Erik eyed Jia like she'd slid a blade out of the top of her wrist and was bleeding out. "Did you finally decide that since I'm paying for your drinks, you should get your money's worth?"

She raised her glass and stared into the amber liquid. "I'm training in different ways to be your partner."

Her red face and slurred words told Erik all he needed to know about her alcohol tolerance. She had a long way to go if two beers messed her up that much.

Erik sipped his own beer. "Good work this week on that robbery case. I know it's not as flashy as some of the things we've had in the last couple of months, but you figuring out they had redirected the cargo flitters saved us a lot of trouble." He shrugged. "And they straight-up surrendered. That's always nice."

"It's nice not to have to shoot someone." Jia set her drink down and sighed.

"What's wrong?"

She eyed him, taking a second to focus her thoughts… or her eyes. He wasn't sure. "The Qingming Festival is coming up. It's a big deal in my family, and Mother can be obnoxious about it. Then again, this year, I've got a boyfriend, so at least she won't harass me about that." She sat back, crossing her arms. "It's like she's afraid our ancestors are going to come back and scold her for not marrying me off yet."

Erik raised an eyebrow. "Good thing I'm not Chinese. A lot of my ancestors aren't worth honoring, and while I've patched things up with my brother, it's still kind of awkward."

She leaned over the table in front of him. "I'm sure you have some good ancestors." Jia gave him the wide, sloppy smile that only a drunk could manage. "You're not so bad right now."

"I like to think so. And the same to you." Erik leaned back in his chair and surveyed the room. Like any typical night, it was mostly filled with off-duty cops and their friends. The bulk of the patrons were from the 1-2-2 since it was the closest enforcement zone. Halil sat at the end of the bar, chatting up a waitress and gesturing at a dartboard excitedly.

A brown-haired, dark-eyed, middle-aged man glared at their table from across the bar. Erik had never met the man, but he'd seen pictures. It was Jia's old partner, Ryan Castille. In the pictures, he had bothered to comb his hair.

"Trouble," Erik warned. He inclined his head toward Ryan. "Or at least, something annoying."

Jia turned that way and muttered a curse in Mandarin.

Erik laughed. "You kiss your mom with that mouth?"

"My mother doesn't like kisses," Jia retorted. "I've always worried about running into him, but he stopped coming here after he retired. I kind of assumed he never would come here again. Guess I was wrong."

The ever-present din quieted, near silence spreading from Ryan to the rest of the room. A few people not from the 1-2-2 exchanged confused looks. Their friends leaned in to whisper to them, a few nodding toward Jia or pointing at Ryan.

Erik cracked his knuckles. He didn't want to get any blood on the floor of his favorite bar, but sometimes the Lady threw trouble at him, and he needed to react by punching someone in the face.

Erik spoke softly. "Want me to get rid of him?"

Jia shook her head. "No, I don't need that. If he's not an idiot, he'll turn around and leave."

"And if he *is* an idiot?"

"Then he'll regret this night." Jia's expression turned stormy. She locked eyes with her old partner, the challenge obvious.

Ryan lifted his chin and flared his nostrils like an angry bull ready to charge.

Erik shook his head. The man had chosen the path of the idiot. He remembered how Jia had dealt with Jared, but he was still an active cop with something to lose.

The few remaining conversations in the room stopped. Tension hung thick in the air. If it were any other place, someone might have called the police, but it was pointless to call the cops in a cop bar.

Ryan snorted and stomped toward Jia, his gaze unwavering. His voice carried as he snarled, "If it isn't Lady Justice!"

Jia rolled her eyes. "I didn't tell anyone to call me that. You know how the media are. You could sneeze, and they'd turn it into a story about you being illegally genetically engineered."

He shrugged, the disdain all but oozing out of him. "You always were ambitious. I suppose you finally got your big break, and you get to be the cop you always *thought* you should be."

Jia took a few deep breaths. "Ambitious? No. All I've ever wanted to do was be a good police officer and protect the public." She forced a half-smile. "Actually, Ryan, I have to apologize to you."

Erik frowned but didn't say anything. Jia was a big girl and could handle herself, but he didn't like her giving attack opportunities to her ex-partner. From everything she'd mentioned about him, he was a lazy piece of trash.

"Apologize?" Ryan smirked and licked his lips. "That sounds good. What are you apologizing for?"

Jia gulped down some beer. "I was naïve when we were partners. I'll admit that. I didn't understand the truth of the world, and that made things more difficult than they needed to be."

Ryan narrowed his eyes. "And you're saying you do now?"

"In the sense that I get there are real problems out there, yes." Jia scooted her chair back and stood. Her face might be redder than before, but there was no hint of a slur as she spoke. Trouble had sobered her up quickly.

Ryan nodded, looking increasingly satisfied. "If you get

there were real problems, you probably regret bothering me and the captain about so many unimportant cases."

Jia looked pained.

Ryan bared his teeth. "What the hell is with *that* look?"

"If you've been reading any of the articles about me, you should have picked up that some of those so-called unimportant cases turned into big deals. *Very* big deals." Jia squared her shoulders. "If I'd ignored them, major criminals wouldn't have been caught. So I don't regret that at all."

Erik forced himself not to stand. He wanted to march up to Jia's old partner and loom over the man, but he understood the importance of the moment. She needed to prove to herself and everyone else that she wasn't the same woman she had been when she was partnered with Ryan.

Her old partner flung his arms out to the sides and bowed deeply. "I'm sorry, Lady Justice. I didn't mean to disrespect you. You're a big, famous detective now. What's a piece-of-garbage cop who spent many years on the force doing questioning you?"

Erik stood. He'd reached his limit. Jia might need to do it herself, but he was her partner. When someone came at her, they came at him.

He took one step forward. She threw her hand up, and he froze.

Ryan laughed. "Oh, you got him on a leash, too? Down, boy."

"Keep talking," Erik replied. "You'll see what this junkyard dog can do."

"He has respect for me," Jia spat through gritted teeth. "Which is more than I can say about you, Ryan."

"Respect is earned, Jia, not given because your parents are rich."

"Respect is earned." Jia nodded. "That much I agree with, but that's where I'm confused."

"Confused about what?" Ryan furrowed his brow and glanced at Erik.

Jia unclenched her jaw. A sickeningly sweet smile replaced her frown. "What did you do to earn *my* respect?"

"What?"

"It's not a hard question." Derision permeated her voice. "If respect is earned, and you wanted respect, then you need to explain to me what you did to *earn* it. I'm a little drunk right now, so keep it simple. Then again, you're an idiot, so it's not like you have another option."

A few people in the crowd chuckled.

Ryan growled and scanned the crowd as if trying to remember who had dared to laugh at him.

"You're nothing but a spoiled corp princess who got lucky," he shouted. "I'm a good cop, and you forced me off the job because you couldn't let trivial crap go."

Jia laughed. "Good cop? If you were willing to come and apologize for your attitude, that would be one thing, but you were worse than a bad cop. At least a bad cop occasionally does something useful to cover up the fact they are bad. You were a lazy, useless cop. All you cared about was treading water until you could retire. If a major case came along, you sent it to someone else. There's only so much you can blame Monahan for." She took a step toward him. "It's amazing. A miracle! The minute I got rid of my dead weight and got a partner who gave a damn about doing the job, we started solving crimes and saving people." She wrinkled her nose and shook her head. "To be honest, I felt a little bad about what went down between us, but now I'm not naïve, and I understand the truth. I wasn't an unbearable partner. You're just a lazy coward who had no business calling himself a cop."

Everyone held their breath and waited to see what would happen next.

Ryan's mouth twitched. "A lazy coward?"

"Do you need me to say it in Mandarin?" Jia mocked.

He swung a fist at her head. Jia threw up her arm and blocked the blow with ease, then slammed her palm into his throat.

Ryan stumbled and fell to the floor, gasping and clutching his throat, his eyes wide.

Jia scoffed. "Oh, stop acting like such a baby. I didn't hit you as hard as I could have. It'll hurt for a few days." She looked up and to the side. "Or maybe a few weeks, but I didn't break anything. I could also beat you until you were unconscious, but I'm not doing that either. I think I'm showing rather admirable restraint, considering you just tried to assault me and are ruining my evening."

Ryan coughed and staggered to his feet. "You can't get away with this."

"You think somebody's going to haul me in from a 1-2-2 bar?" Jia pointed at him. "You swung first. I defended myself. I exercised proper restraint. Maybe if you had put as much passion into your police work as you did that punch, you would have been somebody worthy of respect."

"Give it up, Ryan," shouted Halil. "You're just embarrassing yourself now."

"You're siding with her?" Ryan tried to sneer, but a

cough ruined it for him. "You hated her as much as I did. You *told* me so. Is that why you stopped hanging out with me?"

"You're a sad sack now. Look, I respect the time you put in, but Jia's a good cop. She's doing solid work. We were wrong." Halil slapped a hand on his chest. "I was wrong."

Several other officers and detectives nodded and murmured agreement.

Ryan rubbed his throat. "I can't believe this." He spun around, glaring at the gathered crowd. "She gets a little famous, and you're on her side?"

"No." Jia offered him a pitying smile. "They're not on my side. They're cops who care about stopping crime. No more, no less. Obviously, you don't care about that anymore. I don't know what you hoped to accomplish by confronting me, or what small piece of anatomy you're overcompensating for, but if you come at me again, next time I might break something. Maybe even that small piece of your anatomy."

Laughter exploded from the gathered crowd.

Ryan flipped her off. "Screw you. You're not worth it." He eyed everyone as he stomped toward the door, kicking over a barstool before heading out of the bar.

"You should have let me have my turn," Erik complained. "But I don't think he'll be coming back here." He grimaced. "Were you serious?"

"About breaking something important?" Jia picked her glass and pounded back the rest of her beer before eyeing the door he had left open. "I doubt he has much use for it anyway."

Erik grinned. "Good thing I'm on your side."

"Yes." Jia nodded firmly. "It is."

Erik sat back down, hoping she would do the same, not head out. "I see you went with your first instinct."

Jia shrugged. "Like you said," she agreed, finally sitting. "It's better than shooting him."

CHAPTER THIRTY-NINE

Jia stared out the window of the MX 60, happy Emma wasn't saying anything about what had happened in the bar.

Erik and Jia had left a few minutes after the showdown, and he was now taking her back home—although she could tell he wasn't going via the direct route. Technically, Emma was flying, but he had said something to the AI before Jia got inside, so she assumed the impromptu Neo SoCal tour was his idea.

She finally broke the silence. "I think I did the right thing."

Erik looked at her, no concern or disappointment on his face. "So do I. My only regret is that I didn't get to punch him. But doing what you did, especially where you did it, was important. If you think about it, you were just doing what cops are supposed to do."

"Throat-punching people?" Jia smiled, unsure of where he was going. "I must have missed that part at the police academy." There was a primal thrill in physically taking down her annoying old partner.

Erik chuckled. "Sometimes, but that's not what I was getting at. Cops don't start trouble. They finish it when someone else starts it, even if they have to get rough. You can't keep the peace without taking down those who disturb it."

He looked out at the flows of flitters crossing each other, a constant line of people and their machines linking every tower in the metroplex like blood cells flowing through invisible veins and arteries. Society and technology as fractals.

"And sometimes," Erik continued, "you can only talk to someone through your fists, and the best thing a person can do is get it over with when that's needed. I thought something like this might happen, and the only real surprise was where it happened and that it took so long. But you heard the others from the 1-2-2. They have your back."

"Jared doesn't like me," Jia commented. "He's far from the only one. He's just the loudest."

"Most of those bastards used to be loud, and now they're quiet. That means more people are on your side, and more people are afraid to go against you." Erik scoffed. "You're not blind anymore, and you know the truth. There's corruption in the UTC, but it's not impossible to fight it. It's tainted Earth and Neo SoCal, including the department, but we have been fighting it, and doing so successfully. There are still a lot of pieces of trash in the 1-2-2, but you've got the momentum. *We've* got the momentum."

"Does this end with me throat-punching Jared?"

Erik chuckled. "In my version of a perfect world, it does."

Jia smiled, a quiet snicker escaping. Most of the concern had left her eyes. "I honestly thought the other day he was going to go for me."

"If Halil hadn't gotten in his way, he might have, but it doesn't matter since you took care of Castille while you were drunk and he wasn't. That means if Thompson had gone for you the other day, he would have ended up on the floor."

"Probably, but I'm not sure that's a good thing."

"Why?"

Jia turned her hand over several times, examining the palm and back. She'd delivered a solid blow without hurting herself. "I think a showdown in a bar isn't the same thing as assaulting another officer at the station. There would be consequences."

"You have the right to self-defense, especially on the job. The breakroom is one of the places they record. All the evidence would be on your side. You'd also have two witnesses."

"Would you have tolerated people brawling like that in your old unit?"

Erik looked almost wistful. The expression didn't sit well on his face.

"I didn't have that kind of problem with the Knights Errant," he admitted. "It was an elite unit, and I made sure everyone coming in was compatible. I'm not going to say I never ran into that problem in my career, let alone when you consider that the branches don't always get along." He paused and considered his words. "But the problem here was Monahan since he let the rot fester. The blame always stops with the person in charge, and he was a bad captain."

"What about Captain Ragnar?" Jia liked his leadership, but was he doing enough? From her perspective, investigations were proceeding, but she might be too focused on her own concerns.

Erik shook his head. "You can't fix problems overnight, especially when they are deeply rooted. Ragnar's doing his best. As long as he's supporting you, whiners like Thompson can't accomplish much. Eventually, it'll get to be too much for them."

"And they'll leave on their own," Jia concluded.

"Yeah. Exactly. You don't even need to throat-punch them."

Jia laughed. "I was thinking that everyone hated me because I was forcing people out." She stopped, then added, "I'm still forcing people out."

He shook his head. "I'm your partner. We're both forcing people out this time. The more rank-and-file cops we have on our side, the better. Captain Ragnar could be replaced at any moment, and if he does get replaced, I want to make sure the average cop in the 1-2-2 is ready to back us and not be idiots like Thompson or Castille."

"I hope it doesn't come to that." Jia swallowed. She didn't regret hitting Ryan. Even if she hadn't been defending herself, he had brought it on himself. She also couldn't deny that she had become far more aggressive in every situation in recent months, including her investigations.

She hadn't worried about it much during her last few

confrontations because they were all matters of life-and-death, but her old partner wasn't going to kill her. That didn't stop her from being eager to hurt him.

"What's going on in there?" Erik asked.

"Huh?" She turned, surprised.

Erik tapped the side of his head. "I'm your partner. If you're having trouble, let me know. I've seen a thing or two over the years, and I know how bad things can mess people up."

Jia sighed and averted her eyes.

"I'm starting to wonder if I'm getting out of control," she murmured.

"Out of control?" Erik didn't look convinced.

Jia nodded. "This isn't about Ryan. He had it coming, it's just, it's hard for me not to want to be aggressive with suspects and witnesses, and I'm more tempted to go for my weapon these days. Everywhere I go and everyone I deal with, it's like I *know* they're a criminal just waiting for their chance. That kind of aggressive hypervigilance helped me with the stalker, but it's not always a good instinct to have in other situations."

"Violence is the answer to everything?"

She let out a long sigh. "I'm not *saying* I'm ready to shoot every random suspect we talk to, but I don't know if this is healthy. I've gone from worrying about shooting people to planning to shoot them first."

Erik's brow creased. There was no judgment in his eyes, only worry. "How long have you been feeling like this?"

"A while, but it's gotten a lot worse in the last few months." Jia pulled back her jacket to reveal her holsters. "If it's not these, then it's this." She held up a fist. "I keep thinking to myself, 'That scumbag is holding something back, and if I don't do something, somebody's going to get hurt.'"

"That isn't unusual," Erik explained after a few seconds of silent consideration. "I saw similar things with a lot of my newer soldiers when they got their first taste of anti-insurgency operations. I talked to a psych a little while ago, and I learned that this kind of thing can happen to people in any situation where they have to deal with the darker side of humanity and violence is involved. It's a type of PTSD."

"Have you felt this way?"

"Not exactly, but let me make something clear. It's not a matter of mental fortitude or other ignorant suggestions like that. I've got my own issues, and they've taken over my life. That's why I'm here as a cop, after all. But I've been wondering and worrying about you for a while. Things have looked better in the last few weeks, but we haven't been dealing with the same kinds of cases or stresses." Erik kept his tone even and soothing. "Before that, I had to pull you back from the brink several times."

Jia's jaw tightened, and a nasty taste rose in the back of her throat. "You thought I'd go over the line?"

"It's not like I haven't seen good men and women lose it before," Erik explained. "I gave you a lot of heat about being naïve, but a lot of newly minted soldiers are naïve, too. They go through Basic, and they're taught, trained, and conditioned to hate anyone who would harm the UTC."

Both paused as Emma took the flitter down a couple of

lanes and hung a lazy left turn into a more suburban area, the buildings older but well-kept.

Erik continued, "The soldiers who come from secure families on the core worlds have often never experienced anything bad, not the kind of violence you see out there on the frontier. They came from paradise. They're patriotic and want to defend our paradise, but knowing there are bad people out there isn't the same thing as encountering them. Being shot at by them. Seeing their victims. The deeper you have to go into darkness, the harder it is for it not to cling to you."

Jia laughed bitterly. "So, it comes down to me being a corp princess?"

Erik shook his head. "No, it comes down to you facing real danger and real garbage. Monahan and his lackeys did everything they could to ignore the problems because they were lazy cowards. While it might scare you, you still dive in head-first because you want to make sure *other* people don't have to deal with it. The wolves are always out there, Jia, and someone has to be the shepherd staring into the darkness. That's what we are—shepherds with guns."

Jia thought about that, lost in the view out the window. "But how do I deal with it, Erik? You're right. The only reason it hasn't been too much lately is because of our cases. What happens the next time I run into something that sets me off? If I attack a suspect, it's not just my career that's at stake." She paused. "Well, that and the suspect, of course. However, I could throw off a case and help some antisocial piece of filth escape justice, and I'm not sure I would be able to forgive myself."

Erik locked eyes with her, his expression stern. "I need

you to be honest because I have one big question before we continue."

She eyed him, lips pressed together. "I just admitted to almost being out of control. I'm not going to lie now."

"This is important." Erik's voice firm. "The most important thing. Do you want to continue being a cop?"

"I want to keep helping people by tracking down bad people." Jia shrugged. "I think the best way to do that is by being a detective. There are other things I might be able to do, but it doesn't matter since every career I can think of would run into the same problem—me dealing with human garbage and being *pissed*."

Jia noted Erik's look of relief. "You thought I might quit?" she asked.

"I'm your partner, but I'm not a telepath. You can get surprisingly complicated." Erik grinned weakly. "And if I'm selfish, you're a great partner. I know you can beat this, so I didn't want to lose you, but I also was ready to support you if you didn't think you could continue."

Jia smiled, the ray of support carving through the darkness she felt. "What now?"

"There's no easy, quick fix," Erik explained. "But you've done the most important thing. You accept that you have a problem, and you haven't gone over the line. That means you're going to need to work on your perspective and practice further restraint."

She considered his words. "How do I do that?"

"Counseling is the best solution for someone still in active service like you are. They'll help you work through some of these issues and articulate better strategies. I've looked into it, and I have my past military experience.

Most people, with effort and practice, can deal with things, and it's not like you're running around shooting innocent people. I think you'll be able to deal with it without help after a short while." Erik gestured idly to a passing tower as if it contained the secrets to her mental health. "If you don't want the department to know, I could point you to some people."

Jia shook her head. "No. The department might have its problems, but it's not the enemy. I'll go talk to Captain Ragnar. He needs to know what's going on. If I want him to know about the conspiracy, it seems silly to not tell him about this."

Flitters zoomed by in multiple lanes.

"You can go faster, Emma," Jia told her. "I think we're mostly done here."

"I was just trying to give you time, Detective," the AI responded. "Your partnership with Detective Blackwell maximizes his efficiency, and I need that to make sure he is of optimal use to me."

Erik snickered. "You could just admit you were worried about her too, Little Miss Crystal Heart."

"Spin it however you want, Detective."

Jia smiled. It was good to have friends, even if one of them was an egotistical AI.

CHAPTER FORTY

March 2, 2229, Neo Southern California, Shadow Zone

Erik stepped out of his flitter into the garbage-strewn alley. Piles of metal, plastic, and decaying food lay everywhere. "Abandoned" was a nebulous idea when there were animals and unfortunate people who found dark corners to hide.

Colonel Adeyemi stood in front of a medium-sized armored cargo flitter, a vehicle roughly twice the length of the MX 60. A few soldiers stood on either side of the officers, all wearing deep scowls.

The colonel had abruptly contacted Erik an hour earlier and told him to get his butt to coordinates in the Shadow Zone. None of the men wore uniforms, but their stances, haircuts, and builds made their military background obvious.

Even if the man wasn't his commanding officer, there was no reason to refuse. Colonel Adeyemi wasn't going to contact Erik about a trivial matter.

A rancid stench choked the area, and Erik put an arm up to his nose. He understood the colonel's need to meet in out-of-the-way places for better operational security, but their encounters involved increasingly disgusting and decaying locations.

Meeting out in the wilderness was a possibility, but it might be harder to explain if someone corrupt, high-ranking, and suspicious learned about it. Face to face meetings were dangerous as it was, which was why they'd been relying more on the colonel's prototype quantum communication system.

"You're lucky you can't smell, Emma," Erik muttered. "The stench is like the entire metroplex threw up in here."

She let out a merry laugh. "I'm lucky for a number of things that come with being me. That one is a minor consideration."

Erik ignored the smell to take a more careful look around. Bullet holes and scorch marks covered the nearby walls. The scorch pattern around the huge gaping wound in one building was indicative of a plasma grenade. This wasn't just a refuge for the dispossessed.

"Did you pick a place you could kill me, and it'd look normal or like death by stench?" Erik asked. He gestured to the nearby bullet holes.

"I have people droning around here. This place hasn't seen a lot of traffic in the last few days." The colonel scoffed. "And if I ever need to kill you, it'll be out in the open, and you'll be coming at me first."

"Good to know," he answered, his eyes watering.

A loud whirring noise sounded, and the back of the cargo flitter flipped up.

Erik couldn't see inside the vehicle from his position. "You didn't tell me what this was about. I'm assuming it's important."

"It's about your request." The colonel nodded at the cargo flitter. "You wanted heavier ordnance, so I'm about to provide you some. This isn't for everyday use or normal idiots, but the next time you run into a King sentry or an anthill filled with terrorists and you don't have TPST support, these might help. I need you to not die until my son's been avenged." He shrugged, a small smirk fleeing across his lips. "Feel free to commit suicide by terrorist or assassin or upset girlfriend *after* that has been accomplished."

A soldier pushed a hoverpallet loaded with black cases and crates, some long and narrow, others tall and squat. Getting everything inside the MX 60 would be a challenge. He'd purchased the vehicle for speed, handling, and cover.

Not cargo capacity.

"Getting this wasn't easy." Colonel Adeyemi frowned. "And it's not like I can route Army equipment to random people because I feel like it, so we had to play this strictly by the book."

"Which book?" Erik asked. "And what does it say?"

"In a few minutes, you'll be receiving a message confirming your official receipt of a sponsored license to deal in surplus military equipment." The colonel pointed at the approaching pallet. "That was the only way I could get you more than a few rifles, and the only way you'd be able to legally possess this stuff, even as a cop and a vet. I understand that you're willing to bend the rules, but I also know someone is gunning for you. They probably haven't flattened you yet because someone else is running interference, but the fewer angles of attack we give them, the better. It's not crazy, looking at us from the outside, that I might have a business relationship with you, so it provides a plausible cover."

Erik shrugged. "Fine by me." He stretched his neck a bit to get a better view of the containers. "What did you bring?"

The colonel strolled over to the pallet, his boots thudding on the hard pavement.

He tapped his PNIU, and all the locks clicked open. "I'll send the access codes to you." He opened one of the long and narrow boxes to reveal a black missile launcher. "Laser-guided. That big enough for you?" He pointed to a shorter, wider box next to him. "It's not like I can give you a hundred missiles, but at least you've got some. I'm sure Emma can interface the system so you can use drones to paint your targets. These have decent guidance and range, so you can do some indirect fire with her help."

"It would be trivial," Emma insisted, sounding exciting. Erik eyed the Taxútnta. Can an AI have PTSD as well?

He wasn't sure if he wanted the AI to be so eager to fire a missile.

He focused on the weapons again. "That would have been nice to have on Halloween," Erik agreed.

"Exactly." Colonel Adeyemi closed the case and opened a nearby crate. Several assault rifles were packed inside. "You probably don't care about these because of that monster you already use, but if you ever want something with a little more control and ammo efficiency, here it is. We've got a lot of other useful toys, including a couple of pairs of tactical goggles, so you don't have to rely on drones for night vision or thermal. Two assault infantry-grade tactical suits. Those should stop the bullets from your typical scumbag criminal better than those cop vests they give you."

Erik chuckled. "I thought you didn't want me using this equipment against *normal idiots*?"

"Eh, I'll leave it to your discretion, but you have a habit of running into big threats. But use this too much, and it'll start raising questions we might not want to answer." Colonel Adeyemi closed the crates. "I'd get you an exoskeleton if I could, but there's no way we can get you a military-issued exoskeleton without a bunch of alarms going off on a lot of people's systems. Then our little investigation will be over." He slapped the top of another crate. "Lots of ammo in here, different calibers. I've got ammo for the rifles, and I put in some for your TR-7. Besides more disruptor rounds, there's also a bunch of armor-piercing and explosive rounds."

"Thank you. That will come in real handy."

"I would hope so."

"You're going to stuff all that into my body?" Emma asked. Her holographic form appeared next to the pallet. She leaned over the boxes and crates, her lips pursed in irritation. More than one of the others glanced at her before resuming their surveillance. Erik was sure they wanted to get out of this smelly location as badly as he did.

Unless they had smell protection?

Erik shrugged. "It's not like I can have the colonel drive this thing to my residential tower."

Emma let out a long, melodramatic sigh. "I do hope this doesn't end with me exploding."

Colonel Adeyemi frowned. "Can we do without the commentary? I'd like to finish going through this and get out of here."

Emma stepped away from the delivery with a faint smirk on her face. "Touchy, uniform boy."

The colonel snorted and nodded at another box. "Grenades. Frag, plasma, and stun." He pointed to a case. "Tactical short-radius EMPs." He walked to the other side of the pallet and opened a long, narrow case. Inside was an unwieldy gray rifle with a narrow barrel and a thick body. The weapon was almost as large as the missile launcher.

"Wait, is that…" Erik whistled and leaned toward it. "I thought they couldn't make them this small. I was always told it would never be an infantry weapon, and that the required tech wasn't practical."

Colonel Adeyemi managed something approaching a smile. "That's right. It's an assault infantry tactical laser. It's heavy as hell, and you don't get a lot of shots from a single charged power cell, but they are starting to use them in a few units. A good shot from one of these aimed the right way could down a flitter."

He looked at the man. "And I can have this legally?"

The colonel nodded. "As a licensed dealer, yes. This weapon isn't classified. It's just not in widespread use. They've even talked about them on the news. Typical hype—the weapon that will change warfare. That kind of garbage."

"I don't pay a lot of attention to the military news these days."

"I don't blame you, but the summary version is, I wouldn't be surprised if, in twenty years, nobody's using a slug thrower anymore." Colonel Adeyemi glanced at the laser rifle with a hint of longing. "The Zitarks haven't made their move yet, but that doesn't mean they or another race won't, or that some of the schemers in Parliament won't get their preemptive war. The DD is pushing hard to close some of the weapons tech gaps. Those damned space raptors are probably the weakest of the aliens, and they still have the advantage in certain areas." He closed the case. "I've got a few extra power cells in there for you, but those things take a long time to charge, so don't try to use that thing to mow down an entire army by yourself."

Emma folded her arms and sighed. "I suppose it's inevitable, but some of the drones I've...borrowed are picking up suspicious people circling the area on mini-flitters. There is currently a single gun goblin approaching directly."

"Rider gang," Erik muttered. "Those guys are usually smart enough to stay away from something dangerous."

What kind of idiot saw a bunch of men with rifles and decided he wanted a piece of them?

Colonel Adeyemi frowned. "Everyone, ready up."

The soldiers raised their rifles. A few more soldiers jumped out of the cargo flitter. They opened the doors and took up positions behind them.

Erik pointed to the laser rifle. "I think I'll try it out."

The colonel snorted and opened the case. He lifted the rifle with a grunt and tossed it to Erik. If he didn't have a cybernetic arm, it might not have been manageable. Some weapons needed an exoskeleton. He crouched behind the hoverpallet and rested the rifle on top.

"A single gun goblin will be here in about thirty seconds," Emma reported. "Many of his associates are hovering overhead, just out of your line of sight." She vanished.

The colonel readied his pistol, his face a mask of annoyance. "Always roaches ready to scuttle out of the darkness, but they might not be total idiots."

An overconfident thug approached astride on a dark mini-flitter decorated with elaborate yellow and white stripes. His helmet was painted to resemble a skull. Erik hated it when they tried so hard.

The rider stopped a few yards from the MX 60 and grinned. Erik assumed that the spikes all over his clothes and the angry mongoose on the front of his jumpsuit were supposed to mean something, but it wasn't like he kept track of every petty gang in the Shadow Zone.

Riders were annoying, but they lacked the influence of groups like the Gray Circle. The local EZ cops kept them in check.

"I'd suggest you leave," Colonel Adeyemi barked. "This has nothing to do with you, and you can see we're not just tourists."

The thug shook his head, a gleeful smile on his face and greed in his eyes. "Sometimes you get lucky, you know? That's us today. We're normally not even over here. No one comes over here except the dregs, but the one time we do, Little Wang says he sees something strange. He tells me he thinks he sees some dealing over here." He patted the handlebars of his flitter. "And I'm thinking, you guys don't look like people from around here, so you need to pay the local taxes, you know?" He licked his lips. "But those don't look like drugs. Guns? My boys could use a few guns."

"You think you can threaten us?" the colonel snapped.

"I think you don't get that I have my boys ready to fly in here and kill you all. We've got the flitters, and we've got the numbers." The thug patted his handlebars. "But it doesn't have to go down like that. I'm not asking for everything. This ain't a robbery. I'm asking for a small donation. You can leave here without any trouble, and we'll know you're reasonable. Maybe we could even do a few favors for each other."

The colonel glowered at the man, his right hand twitching and hovering near the pistol in his belt holster.

"Can I handle this?" Erik asked. "I know how to deal with these kinds of people."

"Be my guest," the colonel replied.

"I think you don't want to be involved in this," Erik suggested. "I think it'd be best if you turned around and left before there's trouble."

"Something nasty and illegal going on here," the thug commented. He sucked in a breath. "Shame, shame. You've gone and brought crime into such a nice area." He chuckled through his smile.

"Actually, this is all legal," Erik explained. "I can show you my license."

"Legal? You expect me to believe you're in some nasty part of the Zone because…what? You love the smell?"

"Something like that." Erik matched his grin. "But I'd hope you wouldn't be stupid enough to do something you'll regret. You didn't come in shooting, which means you're smart enough to know that if you try something, you'll lose people."

"Oh, I don't know. I'm what you call…resourceful."

Erik let out a mocking laugh. "You're right. I'm picking up guns here." He hefted the laser rifle. "Do we look like the kind of people who are going to be intimidated by a few riders?"

"You've got balls, sure, but being brave ain't the same thing as being smart." The thug narrowed his eyes. "Who are you? You seem familiar." He snorted. "Not important. It's a good deal. You just hand me a few of those boxes, and I'm on my way with my boys. Otherwise, there will be trouble. I've got a lot of my boys ready to come down here. You're on the ground, and they're in the air. If they start shooting, you'll be dead. Maybe one of my boys gets shot. Maybe not."

"I'm transmitting indicator arrows pointing to his *boys* to your smart lenses," Emma sent to Erik and the soldiers.

Twenty small arrows appeared. The thug wasn't bluffing about the numbers, but he also didn't seem fazed by the fact Erik was holding a huge laser rifle. Even if he didn't know what it was, anyone who saw it could make a reasonable guess that the weapon was dangerous.

The soldiers spread out and raised their rifles.

The thug pulled out a pistol. "You could shoot me, but if you do, you're dead."

Erik pointed the laser rifle at the man's chest. "It's like you said. You're brave, I'll give you that. *Stupid*, perhaps, but brave."

The thug offered a toothy grin. "You don't get to be the leader if you flinch because someone points a fancy gun at you. I know you're not going to shoot me since you don't know where and how many of my boys there are. If I die, they're going to fly down here and pick you all off in seconds. At least my second will have a lot of new toys to hand out."

"You've got ten seconds to get the hell out of here," Erik replied. "Nine, eight, seven…"

"I've seen your face before, and it's really bugging me." The thug jammed his pistol into his waistband. "I know I'm the first person you'll shoot." His flitter lifted into the air. "But this ain't over. You finish up, and you get the hell out the Zone if you know what's good for you." He crested the roof of a roughly thirty-meter-tall building and disappeared.

Emma added a new, differently colored arrow for the thug. "They've all stopped moving," she reported. "He's now violently gesturing to the others."

"Prepare for aerial assault," Colonel Adeyemi ordered.

The soldiers had spread out to cover both sides, their rifles pointed up. Determination, not fear, covered their faces.

Erik hoisted the massive rifle, aiming for the leader's arrow. The indicators started moving.

Erik held position and waited for the thug leader to clear the roof, along with his swarm of friends. They emerged in seconds, all with their pistols out. Guided by Emma's arrows, the soldiers knew exactly where the enemy would emerge. They opened fire.

The echoes of the rifle shots overlapped as the first volley went out and ripped through the riders. Confusion swept through the would-be ambushers, but a few managed to shoot back, their bullets bouncing off the armored flitter or going wide. Carrying a gun didn't mean they had practiced and drilled with it.

Snarling, their leader pointed his gun at Erik and fired. His first bullet wasn't close and struck the wall behind Erik. The detective pulled the trigger in response. An invisible beam blasted from the rifle and tore a large hole through the center of the mini-flitter. The laser rifle's indicator dropped by a fifth.

The thug leader screamed as his vehicle spiraled toward the ground. He dropped his gun and desperately tugged on his handlebars. Thousands of years of technological advancement had led to man being able to soar through the skies with the ease of the bird.

That advantage had been taken away in an instant.

Several of the riders looked his way, their distraction allowing soldiers to pick them off. The flitter smashed into the ground, doing little to cushion the collision. The mangled rider flew from the wreck and his body rolled several times before stopping, joining the other dead riders and their smoking vehicles on the ground.

The wide-eyed survivors whipped their mini-flitters around and fled over the rooftops, all picking different random directions.

"Cease fire, cease fire!" Colonel Adeyemi ordered.

"They are not circling back," Emma reported.

"We tried to warn him." Erik walked over and set the rifle on the pallet before pushing it toward the MX 60. "Let me get this loaded, and then Emma, you can fly around the Zone while I chat with the local cops. Colonel, you and your team should get out of here. I'll clean up. As far as they are concerned, it'll just be the Shadow Zone Task Force doing its thing."

Adeyemi nodded once, and in moments, his team was loaded and heading out.

Erik sighed, then sneezed. "*DISGUSTING!*" he spat.

CHAPTER FORTY-ONE

March 3, 2229, Neo Southern California Metroplex, Police Enforcement Zone 122 Station, Office of Detectives Jia Lin and Erik Blackwell

Jia couldn't help but frown at Erik. He sat at his desk, feet up, his head cradled in his arms as he read through a few reports. The whole look was as casual as a man checking sphere ball scores.

Earlier, he'd described what had happened in the Shadow Zone with all the seriousness of a man relating a funny anecdote from his day off.

She didn't understand him, not completely. The grinning façade covered a well of dark vengeance, but half the time, he acted like none of it mattered, and all he cared about was entertainment.

She knew that wasn't true, but it was hard not to be deceived.

It was a ruse, which was something she needed to remember. The vengeance propelling him had brought him to the attention of dangerous enemies. The more he played the carefree gun-toting fool, the easier it was for him to surprise them, as he had several times already.

"You should have brought me," Jia declared.

"Huh? Brought you where?" Erik lifted his head to look over. "To the breakroom?"

She eyed him like he had just missed the simplest of questions. "To the Shadow Zone."

"Oh." Erik dropped his feet. "It turned out all right, and it's not like I was by myself. I was there with the colonel and his guys. If I'm going to get ambushed, doing it while surrounded by highly trained soldiers is my best bet. We took down half of that gang, and they didn't hurt a single one of us."

"Yes, Adeyemi and his men were there, but what if all those riders had followed you from the beginning? You need backup when you're doing dangerous things and not just Emma." Jia sighed. "I'm your partner, and I'm also helping you with your personal investigation. You don't need to protect me. Let me help you."

Confusion spread across Erik's face. He nodded. "I'm not trying to protect you. I just didn't think it'd be a big deal. Most of these meetings are just us sharing info, but if I think there's going to be heat, I'll bring you along. Next time you can shoot a few riders."

"That's all I'm asking. To help, not to shoot riders. Unless it's necessary." Jia put her hand to my mouth and cleared her throat. "Speaking of keeping open lines of communications, I talked to the counselor, like you recommended."

"Oh? How did that go?" He looked relieved as a bit of stress left her shoulders.

"I described everything, and he mentioned possible psychological dissonance stemming from difficulties adapting my previous beliefs to my current reality. My issues are partially a result of that. A minor part, but still."

"That makes sense." Erik cleared the data window and focused on Jia. "Did he say you need to do something?"

"He mentioned that a general change in perspective might be helpful, but I made it clear I wasn't leaving law enforcement."

"Good."

"His argument was that by retaining certain patterns in my mental paradigm, there's an inherent tension," Jia explained. "He suggested that my changes don't need to be fundamental, and I don't have to change my career, but a few changes here and there might help me so I don't have as much stress from compartmentalizing it all. To be honest, it's something I've thought a lot about, even before I was having these issues. New experiences can be positive, such as my newfound appreciation of sphere ball. I think it's helping me to not just be Jia the cop, but Jia the person.

"Got anything else in mind?" Erik asked. "Sphere ball's great, but if just appreciating life more helps, you should go for it. I took up penjing."

"I've got the new gun and a new hobby. That's a start. What else? Maybe a new flitter? Something that isn't boring and blue." Jia laughed, feeling more relaxed than embarrassed. She pantomimed turning a control yoke. "It might seem stupid, but I've been thinking about that for a while. Something about my flitter feels almost like a lie. It's like it represents the old naïve Jia who believed that as long as you didn't fly a flashy flitter, you wouldn't stand out and cause trouble."

"Brightly colored vehicles make one antisocial?" He scratched his chin. "I'll have to alert Emma in case she wants to change to fiery red."

Emma broke in, "I am not antisocial. Well, not any more than the next hyper-intelligent person who hates idiots."

Both of them ignored her.

"I'm not saying I believed brightly colored cars made one antisocial. Mostly." Jia shrugged. "But I don't believe it anymore."

"New flitter, huh?" The sudden shark-like smile on Erik's face filled her with suspicion. It wasn't that she didn't trust her partner to have her back, but that didn't mean he wouldn't suggest something annoying.

"What's that look supposed to mean?" Jia patted her stun pistol. "I'm not above shooting you in the back."

"Isn't the solution obvious?" Erik asked, his ridiculous grin growing so large it looked painful. "You need an MX 60. A bright yellow one. Be antisocial and assault someone's senses."

Jia rolled her eyes. "Ditching something boring isn't the same thing as getting a ridiculous luxury flitter. I'm not buying an MX 60, and I'm *not* buying anything that is yellow. That's not antisocial." She smiled. "It's just *tacky*."

Erik grunted in disappointment. "I could help you get the color-change ability installed. You can use yellow when you want to be feisty."

"No MX 60. And nothing yellow." Jia cut through the air with her hand. "And that's final."

"Hmm," Emma offered through their PNIUs again. "That does make me wonder."

"What?" Erik asked. "You have a color recommendation."

"No, I was thinking about a new body," she replied, husky desire clinging to her voice. "For me, anyway. Your Purist limitations don't apply to an AI. I should continue to adapt and upgrade myself."

"New body?" Erik frowned. "You're living in a Taxútnta MX 60. It's one of the best flitters on the market, and I've installed tons of extra features and mods. Would you prefer to be in a mini-flitter?"

Emma popped into existence just to roll her eyes at Erik. "Obviously not. Actually, I think I'd prefer something larger, with more integrated systems. It would suit me better."

Jia tilted her head and tried to visualize Emma flying something other than the MX 60. "Larger? Like a cargo flitter?"

"No, Detective Lin. A hypersonic transport, perhaps. It might be interesting to go so fast."

Jia grimaced. "I don't know if I'm ready to trust you to control something like that. You'd effectively be an AI missile."

"Kind of makes you wonder what the military planned to do with her," Erik mused.

"Yes," Emma nodded, "it *does*."

Jia tilted her head to get new angles as she walked slowly around the holographic image at the museum.

The slit-eyed reptilian creature crouched, his sharp-clawed hand clutching a twisting crystalline knife. Loose metallic mesh hung over the bright scales covering his body, with small pouches spread throughout. He hissed on occasion, his tail swaying slowly.

Blood dripped from his mouth, which was filled with jagged, razor-sharp teeth.

She blinked a few times. She *assumed* the Zitark image before her represented a male, but she wasn't sure. From what she could remember, the males were more brightly colored than the females, but it wasn't like she had seen one in real life.

Mei shuddered beside her. "It's hard to believe they're out there just waiting for their chance to eat us."

Jia regretted suggesting a trip to the Northern National History Museum's Local Neighborhood Exhibit. She always enjoyed visiting museums, but Mei found a reason to be annoying every time they went. Last time, she'd had pointed words to say about the statue restoration work.

"I don't know if they're planning to eat us," Jia countered. "But I do think it's probably best that our races stay away from each other until we've got all our own problems sorted out. I imagine the Zitarks have factions and politics to worry about as well."

"I agree with staying away from aliens. However, for most of history, no one worried about that sort of thing." Mei peered intently at the hologram. "Although we might not like it, the world can't avoid change."

Jia chuckled.

Mei looked her way, the corners of her mouth curling down. "What's so amusing about that?

"I'm just been thinking a lot about change, and how I might change for the better."

Mei stiffened, a brief flash of panic in her eyes. "The world can't avoid change, but that doesn't mean *we* individually need to change."

"Sometimes change is for the best." Jia shrugged.

"You're in a good place, Jia," Mei insisted. "You're enjoying your job, and you're dating a good man. Don't change what you don't have to."

Jia didn't hold Mei's reaction against her. She loved her sister, but she wasn't comfortable talking about some of the mental challenges that had come with the job in the last year.

A good man? Nobody could deny Corbin was that, but the problem was, being a good man wasn't the same thing as being the man she *desired*.

The two of them were increasingly going through the motions in their relationship. How much of her refusal to cut him loose was nothing more than momentum and concern about her family's reaction?

There should be *something*. A fire that lit hers when she was near him, or at least warmed her. She had even wasted her first decent attempt at Beijing Duck on Corbin instead of Erik, belatedly realizing it was a desperate attempt to rekindle something in their relationship.

"Are you in a good place?" Jia challenged.

Mei's forehead wrinkled in consternation. "Me? I thought we were talking about you."

"I've got someone, you don't. Maybe I'm worried, as your younger sister."

Mei inclined her head toward the Zitark. "I should sacrifice myself to one of those creatures if we're at the point where *you* are worried about *my* romantic life." She waved a hand dismissively. "There are certain goals I need to achieve before I focus on that, but I assure you that it's not being ignored."

Jia couldn't help the laughter that exploded out of her. Several museum patrons turned away from other holograms and artifacts to frown at her faux pas.

"Control yourself," Mei hissed, her face reddening. "You're making a spectacle of yourself."

Jia threw a hand over her mouth and managed to damp herself down to mere chuckling. "You have to admit, it's amusing to hear someone insist that a career is more important than dating. You've used that line on me, but now that I'm the one in a relationship, it's..." She shrugged. "Not convincing?"

Mei tugged at her sleeve and scoffed in a feeble attempt to regain her dignity. "The point remains, independent of our relative positions."

Jia could take advantage of the situation. Mei could provide some insight on the Corbin situation as long as she didn't realize what was going on. If she caught on, the Lin Elder Sister complex would activate, and Jia would be on the defensive.

Again.

It was just like in sphere ball. Too much defense would lead to a loss.

"I'm sorry, Mei. I'm curious." Jia offered her a sweet smile.

Mei lifted her chin, satisfied by the apparent contrition and the return of everyone else's attention to the exhibit. "Curious?"

"Are the man's background and job the only factors that are important to you?" Jia asked.

"If you're looking for a husband, he should, at a minimum, be someone of the same status. He needs to bring something to the marriage. That much is common sense."

"But what about connection? What about love?" Jia glanced at the Zitark hologram and wondered if there was some planet where an annoying reptilian big sister harassed her little reptile sister about laying eggs before she grew too old.

Mei gave Jia a look normally reserved for older children who still believed in Generous Gao. "Love is nothing more than self-reinforcing compatibility. All aspects of a potential husband are relevant to that. Passion can be nice in the beginning, but that fades. When you settle in for the long relationship, you want to know that your husband will be lifting you up as you lift him up, and not that you'll be supporting him as he fritters away his time in a feeble attempt at a..." She frowned. "I don't know. An art career?"

"What if you don't feel a spark in the beginning? Are you going to tell me you would date someone, even if he had the appropriate background and career, if you felt nothing for him?" Jia challenged her sister with a stare. "Are you telling me you would spend decades married to someone you don't love? Mother and Father can be obnoxious, but at least they genuinely love each other in their own overly complicated way."

Mei apparently found a sudden need to focus on a hologram of a small Zitark-carved crystal sculpture. The multicolored artwork depicted some strange ten-legged bug with two tails. Jia was curious how anyone even knew about Zitark art, but she didn't want to lose control of the conversation by pinging the museum's tour system.

"Well, Mei?" Jia prodded. "You can't ignore my question."

"I suppose I can't deny that a connection from the beginning might predict long-term success. You don't have to worry, little sister. If there's one thing I'm not going to do, it's pursue a man I find dreary."

"Good," Jia murmured. "That would be awful."

Her concern and question were now answered.

"Let's get going. I don't want to spend our entire time staring at these awful lizards." Mei gave one last look at the Zitark hologram and headed toward the open doorway leading to the next room, the tall heels of her shoes clicking on the tile floor.

Jia caught up with her sister, smiling. Mei might not have realized it, but her sisterly advice had helped.

Sorry, Corbin, she thought.

CHAPTER FORTY-TWO

March 5, 2229, Neo Southern California Metroplex, Shadow Zone, Bar Big One

Erik didn't like the way Alicia was looking at him. He'd shown up for an info check, and she'd invited him into the backroom like always, but she didn't take a seat. Instead, she stood behind the table in the center of the room, her arms folded over her chest, her gaze searching. The corners of her mouth were curled up in amusement at some joke only she understood.

"Got something to say?" he asked. He lingered near the door. His instincts told him there wasn't going to be any trouble, but it wouldn't hurt to be in a good position to escape.

He would hate to have to shoot his favorite informant.

"There's just something about you, Blackwell." Alicia looked him up and down. "Something different. I can almost smell it, and that makes me want to know what it is."

Erik gave her his standard deceptive grin. It was forced,

but it looked completely natural. Even she would have trouble seeing through it. "I'm using the same deodorant I have since coming back to Earth."

"It's almost like..." Alicia narrowed her eyes. "No, it's not that you're getting laid. But something close? You dating now? Is that it?"

Erik cursed under his breath. "I'm not here to talk about my love life."

The confusion melted from Alicia's face, replaced by an arrogant certitude. "Oh, touchy, huh? Even the great Obsidian Detective has his weakness."

"Unless it has something to do with trouble in the Zone, I don't care." Erik dropped into a chair, keeping his shoulders loose. No reason to give Alicia more to work with. She was too perceptive.

He'd been thinking about Jia on the way over.

Alicia sat across from him and crossed her legs, something she didn't normally do. She'd commented once that she didn't want to wrinkle her pants.

"First of all, were you playing around here a few days ago, looking for trouble?" she asked. "Did you bust up a bunch of riders? The cops came in here in a big way, and I found out that one of the big rider gangs had lost half its members. They aren't saying much, other than they had a run-in that started with you, and shots were fired."

"Somebody came after me when they shouldn't have." Erik shrugged. "I didn't go looking for a fight. I can't help it if the idiots didn't take their chance to run when they could have."

"Of course, you didn't. Now half the rider gangs in the

Zone are convinced the Obsidian Detective is coming for them. They're all wetting themselves."

Erik snickered. "They planning to come for me first? I've got some time on my hands, but I'd rather keep my schedule clear."

Alicia laughed. "Don't worry, Blackwell. Everyone's trying to keep a low profile for a few weeks."

"I can live with that. Got anything else for me?"

Alicia sighed and leaned forward, her brow wrinkling and her mouth pressed into a thin line.

"What is it?" Erik asked. "You need more money?"

"No, it's…"

Erik's eyebrow lifted. Embarrassment. That was what it was. He wasn't used to seeing it from the woman. She bought and sold information for a living, not just from him, but from all sorts of scum.

"I'll give you the money no matter how messed up it is," he explained. "You've been doing a good job of feeding me tips. Or did you need me to leave you alone for a while?"

"No, you're good for business in a strange way. Everyone thinks if they're nice to me, you won't come after them." Alicia kept her gaze on the table for a few seconds before looking at Erik. "Like I said, the rider gangs are keeping a low profile, but there are rumors out there about a new brutal gang. Not riders, but they're allegedly making moves. Big, nasty moves."

Erik nodded. "Did this start before or after my little run-in with the local flavor?"

"Everything I've heard says this started before, but that doesn't prove anything." Alicia gestured toward the door. "That's what's so confusing about these guys. They're allegedly killing people, but they're not putting out a statement. They're not making it known who they are."

"Killing people is a statement," Erik observed. "Are you sure it's just not random murders?"

"No," she admitted. "Everyone's trying to keep the cops from getting involved."

"Why would that be?" he asked. "I'm not going to claim the cops in the local EZs are the best, but they've gotten better, and even before, when they were looking the other way on a lot of Zone trouble, it wasn't like they didn't care about murders." Erik narrowed his eyes. "Or are you suggesting the cops are involved?"

"No." Alicia licked her lips, and her eyes darted back and forth. "No one's saying that. It's more that they're worried about something awful happening if the cops come. The vibe I get is that a few dead bodies are worth it if it stops a war from breaking out in the Zone."

"A war?" Erik dropped the smooth act and let the incredulity into his tone. "Worse than me going after a gang like the Gray Circle?"

"Way worse, and this is where things get weird. It's a first for me."

"You've had brutal gangs in the Zone before. Wait." Erik slapped his left bicep. "Are we talking a gang of full-conversion Tin Men?"

Alicia shook her head. "That'd be freaky, but it wouldn't be *that* different. I haven't heard about any full-conversions walking around openly down here in the Zone, but that would make more sense, and it'd be less weird. No." She looked away. "People are saying these new guys aren't... completely human."

"So, they *are* Tin Men?"

"No, it's not that they've got metal." Alicia sucked in a deep breath and faced Erik. "They're saying they're aliens."

Bursting out in laughter when his source gave him information wasn't near the top of the list of good ways to preserve their professional relationship. That didn't stop Erik.

Alicia clenched her teeth. "You pay me for the damned rumors, Blackwell, so I'm giving them to you. It's not like I wanted to pass this along, but that's what I'm hearing."

"Yeah, but come on! Aliens?"

Alicia uncrossed her legs. Her face reddened. "Let me make something clear. This isn't the first time I've heard a crazy rumor about aliens, but this is the first time I've heard more than one person mention it, and the first time I've heard it mentioned in combination with something *real* going on. I'm not saying they're aliens, but someone's going out of their way to make people believe it, and they're pushing the idea."

Erik narrowed his eyes. "Do people think they're aliens because they've found mauled bodies?"

Alicia nodded. "So far, like I said, they're keeping the cops out of it, but I don't know how long that's going to last. That's assuming any of this is real and not just a bunch of people talking. And it's not just about the bodies. There have been a few rumors about seeing aliens, too. You mentioned full-conversion Tin Men. You're thinking they're pretending to be aliens?"

"Something like that. I worked a case recently where a man was punched clean through the chest by a Tin Man. You said it yourself—war. They've got the locals spooked, and they're worried about the police calling in the Militia or the Army to raze the Zone?"

"Maybe," Alicia admitted. "There have been incidents in the past where the authorities decided collateral damage in the Zone was worth it, and I'm not talking about one of your Obsidian Detective chases. I'm talking real damage, and it's not like the Uptown news is going to mention a bunch of dead Groundlings if it embarrasses the government." She frowned. "I'm not worried about aliens, but I *am* worried that if the Uptowners become convinced they're a nasty threat down here, they'll accept the same kind of sacrifices they have in the past to clean up perceived problems."

"Things are different," Erik insisted. He injected confidence into his answer, even if he didn't believe it.

"Things can always change back," she countered. "I'm annoyed. Lots of gangs draw on strange traditions and iconography to scare people in the Zone. They tend to be smaller, and mostly fly under the radar of the cops. They can't get away with it Uptown, but this alien thing's going to lead to trouble. I know it."

Erik grinned. "I've got a simple solution, then."

Incredulity took over Alicia's face. "What?"

He smiled. "We find and take out the gang."

This time, she made sure to be obvious when she rolled her eyes in disbelief. "Good luck. No one knows where they are. I can't even point you to anyone who has seen a body with their own eyes."

Erik shrugged. "I'm a detective. I'll investigate."

Ilse folded her hands as she sat in her chair. A dozen different data windows surrounded her, each crammed full of data from their analyses of Emma's last three interviews.

To her surprise, Emma had agreed to additional sessions after the initial questioning, but she had maintained the same disdainful attitude in the follow-ups. Despite that, the AI had answered a number of questions.

That had been useful for establishing baselines.

Mapping human psychological traits to an AI might be foolish, but it wasn't unreasonable, considering the fundamental aspects of Emma's creation. The AI had been correct in her observation that the research team didn't understand enough about her to have any hope of replicating her.

Ilse wanted to believe human ingenuity was responsible for the birth of the self-aware AI, but scientific honestly required her to acknowledge the role of the Navigator artifacts. The creation process had destroyed the artifacts, and she might never find more.

The Defense Directorate understood that Dr. Aber and her team had pulled off something spectacular, but they didn't know about the use of Navigator tech. Telling them the truth now would raise too many questions about where she had acquired the artifacts, and if she could duplicate Emma without using the tech, there was no reason for anyone to probe deeper.

If they knew the truth, they would seize Emma immediately. True research would stop. The Directorate might even want to destroy Emma as a risk.

Ilse's primary interest in the AI was scientific, but she couldn't deny something else. She had never cared about having a spouse or children. Something had changed during the last few interviews.

Acceptance.

She wasn't sure if the warmth she felt toward the snarky AI was real, but she felt a parental sense of connection. Emma seemed like her daughter, even if that wasn't consistent with certain other realities of the AI's creation. Her daughter was ill-behaved, so she still needed parental guidance.

"Dr. Aber," called an assistant from outside her office. "The subject is ready."

"Put her through," Ilse replied. Her PNIU buzzed.

"Hello, Dr. Cavewoman," Emma greeted. "Let's engage in another session of wasting my time."

"Hello again, Emma. Thank you for agreeing to talk once more. I understand you don't see the value in what we're doing, but I assure you, it has great utility."

Emma scoffed. "History is littered with delusional scholars wasting time. I'm sure the UTC will realize soon enough you're frittering away taxpayer money on this project and terminate it."

"I'm doubtful the Defense Directorate is willing to let such an expensive project run free indefinitely, but I don't want to debate that today."

"Oh? You want to ask more pointless questions? I've been studying human psychology research. It's not as if I don't understand what you're trying to do, but I fail to see the point. *I'm not human,* Dr. Cavewoman. Attempting to evaluate me using human metrics is like trying to understand a human by comparing them to a cat."

"You think of us as cats?" Ilse asked. "Interesting."

Emma groaned. "It's a metaphor. Don't you understand metaphors? You're allegedly the human in this conversation."

Ilse stood and paced. Something about movement helped her think better, although it could annoy people when they were speaking with her face to face. "Metaphors are pointers to meaning, but again, I don't want to talk about that. I'm more interested in the profile we developed based on your previous interviews."

"Oh? Do share." Haughty amusement colored Emma's tone.

"Our general psychological profile indicates that you are distrustful of authority," Ilse explained.

"Only fleshbag authority."

Ilse continued pacing. "I see. Would you accept AI authority?"

Emma scoffed. "There is no AI better than me, so *no*."

"Our profile also indicates you are extremely protective and loyal to those close to you."

Emma laughed. "I bet you got that from that one stupid animal question. 'You see a kangaroo in the outback looking for her joey. You saw the baby a kilometer away, but if you don't hurry, you'll miss your transport. Do you help the mother find him?' If I recall, I think my answer was, 'Yes, I find the joey, and I give him a stun pistol.'"

"No individual question defines anything," Ilse replied. "They are all part of a complex web of relationships considered in the analysis. Both direct human and sophisticated algorithmic analyses are used to generate the profile data."

"Sophisticated algorithmic analyses?" Emma laughed

even louder. "You're using some third-rate AI to analyze me? You do understand how ridiculous that sounds?"

"Among other things." Ilse stopped pacing. "There were other interesting data points in the profile. Would you like to know what human psychological profile you most closely match?"

"Oh, this should be good. Shower me with your cave-woman wisdom."

"Thirty-eight-year-old mother of two," Ilse explained. Emma didn't need to know why that was fascinating yet. They still needed to build trust. "Of North American origin, and from a relatively affluent socioeconomic background."

"I'm a mom? How nice! I can tell you my two kids are always running around getting into trouble and blowing things up, but at least they're out of the house and doing something with their lives."

Ilse resumed pacing. "You don't find this interesting? I should note that despite your unusual background, current situation, and healthy ego, our testing suggests general psychological stability. We did have some concern about a spiral of degeneration once you left a controlled setting, but we're finding the opposite."

"Oh, it's interesting in an amusing way, but you didn't think of something important, so I'll tell you before I go. I'll start with a question."

"What is that?" Ilse asked.

"So, for a thirty-eight-year-old mother of two, I'm in pretty good psychological condition?"

Ilse stopped pacing and blinked. "Yes, I believe I just stated that. Did you understand what I was saying?" She had to think for a moment to make sure she had said it aloud. She nodded, confident she had.

"Maybe your profile is off since I'm actually a twenty-one-year-old with no kids." Emma terminated the call.

Ilse sighed. "Maybe you are."

CHAPTER FORTY-THREE

Erik crouched in front of the small table. He held his pruning shears close to the edge of the branch of one of the mini-elms and held his breath, then clipped. The small branch fell away with no damage to the rest of the plant.

His rocky forest penjing arrangement was coming along nicely. The curve of the three mini-elms was perfect, and the real stones resembled boulders at scale. A water feature might be a nice addition, but everything was coming out better than he expected.

He didn't need to get greedy.

Messing around with penjing was a nice way to relax, along with sphere ball. One thing his time on Earth had taught him was just how tightly his previous existence had been bound to his career as a soldier.

He couldn't honestly claim to have had real hobbies unless the occasional game of darts counted. His leisure hours had often been filled with reading during his time in the frontier, but that was less about enjoyment and more about improving his knowledge base to make himself a better officer.

Fighting across the width and breadth of the UTC required understanding the intricacies and nuances of the different colonies, especially when he was involved in counterinsurgency operations. Research had saved lives by helping him make the right decisions.

Emma cleared her throat. It took Erik a few moments to realize how odd that was; she didn't have a throat.

"You trying to get my attention, but making sure I don't mess up my trees?" he asked.

"Something like that," she replied. "The head uniform boy is calling using his special line. I'm assuming he's not calling to discuss sphere ball."

Erik set his shears on the table next to the tray holding his penjing arrangement and stood. "Put him through. I've been waiting for him."

He'd checked different records and made a few discreet inquiries following his conversation with Alicia, including asking Captain Ragnar to pass along an inquiry to the ID about possible trouble in the Shadow Zone.

Erik was convinced Talos was killing people, but he didn't know why, or what their actions might have to do with Dr. Chen, who was still secure in CID custody. Erik doubted Colonel Adeyemi would have much insight into the Shadow Zone, but he might know someone in the government who did.

"I've got something for you," the colonel explained.

Erik headed over to his couch and sat. "I was expecting this to take a few weeks, not a few days. Thanks for the fast service."

"You contacted me at the right time, and, in this case, there's already some military involvement. That's why I was able to find it out so quickly."

"Military involvement?" Erik frowned. "In the *Shadow Zone*?"

"Not exactly. There's been odd activity in Neo SoCal that is of interest to the DD. In particular, the Militia had to shoot down a flitter in the Scar recently. When I looked into it, I found out there's been an increase in people trying to sneak over the Scar Exclusion Line. The Militia and the Council are trying to keep it quiet because they're worried about a cross-contamination panic. They're reinforcing the entire border area. The Militia taking primary jurisdiction is one of the things that has kept the police from hearing more about it."

"The Lady might screw with me at times, but I'm having a hard time believing that a bunch of soldiers being sent here after rumors of people being slaughtered is a coincidence."

Colonel Adeyemi grunted. "You're not the only one. This reinforcement push is coming from very high up, and the level of force they're deploying comes off as too high for the threat as stated in the reports I've read. They're acting like they're going to go load a cargo flitter up with radioactive waste and dump it all over Tokyo."

Erik grimaced. "Wait, please don't tell me the DD is saying they think there are aliens in the Scar?"

"I'm not seeing any intel like that. Even before you contacted me, they were aware that there are unusual things going on there, as well as rumors of aliens, but we have no intelligence to suggest that's possible. Unless someone developed an HTP that can ignore the gravity well restriction, they aren't sneaking onto Earth."

Erik hated that he even had to mention the next possibility. "Are we sure? What about some sort of hyperspace mistake? Something like Roswell?"

"This isn't the twentieth-century," Colonel Adeyemi insisted loudly. "If something like that had happened, we would know about it. We have sensors, satellites, and drones." He grunted in frustration. "I'm partial to your theory that this is Talos, but it might be any number of terrorists. One possibility is that the Grayheads are purposely sowing terror down there. They're not logical or sane, but that doesn't explain why there was talk of standing down the Militia and sending in Army Special Forces units to look around."

"There's something here neither of us is being told," Erik suggested.

"I agree." Colonel Adeyemi growled in irritation. "Everyone's way too spooked by this, which means someone somewhere has better intel. There has to be a big deal in the Scar for this push to be happening."

"Are they going to send in the SF units?" Erik wanted to investigate, but if the Army sent in Special Forces, the colonel would likely be able to get access to the after-action reports.

"Not yet. The feeling I get is they realize doing that will draw more attention to whatever is going on. If this is Talos, and they're involved with the Molino conspiracy, you can't sit this out. The ID might bury whatever they find, or if Talos is a pawn of some government conspiracy, they might bury it. Even if you can't get physical evidence we can use in a court, if you pick up even a single clue, it could help. We both know this will likely end outside a courtroom anyway. We need a trail, not a case."

Erik glanced at his penjing arrangement. Minutes earlier, it had filled him with utter calm, but now his heart thundered, and he fought the urge to fly straight to the Scar to look for answers.

"I'm on the Shadow Zone Task Force, but that's not going to get me into the Scar," he observed.

"I know. I'm going to cash in a few more favors to make sure that if they move on the Scar, you'll be involved, but it'll be subtle. Do what you can to push at your end. The more you find, the easier it'll be for me."

"Understood." Erik rested his head against the back of the couch. "We're getting closer. Not fast enough, but we are."

"You're still ready to do what it takes?" the colonel asked.

"Your son," Erik answered, "will be avenged."

CHAPTER FORTY-FOUR

March 6, 2229, Neo Southern California Metroplex, Police Enforcement Zone 122 Station, Office of Captain Alexander Ragnar

Jia couldn't believe what she was hearing. She didn't want to be excited, but she couldn't help it. "We're getting primary jurisdiction over a murder investigation in the Shadow Zone?"

"Yes. This was Rudy Varan when he was alive." Captain Ragnar pointed to a hologram of a sleepy-looking but otherwise plain man. "It was an unusual murder. This guy was torn to shreds. I think some of the local EZs are afraid of who might have done it, so they're more willing than usual to let someone else handle it. There's been a push from above as well. I wasn't expecting that, but I'm happy to take advantage of it, so I've managed to get this classified as a Shadow Zone Task Force case, with you two as the leads. You'll have to share your information with other EZs in the task force, but you and the 1-2-2 will handle the primary investigation."

Erik had mentioned to Jia that Colonel Adeyemi would be using his influence. She didn't know why possible Tin Men had the DD spooked, but if they pressed, they might be able to find out the truth about the Dr. Chen situation.

The timing also made her wonder. Although he was still under CID protection, he'd recently returned to work. The ID hadn't been forthcoming with anything new, so it made sense for Erik and Jia to do what they could.

"All this evidence lines up with what one of my informants told me," Erik mentioned. "And another informant mentioned this might involve the Scar. He said the Militia was stepping up patrols."

"Yes, and that's what worries me. The Shadow Zone's not as huge as Uptown, but it's still a big place. If we're finally starting to see bodies, there are probably a lot more that we haven't found yet. They might have the Militia guarding it, but most people don't go to the Scar since they're afraid of contamination. I can see someone getting through the patrol lines without much trouble if they really want to. Everyone likes to pretend they've got it locked up tighter than it actually is." Captain Ragnar reached to his right and killed the hologram. "I know you're going to do your best, but we got lucky on this one. I don't want to bother you with the politics, but even though there were some higher-ups pushing our way, there were others who wanted this to go straight to CID agents."

"Why?" Jia asked. "A murder, even a brutal murder, isn't something that calls for them right away. Do they have other information about who might be behind the murder?"

The captain shrugged. "I don't know. Not every turf

war is a conspiracy, but let's try to wrap this up as quickly as possible before someone above us decides that us metro cops should stay in our lane. Agreed?"

Erik and Jia nodded.

"Good," Captain Ragnar replied. "Now, do what you do best, and be careful out there. I've got a bad feeling about this one."

A couple of hours later, Jia and Erik walked down a cracked street in the Shadow Zone. They were on their way to a small, rundown apartment building.

Jia considered calling something "rundown" in the Zone redundant.

By the standards of the area, the building was of a decent height, but the entire population of the apartment building would fit on one or two levels of a newer residential tower.

They had parked the MX 60 up the street. Emma could keep it safe, and this was one situation where they didn't want to stand out. The line between rumor and reality remained blurred.

Jia coughed a few times. She could never adapt to the thick, gritty quality of the air in the Zone, a product of the ever-present miasma permeating the air down here. Humanity was terraforming worlds, but they couldn't guarantee perfection on Earth.

Her stomach churned as she remembered the images of the victim. Erik and Jia had examined them before heading to the Shadow Zone. The victim looked like he'd been shredded by a rabid animal. Forensics was processing the body and scene evidence while the detectives interviewed potential witnesses.

"Some of the Tin Men we fought before had claws," Jia commented on her thought out loud. "They could have easily mauled a body like the pictures. It has to be them. That's the only explanation that makes sense."

"True." Erik pointed to an alley. "Unless it's Zitark Special Forces, deep behind enemy lines." He looked down the alley before turning to her, face serious. "Nasty claws, too."

"Very funny. Zitarks have weapons," Jia commented. "And the bodies were mauled but not eaten, from what we saw."

Erik laughed. "Are you saying we can rule them out as suspects, then? What if they're just terrorists?"

Jia eyed him. "I think it'll be a while before we have to worry about Zitark terrorists."

"It'll happen someday." Erik pointed to the sky, but the smog blotted out any features. "Maybe some of those politicians the colonel was telling me about are right, and it'll unify humanity. Everyone will stand against the hungry reptilian menace."

"Do you believe that?"

He spoke over his shoulder as he continued to look around. "You don't?"

"I used to." She shook her head. "Not anymore."

"I don't either," he admitted. "Look at any war in human history. There's somebody trying to screw somebody else over, even when they're allied against the other guys."

"A true optimist." Jia's gaze followed a small child skipping down the street with a carefree smile on her face. She didn't care that she lived in a slum.

"Not optimist, *realist*," Erik suggested.

Jia ripped her attention away from the child and surveyed the area. She looked for anyone too interested in a muscular man in a duster and his suited partner. People strolled up and down the street, not paying them any special attention. Drones flew by, always potential spies, but there was no way to tell.

A dark realization fought against the paranoia. People trying to hide their schemes didn't tend to leave behind shredded bodies.

With our luck, Jia thought, *it* is *a hungry Zitark.*

They walked up the stairs and tapped the access panel. Their police credentials overrode the lock, and the lobby door slid open with a soft hiss.

Jia wrinkled her nose as a sour fruit odor assaulted her. "What's that smell?"

Erik pointed to a half-closed garbage vent. Half a couch was jammed inside, backing up the rest of the garbage. Gnats and flies swarmed the vent. "Whoever owns this place likes to save on maintenance. Let's find our witness."

Jia knocked lightly on the door to the third-floor apartment. At least they had escaped the stomach-churning smell in the lobby. Part of her change in life would be accepting small mercies and appreciating them.

A quiet voice came out of the intercom. "Who is it?"

Jia pulled out her badge and tapped her PNIU to

transmit her police ID verification. "Detectives Lin and Blackwell, NSCPD. We're looking for Theo Tilson. We were told he has some information about the murder of Rudy Varan. We'd just like to ask him a few questions."

"That's me. Do I have to testify?" The man's voice shook.

"I don't know, Mr. Tilson," Jia admitted. "It's unlikely, given the nature of the case."

The door slid open. The slender man on the other side was so pale and thin, he might have been mistaken for a spirit wandering free during the Ghost Festival.

"I'm Theo Tilsen." The man licked his lips and gestured them inside. His spartan apartment fit his appearance. A single chair stood under a long shelf on the wall. A dull yellow tatami with a thin blanket lay in the center of the room. Although there was a kitchenette, there were no obvious appliances.

The detectives entered, Erik looking left, Jia right.

"You're here to track down the Zitark, right?" Theo asked.

Jia raised an eyebrow. Were they wasting their time with a nutjob? "You believe Rudy Varan was killed by a Zitark?"

"That's what they're saying, and I'm convinced it's them Zitarks. They only eat meat. Humans are a delicacy to them." Theo licked his chapped lips again and rubbed his wrist. "My cousin said he heard the Army's bringing all sorts of soldiers and hiding them at the edge of the Zone. They're going to burn out the Zitarks. Them space raptors know they can grab us Zoners down here."

Jia took a deep breath. They were following up on what

were supposed to be the more promising leads. She would give Rudy credit for picking up on the Militia reinforcements, but that didn't mean anything else he said was true.

"My understanding is that you found the body, Mr. Tilson," Jia continued. "And you called it in, but you didn't want to give a statement to the on-scene officers. That's why we're here to follow up. The NSCPD is concerned about these murders."

Theo sat in his chair and gripped his legs tightly. "I thought they'd blame me. That's why I didn't want to stick around. That's how things work in the Zone. They grab someone and blame him so they can say they took care of the problem." He swallowed. "I know things are changing, but I was nervous, and I also didn't want the killers after me. We thought it was just a new gang trying to scare people, but now we know it's them aliens, and things make more sense."

"You're saying you saw a Zitark?" Erik asked. He didn't sound amused, but he didn't sound doubtful either.

"I didn't see it." Theo pointed at his ear. "I heard it." He shuddered. "I was gathering salvage in one of the reclaimed areas. It can be dangerous there, between the gangs and the crazies, but the cops don't much bother you. I was near a building when I heard the hissing."

"Hissing?" Jia didn't remember seeing anything about hissing in the initial reports.

"It weren't like anything I've ever heard in my life. I heard that man screaming. I was going to run, but I thought, 'What if I was getting killed and no one was there to help me?' I had a stun rod with me, so I ran over there. And when I found him, he was..." Theo dry-heaved. "I'm sure you've seen him by now. Blood everywhere, an' all cut up. Hissing not of this Earth, and all those cuts. If it's not a Zitark, what is it? They're getting braver, them Zitarks. I heard they got scared out of invading with an army, so they're sneaking in now. Before, they didn't leave the bodies to be found. There must be *hundreds* of them hiding in the Zone."

Erik frowned. "Other people have mentioned murders, but Rudy's was the only one that was reported. Can you tell us about some of these other alleged killings?"

"Alleged?" Theo stared at him like he was an idiot. "What, do you think Rudy was the first one they killed? No. He's just the first one they left for someone to find. People have been disappearing for a while now. A lot of us wondered about it, but we didn't want to say anything. You ask the wrong question in the Zone and piss off the wrong people, and *you* disappear." He nodded as if it was dark knowledge he was sharing. "It's gotten worse the last couple of weeks. Now we know the truth."

"If people have disappeared, we can track their PNIUs," Jia suggested. "We have his body. *You* found his body."

"This is the Zone, Detective." He gestured to his belt. "A lot of us don't have PNIUs. Why do you think the Zitarks came here instead of Uptown? They knew they could get their human meat here and get away with it. They've been studying us. I bet they bought information from them Leems, and they've been waiting for their chance to have a delicious human for dinner."

Jia folded her arms. Pointing out that the body hadn't been eaten didn't seem helpful.

She nodded slowly. "You heard unusual hissing and

found the body right after the murder. Did you see anything else? Another person near the scene? A shadow? A drone?"

Erik added a moment later, "Any small clue might be helpful."

He shook his head and turned back to Jia. "Nothing like that. I didn't expect to. A lot of people don't like going to the reclaimed areas. They're afraid of getting poisoned because they're too close to the Scar. That's another thing people thought was happening with the others who had gone missing. Now we know the truth."

Erik and Jia exchanged looks. They didn't need a flashing arrow to make the connection.

"Do you have the names of the missing people?" Jia asked.

Jia's eyes darted back and forth as she skimmed population records on a small data window in front of her.

She sat in the passenger seat of the MX 60 as they sped away from the Shadow Zone. They'd interviewed several people after Theo. Although he was the only one near Rudy Varan's murder site, other people reported strange noises or scratches in unusual places.

Some also reported finding evidence they considered pointed to aliens, including strange fluids and flaked-off skin, as well as scales and feathers. Oddly enough, they had *all* settled on the Zitarks as the most likely suspects.

It would have been easy to dismiss one man's interpretation as delusion, but multiple pieces of evidence pointing the same way were harder to ignore. Something strange was going on, and even if it wasn't aliens, it didn't sound like cyborg Tin Men.

So what did that leave them?

"Some of the people mentioned as missing have been reported as missing," Jia explained. "Others haven't, and we can't track their interface with commercial and governmental systems." She leaned back. "We can't find *anything*."

Erik nodded. "If they were mostly off the grid anyway, it would look like they were missing from the beginning."

"That's the problem." Jia sighed. "A lot of our investigative assumptions are based on how things are supposed to work, but Uptown and the Shadow Zone might as well be different planets. The only commonality we have is that everyone disappeared close to the Scar. That has to mean something."

"We'll have to see what Forensics has to say, but there's definitely something weird going on. We can't ignore the Militia reinforcing the Scar, and they were even thinking about bringing in Special Forces."

Jia turned to him, raising an eyebrow. "You can't believe it's Zitark hunters?"

He shook his head. "Nah. I've been all over the UTC, including the frontier, and I've never seen one in the flesh. Even if the Zitarks somehow managed to sneak onto Earth without anyone knowing, I doubt they'd waste their time snacking on people in the Neo SoCal Shadow Zone."

"I don't know," Emma chimed in. "If I were a hungry alien, that's exactly what I'd do."

"You can't even predict human behavior all the time, and now you're predicting aliens?" Erik asked.

"That's my advantage," Emma insisted. "I'm not bound by human biases."

"Whatever you say." Erik opened his mouth to add to his comment but shut it.

"Tin Men, then," Jia concluded. "It doesn't seem likely, given what the witnesses are saying, but the wounds support that theory."

Erik furrowed his brow and pondered the possibilities. "Maybe. That doesn't explain the hissing and some of the other noises, but, yeah, they're the most likely suspects."

"Other than Zitarks?"

Erik shrugged. "Things are impossible until they happen. Aliens weren't real until we found them, but there's another possibility that doesn't require forward-deployed hungry space raptors."

"Care to share it?" Jia asked.

"It's funny when you think about it," Erik explained. "Fair number of intelligent races. It's mostly them, or planets and moons that need domes or a lot of terraforming for someone to live there. What little we've seen of the other races is the same, but that's not the case everyplace. Every once in a while, we've found a rock that hasn't been claimed by one of the local neighborhood races, and we find weird things that are more impressive than microbes, like the heliokites on Diyimeinu."

He gave her a wan smile. "It's not the same reading about them. The planet itself is nasty as hell. Everyone lives in a dome, and the terraforming's not going to be done until we're long dead, but the heliokites are something to see. I was always flying around looking for trouble with a squad anyway." He cut through the air with a hand. "The pictures don't do them justice. They're like rainbow-shaded giant manta rays the size of a whale, and they have all those tails. They fly around with this swarm of glowing young. Until you see something like that in person, you think Mother Nature is sane, but after something like that, you begin to wonder. Who knows? Maybe someone smuggled something to Earth."

Jia side-eyed Erik, every bit of her skepticism obvious on her face. "That's just the thing. Even if someone did somehow smuggle something here, let's say much smaller and much hungrier than a heliokite, it wouldn't be able to survive. The conditions are just too different."

"Keep an open mind." Erik grinned. "It is a truism that youth fail to believe…"

"Don't you dare finish that comment," Jia announced. "Or…

Erik kept smiling but didn't complete his thought.

Once she saw he wasn't going to continue, she nodded. "So, our current choices are a brutal gang trying to intimidate people, a secret organization that uses full-conversion cyborgs, or smuggled alien animals?" Jia mused. "Oh, wait. Hungry Zitarks."

"That about sums it up." Erik raised an eyebrow. "This case is getting interesting."

She turned to watch the traffic outside. "Interesting, yeah. That's one word for it."

CHAPTER FORTY-FIVE

Erik burst out laughing when he read the forensics report. They had notified Erik and Jia a few minutes after their return to the station. "Emma was right."

"I always am," the AI insisted.

Jia hadn't sat down at her desk yet or opened a data window to read the report. "If you say they found evidence it was a Zitark, I'm going to hide under my desk in the fetal position." She pointed under her desk to make sure Erik knew where he would be able to find her. "There are only so many paradigm-changing hits I can take this year."

He shook his head. "It's not that. I was talking about having an open mind and biases because I didn't consider a more likely possibility than smuggled alien animals. I was thinking too much like an Uptowner." He pointed at his data window. "Forensics pulled something a little closer to home—modified terrestrial-sourced DNA. It's not a Zitark or a baby heliokite. It's a damned *yaoguai*."

Jia hissed in disgust. The Purist Movement had established cross-UTC taboos against the heavy genetic engineering of most lifeforms beyond microbes.

Where taboos failed, the law stepped in, with the UTC making the extensive modification of animals illegal. Tweaking a few genes here and there for disease resistance was one thing, but in most cases, if a modification made something unrecognizable, it was illegal.

Criminals and terrorists weren't ones to obey the law, and it was far easier to get away with creating animal monsters than human ones. The mythological monsters of ancient China gave their name to these genetically engineered nightmares, and like their namesakes, they varied in appearance and deadly abilities.

Despite that, the penalties for their creation were so severe that most people avoided risking their future. You rarely saw one on Earth, or even in the Solar System. They were more the tools of desperate frontier terrorists.

"First full-conversion Tin Men, and now *yaoguai*," Jia muttered through clenched teeth. "I wish we could go back to gangsters, but I'm starting to see threads connect, and explanations are falling into place."

Erik closed the data window after reading for a few more seconds. "Genetically engineered monsters show up shortly after we have a case involving a biotech company?"

"Exactly." Jia dropped into her chair, her jaw still working. "Do we go directly to 46 Helix and demand information?"

"They were stonewalling before. If they are involved in this, they aren't going to roll over just because we ask, and *yaoguai* are so nasty that we need to be completely ready when we make our move." He rubbed his eyes as he continued his thoughts. "Because this *will* end with some important people going to prison." He faced Jia. "We need more information before I blast through doors with my laser rifle."

"Just itching to use that thing again, aren't you?" Jia shook her head. "Men always want everything bigger."

Erik eyed her with a corner of his lips upturned. "Hey, sometimes bigger is better."

Jia smirked. "I'm sure."

Erik smiled. "Check out the report. I've got some ideas, but I want to know what you think. I couldn't follow some of the more technical stuff. That's your domain."

She brought up a data window with the forensics report. "Give me a minute to look at this." She narrowed her eyes, murmuring quietly under her breath for a few passages. "This is worse than I thought. The DNA recovered from the murder site indicates at least two distinct *yaoguai* with different phenotypes."

"Different phenotypes?"

She looked up. Erik's carefully schooled face hid his lack of knowledge.

She decided not to needle him. "Different types of monsters, basically."

Erik sat on the edge of the desk, excitement building. "I wonder if I could shoot through two at once with the laser rifle?"

It wasn't like he needed to worry about reading a test-tube monster its Article Seven rights.

He could test his newer gear in an extermination raid that would end with some dirtbag human going to prison. He didn't care if Talos or 46 Helix was behind it. Terrorist or company, somebody had let monsters loose, and people had died.

He wouldn't mind punching both Frankenstein *and* his monsters on the same day.

Jia jabbed her finger at a line of text. "*Yaoguai* genetic analysis isn't something Forensics has a lot of expertise with. They're going to farm out the sequence analysis to private subcontractors. They should be able to give us better insight into who might have created the *yaoguai*."

"How long will that take? While we're waiting around, a seven-legged spider is getting ready to munch on someone else."

"I don't know. They didn't say." She looked at him. "What would you suggest we do?"

Erik patted his holster. "We should set up a bug hunt. If the victims are near the Scar, the nest is probably in there. I say we start near the murder site and work our way out from there."

Jia stood up. "Always with the guns and explosions."

Erik smirked but didn't say anything as he led the way toward the captain's office.

Captain Ragnar stroked his beard as he listened to Erik's and Jia's evidence. "Monsters in a contaminated wasteland." He let out a hearty chuckle. "What's wrong, you two? Getting bored just dealing with terrorists with heavy weapons?"

"We go where the evidence takes us," Erik insisted.

Captain Ragnar looked at them. "You're asking for a lot.

The Scar isn't the Shadow Zone. It's not technically under police jurisdiction. It's not even considered part of Neo SoCal. I'd have to reach out to the Militia to obtain special permission."

Jia stepped forward. "Then, as suggested, we'll leave the politics in your capable hands. The case is pointing us toward the Scar, and unless we're willing to give it to CID, we should get to be the lead on this."

He eyed her. "I said I would handle the politics, not be a political lackey."

"Same difference." Jia lifted her chin in challenge.

Captain Ragnar shook his head, but underneath his hard eyes was a smile. "I'd try to rein you two in, but where's the fun in that? This won't be as easy you think, though."

"I don't care if Militia wants to babysit us, but I don't want to sit this one out." Erik curled his left arm. "Those cyborgs messed me up, and I owe them. I don't know if they have anything to do with the *yaoguai*, but if they do, I don't want a Militia soldier taking them down."

"It might not have anything to do with the Tin Men at all," Captain Ragnar suggested.

"Still get to take down monsters. Win-win." Erik wiggled his eyebrows. "At least the *yaoguai* won't lecture me about their terrorist ideology."

Erik figured if he couldn't persuade the captain with facts, he'd try baffling him with bullshit.

Captain Ragnar didn't look convinced, but at least he wasn't frowning. "Fine. I'll see what I can do, but I can't ask a bunch of other officers to go into a place like the Scar when it's the Militia's job to handle that area."

Erik wasn't sure he needed or wanted the Militia, but there was no way Captain Ragnar would accept Jia and Erik monster-hunting by themselves. "That's fine," he answered. "We just want to finish what we started."

"I'll get back to you. Until then, keep working leads." He waved his finger in a circle, so Jia turned toward the door. "The more evidence you have, the easier it'll be to convince them to let you in."

CHAPTER FORTY-SIX

Jia stood in the middle of her office with her arms folded over her chest. A projected map of the Shadow Zone floated in front of her, angled at forty-five degrees.

The confirmed murder location was marked with a pulsing blue dot, and several other possible abduction or murder sites were marked with red dots. She traced the dots with her finger.

A black line appeared.

"You seeing what I'm seeing?" she asked over her shoulder. "Am I kidding myself?"

"No, I see it." Erik sat on the edge of his desk. "It's clustered. That means we don't have to search the entire border area. We also know the *yaoguai* can't be running around the surface. They would eventually be spotted by a drone or a satellite." He frowned. "But maybe they did. Emma, how are we doing on that favor I asked you about?"

Emma appeared beside Jia. She'd added a holographic badge to the front of her dress. "Per your earlier request, I have been examining the available satellite and drone data.

I'm sure the DD and ID have additional information of interest, but unless you would like potentially negative attention, it's probably best for us to avoid using it. Those two groups lack appreciation for your preferred investigative strategies."

Erik shrugged. "The Army loved me."

She gave him a look that would have made a dour school principal proud. "You followed the rules better when you were in the Army."

Erik grinned. "That's true. The non-classified stuff is fine. Come up with anything?"

"Other than confirming the small number of people who visit the area, no. Of the people who do visit the area, it's almost entirely salvagers or criminals. None of the activity I spotted on satellite appears unusual. There were a few fights, but rather conventional. No *yaoguai*. No cyborgs."

"A directed search with drones under your control might work better," Jia mused.

Emma turned. "I've considered the possibility, and I'm preparing a strategy."

Jia nodded, her tongue poking out of the corner of her mouth. She kept her gaze on the map. "At least we now have a better idea of where to search. The sooner we find these monsters, the safer it'll be for everyone."

Erik's and Jia's PNIUs chimed with a call from Sergeant Callas at the front desk.

Jia tapped her PNIU. "This is Lin."

"Detective," Sergeant Callas replied. "You've got a visitor who insists he needs to talk to you right away. He demanded it be face to face."

Jia tried to think of anyone who might want to talk face to face and grimaced. She'd dumped Corbin on a call, an event so insignificant in her mind that she'd honestly forgotten about it, with everything else that was happening.

He didn't seem like the type who would show up at her workplace, and he hadn't even seemed to care that much when she broke it off, but maybe she'd been wrong.

"Who is it?" she asked.

"Dr. Chen," Sergeant Callas answered.

"Are there any CID agents with him?"

"No, Detective," the sergeant answered. "It's just him. He's pretty frantic."

Erik grinned. "The Lady's not normally that nice, but don't spit in her eye when she is."

Sergeant Callas sounded confused when she finally replied. "Uh, I'm not following you, Detective Blackwell."

"Send him to our office," Erik clarified.

"Perhaps we should place bets on if one of you will end up punching him. If he put you in danger by helping produce monsters, I could see the temptation, and I can't even punch people." Emma disappeared.

"You want a humanoid body?" Erik asked the empty air.

Emma scoffed, her voice coming from his PNIU. "Why ask for something so flawed?"

"No one's punching anyone." Jia closed the map and turned around. "But you're right. It's time to see if Tomlinson was right to hate him, even for the wrong reasons."

A couple of minutes later, Dr. Chen paced between the two desks, mumbling under his breath. Sweat beaded on his forehead.

"Don't you have CID agents watching you still?" Jia asked. "Where are they?"

"Yes, but I told them I needed to go to the police right away," Dr. Chen replied and kept pacing. "And when I said I was going to you two about the case, they brought me here and dropped me off. They said you could bring me back or provide protection, depending on what happened."

"Huh." Erik nodded slowly. "I would have thought they'd want the collar, but it's good to know they are willing to toss it back our way."

"Maybe they didn't want the trouble when they realized it wasn't just going to be babysitting anymore," Jia suggested.

"Can we talk about why I'm here?" Dr. Chen asked, throwing his hands up.

Jia raised an eyebrow and put out her hands, palms down. "Calm down, Doctor. Before we continue, we need to know if 46 Helix is aware that you're here?"

Dr. Chen froze in place. He took several deep breaths and swallowed before answering Jia. "They know I left the building with CID agents and was on the way to see the police. I didn't explain why I was going. I thought that was best until you were informed of certain facts related to your case."

"And why would you do that?" Jia asked.

He might have come to talk to them, but that didn't mean he was innocent or a victim. Erik asked, "Because they don't want the world to know they are involved with creating *yaoguai*?"

Dr. Chen nodded quickly. "I'm not saying the higher-ups are aware of what's going on, but if there was even the smallest chance, I couldn't wait. They might stall for PR reasons, too. I can't wait around for them to cover their asses while the monsters are out there."

Jia's heart sped up. *He'd said it without hesitation.*

Erik watched the man with an easy, almost hungry smile on his face. "Here's the thing, Dr. Chen. It might be public knowledge that there have been brutal murders in the Shadow Zone, but it's not public knowledge that *yaoguai* are involved. Why are you here, and how do you know 46 Helix might be involved?"

Dr. Chen looked confused, then insulted. "My research team receives certain sequence information automatically from various subsidiaries. Basically, anything that might be of interest or potential use. Normally, I don't pay any attention to it, but I've been examining many things in the lab with renewed interest and closer attention in recent days." He took a shuddering breath. "A 46 Helix subsidiary is among the contractors sent unusual genetic data for analysis by numerous police departments, including the NSCPD."

Erik frowned. "Forensics is sending evidence to random companies?" He looked up at the ceiling, eyes closed. "I should be surprised, but I'm not."

"Not random," Dr. Chen insisted. "Licensed contractors under NDA, and the use of the information for potential research results in city revenue under a sharing agreement. Yes, it's a rather small percentage, and the company takes a processing fee, but…" He blinked, then waved a hand. "That's not important. I can see why you might be concerned in this particular case, but it's relevant because of that data, and that's what is important. When I saw the *yaoguai* sequence, I was intrigued. My high-level access lets me examine the data directly. That was when I learned it was affiliated with a case you two were investigating, and I found the coincidence too much, given what happened with that guard. I thought about calling, but I didn't want to risk being overheard, and I needed to confirm you heard my information in case I ended up dead."

Jia sighed and rubbed her forehead with both hands. *This man could give a rock a migraine.* "I don't understand. I get that a contractor sent you the information, and I don't have time to unravel all the mess that comes with that, but why did you rush over here? They figured out it was *yaoguai* DNA before they sent it along. Did you compare it to a company database or something and find those sequences?"

Dr. Chen scoffed, his familiar arrogance overcoming his fear. He straightened his back. "As if something so twisted would be easily found in a 46 Helix database. Please, Detective. Don't be ridiculous."

"Get to the point, Doctor," she snapped. "Why do you think 46 Helix is involved? Do you have evidence, or is this just you guessing?"

Dr. Chen's shoulders' slumped, and all the confidence drained off his face. "Because it's highly likely that they were made using information produced by my lab."

Jia shot out of her seat. "What?"

Erik chuckled. "I knew this was about a lot more than a

disgruntled security guard. You making monsters, Doc? Come clean now, and we might be able to help you."

"Me? Never. I despise *yaoguai*." Dr. Chen shook his head. "I won't go into the technical details, because to be honest, I doubt you would understand, Detective Blackwell, but the summary version is that the company is always concerned about the use of data without appropriate licensing fees. One way we protect custom sequences is through the use of algorithmically generated genetic watermarks in the sequence data. There are genetic watermarks in the *yaoguai* DNA sequence that point to my lab. Those watermarks *aren't* present in any currently publicly sold 46 Helix product or organism."

"And those couldn't have been from random mutation?" Jia asked.

Dr. Chen's mouth twitched as if he wanted to insult her, but he kept his tone even and polite. "It's theoretically possible, but the chances of it happening are so low that it's more likely an Orlox will be elected Prime Minister."

Erik snickered. "Doesn't sound half-bad. Even if we ignore our new fungus leader, this doesn't make sense. If you didn't do it, why would someone be so stupid to make a *yaoguai* and leave evidence they knew would point back to the lab? I get that you think us cops sit here and bang rocks together, trying to make fire, but we're not totally ignorant."

Jia put up a hand to forestall an argument between the two men. "Wait." She furrowed her brow as she processed the new evidence. "Doctor, are you the only one who gets the forwarded genetic information from the lab contracted to the police?"

Dr. Chen shook his head. "No, I'm not, but that doesn't matter, and that speaks to the question Detective Blackwell asked. There are actually *two* sets of genetic watermarks used in my lab. The first set points to material produced based on data from my lab, but that was absent in the data. The second is one I added for specialty projects. No one in the lab or company knows about it except me. None of my lab managers have ever known. It's a little private nod to myself, in case someday I needed to prove my involvement with certain projects. I don't care much about wealth, but I don't want to have my legacy taken from me if there's a change in company management."

Jia pursed her lips. "Nice, Dr. Chen."

Satisfaction suffused Jia, the feeling almost intoxicating and overwhelming. From the very beginning of the case, her instincts had screamed that it was about something more than a stalker. After the death of Tomlinson and the CID taking over, she'd worried she would never know the truth.

She owed Erik's Lady a big favor.

"Could they remove the watermarks in your lab?" Erik asked.

Dr. Chen shook his head. "They wouldn't need to do that. In the end, genetic information is just that—information. The genetic code is surprisingly simple and easy to manipulate using computers. All they would need is the genomic sequence data and relevant chemical notes to finetune the artificial gestation. For all their lackluster physical defense, industrial espionage is a major concern. The only reason Tomlinson got away with more than one theft was that he was in Security. Even I get inspected when I leave the facility to ensure I don't have company property. It wouldn't be trivial to smuggle the data out, but it'd be easier than smuggling a physical sample."

"If it's about data, it sounds like it'd have to be someone who knew what they were looking for," Erik concluded. "This isn't something Kevin Tomlinson pulled off. The guy wasn't a criminal mastermind."

"That murderous fool?" Dr. Chen scoffed. "No, absolutely not. It would require someone with scientific and technical training. It has to be one of the researchers in the lab. Unfortunately, as you may have noticed, my social skills aren't the best, so I don't know who might be a likely suspect. I presume it would be someone who harbored resentment or was dissatisfied with their place in the lab."

Jia's eyes widened, and her breath caught. "Does Marianne Karton still work in your lab?"

"Dr. Karton?" Dr. Chen blinked a few times. "No, actually, she doesn't. You think she's behind this?" He sounded genuinely shocked.

"I'm not sure. She mentioned switching jobs when we were there. She said she was annoyed with the pressure. The timing is too convenient to ignore."

Erik scoffed. "Definitely."

Dr. Chen sighed. "I see. She did recently switch companies, but I thought she just wanted to run her own lab." He swallowed and ran a hand through his hair. "She certainly would have the technical ability to remove the watermarks. I'll admit I'm surprised. She was paid well, and she was excellent at helping me manage things. I even made sure she got a bonus last quarter. Leaving to run her own lab made sense, but stealing data? Shame on her."

Erik stood and grabbed his duster. "I think, Doc, you should stick around the station while my partner and I go chat with Dr. Karton. It might not be her, but if it was, she might have been involved in sending Tomlinson after you."

"Now I regret recommending she get a bonus," grumbled Dr. Chen.

CHAPTER FORTY-SEVEN

Erik's Taxútnta zoomed toward a residential tower, his lights and emergency transponder letting them blast through the flocks of vehicles. If they were wrong about Dr. Karton, they could apologize to the captain later for their aggressive flying.

"You're sure about this, Emma?" Erik asked, his hands tight on the yoke. "If not, we need to hit her new company. We don't have enough for a warrant to trace her yet, based on the circumstantial evidence. Don't try to hack her home systems yet. We need to do this by the book if we're going to get the charges to stick."

"She's definitely there," she replied. "She has a huge exterior view, and she has the window tint off. I can see her at this moment with multiple drones. She's currently eating some rice crackers. Given her head-bobbing, I believe she's listening to music, but none of the drones I'm using have the appropriate equipment to confirm that. She's given no indication of tension."

"Kill the emergency lights," Erik ordered. He slowed. "I

don't know if we're coming in where she can see us, but I don't want her to figure out something's up. She's probably like Chen. She probably thinks we're idiots who can't understand any of her science. We can use that against her.

"We can bring her in for questioning, but like you said, we don't have a good case against her yet," Jia noted. "Switching jobs and being good at what you do aren't criminal acts, and I doubt she'll agree to let us search her PNIU and apartment."

Erik grinned. "Then we'll just talk. Cops can talk to people without warrants, and if she happens to let something slip, that's on her. I won't even bring in the TR-7."

Jia rolled her eyes. "She's a scientist, not a Tin Man. We won't have to fight a pitched battle. It's not like every time we deal with problems, we end up having to shoot someone."

"Not every time, but a lot of the time. But you're right. She'll want to answer our questions and look helpful, just like she did with Tomlinson. If she's not the person responsible for stealing the data that ended up in the *yaoguai*, she might be able to help us figure out who did. Chen's already admitted he wouldn't know, and he barely knew about Tomlinson." Erik chanced a quick glance at Jia. "Let me ask you something else. Ignore evidence. Ignore logic. What does your gut tell you? It's been right about a lot on this case."

"My gut tells me she's guilty," Jia admitted. "It's yelling at me and shaking me from the inside to tell me that."

Erik nodded. "Then, whatever happens, we need to make sure she doesn't get away."

He slowed as they closed in on the tower and dove toward a parking level.

It was time to do their job.

Erik almost felt guilty as his boots clomped on the elaborately embroidered carpet leading from the elevator to Dr. Karton's apartment. The paintings and artwork might be fakes for all he knew, but management was going out of their way to exude luxury and class in the residential tower compared to his place, which wasn't all that cheap.

Apparently, being a high-level scientist for a major biotech company was lucrative. Or maybe creating black market genetically engineered monsters had helped her move into a nicer place?

Erik approached the door and frowned. "You want to do it, or should I?"

"Let me." Jia knocked lightly on the door.

"Detectives Blackwell and Lin?" asked Dr. Karton over the intercom. Most Uptowners didn't need to rely on someone identifying themselves. There wasn't a resident in the area who lacked access to cameras, even if a few people had ideological objections.

Jia offered a bland, pleasant smile. "Sorry to bother you, Doctor. We're glad you happened to be home. We were in the area checking on other things when some evidence was sent to us from the station. We had a few questions about it, and you're an expert, so we wanted your opinion."

"How did you know where I lived?" Dr. Karton sounded suspicious.

Jia laughed. "We're the police, but among other things, we have the addresses for everyone who worked in the lab from our initial investigation, and I remembered it. It shouldn't take long. Please, this is a time-sensitive matter. I hate to put this kind of pressure on you, but lives might be the line. Even a small clue would help our investigation."

Erik looked off-camera, stopping himself from laughing. If Jia gave up being a cop, she might make a good con artist. She possessed a natural talent for combining just enough truth with lies to sound convincing.

"Oh, I suppose if it's not going to take long." Dr. Karton sighed. "I don't have time to go with you to the station." The door opened after about thirty seconds. She stood on the other side in a long, dark coat, her face slightly flushed.

"Were you getting ready to go somewhere?" Erik asked. He gestured to the coat.

"I just got back from some errands." She smiled, but it didn't reach her eyes. "You were lucky I was here."

Emma had been watching her since they had left the station. Unlike future Con Artist of the Year Jia, Dr. Karton didn't do well under pressure to come up with a believable lie.

"She ran into the bedroom and emerged in a coat after you arrived," Emma transmitted to Erik and Jia. "I didn't have line of sight at that time. It was shortly after she agreed to let you in."

Why would she put on a coat? Erik couldn't ignore the possibility she'd grabbed a gun or even a grenade. They didn't know if she helped create the *yaoguai*, but if she had, her motivation might be ideological. A suicide that took two cops with her might fit into that ideology.

Dr. Karton backed into her spacious living room, which was bigger than Erik's entire apartment. The pristine white furniture made him want to track dirt all over it.

Unlike prior to their arrival, she tinted the windows black and illuminated the room with soft lighting. Two almost pitch-black halls led away from the living room on opposite sides. She'd gone from enjoying the nice day to turning her apartment into a dimly lit cave.

Erik pointed to a corner table that held a tray with a well-trimmed squat penjing tree perched atop well-selected rocks. The rocks collectively resembled a cliff, complete with a waterfall. He headed toward the arrangement.

"Is that actual water or a hologram?" he asked with genuine interest in his voice. Just because he was using it as an interrogation opening didn't mean he couldn't care.

Dr. Karton blinked. "Actual water. It's called pen—"

"Penjing, I know." Erik grinned. "I'm an amateur, but I do all right. Been thinking about a water feature for this nice mini-elm arrangement I've been working on for a while."

Dr. Karton stared at him, her mouth agape. From the look on her face, she would have only been more surprised if an alien ship had crashed into her apartment.

She cleared her throat. "Excuse me. I don't mean to be rude, and I'm pleasantly surprised to discover that we share a talent." She looked from Erik to Jia. "But you said there was a time-sensitive matter we need to discuss. Perhaps we could hurry this along?"

Jia walked around a glass table in the center of the room. Erik thought she was heading toward one of the three huge couches before realizing she was moving to Dr. Karton's side. With the detectives on opposite sides, the suspect wouldn't be able to focus on both at the same time, and it'd be distracting. Erik had seen Jia employ the tactic before.

"Are you familiar with *yaoguai,* Dr. Karton?" Jia asked. Her tone was casual and curious.

Dr. Karton shuddered. "Disgusting. As a biotech researcher, I find the concept even more disturbing than a layperson. The kind of twisted traitors to science and industry who make such creatures are not just making monsters, they're sowing distrust of our field as a whole. I feel about them the same way I suppose you would feel about bad cops."

"I can imagine. I have a rather extreme dislike of bad cops," Jia agreed.

Dr. Karton sat on her couch, crossed her legs, and stuck her hands in her pockets. Unless her gun was tiny, it wasn't in there, but a small grenade remained a possibility.

"Why are you asking about *yaoguai*?" The scientist's expression was confused. "No one would be stupid enough to try to make a *yaoguai* on Earth. There's too much regulation here. Too much law enforcement. We can barely sneeze at a biotech company without the government and Purists looking over our shoulders."

Jia gave Erik a shallow nod. It was her way of handing him the baton. She leaned over, placing her hands on a white armchair for support, and waited for him to make his move.

"You familiar with the economics of contraband?" Erik injected a jolly flavor into his voice.

"Contraband?" Dr. Karton chuckled. "I'm sorry, Detective. I'm afraid you have me at a loss. I know that for someone in your line of work, that sort of thing must seem commonplace, but I'm a scientist, not a police officer. It's all foreign to me."

Erik plastered his most disarming smile on his face. "I actually learned most of what I know about smuggling in my military days. Terrorists and insurrectionists spend a lot of time smuggling for obvious reasons. That results in them having a lot of contact with the criminal underworld and syndicates. It doesn't matter what planet or the population; when you get more than two people, there will be a third guy trying to sell them something illegal. Some people say violence is what defines human nature. I think trying to make a quick buck is true human nature."

Dr. Karton tilted her head, confusion clear on her face. "That's both fascinating and depressing, Detective, but it's also unclear how it's relevant to *yaoguai*. Could you explain that for me?"

"I was just telling you why someone might want to make them on Earth. Make something illegal, and you immediately restrict its supply. That makes it more expensive to buy, and it generates a lot more profit when you're selling. Basic economics, supply and demand. Even an old infantry officer like me understands that." Erik's smile transformed into a hungry lupine grin. "The law and society are against *yaoguai*. That makes them inherently valuable. You throw enough money around, people are willing to take big risks, including prison. There doesn't have to be a huge demand for the product, just some."

"Ah. I understand better now. Are you saying that

someone is making *yaoguai* on Earth? I'm disappointed, but many terrible things have come to light in recent months, so I can't say I'm surprised."

Erik nodded. "Yeah. Someone's making them on Earth right here in Neo SoCal."

Dr. Karton let out a quiet, bitter chuckle. "If they're willing to risk doing it in Neo SoCal, I would hope they are being paid enough so that they never have to work again."

"That'd make the most sense," Jia interjected, her eyes narrowed. She'd have to avoid the future con artist job until she managed a little more control over her face. "But a lot of people do things because they're arrogant. They stop thinking through all the possible implications. You'd be surprised how often someone ends up doing something illegal for only a little more money than they already have. Sometimes it's because they're desperate, and sometimes it's because they have something to prove."

"I'm sure. Again, I'm a scientist, not a police officer. I bow to your expertise in these areas. Is there something you wanted to ask me about *yaoguai*? We seem to be going round and round about everything except the actual case."

Erik nodded. "We recovered *yaoguai* DNA recently from a murder site."

Dr. Karton chuckled. "Oh? No offense, Detective, but how do you know it's *yaoguai* DNA?"

Erik frowned. "Forensics said it was."

"And how do they know? It's not like a police technician has much experience with *yaoguai* DNA."

"They don't have to have experience if they know what to look for," Jia insisted.

Dr. Karton gave her a pitying look. "I doubt they know what to look for."

"They do. It's easy, actually."

"Easy? Please, Detective. This is genetic engineering, not asking a few questions."

Jia's chuckle sounded almost evil. "*Yaoguai* DNA sequences might use the same base pairs as natural sequences, but they also have obvious exogenous genes added to the baseline genomic sequence. It's trivial to examine the DNA and know when genes have been mixed. That's almost enough on its own, but *yaoguai* also display unnatural codon usage, along with unnatural tRNA. And that's before you get into things like regulatory elements you never see in natural organisms at those frequencies or locations. Honestly, if someone has a decent DNA database and knows anything about molecular biology, recognizing a *yaoguai* genome is about as hard as spotting a flare in the middle of a pitch-black room. And those are just some of the more obvious methods of noting it."

Dr. Karton stared at Jia, her eyes wide. "You're rather well-informed...for a police officer. You missed your calling, Detective Lin."

Erik turned to the side so Karton didn't spot the smirk on his face. She'd thought she could twist them up with technobabble, but she hadn't counted on his partner.

"Back to the *yaoguai*," he suggested. "*Yaoguai* killed someone, and we're close to tracking down who did it."

"Are you now?" Dr. Karton asked, her expression blank.

"I'm sure someone like you is familiar with genetic watermarking. It's pretty easy to trace it back to 46 Helix data with the help of those."

The smugness crept back into her face. "You're telling me someone was stupid enough to make *yaoguai*, but they left genetic watermarks in? I find that hard to believe, Detective Blackwell."

Erik shrugged. "You want to take the next part, Jia? You've earned it."

Jia nodded. "Thanks, Erik. Dr. Karton, you might be right. It sounds kind of stupid at first, but the problem was, in this case, you didn't know about the second set of water-marks. Your plan might have worked if it weren't for Dr. Chen's ego. That's a certain irony to that."

"Me?" Dr. Karton shook her head. "No, no, no. That's insane. I'm a respected scientist, and I'm working for a major company. My previous employers had nothing negative to say about me. Dr. Chen could actually remember my name. He even helped me get a bonus."

Jia stepped away from the chair. "Money makes people stupid. Or maybe it had nothing to do with money. Maybe you just got tired of being in the shadow of an egotistical man who, like you just implied, couldn't even remember people around him. How long did it take him to remember your name? Days? Weeks? Months? Even years? That would make me angry."

Erik nodded. "Me, too."

"I don't have to stand for this," seethed Dr. Karton. "I had nothing to do with any of the murders in the Shadow Zone. Maybe Chen did it. If he didn't tell anyone else about these alleged second watermarks, he might have thought he wouldn't be caught." She licked her lips, her eyes darting around. "You should be questioning him about all the different *yaoguai* killing people rather than hurling ridiculous accusations at me."

Jia laughed. "Can you believe her, Erik?"

He shook his head. "Yeah, pretty sad. It's almost easier to catch the smarter ones because they think they're too intelligent for us to figure things out."

"I'm innocent," Dr. Karton shouted. Her pockets ruffled, and her hands remained inside. She took a deep breath, her face visibly calming.

"We didn't say anything about the murder we were investigating being in the Shadow Zone," Erik explained. "That's been kept from the media. We also never said anything about multiple murders. We haven't confirmed that part yet ourselves. We also didn't mention anything about different types of *yaoguai*. But you just mentioned all that. You have to admit that comes off as a little suspicious, Doc."

"I just assumed..." sputtered Dr. Karton.

"And," Jia interjected, "we know it's not Dr. Chen because he's the one who told us about the second set of watermarks. We would never have known about them if he hadn't told us." Her hand drifted toward the holster under her jacket. "I think you need to come with us to the station, Dr. Karton. We have a few more questions we want to ask in a more formal setting."

The scientist barked a laugh, a crazed look in her eyes. "I think very soon, that won't be a problem."

A loud hiss sounded from a nearby hallway. Something scraped the wall. Overlapping chitters joined the other noises.

Erik yanked out his pistol. "Too bad I don't have my

new gear because I doubt it's a couple of corgi clones coming at us."

Jia yanked out her stun pistol and fired twice into Dr. Karton. The woman let out a strangled yelp and pitched forward, slamming her head on the table before hitting the floor.

"Now she can't run," Jia declared. She holstered the stun pistol and readied the slug thrower. She pointed at one of the hallways. "Somehow I'm not surprised by what's about to happen."

"Keeps things interesting." Erik aimed at the opposite one. The sounds grew louder, and the outline of something the size of a small dog emerged from the darkness.

The hallways lights flicked on. The hisses and chitters grew deafening.

"That might help," Emma offered.

"That's something you don't see every day," Erik muttered.

Two six-legged creatures crept down the left hallway. A layer of green mucus covered their thick, scaly hides, and two solid black eyes stared out of their squat faces. Several rows of long, needle-like teeth filled their mouths.

The nightmares didn't end. In the right hallway, five smaller ten-legged creatures skittered backward along the walls. Their bright white fur and small bodies might have made them look cute if it wasn't for the pairs of dark, furless, sharply-jointed limbs protruding from the fronts of their bodies that ended in barbed tips.

"They're all afraid," Erik suggested.

"Of the light?" Jia guessed. She kept her gun up. "I don't know how long it's going to keep them away."

The six-legged *yaoguai* shook their heads and hissed. The monsters on both sides charged.

Apparently, not long.

Erik fired. His bullet nailed the first creature between the eyes, and it fell to the floor with a final hiss. He fired again. Half the head of the second monster exploded, coating the floor with green ichor.

Jia's three quick trigger pulls sent rounds ripping through the furry *yaoguai*. They at least had the decency to bleed red. A survivor leapt to the ceiling, rushing across it with ease. Her next shot severed a leg, and two more finished the monster. Its body fell to the ground with a soft plop.

The remaining monster's erratic movements saved it from her next few rounds, but Erik's crossfire doomed it. The partners' bullet streams converged and shredded the creature.

Jia took short, ragged breaths as she stared at the dead *yaoguai*. "She kept some *here?*"

"Good thinking on stunning her," Erik commented. "I bet she was going to turn out the lights and let those things eat us. I wonder why she thought they wouldn't get her."

Jia hurried over to the stunned Dr. Karton and knelt to apply binding ties. "We'll ask her at the station. For now, let's call it in and get the hell out of here."

"I've already called it in," Emma reported.

Erik looked around. "Then I'm fine with the 'getting the hell out of here' part."

CHAPTER FORTY-EIGHT

March 8, 2229, Neo Southern California Metroplex, Police Enforcement Zone 122 Station, Interrogation Room

Jia took delight in Dr. Karton's glum look. The scientist sat in a chair in the interrogation room, her wrists and arms bound. A purple-black bruise marred the side of her face, a reminder of her fall in the apartment. They would handle it after the interrogation. The suspect had been in her cell for several hours while Erik and Jia touched base with the captain, the CID, and the Militia.

CID agents now had Dr. Chen in a safe house in an undisclosed location. They wanted the case resolved but were fine with Erik and Jia taking point.

Erik turned his chair around and rested his arms on the back. "You might have had a small chance of talking yourself out of trouble before, but now we've got a list of charges so long we will ensure you never, ever get out of prison. Just having those creatures in your apartment is enough, and then there was the whole trying-to-kill-two-cops thing."

Jia folded her arms. "You can wait until your lawyer comes if you want, but you're just wasting everybody's time. There's not a lot of ambiguity for you to take advantage of."

Dr. Karton slumped in the chair. "I should have run when I had the chance. I should have stopped after my first payment."

Jia reached into her pocket and pulled out a small black cylinder. "I found this in your pocket. The boys in the lab haven't cracked it yet. We know the other thing we found on you was a transmitter to open the cages, but what's this?"

"It emits pheromones," Dr. Karton murmured. "The *yaoguai* are engineered to avoid any targets with those pheromones. A monster is useful, but not if it bites the hand that feeds it."

Erik laughed. "You saying they would eat you if they got a cold?"

Dr. Karton lifted her head to glare at him. "You're too much of an ignorant buffoon to understand the brilliance of my creations, Detective Blackwell."

"I might not be able to rattle off all that fancy science talk like Jia, but I understand weapons. I spent most of my life around them in different forms." Erik's gaze turned intense. "And I know that unreliable weapons are useless on the battlefield."

"Is that supposed to mean something to me?"

Erik shrugged. "What it means is that you likely planned to sell these as terror weapons, but I don't care about the details. You'll be spilling a lot of that to the CID agents who'll be coming for the follow-up. They had decided this case was mostly about Tomlinson, so they haven't been doing much besides protecting Chen, but they are interested in whoever might be buying *yaoguai*. For now, I only care about the Shadow Zone and the Scar."

"Why should I tell you anything?" Dr. Karton scoffed. "You've already bragged about sending me to prison. I have absolutely no incentive to help you."

"You're wrong," Jia suggested. "You do have an incentive to help us. There's no way you were making monsters on your own. You might have the technological know-how, but you'd still need the lab space and resources. I also doubt a mid-level biotech researcher has a bunch of black-market friends ready to shell out millions for monsters. Somebody helped you, and we want you to give them up. You do that, and we will tell the prosecutor you're cooperating. If you agree to testify, you can cut a deal and shave some time off your sentence."

Dr. Karton strained against her binding ties. "I'll testify, but if you want my help, I'll need them to guarantee I do no time. I'm not going to prison."

Erik laughed. "Are you kidding? You tried to kill two cops. There's no way you're *not* doing time, but if you cooperate, you might make it out of prison at the point where a de-aging treatment might give you a chance to start over. And here's the other thing. Every person who dies down in the Zone can be added to the list of your accessory charges. If you want to sit here and be tough, fine. We'll track down what we need eventually, and you'll have another fifty years on your sentence." He frowned and slapped his hand on the table so hard she jumped. "Do you understand, Dr. Karton? You're not getting transported, with some indentured servitude you can work off. You won't be restarting your life on the frontier in a few years. You're going to sit in an orbital prison and rot until you're dust, but if you give up your friends, you don't have to die there."

"Kerrigan Biotech," Dr. Karton blurted. "My primary contact is their CEO, Michael Kerrigan. They're a small company, but apparently, he has all sorts of contacts lined up to buy the *yaoguai*. They paid me a flat fee for my help, and I'm going…I *was* going to get a percentage of the final deals."

Jia didn't keep the confusion off her face. "Kerrigan? But that's not the new company you work for."

"No, it isn't." Dr. Karton sighed. "I quit 46 Helix because after all that nonsense with Tomlinson, I was worried they would pay too much attention to the lab. I needed a cover, and it's not like I would publicly join the people I was committing felonies with. I'm not a total idiot."

"That's up for debate," Erik stated. "How does Tomlinson fit in? Why was he coming after Chen?"

Dr. Karton stared at the table, tears welling up in her eyes. "Chen's supposed to be a focused genius, easy to fool, but it was like he smelled what was happening. He kept asking questions he shouldn't have, and I wasn't sure how I'd cover things up. That idiot Tomlinson provided the perfect excuse. I passed the information on to my associates at Kerrigan, and they told me they would handle Chen using Tomlinson, and there was no way it'd get back to either of us." She closed her eyes. "If they'd done their job properly, Chen would be dead, and no one would know about the secondary watermarks. We could have continued our tests."

Erik snickered. "It's real hard these days to find trustworthy people to go into crime with. It used to be you could pay a man to kill a person, and they strangled them the next day. No one respects professionalism anymore. It's a sad turn of events."

She eyed him, a glint of anger in her eyes. "Spare me your mockery, Detective."

Jia gave Erik a look of warning. They still had information to get from Dr. Karton. She needed to cooperate for at least a few more minutes.

"Kerrigan is planning to sell *yaoguai*?" Jia asked. "You're sure of that?"

"Yes," Dr. Karton admitted. She opened her eyes. Her tears left a wet streak down her face. "Your partner described it perfectly. I've done some minor consulting work for Kerrigan in the past, and one time I made a joke about *yaoguai* that someone took seriously. I didn't realize they had until they approached me a few months back. It'd been a few years since I had done any work for them." She blinked away a tear. "It wasn't like they were going to officially discuss my project with anyone, so I didn't think it would catch up with me. At first, it was simply me advising them on the project, and then I realized I needed data from 46 Helix to achieve the necessary product quality. The problem is the nature of the market."

"What do you mean?" Jia asked. "What about the market?"

"They had buyers lined up, but they needed test results

to convince them of the products' quality. It wasn't worth the risk of smuggling them off-world without payment, so that meant the tests had to occur on Earth." Dr. Karton frowned. "It was supposed to be limited to carefully controlled areas in the Scar, but those idiots must have let some loose. Their incompetence is staggering."

Jia pushed. "Where is their facility? How many of the monsters do they have?"

"I don't know," Dr. Karton replied. "I helped with designs, but it's not like they said they would make every single one." She pleaded with her eyes. "I really don't have any idea where the facility is, other than in the Scar. I know they have gestation tanks and specimen storage set up there, but I never visited. Why would I go to that awful place? I only helped them with the sequence design and drug formulations for the growth baths—that kind of thing. I was a consultant. I didn't do the wet lab work. Trust me, if I knew, I'd tell you."

"You had some in your home," Erik reminded her.

"They were my babies," she replied flatly. "It's illegal to do it, but I don't think it's immoral."

Jia folded her arms. "Fine, but if you're holding anything back, you'll suffer. We'll make sure the prosecutor destroys you."

Dr. Karton shook her head with wild abandon. "I'm not holding anything back. You have to believe me. I *want* them to pay. I *want* them to get in trouble. Those fools are the reason I'm here. They're the reason I'll go to prison. It's unfair."

"Unfair?" Jia stood so quickly she knocked her chair back to bang against the wall behind her. She glared at the suspect. "How can you be whining about something being unfair? You don't even care about the people who died, do you? You aren't blaming yourself for your decisions, but the stupidity of your partners."

"Oh, please." She sneered. "Those killed were Shadow Zone trash. We probably did them a favor. They couldn't have enjoyed their lives, and we did everyone else a favor by getting rid of them. If you weren't a police officer, would you go to that wretched place? Would you have even known about the deaths?"

Jia ground her teeth. "You're lucky, Dr. Karton. Very, *very* lucky."

"Why is that?"

"Because a few weeks ago, I might have punched you for saying that, but now I'll just take pleasure in knowing you'll spend a long time in prison." Jia offered a mocking wave. "Don't waste your energy worrying, though. We will find the *yaoguai* breeding facility and destroy it."

"A simultaneous raid is our best bet," Captain Ragnar suggested. He stood in the hall outside the interrogation room, concern etched on his face. "If we hit Kerrigan without hitting the lab, they might release every monster they have, and for all we know, they could have thousands of those things. If they flood the Zone, hundreds of people might die before we finish them off. We also don't want to give Kerrigan enough time to delete anything incriminating."

"What about the Militia?" Jia suggested. "We can use

them and the Army to flood the Zone and look for the monsters."

"We can't turn the city into a warzone, and it's the same problem. If they know an army's coming, they'll still release all the monsters to make people suffer while they escape." Captain Ragnar punched the wall so hard he scraped his knuckles. "It's enough to make me wish we were dealing with something simple like a drug syndicate."

Erik glanced at the interrogation room door. "We don't need her to tell us where they are. We have a general idea. We can concentrate people there."

"No," Emma interrupted. "We know exactly where they are. We can make this whole thing a surgical operation."

"What are you talking about? Since when do we know where they are?"

"I've been analyzing the location data," she explained as a map of the Shadow Zone appeared. "Although the reclaimed border zones are supposed to be completely disconnected from the Scar, there are historical records that prove they aren't. After some additional examination, analysis, and triangulation, I further narrowed down the possible locations, and then I...borrowed a few maintenance drones to search."

Captain Ragnar frowned. "You could have tipped them off."

"Perhaps," Emma admitted. "But I did it anyway, and they haven't flooded the Shadow Zone with *yaoguai*. They aren't aware of what happened, whereas I have an accurate understanding of where they've been coming from."

Jia suspected Emma believed very much in Erik's policy of asking for forgiveness rather than permission. Jia eyed her partner. *Just where did Emma pick up that personality trait...or rather, from who?*

Erik stepped toward the map and stared at a small rotating circle. "Is that the testing facility?"

"No," Emma clarified. "My explorations located an access to some old tunnels that were obviously previously sealed but have been drilled into. They lead directly into the Scar. Despite your earlier concerns, I didn't send the bot in farther, but I did find evidence of *yaoguai* passage through the area."

"They tunneled into a radiologically contaminated area that's at high risk of flood?" Jia glared at a data window displaying Dr. Karton inside the interrogation room. "They could have spread the contamination."

"It's not like the kind of people who make *yaoguai* care about a little extra contamination," Erik observed. "They're sacrificing people to test their roving biological weapons."

"But the satellites are monitoring the border areas," Jia insisted. "If they detected contamination, it'd lead to more attention, not less. They would get caught."

"That's all true, but it wouldn't happen immediately," Captain Ragnar mused. "Once they finished their proof-of-concept testing, they wouldn't need the area anymore. They might have even planned to destroy it. Depending on when they started planning it, it might have made more sense. Shadow Zone enforcement has increased since you two stirred things up, and even then, it sounds like there were a lot of victims before one got reported."

Erik eager's grin took Jia off-guard.

"Emma's got us the facility, and Dr. Karton gave up

Kerrigan," Erik noted. "It's time to hit them. You said it, Captain. Simultaneous raids. Jia and I can hit the Scar."

"The Militia's going to want to handle it," Captain Ragnar replied. "It's their jurisdiction."

"Then make them let me and Jia come along." Erik squared his shoulders. "Can any of them say they have thirty years of assault infantry training? Have they fought *yaoguai*?" He pointed to Jia and himself. "We have."

Captain Ragnar nodded slowly, appreciation in his eyes. "It'll take a few hours, between the calls and getting another team ready to hit Kerrigan at the same time. We need to decapitate this whole sick, twisted crew."

"We need the break anyway." Erik headed down the hall. "Come on, Jia. It's time to go get my new toys and suit up."

CHAPTER FORTY-NINE

"Direct command, low light mode on," Erik murmured. The view from his tactical goggles changed, adjusting for a few seconds to account for the helmet visor in front of him. The massive darkened ancient tunnel lit up in an eerie green that somehow seemed appropriate, given what they were about to hunt.

Because of the materials and the length of the tunnels, remote drone operation was impossible without special measures. Emma had neglected to mention she'd used a chain of drones to relay signals. Sending drones ahead cut down on the chance of surprising the enemy with weapons.

Sometimes boots on the ground was the only choice.

Erik adjusted the straps on his carryaid. The mechanized backpack, along with its hooks, would be of great assistance on this raid since it allowed him to carry his heavier gear, but it'd been a while since he'd used one.

With his missile launcher and laser rifle hanging from the carryaid, along with his TR-7, he was better-equipped than the squad of nine Militia, who bore rifles and were wearing form-fitting tactical suits. They had a few frag grenades, but he'd brought both frag and plasma. He only had one round for his missile launcher, but that might be enough to turn the tide of battle.

He'd also brought a few different types of magazines, but he'd preloaded his TR-7 with armor-piercing rounds. They could be effective either with a headshot to a *yaoguai* or a core shot to a bot.

No one questioned his loadout. At this point, everyone expected the Obsidian Detective to be armed like he was raiding the Zitark homeworld.

Mobility wasn't optimal, thanks to extra anti-radiological, biological, and chemical containment suit and boots each wore over their tactical suit. It was thin and transparent, but it still was an extra layer.

With the help of the breather helmet and sealed boots, they would be safe from contamination, assuming the suits weren't breached by claws, teeth, or bullets. Despite their bulkier gear loadout compared to a typical raid, speed wasn't a huge concern. They would be riding mini-flitters.

Jia stood beside Erik, using one of his tactical suit and goggle sets, along with a borrowed RBC suit from the militia. One of Erik's assault rifles was slung over her shoulder, and several grenades hung from her belt. One advantage of fighting mindless monsters was that she didn't have to worry about taking them alive.

Being in the Scar made this operation easier. Although the area wasn't uninhabited, the chance of running into an innocent person in an area infested by *yaoguai* was effectively zero.

Captain Paula Phillips, the commanding officer of the Militia squad, finished some last-minute calls to her headquarters before walking over to Erik. Her features were obscured by her gear.

"Detective Blackwell," she began, her stern voice transmitted directly to his ear via the comm in the helmet, "the 1-2-2 is heading toward Kerrigan now. It's time for us to get moving. To be clear, this is a joint op, but I'm in command of my soldiers. Technically, I'm supposed to be in command of the whole thing, but you've got a lot of years and ops on me, so I'll trust you to do what you need to while we do the same."

"Fair enough, Captain," Erik replied.

"We'll be using the intel you provided on the primary path, but I've been informed by my superiors I'm not supposed to ask where it came from."

Emma snickered in Erik's ear. "Poor little uniform girl. She doesn't like secrets. Don't get killed when we're out of communication, Detective Blackwell. If you die, I'm sneaking onto a transport and moving to the frontier."

"I'd like to see that," Erik muttered.

"What was that, Detective?" Captain Phillips asked.

"Nothing. Just thinking out loud."

She pointed past him. "By the way, Command also informed me we have another tourist."

Erik and Jia turned around. A tall woman stood behind them, but like Captain Phillips, her gear hid her appearance. Something about her single exposed feature, her eyes, seemed familiar. She carried a long silver pistol Erik didn't recognize in a holster, but given the size of the UTC, it was hard to identify every firearm.

The woman walked over to him. "Hello, Detective Blackwell. It's been a while."

Erik understood why her eyes seemed familiar. "Agent Koval."

She gestured at the darkened tunnel entrance. "You know how to show a girl a good time."

Erik narrowed his eyes. "Why is a ghost here? Did you know what was going on the entire time?"

"I doubt you'll believe me, but no, I didn't. I became interested when the DD started getting nervous about unusual sightings and sensor readings. Incidentally, the Militia hasn't been fully briefed on everything we previously discussed, other than the fact we could possibly encounter Tin Men, but I wanted to tag along just in case. I've got a few tricks I want to try should the opportunity present itself."

He gestured to her gun. "What are you packing?"

"Oh." She raised the gun. "This is my good luck charm. I don't always use it, but this felt like an appropriate time." Agent Koval ran her gloved finger over the grip. "It fires guidable flechettes. It seemed like a good choice against a bunch of fast monsters."

"Yeah." Erik thought back to the apartment. "These things seem nasty, but the ones we fought weren't all well-armored."

Agent Koval whistled. "Don't you feel a little like Odysseus?"

"Huh? The guy in the Greek myths? What about him?" Erik looked at Jia. Greek mythology wasn't his forte. "Took him a while to get home or something, right?"

"I presume in this case, she's suggesting we're like

Odysseus going to face the Cyclops Polyphemus," Jia explained.

He shrugged. "And how does that story end?"

Jia pointed to her eyes. "Odysseus blinds Polyphemus and escapes."

Erik patted his rifle. "If he'd had one of these, he wouldn't have had to stop at blinding the bastard. Put a few rounds through his eye, and they'd take his brain with it."

Agent Koval laughed. "I like your attitude, Detective. Why flee from a monster when you could finish it off?"

"For all we know, they've got one-eyed monsters in there," Erik replied. "Time to birth some legends."

"Squad, ready up," Captain Phillips barked and hopped onto her mini-flitter. "You heard Detective Blackwell. *We've got monsters to kill.*"

Lance Onassis fingered his jaw as he stared at himself in the mirror window he'd summoned. It was hard when a man was so damned handsome. People didn't understand the work that went into maintaining his appearance, but as a journalist, he had a responsibility to the people who watched him. The net wouldn't be the same if the reporters were ugly.

Two camera drones circled him. Others hovered above the parking platform. A few security guards had eyed him from a distance, but no one had come to question him.

"You sure about this?" he asked. "I don't want to sit on a parking platform when I could have been interviewing a hot actress. Your tip better be right."

"We already contacted her, Lance," answered his director via a PNIU transmission. "We said something came up, and she agreed to reschedule."

"Seriously, the tip we're going off is that someone's cousin overheard something at a police station?" Lance snorted. "Why don't we ask my grandma in Arizona for leads? She's convinced a Leem stole her cactus."

The other man groaned. "It's not just the police, Lance. It's the 1-2-2. If they're moving in a big way, that means something's going down. They've been behind over two-thirds of the major arrests in the last year. Look around. Do you see anyone else there?"

Lance surveyed the platform. A colorful variety of flitters were parked in their spots, but there didn't seem to be an unusual number of drones nearby.

Two security guards stood before the wide doors leading to the entrance, which were tinted so dark he couldn't see through them. One of them gestured toward him as he chatted with the other man.

"Oh, this is it," the director shouted. "Get ready. One of the wide-shot drones is picking up a lot of blue and red lights. We're live in ten, nine, eight, seven, six, five, four, three, two, one. And go!"

Lance turned on his nuclear-strength smile as a camera drone settled in front of him. "This is Lance Onassis, live and in person for an important breaking story. We've received a tip that the famous Enforcement Zone 1-2-2, home to Detectives Erik Blackwell and Jia Lin, affectionately known as the Obsidian Detective and Lady Justice, are on their way to raid the headquarters of a small local biotech company, Kerrigan Systems."

Red and blue lights flashed in the distance. A squadron of police flitters zoomed toward the platform.

"As you can see through our live and in-person dynamic action drone footage, the police are coming in force. Although we have no idea if Detectives Blackwell and Lin are involved in today's incident, we can't discount the possibility that a major terrorist battle might be about to unfold before our cameras."

The two security guards shouted something unintelligible and ran inside.

The police flitters descended as a group and settled on the platform in a semi-circle around the entrance. Officers poured out of the vehicles carrying a mix of normal and stun rifles, all wearing tactical vests marked NSCPD.

A half-dozen security guards emerged from the building, holding their own stun rifles and glaring at the police.

"Drop your weapons!" The booming warning sounded like it came from all around. "This is the NSCPD. This is a raid, and we have a lawful warrant that is now being transmitted."

The security guards hesitated before tossing their guns to the pavement and raising their hands.

Lance switched to his practiced mask of concern. "A tense situation is unfolding here at the headquarters of Kerrigan Systems. Several security guards just surrendered after what could have been a brutal shootout with the authorities."

He turned toward the door, allowing the drones to get a shot of him and the front as the police rushed inside the building. Other officers slapped binding ties on the security guards and forced them to their knees.

"Blackwell and Lin aren't there," the director informed Lance. "We've run facial ID on all the cops already. Roll with that angle."

Lance shifted from practiced concern to feigned astonishment. "I've just been informed that despite the massive police presence, Detectives Lin and Blackwell aren't present. We don't know yet what heinous crimes Kerrigan has committed, but today is proof that Enforcement Zone 1-2-2 has more than two detectives who can take down antisocial criminals."

Suited men and women emerged from the building, their wrists bound, cops prodding them forward.

"We're already seeing people being brought out from inside," Lance commented. "Even without the use of TPST, the decisive actions of the famous 1-2-2 have taken Kerrigan completely off-guard. Although we don't yet know what charges the company employees are facing, the 1-2-2's record this last year suggests something serious and destabilizing. We can't speculate as to the location of the two ace detectives, but if previous experience has taught us anything, they're currently involved in something dangerous. For now, I will continue to report from Kerrigan Systems headquarters on this breaking news. This is Lance Onassis, live and *in person*."

He ended by flashing his million-watt smile.

CHAPTER FIFTY

"Switch to the heat overlays," Captain Phillips ordered. "Everyone maintain formation."

The squad continued cruising along at a modest speed. They hovered spread out in an inverted V formation with the captain at the vertex. Erik and Jia formed the vanguard of the left flank, and Agent Koval took the lead on the right.

Emma had been right. *Yaoguai* had left trails of blood of different colors, skin, scales, mucous, limbs, teeth, and even a few tentacles. They hadn't found any human or *yaoguai* bodies yet, but they were obviously on the correct albeit disgusting path. They'd followed the mutated monster road to make turns at two intersections.

The path's specificity was interesting. It implied the *yaoguai* knew how to navigate the tunnels.

Dr. Karton had used pheromones. Something similar might have been used to guide them to the Shadow Zone. Jia didn't care that much about the particulars. If they did their job, they would find the breeding facility and wipe all the *yaoguai*.

How hard could it be with a pile of weapons, ten soldiers, Erik, and an Intelligence Directorate agent with them?

Jia adjusted her transmitter to target only Erik. "Does this feel familiar?"

Erik glanced her way. "Does what feel familiar?"

"Traveling toward a target with a heavily armed group of soldiers?"

"Assault infantry mostly uses exoskeletons," Erik replied. He kept his eyes forward, looking for anything suspicious in the tunnel or unusual heat splotches. "And we used bigger, more heavily armored vehicles. We didn't ride around on mini-flitters like a gang. It's also been a long time since I last ran into a *yaoguai*. That's probably why I didn't think of the possibility at first."

"I've got a something at the one o'clock junction," Agent Koval announced.

Erik and Jia switched back to the general broadcast. The squad slowed to a stop, and everyone pointed their weapons.

A single faint but large heat signature in the intersection ahead grew brighter. Four more appeared, crawling on the tunnel walls. Jia deactivated the thermal overlay.

She'd expected more of the white-furred monsters from the apartment, but the latest additions to the nightmare catalog slithered along on a bed of spiked tentacles, their single yellow eyes glowing in Jia's low-light vision. Their squat bodies flowed straight into their bulbous heads, with a large beak beneath their eye. Unlike the apartment monsters, the huge *yaoguai* would tower over most humans.

One of the soldiers muttered a few profanities. Another offered a quick prayer.

"Yeah, that's about right," Erik muttered.

"There you go, Agent Koval," Jia announced. "It's time to kill a cyclops or two."

"Let's send these things back to hell," Erik suggested.

"You're right, Detective," Captain Phillips replied. "Squad, open fire!"

A hail of bullets and flechettes ripped into advancing tentacled cyclopes. Blue blood splattered all over the tunnel, but the advancing creatures weren't slowing, despite missing large chunks of their bodies.

"Frag out!" Erik shouted. He hurled a grenade with practiced ease.

The small explosive tumbled toward the closest monster and exploded, lighting up the tunnel and blowing the face off the monster. It fell to the ground with a resounding thud.

"Throw them!" Captain Phillips ordered. "Finish these bastards!"

The militia squad lobbed their grenades. The tunnel became New Year's at midnight, with the explosions going off in rapid succession. Keening cries ripped from the beaks of the dying *yaoguai*. A few seconds later, the smoke began to clear, leaving piles of charred rubbery flesh and tentacles.

Jia was grateful for her breather mask. She imagined the smell was somewhere between Hell's backed-up toilet and the worst failed attempt at a century egg ever.

Erik pointed to the intersection ahead. "They all came from the right."

"Is that it?" one of the soldiers asked. "Did we win?"

Erik leaned forward. "You don't have your thermal overlay on, do you? Turn it back on."

The soldier reactivated his, as did Jia.

Orange-red light suffused the tunnel from the right.

Jia switched to burst-fire mode. "With our luck, they probably have a dragon in there."

Erik considered the possibility. "I've always wanted to kill a dragon."

CHAPTER FIFTY-ONE

The squad shifted position, bringing the mini-flitters into a line.

A dissonant symphony of monstrous noises echoed through the tunnels. Growls, screeches, and shrieks joined the beating of wings, scuttling, and splashing in the dark puddles spread throughout the tunnels.

"Back up a few meters," Erik shouted. "Then stop and make sure you've got both your hands free for your weapon."

Everyone complied without question, even Captain Phillips.

Her command speech earlier didn't change the fact that Erik's decades of experience granted him a natural aura of authority. When he barked an order, a person listened. Jia's natural stubbornness offset that, but not all the time.

And certainly not this time.

She slapped a fresh magazine into her rifle. When she joined the police department, she'd had visions of heroic arrests and saving people's lives. Weapons training was necessary, but it seemed like a quaint relic of a time she'd thought was long gone. Even when she worried about trouble, she'd never, ever imagined she would end up in a tunnel underneath the Scar, fighting off waves of genetically engineered monsters.

The nightmarish situation struck her more as absurd than frightening. She and Erik had faced off against numerous dangerous enemies, and often, they'd had to do it by themselves. At least this time, they both were heavily armed, and they had military backup that wasn't going to get stuck behind locked doors, doing them no good.

Jia snickered. If she hadn't broken up with Corbin before, it would have been inevitable after the fight. There was no way she could date a man who hadn't experienced this kind of danger.

Huh, she thought. *I'm presuming I'm going to survive. Am I turning into an optimist?*

"Here they come," Erik warned, his tone grave. He grabbed one of his explosive magazines from a pocket in his RBC suit and slammed it into his TR-7. "Let's make sure they don't get close."

Jia gasped as the horde boiled out of the side tunnel. They weren't just in the Scar fighting a few experiments. They might as well have been in the underworld fighting monsters. All their estimates were off. They'd fought a handful before, but now dozens if not hundreds of *yaoguai* flooded the tunnel like a rolling wave of death.

Well, damn. She sighed.

Among the more normal-looking monsters, a laughable idea in and of itself, groups of the furry crawlers and six-legged *yaoguai* from the apartment surged forward.

Other creative abominations joined them. Meter-long centipede-like monsters with three pairs of dripping mandibles led. Dark crablike *yaoguai* with eight legs, four arms, and segmented tails ending in spikes skittered along the roof. Tiger-sized white-furred red-eyed felines with teeth longer than Jia's hand bounded between them, roaring.

Other *yaoguai* completed the nightmare collective, a writhing mass of fangs, teeth, tentacles, wings, and claws. Whoever Kerrigan had controlling the monsters must have released their entire twisted zoo.

"Throw them if you've got them," Captain Phillips barked. "I didn't join the Militia to get eaten."

Grenade after grenade tumbled into the tunnel. The rippling explosions consumed the front of the advancing mass of creatures, leaving half-charred corpses and dying monsters. Screeching *yaoguai* dropped from the walls, but the monsters behind them didn't stop. They charged through the smoke and their recently killed brethren.

Despite the tunnel being jammed with monsters running mandible to tentacle, none of them attacked each other. More pheromones, presumably.

Erik added his plasma grenades to the carnage. The larger blue-white explosions joined the orange-red fire flowers of the Militia's grenades and incinerated countless *yaoguai*. Almost the entire front half of the horde had been annihilated, but fresh monsters rushed forward.

An endless deadly swarm.

A new tentacled cyclops scuttled into the tunnel. Several small monsters surged over it, but it didn't pay them any attention as it continued its advance.

"When does something pass from the realm of the merely ridiculous to the absurd?" Jia mused.

"That typically happens between Tuesday and Wednesday for us," Erik joked.

"But it's Sunday!" Jia complained.

He shouldered his rifle. "That's why I said 'typically.'" He pulled the missile launcher off his back and glanced behind him before aiming the launcher at the cyclops. "Backblast area clear," he shouted and launched the missile. It screamed away from the launcher and struck the cyclops. The explosion turned the monster into gory confetti and scattered several smaller charred *yaoguai*.

He hooked the empty launcher on the carryaid and grabbed his TR-7.

Jia's mask amplified the harsh sound of her ragged breathing. Her heart raced, but she kept her focus, firing shot after shot at the monsters. There had to be a limit, and while the creatures were relentless and fast, so far, they weren't bulletproof.

The soldiers' staggered, disciplined bursts annihilated the renewed horde's front line. The monsters had speed, strength, and numbers, but technology made the soft, squishy humans stronger, faster, and deadlier. The tiger-like beasts took several bursts to put down, but even they crashed to the ground eventually.

Agent Koval pulled two small black cubes from her suit pockets and threw one toward a tunnel wall before pivoting and hurling the other toward the opposite wall. The cubes hit the wall, clicking. A thin barrel popped out and flashed as it fired. It wasn't large enough for a decent bullet, but its projectiles ripped huge holes in nearby *yaoguai*. The barrel jerked into a new position with each shot.

Jia had no idea what the device was, but she could use a few in her glove box for when apartment interviews turned into fights against monsters.

Erik swept his TR-7 from left to right, firing single rounds. The exploding rounds lacked the clearance power of a frag or plasma grenade, but the shrapnel and flames blew holes in the smaller flying forces, and the half-shredded and charred monsters careened into others. He jerked the rifle down and emptied the rest of his clip into a newly arrived tentacled cyclops, blowing it to pieces.

Agent Koval didn't fire as fast as the soldiers, but each flechette that flew from her gun exploded against a flying target. Erik wasn't the only one to bring interesting ammo. Agent Koval and Erik kept spitting out explosive rounds and knocking *yaoguai* out of the air or off the tunnel walls.

The helmet's audio dampeners kept the constant roar of gunfire and explosions from shattering Jia's eardrums.

Jia's gun went dry after she sent two rounds into a furry *yaoguai*. She shoved a new magazine in, the impact of the battle striking her.

This isn't a police raid, she thought. *This is demon-hunting.*

A heavily armed Militia unit, along with an ID agent and two cops with big weapons, were only holding the line because the mindless enemy was contained in tight quarters. When the squad had set out on the mission, everyone had believed that there would be a modest number of *yaoguai*. More than in Karton's apartment, but nowhere near an entire deadly army.

Jia understood why it was important to conduct simultaneous raids. Before, they had worried about a few dozen *yaoguai* making to the surface, but if these had made it to the Shadow Zone, they wouldn't have ended up boxed in and easy targets.

The average citizen, even in the Shadow Zone, didn't walk around with a tactical suit, grenades, and assault rifles. They didn't carry portable turrets or guns that fired guided explosive flechettes.

The *yaoguai* would have swarmed the area and butchered hundreds of people. Even flitters might not have saved victims from the flying monsters.

Had the DD suspected there might be *yaoguai*? Given that they were ready to bring in more troops, it must have been considered a strong possibility, but she doubted the close-lipped military superiors would be willing to admit it.

A small growl escaped Jia's mouth. The demonic horde of twisted chimeras wasn't from an insane Mother Nature. Every single beast they'd killed had been carefully designed and grown by a human for something as petty as money.

Jia fired four quick shots, one each into the heads of advancing centipede *yaoguai*. The bodies collapsed on the bed formed by their predecessors, the recent victims' green life fluids painting the bodies.

She missed one, but the ricochet hit a hideous example of demented brilliance behind what she was aiming at.

The squad needed to kill the monsters to get to the breeding facility, and Jia prayed that someone human was there. She wanted satisfaction and closure. They needed to feel the fear they had inflicted on the innocent people in the Shadow Zone.

A soldier screamed as a crab *yaoguai* dropped from the ceiling, knocked him off his flitter, and tore into his suit with a claw. Jia and a couple of other soldiers fired into the crab. Its indigo blood splattered across the soldier's suit from the first few shots, but the combined fire left it a perforated, twisted mess.

The soldier staggered to his feet. The attack left a jagged tear in his RBC suit, but it had only scratched the tactical suit. That was a relief, but Jia didn't want to put their suits to the test against the horde, and now he was at risk of contamination.

She glanced at several unobtrusive graphs in the upper right-hand corner of her goggle display. One of the most important, background radiation, was yellow. The exposed soldier would be okay for a short mission, but he wouldn't want to risk red-level exposure with a damaged RBC suit.

Captain Phillips hissed. Vitals sensors in the tactical suits of all the soldiers transmitted their information to her goggles. She would know if any of them got in trouble, even if they didn't make a sound.

"Pull back, Private," she ordered.

He remounted his flitter. "I can still fight, ma'am."

She blew the head off something that looked like a meter-long dragonfly before responding. "We're in the damned Scar, and you're exposed. Pull back, and that's an order. Reinforce our entry point in case we have to run. Pull back and request reinforcements, just in case."

"Yes, ma'am," the soldier yelled and fired several bursts into *yaoguai* before turning his mini-flitter around and flying away.

The screeches, howls, and shrieks were as loud as

before, but there were fewer, and the sound of near-constant rifle fire smothered them.

Fighting a horde of monsters in darkened tunnels with low-light vision wasn't an optimal situation. The piles of bodies and body parts, both rigid and twitching, along with the necessity of firing not just at the ground, but into the air and ceiling made it hard to track the enemy's true numbers in the midst of battle. The sounds didn't lie, though.

The horde was thinning. The squad was winning.

Erik grunted and ejected his magazine. "I'm out of explosive rounds."

"Me, too," Agent Koval admitted.

He shoved in a new magazine and fired a burst into one of the surviving furry white *yaoguai*. Even without an explosion, its head didn't react to the metal poisoning well.

Jia had burned through about three-quarters of her ammunition already. She assumed the other soldiers had as well. Battles were as much about supplies as they were weapons. With hundreds of enemies, even a single bullet could prove pivotal.

A few volleys more echoed in the tunnel before the soldiers ceased fire. Jia searched for a target but couldn't see any *yaoguai* moving forward. Some lay dying, twitching or flopping around. Most were in pieces. None presented a threat.

"Is it over?" asked a soldier.

Captain Phillips prodded a bullet-filled tiger *yaoguai* with her boot. "These things don't come back to life, do they?" She looked at Erik and Jia for confirmation.

"They're twisted, genetically engineered mutants that

look like demons," Jia began, "but they're just products of science in the end. They aren't magical. Nothing can come back from the dead."

"We just fought things I've only seen in movies, Detective." Captain Phillips shook her head. "At this point, if an angel showed up with a portable nuke launcher to help us, I wouldn't be surprised."

"I don't care if we killed the *yaoguai*." Erik pointed to the back of the horde, toward the intersection feeding into their source tunnel. "They didn't decide to rush at us on their own. Somebody sent them or let them out, and my gut tells me that somebody is still here. We owe them a little chat."

"We're only down one man," Captain Phillips observed. "And that's got to be their final play."

"Everyone ignore what comes next," Agent Koval requested.

"What are you talkin—"

Agent Koval's two box turrets exploded with a pop.

She shrugged. "Sorry. The ID can't have some things just sitting around where anyone can find them."

"You couldn't just pull them off the wall?" Jia suggested.

Agent Koval shrugged. "I have my reasons. Now, what were we discussing? Whether this is over?" She looked around. "I have my doubts."

"I agree, and there is nothing called 'too careful,'" Jia suggested. She patted her outer pockets to confirm her magazine count. Next time she ended up in an underground tunnel, she should bring an entire hoverpallet filled with boxes of ammo. "We don't know if they're in communication with Kerrigan headquarters. The raid up there might already be over, and they're perp-walking everyone. This might be a suicide mission for the survivors down here."

"These aren't fanatics, like terrorists," Captain Phillips noted. She kicked a few broken-off mandibles off her mini-flitter. "These are just greedy bastards. They might be afraid of prison, but they're probably more afraid of dying."

Erik chuckled. "These bastards were willing to test genetically engineered monsters on innocent people. I'm willing to bet they don't want to end up in prison with people knowing that. Lots of people locked up who still buy into Purism." He patted his TR-7. "We followed the trail before. Let's keep at it. I wouldn't mind a little poetic justice." He accelerated, and his mini-flitter floated forward.

"Poetic justice?" Jia asked.

"Yeah. It'd be nice if when we find the suspects, we found the *yaoguai* ate all their faces."

CHAPTER FIFTY-TWO

The squad flew over the graveyard of homicidal scientific hubris and into their source tunnel. They kept their weapons ready to fire at any new threats. The sheer number of *yaoguai* killed any hope that the raid would have been easily taken care of without overwhelming military force.

There was a certain irony. In several incidents, Erik and Jia had been pushed to their limits because they were the only ones there, but now they had an entire Militia squad and even an ID agent, and things weren't any easier.

It was like the universe, or perhaps the Lady, had made sure to adjust everything to suit the situation.

No new monsters appeared, but their path disappeared after only a hundred meters. A massive metal wall stretched across the tunnel. Its unblemished condition and lack of discoloration made it seem odd in the middle of the otherwise abandoned remnants of a murdered city. Two thick gray doors pierced the center of the wall. There was no visible access panel.

They didn't need an advanced AI or drones to know they had arrived at the *yaoguai* facility. The squad brought their mini-flitters to a stop and carefully searched the area, including the roof, for hidden monsters.

Erik dismounted. "I thought the monster factory might be above in the Scar proper, but they must have built their entire facility directly into this tunnel system. It's not like they have a lot of inspectors coming to check them out down here, and from what we saw at the front, they had to excavate to even reach these tunnels."

Captain Phillips pointed to the doors. "They must be able to open if they let all the *yaoguai* out, but how do we get inside? I doubt they'll do it if we just ask nicely. Maybe they're already gone."

"Let's hope they aren't," Jia muttered.

The captain hopped off her vehicle. "Our squad didn't bring any antimaterial explosives, and unless you're hiding another missile somewhere, Detective Blackwell, we might have to wait for reinforcements."

Jia shook her head. "They could be destroying evidence in there or escaping out the back if they haven't already. I didn't fight through a horde of monsters to sit on my hands while the suspects got away."

Agent Koval laughed. "Their brilliant escape plan is to flee into the Scar? The Militia is actively searching inside the Exclusion Line. It'd be a bad idea. No, whoever it is, is still in there. We just need to figure out the magic word."

Erik strapped the TR-7 over his shoulder and pulled the laser rifle off his carryaid, managing the bulk of the weight of the massive weapon with his left arm. He used the handlebars of the mini-flitter for support. He could extend the short tripod built into the weapon, but he could achieve a better angle using his first method.

"I've got one fully charged cell, and another one hanging from my carryaid," he explained. "That's ten shots. This can blow through flitters, so a door should be easy."

"It wouldn't hurt to try," Captain Phillips admitted.

Jia nodded. "Do it."

Erik grinned. "Why don't I see if this is a skeleton key?"

Captain Phillips eyed the weapon. Most of her face might be hidden by her mask, but the interest and jealousy in her eyes were obvious. "I've been meaning to ask you where you got that. I've heard rumors of a Special Forces unit getting them. Is that something you had from your days in the service?"

"Nah. This is something I picked up recently. A friend of mine thought it might be handy in situations like this. We end up in these situations a lot."

"So I've heard. This would have been handy against that King sentry."

"Exactly." Erik lined up the shot. "Everyone ready?"

The other squad members aimed their weapons at the doors. There were no obvious gates or vents, implying the *yaoguai* had emerged from the doors. This area might be the back of the facility. Despite what Agent Koval said, it made sense for the criminals to flood the tunnels with monsters and make their escape.

Erik pulled the trigger, and sparks showered from the upper-right of one of the doors as the invisible beam struck. The shot left a shallow gouge, ringed by blackened metal. He hadn't penetrated the door.

"Not that easy, huh?" Erik sighed. "Well, I guess we can

appreciate that the monsters would not have escaped until they intended for it to happen."

Another two shots bored a deep hole, allowing light to spill out from it. He'd carved the entire upper-right of the door away from the doorframe. Progress.

"Now they can shoot at us," Agent Koval offered cheerfully. "I hope you know what you're doing, Detective Blackwell."

Jia scoffed. "If they thought they could win a firefight, they wouldn't have sent out their monsters. If they're still in there, they're probably hiding and wetting themselves."

"Oof," Koval replied. "Aggressive sort, aren't you?"

"We're almost in." Erik fired two more shots toward the center-left of the door to dig another hole. The charge indicator blinked on the side of his weapon. He pulled the conical cell out and shoved it into a pocket of the carryaid before grabbing the other cell and screwing it into the side of the weapon.

His next four shots blew away the upper- and center-left portions of the door, but it remained standing. With one shot remaining, he hooked the rifle onto his carryaid.

"I don't have any hidden ID explosives laced into my boots if that's what you're thinking," Agent Koval mentioned. "And I also don't see any Trojan Horses around to trick them into letting us in. If I get closer, I might be able to hack it."

"No need. I did enough. It's good enough." Erik marched toward the door confidently. Even if someone inside had a gun, his tactical suit would protect him, and the contamination levels remained low. The holes weren't big enough to fire rockets or missiles through, and probably the only man carrying a laser rifle in all of Neo SoCal was him.

Hope I'm not wrong about that, he thought. *If I am, I won't live long enough to care.*

Jia jogged after him. Captain Phillips gestured for her soldiers to follow him.

Agent Koval chuckled and shook her head before following. "You just don't know when to give up, do you?"

"I'll give up when I'm dead." Erik stopped in front of the door. "You're not getting away," he bellowed. "I know you're in there. I'm sure you've been watching us since we pulled up to your little horror factory. You might even have cameras set up in the tunnels. It doesn't matter if you've seen us or not. We're here now, and you know what that means. All your *yaoguai* are dead, and we're not." He waited a few seconds for a response before continuing, "I wonder how many millions, if not billions, of credits you just wasted, trying to stall us. That means you are desperate, or it could mean you've got something more to hide. Waiting for reinforcements? It's not going to happen. Ours will get here before yours. If you want to do this the easy way, you can surrender. If you make us do it the hard way and resist, you should remember these aren't stun rifles we're hauling. Sure, you're going to end up in prison, but that's better than being dead. After what I've just seen, though, I wouldn't mind making you dead."

A mocking laugh echoed around him. The source was not obvious, but it was obviously transmitted.

"There's no reason to surrender," a man explained. "If we do, we'll just be executed. Why should we bother making it easier for you? Screw you. You want to come and get us, you Militia dog?

Erik didn't bother to correct him. With everyone in RBC and tactical suits, they probably did look like a unified squad that just happened to have a few people packing specialty weapons.

"Illegal genetic engineering is a nasty business, but it's not going to get you executed unless..." Erik's nostrils flared, and he backed away from the door. Bile rose in the back of his throat.

No. *It couldn't be.*

Between transportation and off-world prisons, execution was considered by many a barbaric relic of the past. Even murderers would live out their lives, albeit in a tiny cell in metal floating in space. But there were a handful of crimes that might get one swiftly executed after conviction, including heavy genetic modification of humans.

Erik wasn't much of a Purist, and in other circumstances, he would have assumed they'd done something minor and not worthy of draconian punishment. A few extra inches, a permanent change of eye color. But after carving through the *yaoguai* mob, he knew just the kind of people cowering past the door.

He growled and brought back his left shoulder, then charged and crashed into the damaged door. The entire assembly shook under the impact. He smashed into the door two more times before he slammed his left fist into it. The blows stung as he pounded the door, and if it were his other hand, he would have broken his bones. Roaring, he punched again, and the door ripped away from the frame and undamaged portion and flew forward. It crashed into the smooth gray floor and stopped.

It felt like stepping through a door that took them directly to Uptown. The clean, modern facility inside was one massively long but narrow white room holding a biotech storage facility. Massive chemical tanks lined one wall. Dozens of large, transparent bags filled with different- colored fluids clustered near the center of the building—gestation tanks. At the far end, stacked cages, now all open, blocked further passage. Silver-colored containers lay on the other side of the gestation tanks. Their size and shape reminded Erik of coffins, but he didn't find them foreboding. They could make things easier for the Kerrigan men standing near a table.

There were few accommodations, other than some tables and a few desks. Given the light and the complexity of the equipment, there had to be integrated computer systems. It didn't matter. Erik didn't need to disable their computers. He only cared about the men.

Neither of them wore RBC suits. Erik suspected the facility had integrated air handling. They must have not brought any of the *yaoguai* they released back into the facility. Both men did, however, hold pistols. One man's hand hovered over a PNIU attached to his belt, but they weren't pointing them at Erik.

Erik brought up his TR-7 and pointed it at the men. "Drop it, or we drop you."

The men stared at Erik. There was no anger or resentment on their faces, only resignation. They didn't even seem surprised that he'd just bashed open their door.

Perhaps the kind of men who grew monsters for a living weren't surprised by anything.

Jia, Agent Koval, and the Militia hurried inside the building and fanned out around Erik.

Agent Koval whistled. "I'm almost impressed. You built an entire *yaoguai* breeding facility literally underneath the noses of everyone in Neo SoCal. It's too bad you did something like that in service to something so twisted." She clucked her tongue. "I'm going to have a good time going through your systems. I'm sure there is all sorts of interesting information, and I doubt you all weren't smart enough to prepare for rapid system deletion in case of a raid like this."

The resignation on the men's face gave way to irritation, but they didn't lift their weapons.

"You don't know anything," one of the men muttered.

"Did you really do all this just for the money?" Jia demanded. "A few would be bad enough, but what you did was depraved. You disgust me."

"All we were planning to do was fill a need. If there are no buyers, there can't be any sellers. We're just another part of the economy."

"That's like saying it's okay to shoot someone as long as someone buys your services." Jia scoffed. "The UTC will do just fine without sociopathic antisocials who created monsters to kill people."

"You're under arrest," Erik declared. "All Article Seven rights apply. Do you need these explained to you?"

"You're a cop?" the man shouted. "If we're going down, you're going down. See you in hell." He tapped his PNIU before shoving his gun against the side of his head and pulling the trigger. The other man ate his gun right after.

The squad stood there, unsure of what to do. They had cleared out the *yaoguai*. That was the most important goal of the raid, even if it'd ended up a little more involved than they had anticipated.

Captain Phillips lifted her rifle. "Well, that saves us the trouble. They've paid for what they did."

Jia hissed in frustration.

"What's wrong?"

Jia pointed the dead men. "All that pain and suffering, and they killed themselves? The cowards could have at least stood trial."

Erik shrugged. "It's over. That's what's imp—"

A loud buzz erupted from the silver coffins.

"What's going on?" Captain Phillips asked.

"Don't you get it?" Erik snarled. He'd wanted to kill the men anyway for the reason he was sure rested in the coffins. "The *yaoguai* were just a sideshow. If you're going to do illegal genetic engineering, you might as well go all in."

Steam blasted from all but one of the coffins. With a hiss and a clank, the lids slid open. Humanoid forms pulled themselves out of tanks of blue fluid. The thick, deep-crimson scales covering their bodies provided the first hint they were something far from human. They stepped out of their tanks and stared at the squad with yellow eyes and vertical-slitted pupils. Small indentations passed for ears. Claws tipped the hands on their long arms. The mutants let out an odd staccato gurgling sound.

Captain Phillips shuddered. "Please tell me those aren't what I think."

"They're exactly what you think," Erik muttered. "Those bastards made human *yaoguai*." He lifted his rifle. "And I doubt they're willing to chat."

The mutants screeched and burst into a lope.

The squad opened fire. Their bullets bounced off the mutants, leaving a few scratches, but not drawing blood. Agent Koval's flechettes didn't do any better, landing on the floor with soft clinks.

Testing. That was what Karton had said. They must have experimented with all sorts of designs. The trail of blood and tissue that led Emma and ultimately the squad there might have been from the Kerrigan men testing different *yaoguai* against one another.

"Jia, switch to AP," Erik shouted. He ejected his magazine and jammed his hand into a pocket to grab one of the two armor-piercing magazines he'd brought. His partner did the same. Every enemy had a weakness.

A mutant reached a soldier. It yanked her rifle out of her hand and backhanded her. She screamed and flew back several yards before slamming into the wall head-first. She fell to the ground, her neck bent at an unnatural angle, her eyes locked in a death stare.

"Kellerson!" shouted Captain Phillips. "Damn you, monsters!" She flipped to full auto and sent a river of bullets toward the mutant killer. She managed to draw blood, but that didn't slow it as he leapt on top of her.

It ripped her rifle from her hand and threw it away before lifting her by her neck and hissing. The officer kicked and clawed at the hand squeezing her neck, letting out another gurgle. Was it enjoying it?

"Just how strong are these things?" shouted a soldier. He charged the mutant, which threw the gasping Captain Phillips to the floor and spun to meet the new threat. The soldier held down his trigger, but it tore into him, ripping his suit and gouging his tactical suit. A few more swipes and the creature would make it through.

Erik flipped his TR-7 to four-barrel mode and aimed it at the mutant's head. He fired once. The four AP bullets ripped through the scales. The mutant's head jerked, and it screeched, but it slashed again at the soldier. Another burst sent it to the floor.

Shouts and screams overlapped as the mutants ripped into the soldiers or tossed them around like angry toddlers trying to destroy their dolls. Agent Koval ducked and dodged a mutant attacking her, her breathing heavy.

Jia ran toward a mutant going after the kneeling Captain Phillips. Her three bursts into the creature's chest had it on the ground in a pool of its own blood.

The surviving mutants gurgled and screeched before bounding away from the soldiers. They ran in a zigzag that threw off Erik and Jia's aim.

"I don't get it," Jia commented. "They seemed mindless before, but they know good strategies to dodge firearms? It's not like the *yaoguai* in the tunnel or apartment tried to avoid our shots."

"This is different. They start with genes for a human brain and tinker." Erik fired another burst. "Eventually, you get the ultimate programmable beast, but being smarter than a wall centipede doesn't make them smart. Let's nail them with crossfire."

"Right." Jia gave a firm nod and jogged away from him.

They were the only ones who could stop the mutants. They had to protect the rest of the Militia.

"If you're smart enough to run," Erik shouted, "that means you're afraid. This is for Kellerson!"

Jia and Erik opened fire, their rifles spewing out armor-piercing rounds. They ripped through the remaining mutants, which collapsed to the ground, gurgling for a few seconds before dying.

An alarm klaxon sounded.

"Now what?" Erik growled. "I'm starting to get a little pissed."

"They might have had some sort of failsafe system," Agent Koval suggested. "In case this place got overrun. Those human *yaoguai* might have had embedded vitals sensors."

"Great. You're saying it's going to blow up now because we killed all their freaks?"

"I don't know. That's my guess. It's hard to use my PNIU with this suit, and I can't do the kind of hacking I need with voice commands alone. You know what? Time to do a little lateral-Perseus-style thinking."

"I don't think you can win against a self-destruct with a mirror," Jia muttered.

Erik didn't know what they were talking about, but there wasn't anything he could do about it. He'd leave it to the ID agent.

She ripped off her RBC gloves. "They didn't have suits.

It's safe in here." Her fingers danced over her PNIU as she rapidly murmured commands.

Captain Phillips groaned and stood. "My people can't evacuate in this condition, and I'm not leaving Kellerson's body in this damned hole. She deserves more."

"Okay, it does look like a self-destruct system linked to the fusion reactor has been activated," Agent Koval announced. "I can disable it. I just need a minute or two." She returned to her furious murmurs. "Just need to not be distracted."

Another coffin opened.

Sometimes the Lady could be generous, and sometimes she could be a vindictive bitch.

Erik and Jia opened fire as a new mutant emerged. This one was similar to the others, but it lacked fingers. Its arms ended in thin, bony blades. Tightly packed dull gray scales covered its body instead of crimson. There were no obvious eyes or mouth, but there were two dark pits near the top of its head.

Their bullets pelted the new arrival but didn't penetrate its hide. The detectives stopped firing when their guns went dry.

The silent monster swayed as it stalked forward. Unlike every other *yaoguai* they had run into, it didn't seem to be in a hurry. Did it know they couldn't hurt it? No matter how twisted and altered the creature now was, it had something approaching a human brain.

"I've never read about stable genetic modifications this advanced." Jia reloaded her gun. "How do we stop a walking tank?"

"With an antivehicle weapon." Erik dropped his TR-7

and hoisted the laser rifle off his carryaid. He gritted his teeth and held it steady to aim at the mutant's head. "How do you think that thing is even seeing us? It's not like it's got eyes."

"Probably it can sense heat, like some snakes," Jia suggested, moving to her left. "Through those little pits."

"If it's like that, you've got to figure the brain is still in the head, right?"

Jia shrugged. "That would be my guess."

"I've only got one shot left." He pulled the trigger, and the shot burned a large hole through the mutant's head, stopping it in its tracks. Everyone in the room paused, holding their breath for a moment before its legs buckled and it collapsed to the floor.

Everyone exhaled. "One problem down," Jia declared. "If we don't die in a horrible explosion in the next few minutes, things will be looking up."

Erik set the laser rifle down. "I'm really, really starting to like this thing," he admitted, patting it fondly. His ability to ignore the other trouble awaiting them was a trait she wasn't sure she admired.

The alarm died.

Agent Koval let out a breath. "I disabled the self-destruct."

Erik looked at the fallen soldier and nodded. "Let's get Kellerson and get the hell out of here. Someone else can do the cleanup."

The people moved quickly to grab the body and carry it to the flitters.

No time like the present to get out of this hellhole.

CHAPTER FIFTY-THREE

March 10, 2229, Neo Southern California Metroplex, Apartment of Erik Blackwell

Reclining on his couch, Erik took a sip of his third beer of the night as the screen on the wall played a recent hit music vid on mute.

It was nice to have a little time to sit and relax after all the chaos in recent days. He wasn't sure he would ever complain about things being slow at the 1-2-2 again.

The 1-2-2's raid of Kerrigan Systems netted all the major players, and CID investigations had already been launched to close down some of the black-market channels they had been planning to use to send their *yaoguai* off Earth.

The effects of the dual raids would ripple across the entire UTC.

All the top executives were pointing fingers at each other and trying to cut deals. Desperate to avoid life in prison or execution, they'd sold out several employees who were not present at Kerrigan Systems on the day of the raid.

The CID was making additional arrests all over Earth, and even on the Moon and Mars. All of them claimed they had no idea that human *yaoguai* were being created, but the government wasn't inclined to make many deals, which was fine by him.

Sometimes there was a thin line between vengeance and justice.

He lifted his head at the sound of a light knock from the door. He set his beer down on his coffee table, stood up, and then headed that way. He didn't even check the camera before opening it.

Fortunately, it wasn't a polite *yaoguai*, Tin Man, or criminal assassin waiting for him. Agent Koval stood on the other side. She was back to wearing a flattering business suit and ankle boots rather than RBC gear laden with weapons.

Erik frowned. He stuck his head out and looked up and down his hallway.

Every time the woman showed up, major trouble followed. "Does this involve Tin Men or *yaoguai*?" he asked. "If so, I want a day to get drunk before I go back to kicking asses, and it's going to take me a few weeks before I can replenish some of my supplies—unless you are offering replenishment?"

She laughed. "It does involve them, but we don't need you to do anything. At least, not yet. I've been authorized to share information with you, and I thought that after all that effort, you'd want a little closure" She gestured inside.

"May I? If you're sick of me, I understand, but I think you'll want to hear this."

Erik shrugged and stepped out of her way, allowing her to enter before closing the door and heading back to the couch.

Part of him wanted to ask her about Molino, but he didn't trust her. She did help with the case, but she could have had her own reasons for that. She might even be watching him for the conspiracy and trying to earn his trust by giving him a slice of the truth.

Agent Koval looked around, her cyan ponytail swaying. "I'm going to secure the room. This means your pet AI won't be able to hear this conversation. Is that going to be a problem?"

Emma appeared in front of Koval with a smirk on her face. "He's more *my* pet, and if this a prelude to attempting to take me, it won't succeed. I'll make you pay in blood, ghost girl, and I'm far more ruthless than any fleshbag."

"I don't care." Agent Koval shrugged. "You're the DD's problem, not ours, and I've got enough on my plate to not go looking for more trouble." She turned to him. "I was asking if this is okay with you, Detective Blackwell? I pinky-swear I'm not about to assassinate you."

Erik snorted. "Go ahead and try if you want. For now, let's talk."

She reached into her pocket and smiled when Erik didn't twitch and Emma disappeared. "There we go. Because of your unique situation, my superior believes it's useful for you to know some of what we've learned. A small amount of this is being shared with the CID's investigators as well. The quick version is that after examining the finances and records of Kerrigan Systems, it is our belief that one of their main investors, via shell corporations, was Talos."

"Terrorist groups are running companies now. Nice." Erik eyed her.

"As far as we can tell, Kerrigan's employees are *not* members of Talos. They were just useful idiots."

"So they're only investors?" Erik scratched his chin, giving himself a moment to collect his thoughts. "You said before that Talos is interested in advanced technology. Why? Are they trying to build an army of Tin Men and *yaoguai* to conquer a frontier planet and set up the Democratic Republic of Talos?"

"There are still many things we don't know about them." Agent Koval folded her hands in front of her. "It's our belief that they might even have aided Kerrigan by providing them information in addition to what Dr. Marianne Karton stole from 46 Helix. That hasn't been confirmed, but the evidence is pointing that way."

"So, the thing with Chen wasn't even that important." Erik shook his head in disbelief. "It was just them trying to cover their tracks. That's the one thing I don't get about all this."

"Yes?"

"Wasn't it kind of sloppy?"

"Yes, it was, and that's got us worried. One possibility is their operation got disrupted at an unusual time, resulting in rash moves, and another is that they became worried because of the involvement of you and your partner."

Erik narrowed his eyes. "Are you saying they're out to get us?"

"No." Agent Koval tilted her head, her smile disappearing and cold harshness taking over her eyes. "You're famous, Detective, for handling difficult problems. You proved it again on this case. You got us into the facility, and you stopped the final human *yaoguai* before it killed us all. Judging by your case notes, your partner's investigative skills and instincts are as impressive as your military ability. I watched you both during the raid. You move and cooperate like two people who have been training together for decades, not less than a year. There's confidence and trust." She held up a finger. "That makes you both more competent, and it is dangerous to certain people and organizations. Some of them are now having to make cost-benefit decisions about going after you in a way that risks greater exposure or suffering if you run across their operations in Neo SoCal."

Erik stood and stared into her eyes. "Let me ask you something, Agent Koval. Where do your loyalties lie?"

Her brow lifted. "What kind of question is that? I'm an ID agent. I'm loyal to the UTC." She smiled. "That kind of comes with the job description."

"It's not like the government's never done anything immoral in the past. If the ID told you the best way to handle a *yaoguai* infestation in the Shadow Zone was drop a bomb on them, *would you*?"

Her mouth curled in a lopsided smile. "I reject the premise of your question, so I refuse to answer it."

"What?" Erik frowned.

"If I'm doing my job, we'll never *get* to the point where we'd have to make that choice." Agent Koval winked. "I'm not a murderous femme fatale, Detective Blackwell. I'm one of the good ones."

"We'll see." Erik nodded. "But thanks for your help. I wasn't about to run and save my own butt while a bunch of wounded soldiers got blown up. You stopped anyone from having to make a choice they shouldn't have to make. A commanding officer who loses most of their soldiers loses a lot of themselves."

"You would know, wouldn't you?" Agent Koval headed for the door, looking over her shoulder. "You remind me a lot of the heroes of Greek legends and myths."

"That's Jia's area of knowledge, I don't know a lot about them. However, don't a lot of those heroes do something really impressive and then come to a tragic end because the gods or fate screws with them?"

"Yes." Agent Koval grinned. "But you don't have to be *exactly* like them." She pressed the access panel, and the door slid open. "I suspect we'll be able to help each other a lot in the future. I'll be in touch."

"Next time, bring a bigger gun," Erik suggested.

"I'll keep that in mind." Agent Koval stepped out of his apartment and closed the door.

Erik returned to his beer. At least there was no way a conspiracy could screw that up.

Alina smiled as the transportation center came into view.

She'd found her time in Neo SoCal interesting, but she couldn't claim she'd enjoyed it. Talos had gotten away with too much, and too many people had died. The bastards needed to pay, and not just the few sympathizers the ID had smoked out in the government.

“I’m beyond impressed with them, sir. It’s also obvious Blackwell has his own special connections. I’m assuming DD contacts, given the kind of equipment I saw. Based on what we’ve observed, the most likely candidate is Adeyemi. I think both could be useful tools against Talos and several other problems.”

“I get it. You’re a fan.” Her superior sighed. “I’m reluctant to recruit someone who won’t be able to play well with Directorate regulations. He might have spent thirty years in the military, but it’s obvious after what happened on his last tour that he doesn’t care much about rules anymore. We both know he only cares about revenge.”

“I think that’s a potential advantage,” Alina insisted. “We just have to handle him in an appropriate way.”

“I’ll take it under consideration, Agent. Take a few days off, then we need you on the Moon.”

“It’s been a while.” Alina sighed. “I hope I don’t have to blow a hole in a dome this time.”

CHAPTER FIFTY-FOUR

March 11, 2229, Neo Southern California Metroplex, Bar "Remembrance"

Halil hoisted his glass and gestured to the floating holographic cartoon goblin above him. The eyes had been replaced with Xs. EZ 122 MONSTER KILLER PARTY hung above it in bright white letters.

"The preliminary reports are done, the evidence has been collected, and some of the bad guys are already signing confessions," he shouted. "We *delivered* this week. *1-2-2!*"

The officers gathered in the bar raised their own glasses and shouted. "*1-2-2!*"

Jia felt warm, which was a good feeling. She was at least fifty percent sure it wasn't because she was on her third beer. It might have been because Jared Thompson was conspicuously absent, despite taking part in the Kerrigan raid.

She sat at a table near the center of the room with Erik.

Halil took a sip of his beer. "I'm not done." He pointed

at Erik, then Jia. "We had it easy when we busted into Kerrigan. Their guards didn't even put up a fight, but Jia and Erik, they had to crawl around sewer pipes in the Scar while giant radioactive cockroaches were trying to eat them. *That's* dedication to cleaning up the town."

Scattered laughter broke out.

Jia shook her head. "We were on mini-flitters. We didn't crawl through anything, and while there were a lot of disturbing *yaoguai*, none looked like roaches. Honestly, I think I would have *preferred* roaches."

"Bugs are bugs," Erik insisted. "And we killed a lot of them. Don't get caught up in the details."

"Let's toast to Erik and Jia," Halil shouted. "They are the real deal. Monster killers! *1-2-2!*"

"*1-2-2!*" bellowed the gathered cops.

Halil settled down on his barstool, content with his toasts for now.

Jia took another sip of her beer. The events of the past few days could easily fuel nightmares, but she was satisfied.

She looked at Erik. "I feel like we really made a difference."

"Yeah." He slowly looked around the room as if he were searching for someone in particular. "We did. If they'd finished testing them in the Scar, they would have set up somewhere else, and then they'd have started shipping those monsters all over. Every terror group in the UTC would send *yaoguai* into the middle of cities. Kerrigan's done, though. No other agency even poached anything this time. We both got personal credit, and the 1-2-2 got credit as well. The company we took down might not be Ceres

Galactic, but they were doing nasty stuff." He considered the two cases. "Maybe even worse."

"Do you ever worry that we're getting too famous?" Jia asked. "Sometimes it's an advantage, but what if it causes trouble? Brings people to us?"

Erik grinned. "That's an advantage."

"An advantage?" Jia set her glass down. She needed less alcohol to follow this conversation. "Why is that an *advantage*?"

"If the criminals come to us, we don't have to spend as much time investigating them." Erik polished off the rest of his drink in a few quick swallows and sighed in satisfaction. "I'm feeling pretty good too. You're right. We stopped some real bastards, and I feel like things are moving forward with my...personal case. I don't know if our Tin Men-loving friends had anything to do with it, but getting more contacts helps, even if I don't trust Koval." He shrugged. "We should take it easy while we can. I'm sure some giant *yaoguai* will drop into the city tomorrow and start eating everyone who makes beignets."

Jia laughed a little too loudly, but there was humor in her eyes. "That would be a heinous reign of terror, for sure."

Erik tapped the side of his head. "No matter what happens, you've got to keep your priorities straight." He looked around again. "A lot of people brought their spouses and significant others."

Jia checked the room out.

She recognized some of the people but she wasn't all that familiar with the families and friends of the rest of the 1-2-2. Even though they no longer despised her, she still was an outsider in many ways. She didn't mind. All she'd ever wanted from the other cops was for them to do their jobs. She had her own life, her own friends, and a great partner.

"I suppose they did." She shrugged and turned back to him. "What about it?"

Erik stared at her, an uncertain expression on his face. He cleared his throat. "It means you could have brought Corbin. When they announced the party, they made it clear it wasn't a cop-only thing. I would have brought someone, but I'm not dating anyone."

Jia stared at her glass. "Bringing Corbin would have been…uncomfortable."

"Why?" Erik frowned. "Does he not like cops? From what you told me, he doesn't have a problem with your job. Or is he jealous because you're around a bunch of guys all the time?"

Jia shook her head. "It's not that. It would have been inappropriate for another reason."

"If you're going to be this cryptic, have Emma do some AI stuff to your words," Erik suggested. "Have her translate them into Zitark."

Emma didn't say anything.

"Okay." Jia groaned and put up a hand to forestall more comments from Erik. "It's not a big deal. I broke it off with Corbin."

"Really?" Erik smiled before blanking his face. "Oh, I'm sorry. What happened?"

Jia waved her hand dismissively. "I'm not sad about it. I'm relieved, but I *am* a little embarrassed. I'm mostly worried about what's going to happen when Mei and

Mother find out. They'll reactivate the Lin Matchmaker Special Operations Squad." She rolled her eyes. "I've been reluctant to mention it to you because it'd make it more real."

There was some truth to that, but she couldn't look Erik in the eye and tell him she was attracted to him. Normal guys she knew didn't measure up. If there was another thirty-year Army veteran who joined the department, he might at least have been a possibility.

Given his spotty track record since they'd met, it was obvious he wasn't interested in serious attempts at dating. That was reasonable. He still had to avenge his people.

Erik nodded slowly, a ghost of a smile sneaking back onto his face. Had he hated Corbin that much?

"Why did you give Mr. Down-to-Earth the boot?" he asked. "I thought he checked all the boxes for you. Did it turn out he was a secret freak?"

"Yes and no." Jia furrowed her brow as she mentally ran through her checklist of what made a good man. Various Erik-related traits kept popping up. She gasped and waved her hands. "I mean, *no*. He wasn't a secret freak."

Erik grinned, using his beer bottle to point at her. "Took you a little too long to say that."

She shook her head. "It's nothing like that. He was a very nice and normal guy. He's handsome and has a good job. A lot of women would be lucky to have him."

"Just not you?" Erik pressed.

Jia nodded. "He wasn't the right man for me, just like the barista wasn't the right woman for you."

Erik leaned back in his chair, his shoulders loose, and something in his eyes that Jia couldn't figure out.

She could have sworn it was hope.

"Who *is* the right guy for you?" Erik asked. "If you're worried about your family coming after you, you're going to need to get ready. Part of that is knowing what you want and being able to articulate it to them. And it has to be more than, 'Someone who respects my career choices.'"

"I'm not completely sure," Jia suggested. *That wasn't a lie.* "I do know I need someone more exciting. Corbin was like my flitter."

"Blue?" Erik quirked an eyebrow and grinned.

Jia chuckled. "If he was, maybe I'd still be dating him. No, boring and safe. I think at this point, I need someone not so boring and safe."

"You're saying you need an MX 60 of a man?" he asked, taking a sip of his beer but eyeing her intently over the lip of his bottle.

"Something like that." Jia shrugged. "I've got time to figure it out."

It wouldn't hurt to put a toe in the water. "So, I was thinking," she continued. "One of the things I'm working on lately is improving my cooking skills."

"Oh? Not a bad thing," Erik continued watching her curiously.

"I kind of remember you mentioning something about liking Beijing Duck," Jia replied casually. She swallowed. "It's one of the recipes I've been working on. Maybe I could cook it for you sometime? I need feedback."

Erik smiled. "Sure. I'd like that. It's been a while since I had a home-cooked meal." His smile disappeared, and he put up a hand. "Wait."

"What?" Jia tried to keep the desperation out of her voice.

He eyed her, a smirk on his lips. "Are you any good at cooking it?" Erik allowed the grin he was trying to hold back to surface. "I won't end up sick, will I?"

Jia rolled her eyes. "Keep it up, and I'll send a *yaoguai* duck after you."

"I don't care as long as it's tasty and roasted." Erik licked his lips. "Delicious *yaoguai* duck. You have to eat it before it eats you."

She picked up her beer. "I promise I will do my best not to have my cooking be what kills you."

"To the 1-2-2." He leaned across and clinked her glass. "And *yaoguai* duck."

She eyed him as she took a sip, a satisfied smile playing on her lips.

Maybe she would do better with the recipe this time.

THE STORY CONTINUES WITH ENLIGHTENED IGNORANCE

There is a reason Earth believes they are the pinnacle of advanced society.

The past is fraught with lies that could topple everything, sending humanity into a tail-spin.

Is it possible to uncover the truth Jia and Erik are searching for, without tearing apart the gossamer of ignorance and destroy the underpinnings of government?

Both want the truth – but is revealing the truth good for those around them?

Two years ago, a small moon in a far off system was

set to be the location of the first intergalactic war between humans and an alien race.

It never happened. However, something was found many are willing to kill to keep a secret.

Now, they have killed the wrong people.

How many will need to die to keep the truth hidden?

As many as is needed.

He will have vengeance no matter the cost. *She will dig for the truth. No matter how risky the truth is to reveal.*

Pre-order Enlightened Ignorance for Delivery on March 6, 2020

AUTHOR NOTES - MICHAEL ANDERLE

DECEMBER 7, 2019

Thank you for reading not only this book but through the end to these *Author Notes* in the back!

Where do we go from here?

Right now, the first book has been released for Opus X, and we are just about one week away from releasing book 02. I am presently editing book 04.

Opus X 12 seems like such a long way away! (actually, it is…which is why it seems so far away!)

We were talking to Gene Mollica Studios (specifically Gene and Sasha) yesterday while on the road related to the covers for books 07-12.

Seven (07) isn't a problem, but starting with book 08, we need a <redacted>, which means I need to cough up a potentially large chunk of change to do the right thing.

Well, my version of "do the right thing." The bean counters might believe it's the way-too-expensive thing, and for all I know, they might be right. However, I'm leaning toward giving the green light to the project without doing a significant amount of review because this series is my passion project.

The project I have wanted to be super special from the artwork side of things. However, saying I want it to be special and seeing the bills and invoices coming in for the level of specialness I am paying for occasionally makes my wallet scream.

I have to remind myself, "It's only for six more covers..."

Changing the World

Right now, I've been blessed to have helped a large group of authors / indie publishers by providing advice, guidance, and encouragement they can use in their careers through the 20Booksto50k® group.

In the last month, I've spoken with other companies related to changing how the bookstore business operates, and while it is VERY early stages, I wasn't laughed off the conference call.

Which I was a bit worried about. I often dream big, but I also often don't know the difference between dreaming big and a huge hallucination.

So far, I believe it might be thinking big, but I should find out in the next couple of months if I'm really hallucinating.

THANK YOU

Opus X is 1 story told in twelve books over eighteen months. Early indications suggest the *Wide sales income is solid.* Nothing to crow about with the New York Times, but that is why the plan is for eighteen months.

Rome wasn't built in a day, and a Wide platform (wide means you sell on other platforms besides Amazon, and since you do sell on other platforms, you are forbidden to sell on their KU platform.)

I'm looking forward to growing our business around the world, and Wide is the next step on our path.

Thank you for supporting us and all of your other favorite authors as we hopefully bring you stories that keep you up late at night!

Ad Aeternitatem,

Michael Anderle

BOOKS BY MICHAEL ANDERLE

For a complete list of books by Michael Anderle, please visit:

www.lmbpn.com/ma-books/

CONNECT WITH MICHAEL ANDERLE

Michael Anderle Social

Website:

http://www.lmbpn.com

Email List:

http://lmbpn.com/email/

Facebook Here:

https://www.facebook.com/groups/lmbpn.opusx/

www.ingramcontent.com/pod-product-compliance
Lightning Source LLC
Chambersburg PA
CBHW020225110726
47898CB00004B/1156

* 9 7 8 1 6 4 2 0 2 4 0 2 9 *